A DATE WITH HER BEST FRIEND

LOUISA HEATON

STRANDED WITH THE PARAMEDIC

SUE MacKAY

MILLS & BOON

First published in Great Britain 2022
by Mills & Boon, an imprint of HarperCollins*Publishers* Ltd,
1 London Bridge Street, London, SE1 9GF

www.harpercollins.co.uk

HarperCollins*Publishers*
1st Floor, Watermarque Building,
Ringsend Road, Dublin 4, Ireland

A Date with Her Best Friend © 2022 Louisa Heaton

Stranded with the Paramedic © 2022 Sue MacKay

ISBN: 978-0-263-30138-0

09/22

MIX
Paper from
responsible sources
FSC C007454

This book is produced from independently certified FSC™ paper
to ensure responsible forest management.
For more information visit www.harpercollins.co.uk/green.

Printed and Bound in Spain using 100% Renewable Electricity
at CPI Black Print, Barcelona

A DATE WITH HER BEST FRIEND

LOUISA HEATON

MILLS & BOON

To my three older brothers.

Thanks for sharing all the mud and drama!

CHAPTER ONE

CARA MADDOX WAS two sets in on a five-set high-intensity weights workout when her phone went off. The scary ringtone she'd allocated to her father filled the fire station's small gym and she debated whether to ignore the call. But familial duty got the better of her and she set the weights down with a sigh.

Wiping her face with a soft towel, she accepted the video call. 'Hi, Dad.'

Her father smiled at her. 'Hello, darling, how are you doing?'

He was sitting in a comfortable leather chair, and his background told her he was in the library of Higham Manor, her childhood home. Shelves and shelves of leather-bound books behind him reached from floor to ceiling.

He peered closer, then frowned. 'You look shattered. Are you taking care of yourself?'

'I'm in the middle of a workout, Dad.' She checked her watch to note her heart rate and then paused her workout.

'Right. Of course. Got to stay fit in your type of job, I guess.'

'That's right.'

She stiffened slightly when he mentioned her job. Felt herself instantly go on the defensive. Her father had never been a fan of her joining the fire service. If he was calling just to have another go at her about it, or to suggest she change jobs, then she'd end the call. She really didn't have any time for that kind of non-sense any more.

'What can I do for you?' Best to get right to the point.

'I was wondering if you were going to come back home at the end of the month, for your mother's party? We haven't seen you in a long time, and it would be nice to see you.'

As he finished speaking, Michaels, her dad's butler, came into view, carrying a tray with coffee and biscuits.

'You're seeing me now.'

'Come now, Cara, you know it's not the same. It's your mother's birthday. She'd want you to be there.'

'She's been dead for years, Dad. She's not going to know whether I'm there or not.'

Her father bristled, waiting for Michaels to leave the room before he began speaking again. 'But your family will. Our friends will. The *servant*s will. What will they think?'

'It doesn't matter what they think. I don't know them. They're your friends and associates. Not mine.'

'It's her *birthday*, Cara,' her father said, as if that should be enough explanation for everything. As if that should be enough motivation to get his daughter to do everything he wanted.

She felt guilty for trying to avoid it, but she'd been to many of those evenings before. They were meant to be about her mother, but all they were was a huge chance for her father to network with his friends and/

or try to fix her up with the son of one of them. There would be a speech. Her mother would get a token mention. Heartfelt but short. Everyone would raise a glass and then her father's pals would go back to whatever business deals they were arranging, exchanging cards and contacts over cigars and brandies. And the entire time Cara would stand there, feeling awkward, trying to make conversation with a Tarquin or a Theodore—people she didn't know, who were all rather surprised that she did the job that she did.

It wasn't what they expected. She was the daughter of an earl, and they expected her to be something other than a firefighter. The patron of a charity, perhaps? Someone who had a lot of lunches with her lady friends and cared way too much about handbags and nail polish. She was Lady Cara Maddox, after all.

But Cara didn't care for titles, or expectations, nor did she have lady friends. Most of her friends were guys. Her best friend was a guy. Tom Roker. Sweet, dear Tom. Handsome Tom. Paramedic. Father to a beautiful little boy called Gage. And widower of Victoria, who'd been willowy and tall and exquisite. Preened to perfection. The kind of woman Cara's father obviously wished his daughter would be more like. The kind of woman Cara could never be, which put Tom—dear, sweet, lovable, handsome Tom—completely out of her league.

Cara had always preferred the company of men. But that was what happened when you grew up with three older brothers and didn't quite fit in with the young ladies at your posh school. You hung around at rugby and polo matches, you laughed and joked with the boys, you competed with them, wrestled with them. You got to know your brother's friends and they were mostly guys. On the odd occasion when one of her brothers had brought home a friend who was a girl, Cara had had no idea how to talk to them! They'd seemed a different breed. Alien! Not interested in the slightest in Cara's topics of conversation, such as rugby or whether they wanted to arm wrestle! Clothes and designers and parties had been completely off her radar.

'I know. You don't have to remind me. I can remember all by myself.'

Her mother's birthday had also been her death day. For many weeks Serena Maddox had lain in bed, trying vainly to fight the ravages of breast cancer that had metastasised to her lungs, liver and bones. Cara had sat by her mother's bedside in those last few days when she was mostly asleep, listening to the fluid building up in her mother's lungs and throat, sponging her dry lips as her breathing got slower and slower, and she'd held her mother's hand as she'd taken her final, agonised breath.

It was a day etched into her brain. A memory filled with so much pain and so much guilt that she had never been the daughter Serena had dreamed of. Cara had let her mother down, and her father knew that, and she hated it when he used that to his own advantage.

'Come home, Cara. Your brothers will be here. Clark is flying in from New York next week. Cameron will arrive a few days after that,' he said.

'And Curtis?'

'In Milan, still, but he promises he'll be back for the party.'

She could hear the tone in her father's voice. The tone that said, *I'm glad my boys have flown the nest and are upholding the Maddox name, but I do wish they lived closer to home.*

Her father, Fabian Maddox, Earl of Wentwich, was a proud man, and often boasted about his three sons, but Cara knew he would prefer to have them close by, so that the Maddox men could be a force to be reckoned with. Instead they were spread out across the globe, and their father could only preen, in their absence.

Clark ran a prestigious law firm in New York, specialising in family law and pandering to the rich, Cameron was in Cape Town, South Africa, running a business that built cruise ships, and Curtis was the CEO of Maddox Hotels, whose head office was in London. But she knew they were currently constructing a new hotel in Milan, which he was overseeing.

She spoke to her brothers often, and though she'd never felt any judgment from them, she wondered if they, too, questioned her choice in jobs.

But being a firefighter was all she'd ever wanted to do. Ever since she'd been little, when a fire had broken out in the kitchens and her family and the staff had rushed from the building, only to watch in awe as firefighters rushed *towards* the flames. They'd arrived in huge fire engines, unloading equipment and hoses, and the flames licking out of the downstairs windows had soon been transformed into thick, grey smoke, billowing up into the sky.

She'd felt a nervous excitement at seeing them, had felt herself come alive watching them. It had been a heady feeling, and one she'd wanted to chase from an early age, even telling her parents, when she was just six years old, that she was going to be a firefighter. Oh, how they'd laughed at that, and Cara had felt flummoxed and confused by it. Why was it such a funny suggestion?

Why did they all keep telling her that she'd change her mind when she got older?

She sighed. If all her brothers were coming back, if they were making the effort... She'd not planned on going this year. She'd done her duty, honouring her mother's birthday over the years. She'd been ready to start missing a few. Remembering her mother in her own way instead. Laying a wreath at her grave. Saying a few words, perhaps. Just...*remembering*, without having to stand around feeling uncomfortable, with people she didn't know, in order to fulfil some duty that her father had imposed.

Thankfully, she was literally saved by the bell.

The siren blasted out through the station. 'Gotta go, Dad.'

'But you've not given me your answer!' He leaned forward in his chair, filling the screen with his face.

'Sorry! Speak later!' And she ended the video call, pulling on a navy tee shirt and trousers over her workout clothes.

When that siren sounded you dropped everything. Including any guilt.

In fact, she was grateful for it.

The siren meant that whatever was happening with her right there and then had to be put to one side for later. It wasn't important. What was important were the people who needed help. Those trapped in cars after an accident. Those who watched their businesses and often their livelihoods burning to the ground.

Green Watch often couldn't save someone's car or house or factory, but they could try to save lives—and that siren meant someone or something needed to be saved.

And that was what Cara lived for.

* * *

Tom Roker had just finished eating his sandwich when the call came through from Control about a house fire in Wandsworth and he was asked to attend.

'Roger, Control. ETA three minutes.'

'Roger that, four, three, two. Take care.'

He started the engine of his rapid response vehicle and reversed out of his spot, switching on the blues and twos as he raced towards the destination provided by his onboard computer.

The traffic was light today. The kind of traffic he wished he had to deal with most days. People got out of the way, they pulled over in the right place, the traffic lights were kind and he got to the destination quickly. His only problem was that cars lined both sides of the street. Pedestrians, neighbours—all had stopped or come out of their homes to gawp at the flaming spectacle of a house in full flame. Two fire engines blocked the street, and he could already see the fire crews doing their best to tame the fire. He wondered if Cara was on duty today?

It was a strange thing. He always hoped to see her, and yet also feared that she would be there. The idea of her running into a burning building… She might get a thrill out of it, but he didn't. Not until she was out again.

Tom sounded his horn to make people get out of the way, so he could get closer, and in the end managed to park behind one of the fire engines. Behind him, a normal ambulance arrived, and by the sound of the sirens he could hear many more emergency services were on their way.

He looked over at the house that was burning. It was a mid-terrace house, and the two front top windows were full of flame. It was licking at the bricks and there were holes in the grey slate roof through which more flame could be seen. Maybe the fire had started on the upper floor? On the ground floor the windows looked dark with smoke, occasionally strobed by torchlight as the fire crew made their way through the property, most probably looking for someone not accounted for.

His heart thudded at the thought.

People were crowding around the perimeter established by a police officer, filming it on their phones, their faces masks of awe and fear.

A firefighter wearing a white helmet came to meet him. He realised as he got closer that it was the Chief Fire Officer of Green Watch, known simply as Hodge, so Cara was most probably here somewhere, doing her thing.

'I've got Mum and Dad out, as well as two of the kids, but we're still looking for the third child. I think we're dealing with some basic smoke inhalation for most of them, though Dad's a COPD sufferer. He's also got a decent burn on his arm and left hand. They're over there in that appliance, receiving some oxygen.'

Tom nodded. Smoke inhalation could cause all manner of problems, from the simple to the most severe. Especially if the sufferer had medical issues to deal with, like asthma or COPD—chronic obstructive pulmonary disease. A patient with a respiratory issue could crash quickly, so it was important to keep a close eye on them.

'I'll do what I can.'

'Cheers, Tom.' Hodge headed back to co-ordinate efforts.

Tom made his way to the fire engine. Liam Penny,

one of Cara's crew mates, was inside monitoring his patients. 'Hey, Liam. Whatcha got?'

'This is Daniel Webster and his wife Maria. The little one on her lap is Teddy and the brave girl over on your right is Amy.'

The mother removed her oxygen mask. 'Is there any word on Joey? Have they found him?'

Tom clambered in. 'They're still looking.'

'I need to be out there!' The mum tried to get up and push past him, but he managed to stop her.

'They'll come and find you if there's any news. Right now, I need you to stay here.' He replaced the oxygen mask. 'It's safer for you in here. The fire crews are doing their utmost to find him, but what I need you guys to do is try to stay calm and breathe in the oxygen for me.' He didn't need any of them running out there, getting in the way of the rescue operation. It was dangerous out there. 'I'll just put this SATs probe on your finger.'

The SATs probe measured oxygen and pulse rate. Normal oxygen levels for those without COPD were between ninety-four and ninety-eight percent. As he waited for the reading to appear, Tom used a tongue depressor and a pen light to look at the back of the dad's throat. The smoke inhalation and the COPD were more of a concern than the burn on his arm and hand and would need to take priority. He saw soot deposits. He'd need to be kept under observation in hospital for a while.

More than half of all fire deaths came from smoke inhalation. The smoke could cause inflammation of the airway and lungs, making them swell up and become blocked, and depending upon what types of gases were inhaled some of the inhalations would be toxic or poisonous. This dad was lucky he'd got out.

He began to cough, his eyes reddening and watering with the effort to try and clear his lungs, so Tom set him up with some extra oxygen and tried to coach him through his breathing. The two kids didn't look too bad. Shocked more than anything.

'Do we know yet how the fire started?' he asked Liam.

'We think it began upstairs, but the flash point... We're not sure.'

'I was burning candles,' the mum said, crying. 'And I... I think I might not have switched off my curling iron. Could that have started this? Is this my fault?' She looked at Tom in fear. Fear that he would tell her that it might be. But no one knew. Not yet.

Tom noted that her oxygen SATs weren't too bad at all. Ninety-three to ninety-four. On the lower end. 'We don't know for sure. Accidents happen all the time. You'll have to wait for the investigation results.' He moved the SATs probe from her finger to the dad's, whose laboured breathing sounded much more exhausted. He didn't like the man's colour.

At that moment a couple of paramedics arrived, dressed in their neon yellow jackets. 'Hey, Tom, what have we got?'

Relieved to have back-up, Tom handed over his patients, explaining about the dad's medical history and soot-covered throat. The paramedics offloaded the small family and escorted them to the ambulance, even though the mum kept protesting that she wasn't going to leave without knowing if Joey was okay.

Tom ached for her. But at that moment he saw a fire-fighter emerge from the building, carrying a dog.

'Bella! Oh, my God, Bella! How could we have forgotten about you?' The mum ran free of the paramedic and towards the Boxer dog, which was limp in the firefighter's arms.

Judging by the firefighter's walk, Tom knew it was Cara and, as always, he felt relief that she'd got through this fire okay. He knew it was her thing to run into the flames to help. It was her job, after all. But he always worried about her. She was a tough little cookie, who could hold her own, but that still didn't stop him from feeling he needed to protect her. Feelings of gratitude that she was out of the fire washed over him as usual. He wanted to see her face, but she still wore her re-breather mask.

Cara laid the dog down by the appliance and pulled off her own mask to get out some of the special equipment that he knew had been donated to them by an animal charity—a mask to fit around a dog or cat's face. He didn't realise he was holding his breath until he saw the dog trying to fight the mask and wagging its tail at its owner's approach.

'You might want to get her checked out by your vet,' Cara said as she gave the dog oxygen, pulling off her helmet and laying it on the side of the appliance.

Her hair was sweaty. Some of it was plastered to her skull, dark, as if it had been dipped in molasses, the rest was wispy and golden, almost auburn. Her hair, he often thought, was like flame itself. A mass of burning colours. Autumnal.

The first time he'd ever seen her with her hair loose and hanging down her back he'd realised he was staring,

mesmerised by how beautiful it was. But that had been
ages ago. In another time, it seemed. Back then…before
he'd known her properly and they'd become the best
friends they were now, he'd been attracted to her. How
could he not have been? Cara Maddox was a stunning
young woman. The sight of her had taken his breath
away, but he'd been in no place back then to do anything about it. He'd been a married man. It would have
been wrong.

So they'd just been associates. People who met at
emergencies, until slowly they had become friends.

At that moment she met his gaze, noticing him, and
her face broke into a hesitant, almost shy smile. 'Hey,
Tom.' She touched her hair, as if ashamed of how it
looked. As if she knew that it was sweaty and plastered
to her head, that her pale skin had dark smears from the
smoke upon it, that there were red marks on her face
from the mask. That maybe she didn't look her best.

But to him she looked beautiful. The only problem
was he couldn't tell her, in case she thought he was hitting on her.

'Hey. How was it in there?'

'Hot. Like it always is.' She laughed and unzipped
her jacket a little.

'Any idea of what started it?'

'Not sure. But something upstairs in one of the bed-
rooms.'

One of the woman's neighbours had taken the dog,
Bella, offering to look after it for the Webster family,
so they could go to hospital in the ambulance and get
checked out.

'How are all the patients?' Cara asked.

'Not bad. Smoke inhalation, minor burns. Dad will

need an eye kept on him. He's got COPD, his SATs were low, and he has soot deposits on the back of his throat. Any sign of the missing boy?'

'House was empty apart from the dog, which I found whimpering under a bed.'

'Then where is he?' Tom frowned.

'Don't know. He could have gone out and not told anyone he was going, so they thought he was still inside.'

At that moment they became aware of a commotion amongst the crowd of onlookers. They both turned to look and noticed a young teenage boy struggling to get past the police presence.

'Mum? *Mum!*'

'Joey!'

'Mum!'

Mother and son ran into each other's arms, the mum bawling her eyes out with relief.

Tom and Cara both let out a breath, small smiles creeping onto their faces.

Cara turned to Tom. 'Happy ending in that respect.'

'Yeah... Ever feel like happy endings only happen to other people?' Tom mused.

Cara laughed. 'Oh, yeah.' She looked down at the ground, almost as if she couldn't think of what to say next. 'Are you okay?' she asked.

He shrugged. Everyone still expected him to be riddled by grief. 'Oh, you know how it is.'

She nodded. 'I do. How are things with Gage? All okay?'

'He's asking a lot of questions about his mum lately.'

'What do you tell him?'

Tom looked at the remains of the burnt house. The

blackened bricks, the holey roof. Windows blown out from heat. The flames were gone and all that was left were plumes of thick, grey, swirling smoke, billowing up into the sky. Nobody had died today. Not here. And for that he was grateful.

'I tell him that she loved him very much. He doesn't understand if I tell him she got sick before she died, because he doesn't remember that. It happened so quickly sometimes even I struggle to understand it.'

'In those early days of Covid we all struggled to understand it. Don't be too hard on yourself.'

Cara laid a reassuring hand on his, before turning to look at what was happening with her crew. She had no idea what her touch meant to him.

'I'd better go. You going to be at The Crusader tonight?'

The Crusader was the preferred pub that all the fire crews attended—situated, as it was, just half a mile from their station.

'You bet. My parents have got Gage for a sleepover, so I'm free.'

She pulled her helmet back on, and gave him a warm smile and a wave before jogging back to her team. He watched her go, kicking himself for not saying anything to her.

Yet again.

The ambulance was pulling away, with the Webster family on board, and all Tom had to do was return to his rapid response vehicle and write his notes on the call.

The Websters had survived this terrible event and he was glad for them. It could have turned out so differently. A house and possessions could be replaced. People couldn't.

He thought about his son. How did you fully explain Covid to a near four-year-old? It would get easier, he hoped, as Gage got older and could understand more, but right now all his son knew was that he was the only child at his pre-school who didn't have a mummy. There were a few who didn't have dads, but mums…

Am I enough for my son?

Could he give Gage the cuddles and hugs he needed, the way his mother would have? He hoped so. Victoria had always shown her son affection. And he missed her, too. Missed her voice. Her presence. Which was strange, considering how they'd been with each other towards the end.

They should never have got married. They should never have got carried away with the romanticism of having been together since they were so young. The signs had been there, but they'd ignored them, because Gage had been on the way and Tom had wanted to do the right thing by Victoria and his unborn child.

Gage was his utmost priority now.

He couldn't be getting carried away with how he felt about Cara. He wasn't the best partner in the world for anyone to have, quite frankly. He'd failed Victoria and he couldn't go getting involved with anyone else right now. Gage wouldn't understand that.

And Cara? She would no doubt think badly of him if he declared his feelings for her so soon after losing his wife to Covid.

As the appliance pulled back into the station, the members of Green Watch descended from the vehicle and got into cleaning and maintenance mode. After every job they checked and maintained all equipment and cleaned the appliance if they'd attended a fire.

Cara began an audit of the equipment and checked the breathing apparatus supplies. She was glad of this respite. It was always a confusing moment after seeing Tom. Her feelings for him were confusing. He was her best friend, yes. Absolutely. She would give her life for him. But if she was being honest with herself then she had to admit that deeper undercurrents ran beneath the surface. Like a riptide of attraction that she had to fight every time they were together. But she was being respectful to his late wife. Acknowledging that he'd married his childhood girlfriend and had never looked at anyone else in his life so far.

Also—and she didn't like admitting this—she knew that she could never be as good as Victoria.

She'd known Tom when he was married to his wife. Had socialised with both of them. She'd liked Victoria. Had seen why Tom was so in love with her. She'd been funny and warm. Friendly.

Cara had met Tom just half a year before Victoria had died. Their eyes meeting over the crumpled, steaming bonnets of two cars that had been involved in a head-on collision. At first she'd been startled by her reaction to a man she'd only seen for a couple of seconds. A man she had not yet heard speak. Whose name she didn't know. A man she had not spent any time with, nor yet seen smile.

She'd watched him clamber into the rear of one of the vehicles, to maintain a C-spine in an unconscious female driver who had suffered a head injury, and for a brief moment she had just stood still, watching him, mesmerised, her eyebrows raised in surprise at how she'd been frozen into place, stunned.

Is this lust at first sight? she'd mused, before her brain had kicked in and allowed the rest of the world to re-enter her consciousness. She'd heard instructions from the Green Watch Chief Fire Officer, Hodge, on how to tackle the incident. As she'd covered the driver with a blanket, to screen her from the glass of the windshield breaking as the Jaws of Life were applied, she'd stolen another glance at the paramedic who had intrigued her at first sight.

Dark hair. Dark lashes around crystalline blue eyes. High cheekbones. A solid jawline and a mouth that looked as if it was made for sin.

Cara had had to look away from him, pulse racing, face flushing, and she'd had to concentrate on what she was doing. Once the roof of the car had been cut off, she'd worked with Tom to co-ordinate the extrication of the driver. He had C-spine control, so he'd taken charge—counting them down, telling them when to get the backboard in. She'd helped to slide the patient on, then levelled the back board and helped carry her out of the car and onto a waiting ambulance trolley.

Then she'd turned away to help with the extrication of the second driver and her passenger, who were less injured, and conscious still, but who would no doubt have horrible whiplash injuries and dislocated shoulders to endure through the next few weeks. The engine block of their vehicle had crumpled inwards, trapping the legs of the driver, but thankfully had broken no bones. She'd been extremely lucky.

With the patients off to the hospital, and the crew

organised to begin clearing up the equipment, she'd heard a voice behind her.

'Thanks.'

She'd turned. It had been him. Cara had done her best to keep her breathing normal, but it had been hard when he'd placed the full force of his gaze upon her. It had done alarming things to her insides. Her heart rate had accelerated. Her blood pressure had risen. Her mouth had dried to the consistency of a desert.

'Thanks to you, too.' She'd smiled. 'A job well done.'

She'd been pretty impressed that her tongue had still worked and that she'd not stuttered or tripped over her words. Because she had never felt this before. Not even with Leo.

He'd nodded. 'Absolutely. I'm Tom. I'm new.'

He'd held out his hand for her to shake and she'd taken it, glad that he couldn't ascertain that inside she felt molten.

'Cara. Nice to meet you. You've just moved to this area?'

'To be near my wife's family.'

My wife. Ah. Of course. A man like this wouldn't be single.

Disappointment had washed over her.

'Great. Well, welcome to the area.'

He'd thanked her and then headed back to his car, and she'd watched him go like a love-sick puppy. It had been then that Reed Gower, one of her Green Watch crew mates, had sidled up beside her, draped an arm around her shoulder and said, 'You know, if this were a cartoon your eyes would be on stalks and there'd be little love hearts on the end of them.'

She'd shrugged him off, annoyed that he'd noticed.

'Don't be ridiculous! He's new—I was just introducing myself, that's all.'

Reed had laughed as he'd walked away. 'Sure you were! Keep telling yourself that.'

After that she'd done her best to try and keep things distant, but he'd kept turning up at most of their shouts and eventually, as these things happened, someone on Green Watch had invited him to join them at the pub— The Crusader.

And Tom had turned up. With his wife, Victoria, in tow.

A small part of her had hoped that his wife would be an ugly toad, but of course she wasn't. Victoria had been tall, long-limbed, gazelle-like, with wave upon wave of shiny honey-coloured, hair. And she'd had a very worthy job—but what else could Cara have hoped for? It had turned out that Victoria was a paediatric nurse. An *angel*.

Her perfect figure and shiny white teeth had been a hit with the guys, that was for sure, and very quickly Tom and his wife had become part of their group.

Until Covid had hit.

Emergency services had been classed as essential workers, so they'd still had to work, and somehow— terribly—Victoria had got Covid. The stunning Amazon Cara had considered her to be had been struck down, her fight against the disease complicated by asthma, and Victoria had been taken into hospital and placed on a ventilator.

Cara hadn't seen much of Tom after that. Understandably, he hadn't been at any of their shouts. She'd hoped he was at home, looking after his son, and not ill with Covid himself. There had been some talk of developing a vaccine, but the government had said it was at least a year away.

And then had come the news, passed down from someone in the ambulance crew to Blue Watch, to Green Watch. Victoria had succumbed to Covid.

She was the first person Cara had personally known who had died from the disease and it had struck her harder than she'd ever imagined. It had come close, this invisible disease, and it could be fatal.

She had only been able to imagine how Tom had felt.

She hadn't wanted him to think that she didn't care enough about him to ring. So she'd rung Tom's house, left her condolences as an answerphone message. She'd hand-delivered a card through his letterbox, called his name, but there had been no answer and nothing else she could do.

When the funeral had been announced, she hadn't been able to go. Numbers had been extremely limited. But the funeral home had offered to stream the service online, so she'd watched it that way—attended that way whilst on duty at the station, watching on a laptop. Wishing she could be there to support her good friend Tom. She'd only seen him briefly in the stream, but he'd looked pale and shattered and her heart had ached for him and Gage.

He'd been off for about a month in total. The first job she'd seen him at, she'd gone to him and wished she could wrap her arms around him tightly, hug him and hold him in her arms for ever, but due to Covid restrictions the most they'd been able to do was bump elbows.

It hadn't seemed enough. Nowhere near enough. Her heart had still ached for him.

'How are you?' she'd asked him, standing a good two metres away.

'I'm okay. Thanks for asking.'

'You and Gage doing all right? Is there anything I can do?'

He'd shaken his head. 'No. Thanks. I got your card. It meant a lot.'

'I wanted you to know you were being thought about. I couldn't come to the funeral because of the restrictions.'

'I know.'

'I watched it online.'

'You did?'

She'd nodded, smiled warmly at him. 'If you ever need anything…even if it's just someone to talk to… I want you to feel you can call me. Any time and I'll listen. Rant. Rave. I'm here for you, okay?'

She'd seen his eyes redden and water, and had been touched that her offer had affected him so. If only she'd been able to reach out to hug him!

That all felt so long ago, but it wasn't. Not really.

So, yes, her feelings for Tom ran deep. There was attraction, but there was respect for all that had gone before—and the knowledge that no matter what she felt for him she could never live up to Victoria.

Cara was everything that Victoria had not been. Cara was a good head shorter than Tom's late wife. She had thick, strong muscles, from weightlifting at the gym every day, whereas Victoria had been lithe from Pilates. Cara had tattoos around both wrists and running up her forearms. Tom's wife had had none, and her only body modification had been pierced ears. Cara considered herself to be stocky, and there was nothing she loved more than to hang out in her gym clothes, or in boots and jeans and a tee. She'd never worn a heel in her life. Had never worn a pretty dress. Cara was a tomboy, through and through. Victoria…? She'd seemed to go everywhere in long, silhouette flattering dresses, that flowed and billowed around her, as if she was some sort of ethereal nymph. Graceful and elegant. Something Cara could never hope to be.

They were chalk and cheese.

So any feelings she had for Tom could never be reciprocated.

He just wouldn't see her the way she wanted him to.

CHAPTER TWO

RAIN POURED DOWN as Cara ran from her vehicle towards The Crusader, her jacket held over her head so that she didn't get wet hair. There was nothing worse than trying to enjoy a nice drink, but having cold, wet rain, dripping down the back of her neck.

She pushed open the heavy wooden doors, decorated with multi-coloured stained-glass, inhaling the familiar scent of hops and bar food. She shook her jacket as she scanned the bar area, searching for Tom.

Most of Green Watch were already there, and had command of both the pool tables and the darts board. She spotted Tom and a couple of other paramedics sitting at the games room bar, chatting. A few colleagues turned and greeted her, asking her to join them, and to add her name to the list at the pool table as she was such a good player.

'I'll just grab a drink first, then I'll be over.'

'We'll put your name up for you.'

'Thanks.' She smiled and headed over to the bar, deliberately going to where Tom was to say hi. Her heart fluttered in anticipation. He looked up as she came over and a broad, genuine smile broke across his face, lighting up those gorgeous blue eyes of his.

'Hey…look who it is. What can I get you?'

'Just a dry white wine, please.' She gave her order to the barmaid, Kelly.

'Still raining?' Tom asked.

She nodded. 'Cats and dogs.'

Kelly placed Cara's drink on the bar and Tom handed the barmaid a note.

'You playing pool tonight?'

'Always. You?'

Tom looked over at the chalkboard on the wall to check his name. 'Looks like I'm on just before you.'

'Ah, okay… Well, I'm planning to wipe the floor with you this evening. Make up for the last time.'

He laughed. 'You're going to have to bring your A game.'

'I know no other kind.'

They clinked glasses, then both took their drinks and walked over to the high tables and stools that surrounded the pool table area, taking a place by the window, which was steamed up on the inside.

'How's that family? Have you heard any more? The Websters?' she asked.

That was the thing with her job. You could be there for people, at the worst time of a family's life, but you didn't always get to hear the end of the story.

'The kids were sent home with an aunt, I think. Mum and Dad were kept in for observation, and I think the dad might be in there for a while.'

'What about his burn? Superficial? I never got a good look at it.'

'Second degree. The plastic surgeons were going to take a look, last I heard, because of how the burn was over his arm and hand. They don't want him to lose any movement or function.'

'Good. Well, I hope they're able to move on from this. It's going to be tough, losing their home, but the most important thing is that everyone survived. Houses can be replaced. People can't.'

'I think they may have some trouble moving on, though.'

'How so?' she asked.

She saw that some of the Green Watch crew were listening in to their conversation.

'They didn't have insurance.'

'What? Oh, no!' That was awful! Without insurance, they wouldn't have any money coming in to help get them somewhere else. Or to replace furniture. 'There must be something we can do for them?'

Cara's colleague Reed stepped away from the table and said, 'We could always do a fundraiser for them? Throw a party, or something? Ask for donations?'

Cara looked to Tom. 'Maybe... Do you think we could?'

He shrugged. 'I don't see why not. It would help them out, for sure.'

She thought about it. 'What sort of fundraiser, Reed?'

He took a shot, pocketing a striped ball, lining up his white cue ball perfectly for him to take on the black and win the game.

'Let me think...' He stooped low over the table, sank the black and won the game, commiserating with his opponent. 'We could ask for donations from local businesses? Auction them off?'

'We could auction promises,' Tom said. 'I saw this show once on TV where they did that. It was quite fun.

Businesses donate a meal for two, for example, or a cleaner for the day, and people just auction something they're good at.'

Cara nodded. 'Like what? I guess I could run someone through a gym training session. What about you?' she asked both Tom and Reed.

Reed smiled. 'I could auction off a kiss.' He wiggled his eyebrows suggestively, causing everyone around them to laugh.

Hodge, their chief fire officer, who'd been listening over by the darts board, called over. 'Better offer an STD testing kit for afterwards, then!'

Reed pretended to be insulted, but he was smiling. 'Hey, that's…fair.' He laughed. 'I suppose we could always do one of those naked firemen calendars?'

Cara blushed at the idea.

Tom shook his head. 'They can't wait ages to get the money. They need it quickly. Whatever we arrange, it would have to be sooner, rather than later.'

Hodge nodded, thinking. 'I like the auction of promises idea. And getting companies to maybe donate items that the Websters need.'

Cara smiled. 'What do you think, Tom?'

'I'm happy to help in any way I can. I'm sure I can get a lot of the other paramedics to join in and spread the word if we have some sort of special night planned.'

'You could be a naked gardener, Tom!' Reed called, winking at Cara.

Cara felt her cheeks flush wildly at the suggestion. Tom? *Naked?* Now, that was usually an image she tried *not* to think about. Not because she didn't think he'd look good—because there was no way Tom wasn't beautiful all over—it was just because… Well, if she started thinking that way she'd never stop. And she was always trying to be respectful. Respectful of Victoria. Of Tom's loss. Of Gage. Thinking naughty thoughts could lead them down the wrong path, and there was no way in hell she was going to stupidly jeopardise her friendship with him by blurting out that she fancied the pants off him.

She hoped Tom hadn't noted the suggestive wink Reed had sent her way. She would have to have a word with him later and tell him to back off.

Cara sipped at her wine and just smiled at Tom, shaking her head as if to say, *What is he like, eh?*

'Tom. You're up next to play.'

Tom got up to the table and started racking up the balls for the next game. She watched him, wishing she could just look at him and see him as a friend, but these feelings for Tom were getting stronger every day. She had to find a way to control them!

Just as she was wondering whether she might have to avoid him for a bit—although did absence make the heart grow fonder?—the doors to the pub opened up, bringing in a burst of rain, and cold wind, and the sudden surprising outline of her father, hunkered down under an umbrella being held by his uniformed chauffeur!

At first Cara thought she was imagining things. Her father the Earl of Wentwich in a London pub? It couldn't be. Her eyes had to be deceiving her. She even gave them a rub—only to realise as she took another sip of her wine, that her father's doppelganger was headed straight for her.

'Cara, darling!'

Her cheeks flushed and she looked about her, keen

for her crewmates not to realise who this was. She'd always tried to hide the fact that she was an earl's daughter, and although Hodge knew, he respected her enough to keep her secret, as she'd requested.

She'd worked damned hard to be accepted as someone who could give as much to being a firefighter as a man and prove to her crew that she could do exactly what they could. Run into a burning building? *Check*. Carry a one-hundred-and-seventy-pound man in a fireperson's lift? *Check*. Keep up with the drills and the work and not expect any leeway for the fact that she was a girl? *Check*.

Cara dragged hold of her father's arm and quickly steered him in the other direction. 'What are you doing here?' she asked him in harsh whispered tones.

'I wanted to make sure you're all right.'

'Of course I am! How did you even know that I was here?'

'I tracked your phone using that app thing.'

Dammit! How had she forgotten to remove that after showing him how it worked?

'Dad, you shouldn't be here.'

'Why not? I thought it was time I met your team. Or are you ashamed of me?' He lifted his chin, smiling at her.

'Of course I'm not ashamed. But there are ways and means, Dad, and this isn't one of them.'

'No?' He stepped past her and headed straight for Hodge, reaching out his hand for a handshake. 'Hello. I'm Cara's dad.'

Hodge glanced at Cara. 'Lord Wentwich! Pleasure to meet you, My Lord. You have a fine daughter.'

Her father beamed. 'I like to think so, but I wouldn't

know because I hardly ever get to see her.' he said, directing his words in her direction, eyebrow raised.

Cara swallowed hard. All her work, all that time spent proving that she was just like everyone else, was about to crumble. She could sense it happening. It happened every time someone found out about who she really was. It changed people. It changed their behaviour towards her. And she didn't want her crew joking around, bowing and scraping every time she came into the room. It was stupid, and something she'd never liked.

When Leo had found out who she was, at first he'd been impressed. And then she'd quickly discovered that he was only staying with her for the fact that he could use her money and name to get the things that he wanted. He'd never been there for her. He'd never even been *attracted* to her. Something she'd realised in the most horrendous way. The things he had said...

'We were just talking about organising an evening to help a family that lost their entire home in a fire today,' Hodge told her father.

'*Really?* How awful. Our kitchens caught fire once. Terrible thing. I can't begin to imagine how they must feel.'

'We were thinking about a fundraiser. Getting businesses to donate furniture or goods, or raffle prizes. If you know of anyone who could help us out with that we'd very much appreciate it.'

Her father nodded, clearly thinking. Then his eyes lit up brightly as a thought occurred to him, and Cara knew instinctively that she was not going to enjoy the words that came out of his mouth next.

'The problem with those sorts of evenings is that you

have to have the right kind of people attending. People with lots of disposable income, who are willing to throw crazy amounts around.'

'Dad—'

'You could hold it at my place—Higham Manor. In fact, we're holding an event at the end of the month to celebrate Cara's mother's birthday. We could make it a fundraising event and this family…the…er…'

'The Websters.'

He smiled his thanks to Hodge. 'The Websters could attend, too. In fact, let's invite them as my special guests.'

'That's amazing, Lord Wentwich! Thank you! That will certainly help keep our costs down.'

'Don't mention it. I'm pleased to help. Let's make it a masked ball. We could have music, dancing, and then the auction fundraiser. You'll be there, Cara. Won't you?' He faced her with a smile.

Her father knew she wouldn't be able to refuse him now. He had her snared in a corner with no way out.

She would have to go. This wasn't just about her mother any more—it was about both her families. Her blood family and the people she thought of as her *real* family. Green Watch.

And Tom.

'Of course I will,' she said through gritted teeth as she stared at her father, both hating him for pulling this trick to get what he wanted—her at Higham Manor—but also grateful to him for coming up with what had to be the best way for the Webster family to get funds for a new home.

Who was she to get in the way of a family rebuilding their lives?

Hodge, Reed, Tom and all the others beamed, but she could sense the questions from some of them, and could already see Reed and James Blake and David Garcia looking at her differently.

They'd learned something new about her tonight. That her family had a manor house. That her father had a chauffeur.

That she was *different* from them.

Tom knew about her family already. It wasn't a secret to him. But he knew how much she didn't want the others to know. She hoped he would help protect her from their probing questions once her father had returned to his chauffeur-driven car.

'So it's settled, then!' Hodge beamed.

'Cara knows the time and date—don't you, darling?'

She nodded.

'I'll get my PR man on it first thing...start working on the donors in advance and seeing what prizes we can come up with.'

Hodge nodded. 'If you need us to help, just let us know.'

Her father clapped his hand to Hodge's shoulder. 'Don't worry. I can take care of everything. You guys continue to do your important work and concentrate on saving lives. I'll do the rest.' Her father shook Hodge's hand, then turned to her and kissed her on both cheeks. 'I'll leave you to your evening, then. It's been good to see you, Cara. I can't wait to see you at the ball. I know you won't let me or your mother down.'

And then he was gone, before she could say anything, and before she could blow her top. He did this every time. Took charge. He was used to it, of course, but it was one of the main reasons why she had left home as quickly as she'd been able to—to try and forge her independence. Why she'd tried to distance herself from her father's crazy influence.

They'd all left home. Cara and her three brothers. But of course her brothers were left alone to deal with their own lives. It was different for her. It was as if her father couldn't let go and kept interfering.

'Your Ladyship!' Reed bowed. 'I never knew I was in the presence of such class!'

'Give it a rest.'

She turned away and headed for the loo. She just needed a minute to gather herself. Splash her face with cold water and adjust to the fact that now everyone knew. It would no doubt get even worse once they'd actually been to Higham Manor and seen how she'd grown up. But what could she do?

As she stared at her reflection in the mirror she tried to tell herself that maybe it was better that it was all out in the open now. She waited to feel better about it, but nothing changed. She could still feel that tight, twisted feeling in her gut, and a rage against her father she knew she ought not to have. He was her one remaining parent, and she should be grateful for him, but his tight grip on her was like a chokehold sometimes.

Cara splashed her face with cold water, patted it down with paper towels and then girded herself for heading back outside. She yanked open the door and waiting outside for her was Tom. Dear Tom. Because he knew. Knew how she must be feeling.

Why wasn't she allowed to run straight into his arms?

'Hey. Want to get out of here?' he said, looking deep into her eyes. 'I have a getaway car waiting just outside.' He smiled.

He was so sweet. So perfect.

'Thanks. But, no. I need to face it. They were going to find out sometime, right?'

He nodded.

'Besides, I promised to thrash you at pool.'

She could think of nothing better than getting into Tom's car and driving away with him somewhere. Just the two of them. Pretending time didn't exist, their lives didn't exist, and it was just the two of them in each other's company for ever. They could park somewhere nice. Eat fish and chips together and stare up at the stars, holding hands or…

No. I shouldn't think of the 'or'.

He held out his hand and she looked at it as if he was offering her poison. *Take this and you'll be mine.* She wanted to take his hand so much! She often dreamed of it. The two of them walking in a park, as if they were a couple…

Only he wasn't offering his hand in that way, was he? This wasn't romantic. This was friendship. Support.

I'm with you. You've nothing to fear with me by your side. I'll protect you from their comments.

But she also knew that some of the crew—Reed, in particular—suspected she might have feelings for Tom, and if she returned to the pool table holding his hand she'd never hear the end of it.

'I'll be fine.'

She walked past him, towards her crew, head held high. Hoping that Tom understood.

Tom dropped his hand and watched her go. He had some idea of what she was feeling. Cara had always tried to forge her way through the world on her own merits, for which he was proud of her. He knew she hated it when her father railroaded her back into the world she'd used to exist in. A world in which she'd felt stifled and from which she had rebelled.

He followed her back to the pool table. It was set up, ready for him to break. Cara waited with her cue, determinedly chalking the tip.

Tom selected one from the rack on the wall and hefted it, feeling its weight, how it felt in his hands. Happy with his selection, he took the small cube of blue chalk that Cara had put down on the side, near one of the pockets, and chalked the end before bending down and lining up his white ball. He broke up the triangle of stripes and solid balls, sending them in all directions, pocketing a solid ball and giving himself another go.

'Are you rich?' Reed was asking Cara, downing the last of his pint.

Cara shook her head. 'No, I'm not. Look, I know you must all have questions, but there's a reason I've not spoken about that part of my life, okay? I'd prefer it if you all just left it alone.'

Tom had an easy shot he could take, but a part of him wanted to annoy Reed, so he went around the table to take a more difficult shot—which meant moving Reed from his position next to Cara.

'Excuse me.'

Reed backed off and headed over to the bar to refill his glass, and Tom smiled at Cara before taking his shot and missing.

Cara smiled back at him. 'Get ready to be thrashed,' she said.

He watched her pot ball after ball. She was very good. And he admired her for rolling with the punches and not leaving the pub after her father's visit. It would have been so easy for her to grab her jacket and run, but she hadn't. She'd faced it out. And he knew it was because she felt Green Watch were like her family. The family she'd always wanted. There was no way she was going to run from them.

Cara was down to her last ball before the black, but the striped ball rattled in the corner pocket and refused to go in. 'Damn!'

Tom laughed. His turn now. He looked at the lay-out of the balls on the table, planning his route of play. Each ball went in, one by one, with the white ball lining up for the next shot exactly as he'd intended, until he'd potted all his solids and was left on the black. It was at a tricky angle. If he missed it he would leave the table open for Cara to win the game.

'No pressure!' Cara said teasingly.

He glanced at her, warmth filling him at the smile on her face. The way her eyes gleamed in the light. He enjoyed his time with her immensely. Hours with Cara were never wasted. She made him feel strong again. Something he'd lost since Victoria died. Losing her had left him feeling in limbo, struggling to be everything for his son Gage. And when Gage was finally asleep in bed there was hardly any energy left for him at all. He was exhausted.

Cara was helping to carry him through his grief. Always there for him. Speaking to him on the phone, or in a text, even in the later hours of the night when he was feeling particularly alone. He owed her a great deal that he could never repay.

That said, he wasn't going to throw this game. It would insult her, for a start.

Tom lined up the shot, steadied his breathing and struck the white ball. It connected with the black. Perfect angle. And the black headed over to the bottom right corner pocket and dropped in. Game won.

'Yes!' He turned in triumph to Cara, who laughed, and he pulled her into a hug, kissing the top of her head and trying not to be affected by the way her hair smelled of flowers, or how she felt in his arms. Fighting the urge to keep her in his arms longer than he should.

I need to let her go. Others are watching.

He stepped away from her, smiling, grabbing their glasses from the table. 'Another drink?'

She shook her head, looking strange. 'Just a lemonade or something, please.'

'Okay.' And he headed to the bar, determined not to look back at her, because his body was reacting in ways that it shouldn't do with a friend.

His mind interpreted the maelstrom of thoughts and feelings he was having.

He wanted more of Cara.

Only he couldn't.

And he would need to be strong to fight the feelings that were coursing hotly through his blood and toying with his concentration.

The call had come through as *'Person trapped'*. Which could mean anything. But the address was at a children's play park.

Green Watch clambered into their appliance and set off to their destination, lights flashing to get them through the burgeoning traffic.

Cara watched the houses and cars flash by, thinking over the events of the previous night. Her father

showing up, playing the magnanimous hero and helping them out of a spot by offering to have a fundraising night at Higham Manor. Revelling in his role as a
saviour. It was the sort of thing that he fed off, but the
part he enjoyed most was interfering in her life. Why
did he do it? And so often? Cameron, Curtis and Clarke
didn't have the same problem.

As they pulled up at the park they jumped out to assess the situation, and quickly discovered that the person trapped was a teenage girl who had inserted herself
into a baby swing as a dare. All her friends stood around
her, drinking from cans and smoking, laughing at her
predicament. Clearly, they all thought it was hilarious.

Hodge took point as always, forging his way through
the girl's friends to assess the situation.

'What's your name, love?'

'Sienna.'

'And how did you end up in a baby swing?'

The baby swing was suspended by two thick metal
chains, but the seat itself looked to be of moulded black
rubber. Flexible, somewhat, but strong, all the same.
Cara knew they wouldn't want to cut the chains or the
seat, causing damage to the play park and therefore a
headache for the local council, so this was probably
going to be a pretty easy extraction by Green Watch
using a bit of muscle power.

Once Sienna had explained the dare, Hodge asked
her one final question. 'And are you hurt anywhere?'

'No.' Sienna's cheeks were inflamed and red as her
friends recorded the situation, no doubt to put on so-
cial media later. 'Are you gonna cut me out with the
Jaws of Life?'

Hodge shook his head. 'No need for that. We just

need a couple of strong arms to get you out of this pickle.' He turned and motioned to Cara and the others. 'Cara? You and Reed can lift and I'll hold the seat in place.'

'Okay.'

There was a lot of squealing from Sienna. Laughter. Complaining that they were tickling her or pinching her as they hauled her upwards so Hodge could pull downwards on the rubber seat. The chains clanked and clanged as they swung this way, then that, until eventually they freed the embarrassed teen and set her back on her feet.

'There you go,' said Hodge. 'And next time you want to play on the swings stick to the ones meant for older kids, yes?'

Sienna nodded. 'Thanks.'

They headed back to the appliance. If only all their jobs could be so easy. If only all their calls could be as simple as getting people out of sticky situations.

Perhaps Cara needed a fire crew to help her out of the situation with her dad?

Back at the station, Cara had barely got the kettle on when her mobile phone, which she'd set on silent, vibrated in her back pocket. She pulled it out and saw her dad's name. She let out a breath, not sure that she wanted to read the message. What could it be now?

Hey, Cara. Just a reminder about the fundraiser. It may be for the Webster family, but it's still your mum's evening, too, and she would have loved to see you attend dressed as a lady. It's what she would have wanted. A dress and heels, please. Have your hair done. Makeup. I'll pay. Just do her proud.

Cara stared at the phone in disbelief. He'd had to go there! Getting right to the one thing that he knew Cara felt guilty about!

Serena Maddox had *dreamed* of having a daughter after three boys. She'd loved her sons—of course she had—but she'd longed to have a daughter she could dress in pink and play dolls with, have a special bond with. And Cara disappointed her from the get-go. She'd very much been a tomboy—playing in the mud with her brothers, going hunting, making dens, playing rough, happy in jeans, not interested in anything remotely pink, and certainly not in dolls or dresses or shoes or handbags.

She'd refused to be railroaded in such a way. It had always been a disappointment to her mother. And when her mother had died Cara had felt the guilt of never giving her what she'd wanted. Not even for one day. And that guilt had caused her to stay in her own lane even more. Because what was the point in doing anything different now? Her mum wouldn't get to see it.

She'd started going to the gym even more, working out, lifting weights. Punishing herself. She'd got tattoos. Hey, she'd already failed at pleasing her mother—why not go for it?

But it had all been grief. Just her way of coping. She wasn't that bad now—though she was still a stranger to anything other than boots or trainers. And pink? There was nothing in her life that was pink. Cara liked black and grey. Didn't own a single handbag. She would feel like a complete alien from another planet if she had to go dress-shopping. Or shoe-shopping! She'd much rather hang out at the gym. The only shops she frequented were grocery stores and bookshops.

At that moment in time, she hated her father.

So she punched in the number of the only person she knew she could talk to about this.

Tom.

He answered on the first ring. 'Hey. How are you doing?'

It was so good to hear his voice. She'd not seen him since the night at the pub and she'd missed him. Just hearing his warm voice now made her want to hug the phone tight to her ear and cry.

'Not great,' she said.

'Oh. What's up? Anything I can help with?'

'I hope so. Can I pop round later? I'd like to see you.'

There was a pause as she heard him talk to someone. Gage's voice in the background. 'Sure. I'm just getting Gage ready for bed. When is your shift over?'

'In half an hour. Can I come straight round?'

'Course you can. But Gage might be sleeping, so text me when you're here, so the doorbell doesn't wake him up.'

'Thanks, Tom.'

She ended the call, feeling a little better. Tom always made her feel good. Always listened when she had a problem. And she thought that he got a lot out of their friendship, too. She was company for him, she thought. Female company…which he had to miss after losing Victoria, right? Someone to talk to in the evenings after Gage had gone to bed.

When she got to his house he let her in, and she went straight into his arms for a long hug. It was as if he knew she needed comfort, and for a while she just stood there, head pressed against his chest, listening to the regular, methodical beat of his heart, her eyes closed in bliss, just breathing him in. He felt so strong. So sturdy. A steady presence.

She wasn't sure how long they stood there in silence, but eventually Tom asked her if she wanted to go into the lounge and he'd make her a drink.

If she was honest, she could have stood there in his arms all night. Not talking. Not speaking to each other. Just communicating through the hug. The need to be held. To be comforted. To feel safe and loved and not judged. For there to be no demands made by either person.

'Sure. Okay.' Reluctantly, she let go of him and followed him into the lounge, where she sat down on one of his comfy sofas.

'Tea? Coffee? Something stronger?' he asked with a smile from the kitchen doorway.

'Tea's fine, thanks.' She let out a sigh.

'Is it your dad?' he asked when the kettle was on and he'd come back to the lounge whilst waiting for it to boil.

She smiled wryly. 'Who else?'

'What's he said now?'

Cara pulled her phone from her pocket and showed Tom the text.

'Emotional blackmail. Nice.' He handed the phone back. 'What did you say to him?'

'I've not answered yet. I know he's not asking for a big thing. Wear a dress. Wear some heels. Look like a proper fricking lady for a change! But it's just the way he brought my mother into it, you know? He knows how I felt when we lost her and he's using that guilt against me.'

Tom was silent for a moment, as if searching for the

right words. 'I wouldn't be happy if someone used me like that either. I'd probably not speak to that person for a while. But this is different. It's your dad. He's the only parent you've got left.'

'Yeah…'

'If you want to turn up at that evening wearing camo paint and army fatigues, I'll back you one hundred percent…' He smiled.

Cara laughed.

'But if you do decide to give him what he wants, to get him off your back, then I'll back that decision also.'

She sighed. 'What do you think I should do?'

'It's not my decision to make. But if you do go the dress route, I'd take the opportunity to tell your father he can never use your mother against you ever again.'

'Agreed. But how would I even know how to wear heels? I'd probably break my ankle.'

'Hey, come on. It's one night. A couple of hours at the most. You run into burning buildings, Cara! The bravery that takes? I couldn't do it. But I have no doubt that you can do this.'

She looked into his eyes. Saw the warmth there. The love. The support. If he had belief in her, then maybe she should have belief in herself too.

'Okay.'

'You're going to do it?'

'I'm going to do it!'

She laughed with relief. Glad that Tom had helped her see sense. He was right. It was one night. Three hours? Four? And then it would all be over and she could tell her father that she'd done her bit and he needed to let her live her life as she pleased in future.

'Let's have biscuits with that tea,' said Tom. 'I think I have some chocolate digestives to celebrate.'

'Rock and roll.'

CHAPTER THREE

TOM HAD JUST got back into his rapid response vehicle, after treating a suspected cardiac arrest, when a call came through that there had been a multi-car pile-up on one of the main roads in Battersea. He flipped the switch for his blues and twos and told Control to show him as attending, ETA five minutes.

'Roger that. Police and fire crew are also en route.'

The streets were thick with traffic, and in some parts he had to wait as vehicles already in the jam tried to find a way to move aside, to let him through. Moments like this taught him patience. There was nothing he could do, and it was too late now to go back and try an alternative route. In front of him, drivers tooted their horns at one another, and a few wound down windows to make hand gestures to other drivers, telling them to move over a bit more. And slowly, slowly, the cars parted and created a very narrow lane for him to drive down.

He inched his way along until he was finally able to get through the lights, hit a right and drive down a road that was thankfully much clearer and traffic was flowing. This was better. But his anxiety was high. The traffic jam had caused him a significant delay and time counted. Someone could be trapped inside a vehicle, losing blood, losing precious seconds in which their lives might be saved.

But despite this he knew he had to use caution still. Every junction, every crossing, every school that he passed could be a potential site of danger for pedestrians or cyclists or other motor vehicles that simply didn't see or hear him. Despite the lights and sirens, it was amazing how many people could be in their own little world when they were out and about. It wasn't unheard of for emergency vehicles to end up in a pile-up themselves.

But he was getting closer.

Then the traffic was beginning to snarl up again, and he had to inch through, until he managed to park behind a police car that itself was parked behind a fire engine.

The street was lit with strobing red and blue lights as he grabbed his jump bag, slipped on a high vis vest and walked towards the accident.

He sucked in a breath at the sight of it.

A blue car lay on its roof, facing in the wrong direction, steam hissing out of its engine. A silver car was on the other side of it, its front crumpled in, airbags deployed. A white van was parked askew to the left of them, the driver's door hanging open, and behind them a lorry that had obviously skidded to avoid them had crossed over into the wrong lane, hitting a small red car.

He could see Hodge, striding around in his white helmet, which told him that Cara had to be on the scene somewhere. Maybe one of the team currently gathered around the blue car. All around police were trying to establish a perimeter, as nosy onlookers gathered. Some officers were comforting people kerbside. Were they drivers? Walking wounded?

Tom got Hodge's attention and the chief fire officer came over to him.

'Hey, where do you want me?'

Hodge pointed. 'The driver of the blue car needs the most attention. She's trapped inside the vehicle, unconscious, breathing sounds bad, respirations are really low. We've got her on oxygen and Cara's holding C-spine. There was a child in the back, strapped into a baby seat. We've got her out. Seems fine, just a little shaken up, but she will need a check. Driver of the white van is fine—he avoided impact, as did the lorry driver. The guy driving the silver car has whiplash, and the passengers of the red car are in shock and have a few cuts and bruises.'

'Most of them have been lucky, then?'

'If you call a car crash lucky, yeah.'

Tom hurried forward towards the blue car that was upside down on its roof. He acknowledged Cara with a quick smile. 'Morning.'

'Good morning,' she said.

'We really need to stop meeting like this.'

She smiled at him as she lay on the road on her side, her arms within the car, holding the driver's neck. 'We must.'

'Was she unconscious when you got here?' asked Tom.

'Yes.'

'And hasn't woken up?'

'No. And her breathing has been slow and erratic. I can hear a wheeze.'

Thankfully, Cara and her crew had already got the driver on oxygen. Tom reached through the broken glass and past the deflated airbag to place his stethoscope on the patient's chest.

'Agreed. I think she's asthmatic.'

He felt dread wash over him. Something he always felt now, when he had to attend to an asthmatic, since the death of his wife.

Asthma was the complication in Victoria's medical history that had led to her death from Covid at the beginning of the pandemic. Hearing this woman wheeze, seeing her pale face, reminded him of his wife's attacks.

There'd been one time when she'd totally collapsed. It had been Christmas, and they'd invited both sets of parents over to their house. Victoria had woken that morning feeling breathless. They'd argued, because Tom had said they should cancel their guests, as clearly she wasn't well, but Victoria, not willing to let people down on Christmas Day, had simply shaken her head, used her inhalers and said she'd power through. He'd helped her peel veggies and prepare the table, and then he'd set off in the car to fetch his parents, who didn't have a vehicle, leaving Victoria at home.

She'd promised, she'd stay sitting down, reading a book or watching TV, until he got back. Only when he had returned they'd walked in, full of Christmas cheer, with his parents calling out 'Merry Christmas!', only to find Victoria lying on the floor of the kitchen, face pale, wheezing terribly, close to losing consciousness.

He'd called an ambulance so fast! His parents had taken over the cooking and when Victoria had got better and was finally allowed home, they all had Christmas dinner really late that night.

Had *this* woman been suffering, but thought she was

okay to drive her car? Or had the attack started in the car? Maybe even caused the crash?

Tom didn't know, but the woman's airway was his primary concern. ABC. Airway. Breathing. Circulation. Airway came first. He organised a nebuliser first.

'Let's get a cervical collar on.'

He pulled the one he had from his bag and positioned it around the woman's neck. Then he could continue with his primary survey.

Cara, now free from holding the C-spine, joined her crew to help with prepping the vehicle for extraction.

Tom could see cuts on the woman's face and arms, but had no idea if she'd sustained any broken bones, and he wouldn't know for sure until they got her free of the vehicle. He attached a SATs monitor to her, checking her oxygen levels, and then Cara was asking him to move back, so they could safely break the glass around the vehicle, ready for cutting.

He stood back, knowing he could do no more until she was free, but he was worried. Focused. He wanted her out of the vehicle so he could treat her properly, but this next bit would take some time.

Cara's crew had already stabilised the vehicle, so that it wouldn't move as they cut through the metal. They were cutting through the struts to take the stress off the roof of the car, freeing it to make it easier to free the patient.

Cara used power tools to cut through the fender and expose the door hinges, before Reed removed the doors all round. Then they cut the post above the door hinges and began using another power tool to lift the car free from the dashboard and create even more room, whilst Hodge continued to stabilise the vehicle from the rear.

All Tom could hear was the crunch of metal. He checked his watch. This was time-critical. The woman could stop breathing at any moment. Behind him, other ambulances had arrived and were checking the walking wounded, so he could retain his focus on the asthmatic patient.

He wondered what her name was. Where she was going. What she'd thought her day would involve when she'd set off this morning. Had it just been another day? Who did she have worrying about her?

Cara's crew had secured the vehicle once more, then moved the car seat out of the way, and were now calling for the backboard so they could slide it in through the rear of the vehicle to get the patient out without causing more damage to the spine or neck.

'Easy now!' Tom called as he helped them guide her out.

Thankfully her legs weren't trapped, and they looked in reasonable shape, though there were cuts to her knees. He had to hope there weren't any internal injuries, but he wouldn't find out until later.

Once she was free and on a trolley, he rechecked his primary survey. Her oxygen levels were low and she was at risk of going into serious respiratory arrest.

'Get her to the hospital now!' he instructed the paramedics helping him.

He had to stand back and watch them take her. He'd done all he could, though he felt, as he often did when seeing an asthmatic patient, that he hadn't done enough. He'd given her medication in the oxygen, but that seemed pathetically little help. It always did— especially if the patient was too far gone into their attack and didn't respond to it.

Would she survive? He didn't even know her name. He hated feeling this way.

He felt a hand on his arm. 'Tom? Are you all right?'

Cara. Her soft voice was balm for his soul.

He nodded. Smiled.

'Are you sure? I know this must hit home for you. I'm sure she'll be okay.'

'Thanks. I hope so.'

'Hey, do you want me to pop round later? I could bring a takeaway. Your choice.'

'I don't think I'm in the mood for takeout.'

'How about I come round early and take Gage off your hands for a bit? We haven't played footie together for ages.'

'He'd love that. He loves it when you come. Maybe we should all go out? The fresh air will do me good.'

She smiled. 'Okay. I gotta go now, so I'll see you later? About five-thirty?'

'Perfect.'

He watched her return to her team. They had work to clear up. Their job wasn't over just because the patients were all out.

He was thankful for Cara. Thankful for her friendship. Her insights into his emotional wellbeing. She'd realised how treating an asthmatic would affect him. How the sound of an asthmatic wheeze often chilled his blood, because it reminded him of Victoria's battles with the condition.

He headed back to his car, exchanged his empty oxygen tank for a full one from an ambulance that had not yet left the scene, and then sank into his vehicle to write up his notes.

But as he sat in the car he tried to remember the

last time he'd spoken to Victoria. What had their last words to each other been? He couldn't remember. *Why* couldn't he remember? Was his brain trying to protect him from something? Or was it something mundane? He felt their last words ought to have been important. *I love you. I'll miss you. Get well soon.* Only he had a sneaking suspicion it hadn't been those. He'd been panicking over her worsening breathing. Insisting she call a doctor. But she'd refused, saying it wasn't that bad, and had isolated herself in their bedroom whilst suggesting he slept on the couch—so he didn't get sick, so he could take care of Gage.

By the time he'd got an ambulance and the crew had assessed her, she'd barely been able to talk. Her eyes had been wide with fear from the strain of breathing and trying to get desperately needed oxygen into her lungs. The paramedics had talked to her as they'd carried her down the stairs in a portable chair. Reassuring her. Telling her she was doing fine. Not much further to go. Then Gage had begun to cry, frightened by these strange men in his home, no doubt sensing the tension and upset, and Tom had been trying to soothe their son. Holding him tight, stroking his hair, telling him to say goodbye to Mummy.

Had he said anything important to Victoria? Or had he missed the opportunity, believing that he would be able to speak to her later, on the phone? An occasion that had never materialised, because when they'd got her to the hospital they'd anaesthetised her and put her on a ventilator and she'd never come off it.

So their last words to each other must have been before that. They could have been anything!

'I'd better sleep downstairs, then, so I can look after Gage.'

'Do you need anything? A cup of tea?'

'I'll leave your plate just outside the door. Try and eat.'

Maybe those words said *I love you*, only in a different manner?

He hoped so. He hoped she'd interpreted them in that way. Because he knew that when he *had* told her that he loved her she hadn't been able to hear him. Because she'd been unconscious, with a tube down her throat, and dying. He'd had to say it over the phone, with a nurse holding the handset to her ear. But by then it had been too late.

He hoped the lady today had someone who would sit by her bedside. Someone who loved her. That they would get the chance to say to each other all the things they wanted to say.

Because it was awful when you couldn't tell someone how you really felt.

Cara rang the doorbell, smiling in anticipation of hearing Gage race his father to the door, so that he could greet their guest first.

She saw his little figure through the glass and felt her heart swell. Gage was a wonderful little boy, delightfully happy and curious and funny, despite all that he had gone through.

He stretched to reach the door handle and finally swung the door open. 'Cara!' He leapt up at her and she caught him in her arms, swinging him up high, easily, and whirling him around.

'Hello, you! Are you ticklish today? Let me see!' And

she put him down on the ground and began to tickle him under his arms, causing him to giggle and laugh and collapse on the doormat hysterically. 'Hmm... Maybe... What about here? Or here?'

Gage laughed and laughed, squirming, enjoying the game, and then suddenly Tom was there, looking great in dark jeans and a white tee, and she felt the usual wave of heat and awareness wash over her, taking her breath away.

She released Gage and stood up straight. 'Hey.'

'Hey.' He smiled back, and she was glad to see he seemed a little brighter than earlier at the accident.

'Want to come out and play?' she joked.

'Let me just grab our jackets.'

'And a ball?'

'Ah, yes. Of course. Gage? Go and fetch your football from the box by the back door, please.'

'Yes, Daddy.'

Tom ruffled his son's hair as he ran past.

'He's getting big,' said Cara. 'What are you feeding him?'

'He'll eat anything. The boy's not picky. Must be a growth spurt.'

Gage came back, ball tucked under his arm. 'Are we going to the park?'

'We certainly are,' she answered. 'Come on, you. I need you to show me your moves and what you've learned since I saw you last.'

As they walked down the street to the park, Gage in the middle, holding Cara's hand on the left and Tom's hand on the right, Gage talked non-stop. About keepy-uppies, how many goals he'd scored against his dad at the weekend, how he was going to be a pro footballer when he was older.

Cara looked over his head at Tom to smile and share in the wonder of this little boy. She loved little Gage. He was perfect. Just the kind of kid she'd wish to have herself, if she was ever lucky enough to have a family of her own. Not that that was looking likely. Men didn't seem to notice her, which only reinforced her doubts about her own attractiveness.

Besides, she was always at work, her body and face hidden behind her firefighter's uniform and helmet. The only men who did notice her were her crew, and none of them were single. They were all married or in long-term relationships, apart from Reed, and they only saw her as a friend and colleague. Someone they could trust with their lives. Who had their backs. They didn't see her as potential love interest. Did they even think she was pretty?

They were protective of her, though. Like extra big brothers. Which was kind of nice, but could be scary for guys who did take an interest. Like Leo, for example. Her crew mates hadn't been fond of him. *Suspicious* might be a better word for how they'd felt about Cara's ex. And when Leo had ripped out her heart and walked away without so much as a backward glance, they'd been queueing up to go visit him and *'have a word'*.

She'd appreciated the offer, and the sentiment…but by then she'd felt so humiliated, she'd wanted nothing further to do with him.

Cara stole glances at Tom as they chatted with Gage and wished that he saw her as more than a friend. There'd been moments where her hopes had been raised. Once, she'd caught him looking at her oddly as she'd helped him put together a treehouse in the back garden. The way he'd been looking at her had made her feel self-conscious.

'What?' she'd asked.

'Oh...nothing. I was just daydreaming.'

'About what?'

He'd shaken his head. *'Nothing.'*

She'd returned to hammering in nails, holding two of them in her mouth, but it had been enough to make her feel that she'd been assessed and found wanting.

Would Victoria have helped him build a treehouse? No. She'd have left him to it. Brought out the occasional cup of tea and told him how good it was looking, but that would have been all. And yet there she'd been, in the scruffy tee shirt she used when she was decorating and some cargo pants, covered in sawdust and sweat!

Hardly attractive!

Tom was so handsome and so deserving of some happiness and she felt she could provide it. But she didn't have many friends outside of the fire service, and she didn't want to ruin the friendship she had with Tom by complicating it. Besides, he probably wasn't ready to date yet. He was too busy being a father to Gage and he would *never* be interested in her. No matter how much she wished he would.

The park wasn't that busy, and they managed to find a space where they could kick around the ball. Gage and Tom used their discarded jackets as goal posts and Tom went into goal, leaving Cara and Gage as opposing team members, desperate to score. Around them, birds sang in the trees and squirrels searched the ground for acorns or whatever it was that squirrels searched for. Gage sent one shot wide, the ball flying over to a bunch of oaks, and a grey squirrel shot halfway up a tree trunk and peered at them as if in reproach.

'I'll get it!' Gage said, running after it, his little legs pumping hard. He picked up the ball and came back, throwing it past her to take a shot at goal.

'Hey!' Cara laughed and let him take his shot.

Tom paused and let the ball roll past him and score, pretending he'd been too slow to stop it.

'Yay! One nil to me!' Gage lifted his tee shirt above his head, like footballers did on television, and ran around until he fell over, collapsing with laughter.

Cara scooped him up, righted his tee and then tried to dribble the ball past him. Gage tackled her. She let him have it and he scored again.

'Oh, you're too good for me!' she said, hands thrown in the air, and then she, too, collapsed onto the grass.

Gage jumped on her and she scooped him up above her, whirling him around like an airplane. Eventually Tom took him from her arms and whirled him to his feet.

'I'm exhausted. Who fancies ice cream?'

'Me, me, me!' Gage said.

Tom raised an eyebrow at Cara. 'Fancy a mint choc chip?'

'You know the way to my heart!' she joked, wishing that he really would find the way.

Maybe he would one day. Maybe she was wrong to think he would never see her in that way. One thing she knew for sure was that Tom was worth waiting for…and if it was meant to take some time, then she was okay with that. Being his friend for now would have to be enough. She just hoped he wouldn't do something stupid, like fall in love with someone else, so she'd have to stand there on the sidelines and watch him with another woman.

Tom held out his hand, which she took, and he hauled her to his feet.

They gathered the jackets and headed towards the ice cream van at the other end of the park. One mint choc chip, one strawberry and one chocolate ice cream later, they were sitting on the benches by the public aviary cages, watching the budgies flit from perch to perch as they licked their ice creams.

'So, have you decided what you're going to wear yet for the ball?' Tom asked.

She sighed. 'No. I keep trying to ignore it.'

'You've only got to the end of the month.'

She changed the subject. 'What are *you* going to wear?'

'I have a tux tucked away somewhere. All I have to do is find a mask.'

She stared at him for a moment as an idea formed. Was she brave enough to ask? Would this be expecting their friendship to go to places it wasn't ready to go?

'Would you help me?'

'With what?'

She blushed. She didn't normally ask for help, and for some reason this seemed like a really big thing to ask of him. It seemed…intimate.

'Help me find a dress? I have no idea what type of thing to look for and I'm just not used to going into those types of places.'

He laughed nervously. 'You mean shops?'

'Girly places.'

'You think *I am*?'

'Well, you must have sat around waiting for Victoria

to shop sometimes? Offered an opinion on an outfit? I would like a male opinion.'

She honestly thought he was going to say no. He seemed to think about it for an inordinate amount of time. Looked as if he was going to turn her down. As if he was trying to think of an excuse without hurting her feelings. Maybe she should just let him off the hook? Tell him she was being silly? Of course he didn't have to go shopping with her! What kind of man enjoyed going clothes-shopping with a girlfriend? None that she knew.

'Okay.'

'You will?' She brightened. At the fact that he'd said yes and the fact that it meant spending a lot more time with Tom.

'Sure. Why not?'

Cara flung her arms around him and kissed him on the cheek. 'Thanks!'

She released him to lick her ice cream, her body thrumming with excitement. One question down. Now to ask the next.

Gage got up and idly dawdled over to the bird cages for a closer look.

Cara lowered her voice. 'Could I ask you one more thing?'

'Sure. Go for it.'

She hoped she wouldn't blush. She failed. Miserably. 'Would you come as my date?' Her cheeks bloomed with heat and she almost couldn't make eye contact with him. 'Only my dad will try to pair me off with someone if I turn up alone. Last time it was with this dimwit called Hugo. The son of one of his best friends. All he could talk about all night was stocks and shares. I was

bored rigid and totally embarrassed. With you there…
I could avoid that.'

'You mean you don't want to hear my scintillating
take on the stock market?' he teased.

He could read her the phone book and she wouldn't
mind.

'No, thanks.'

They both laughed, tension released, but she crunched
into her waffle cone, painfully aware that he hadn't said
yes yet.

'So…you want me to pretend to be your boyfriend?'

She checked to make sure Gage couldn't hear what
they were saying, but he appeared to be enamoured of
the brightly coloured birds flitting from perch to perch.
'Yes. I know it's asking a lot, and if it makes you uncomfortable then please feel free to say no. I'd totally
understand. I'd—'

'I'd be honoured.'

Cara stared at him, fighting the impulse to drop her
ice cream cone and plant her lips directly on Tom's. Her
heart pounded in her chest.

'Thanks.' she said, instead. 'That means a lot to me.'

Tom shrugged. 'It's no big deal. It's just pretend,
right?'

She nodded. 'Right.'

'It's just pretend, right?'

That sentence kept repeating over and over in Tom's
mind all night. Condemning him and teasing him in
one stroke.

Cara was amazing. Beautiful, clever—and she loved
Gage almost as much as he did! But…what would people say? It hadn't been two years since he'd lost Victo-

ria, and everyone had assumed everything was great between them. Childhood sweethearts? What could possibly go wrong?

People had fallen in love with that idea. They'd thought it was sweet and romantic and perfect. How would they react if they knew what had truly been going on?

He'd believed at the time that marrying Victoria when she discovered she was pregnant was the right thing to do. And it had been! It had allowed him to watch Gage grow up in the same house as him every day. To experience his milestones first-hand. He'd been there for his first word—*Dada*. His first faltering steps. But he'd also seen Victoria change. Almost as if she'd resented having become a mother so soon.

She would palm Gage off on him the second he walked through the door, so she could go off and have 'girl time' with her friends. They'd argue over simple things Her appearance had mattered to her more than anything else sometimes. She'd spent crazy amounts of money on hair extensions and dresses and heels she never wore, when he'd given her that money for the things Gage needed.

He'd tried so hard to be the best partner he could, but it had never seemed to be enough. She'd always found him wanting, no matter what he did to try and make her happy, and so he'd given up trying. Working long hours. Taking extra shifts. He'd told himself he was doing it for his boy, so they could afford everything he wanted in life, but really he'd been doing it because it was easier to be at work.

What would people think if he started to show that he had feelings for someone else so soon? He didn't want to dishonour Victoria's memory. And Cara? She'd think badly of him for fancying her, surely.

Maybe he was reading more into his feelings for her than he should? Maybe he just *thought* he had feelings for her because she was such a good friend? Because she was so supportive and kind and enjoyed spending time with him and Gage?

I'm just misreading the situation. Grateful for her kindness, that's all.

That was why he hadn't turned down her offer to go dress-shopping with her. He'd thought about it! Going dress-shopping with Victoria had been downright exhausting! Sitting in chairs, watching her go in and out of changing rooms, hearing her asking him if he preferred the scarlet or the crimson...

'They're both red, Vic. Just pick one!'

He had been going to say no. Initially. Watching the woman he had strong feelings for putting on pretty dresses? What if he slipped up and said something incriminating?

And then he'd thought about that idiot ex-boyfriend of hers—Leo. The one who had said all those horrible things about her. About how she wasn't feminine enough. Wasn't woman enough to hold a man. And he'd just known he wanted to go, so that he could see her in all those pretty dresses and build up her confidence a little. If she needed it.

She didn't really want to go out with him. It was just to stop her father interfering again and trying to matchmake.

No. They were just friends. Even if his feelings for her were confusing. He loved Cara, yes—as he loved all of his friends. But he wasn't *in love* with her. At least, he didn't think so. It was just confusing because of how good they were together. How Cara reminded him of who he'd used to be.

So he'd agreed to go shopping with her. Find her a dress. Pretend to be her date at the ball. Maybe as long as they arrived together and were seen together by her father that would be enough. He could leave her to do her thing, and he would go and do his thing. Chat to whoever he knew there. The word about the ball had been spreading, and most of the paramedics who were going to be off duty had agreed to go. Why wouldn't they? They didn't very often get invited to a posh manor house and have the chance to get dressed up, all in the name of a good cause.

He was intrigued himself about the idea of going to Cara's family home. She didn't often talk about her childhood, and he wondered if, by going, he would understand her more. Cara had no airs and graces. She didn't expect to be treated differently because she was the daughter of an earl. She was just one of the guys to most people.

To him... She was that and more.

Tom gave Gage a bath and then read him a bedtime story. His son nodded off halfway through, no doubt exhausted by the football, so Tom left the book on his son's bedside cabinet so they could finish it off tomorrow. He switched off his lamp and crept back downstairs and sat in his lounge alone.

These were the moments he hated. When his son was asleep and it was late at night he felt more alone than he ever did at any other time.

He missed the simple act of sitting on the couch with someone, watching a movie, maybe having a nice glass of wine… He missed that feeling of connection, of having someone stroke his arm absently, or someone resting their head upon his shoulder. He hated going to bed alone. The bed seemed so big without anyone else in it. So empty.

Later Tom lay in his bed and stared up at the ceiling. He thought about Cara. About the way she'd looked playing football with his son. Her smile. Her laughter. The way the sun had caught the auburn tones of her hair, flashing fire. The way she'd looked at him, her eyes aglow, brightly gleaming with happiness. The way she'd made Gage laugh. The way she'd brightened his son's world.

And his.

What am I doing? I'm reading more into this than I should. She's just a friend. That's all she will ever be.

CHAPTER FOUR

'DAD, NO.' CARA had been hanging her things in her locker at work when her mobile phone had rung.

'Why not? Carenza can fit you in this weekend—she's already told me. All she needs are your measurements and she can whip you up something special for the ball.'

'I don't need a designer to make me a bespoke dress. I'll buy one from a shop. In fact, Tom is taking me out to find a dress later on today.'

Her father sounded doubtful. 'The *paramedic*?'

'Yes.'

A pause. 'You two an item, then?'

'Yes,' she lied, gritting her teeth, wishing she could be saying it with a smile, as if it were actually real.

'Oh, that's a shame. I'd rather told Henry that you're single. He's bringing along his son Xander to meet you.'

She rolled her eyes. 'Well, Xander can say hello, but that's all he'll get from me. I'm with Tom.' She glanced around to make sure none of her crew mates from Green Watch were within hearing. There'd be no end of questions if they heard that. Not to mention the teasing she'd get. And if they found out it was fake…? It didn't bear thinking about.

Her father sighed. 'All right. But make sure the dress is something special. There's going to be a photographer, and I'm going to want official pictures of the only time my daughter wore a dress.'

'You're getting a photographer for *that*?'

'Not just for you, darling, don't worry. It's good publicity, what we're doing for the Werther family.'

'The Websters.'

'Ah, yes. Well, I've got to go. Do ring me and let me know when you've found something.'

'Fine.'

'And, darling?'

'Yes?'

'Just be careful. With Tom. A lot of men might be interested in you for reasons you don't suspect.'

Poor Dad. He thought lots of men were interested in her because she was a Lady! If only he knew that men didn't see her that way.

'He's not with me because of money, Dad.'

She sighed, wishing she could end this call, because it was becoming awful, and she hated lying to him, even if he was the one who had put her in this position in the first place.

'Just make sure—that's all.'

He said goodbye and ended the call.

Cara stood there, feeling an anger that boiled inside. It was so unfair! Her father was interfering in her life again. As she passed through the gym she gave the punchbag a thump, sending it swinging one way, then the other, before she headed to the canteen to make herself a drink before parade.

Reed and the others were already there, propping up the kitchen counters, slurping their tea from mugs.

'Morning, Cara,' said Reed.

'Morning.'

'Ready for another day?'

She nodded, smiled. 'Absolutely.' She filled the kettle with water, but before she could reach for a mug the station bell sounded. They had a shout.

They headed for the fire engine as Hodge collected the call report. He met them as they dressed themselves in their uniforms.

'Male trapped in an industrial machine. That's all we have.'

Cara grimaced. That didn't sound good. But she switched herself into work mode and the fire engine, with sirens blaring, pulled out of the station, stopping the traffic, and went roaring in the direction of town.

As they passed the park that she and Tom and Gage had played football in she glanced out of the window, remembering the previous night. It had all been a little awkward after she'd asked Tom to accompany her to the ball as her date. Though she'd made it quite clear it was a fake date, she'd hated lying to Tom.

Why couldn't she just be brave enough to tell him the truth?

Because Victoria was an Amazonian goddess, that's why.

She'd distracted herself from her self-loathing and asked Gage to point out his favourite budgies in the aviary. She'd walked over to the birdcages, embarrassed to turn around and look at Tom. What on earth was he thinking? But eventually they had walked home, neither she nor Tom being overly chatty. Perhaps he was already regretting saying yes? Perhaps she was just being overly sensitive over this issue? Perhaps it was abundantly clear to Tom that this could never be anything but a fake date and so he wasn't worried at all? Because clearly he had no idea about her hidden feelings for him.

Which was just the way she wanted to keep it, thank you very much.

In a strange way she was looking forward to the dress-shopping tonight. Not because of the dresses. No. That part she was dreading. But spending time with Tom was always her favourite thing to do, and tonight he had a babysitter for Gage.

The fire engine sped through the traffic.

Hodge turned. 'Ambulance crew and rapid response are also on their way.'

Reed nudged her. 'Maybe lover-boy will be there.'

She glared at him.

They pulled into an industrialised area. Lots of lorries and vans loading up. A man in a bright yellow high vis jacket stood in the road, directing them to the place they needed to be, which was very much appreciated. He ran to greet them as they pulled up.

'Hi. I'm John—the manager. We've got one of our workers with his arm trapped in an industrial printing machine. It became jammed, and he was trying to clear the blockage, but got his arm trapped inside when it started up again. He's lost a lot of blood and is barely conscious.'

At that moment the rapid response vehicle turned up, with an ambulance and a police car following quickly behind. Tom got out, and he and the other medics were quickly filled in on what had happened.

John led them to the site of the accident.

'Has all this been turned off?' Hodge asked.

'Not all of it.'

'I want everything shut down whilst my crew are here. We don't need any further accidents as they try to help your man here. What's his name?'

'Pete.'

'Okay.' Hodge went over to the man, who was trapped in the machine up to his mid-upper arm and looking pale and weak. 'Pete? We're going to get you out of there, okay?' Hodge turned to John. 'Any chance you can get him a chair or something to sit on? If he passes out he's going to pull on that arm and maybe make his injury worse.'

John nodded and disappeared to get a chair.

Hodge took the opportunity to look at the machinery intently. To see where the arm was caught and if there was any easy way they could extract him.

'Okay, the machine's off Tom, do you want to take a look? It's safe for you to approach now.'

Hodge stepped back and Tom stepped forward. He'd already got an oxygen mask prepped and ready and he secured it to Pete's face.

Cara watched. The poor man! This was going to be a life-changing injury. He'd probably come to work this morning, thinking it was just going to be another ordinary day, but this had happened.

As Tom did his assessment, John came back with the chair.

'Where are your engineers?' asked Hodge. 'We're going to need people who can dismantle this machine, because I don't think you want us just cutting our way through it.'

'Er…no. We don't. I can call Carlos, but he's at home.'

'Anyone else?'

'The business down the road has the same machine

as us. I can call them and ask if their engineer is on site? He'd get here quicker than Carlos would, as he doesn't have his own car and would have to rely on public transport.'

Hodge nodded. 'Call them.'

Tom was inserting a cannula for an IV into Pete's arm. 'I'm giving you fluids and a painkiller, okay?'

Pete nodded, his eyes barely open. Was he shutting down?

Tom grabbed his mobile. 'Control? I'm at the entrapment call. We need a doctor on site. This guy's going to want stronger painkillers than I can give him.'

'Confirmed. Heli-med en route.'

'Thank you, Control.' He turned to Hodge and the team. 'I can't do anything more until we get him clear of this machine.' He lowered his voice. 'Looking at the arm, I'm thinking we're looking at a possible amputation.'

Cara's heart sank. Pete was young. He had a wedding ring on his finger. She stepped forward. 'Pete? Can you open your eyes for me? Is there anyone we can call for you?'

Pete blinked, bleary-eyed, then nodded. With his free hand he pulled the oxygen mask away from his face. 'Sal. Call Sal. My wife.'

'Give me her number.'

Once he had, Tom put the oxygen mask back onto the man's face and checked his pressures and his pulse. 'He's going into shock.'

At that moment they heard running, and Cara turned to see a guy in dirty navy overalls appear, puffing, out of breath, his eyes widening at the sight before him. 'You need an engineer?'

Hodge stepped up. 'Yes. We need this machine dismantled so we can free this man. What's your name?'

'Charlie.'

'Okay, Charlie. We need this done quick.'

'I've put on a tourniquet,' said Tom.

'Okay…' Charlie paused.

'Problem?' asked Cara.

'I'm just not very good with blood, and there's… um…a lot of it.' Charlie was starting to turn pale.

'Try not to look at that. Focus on what you need to do. I can help you.' Cara guided him forward with his toolbox and they set to work. They'd been working on the machine for maybe five minutes when a doctor arrived in an orange Heli-med jumpsuit.

'Can everyone just stand back so I can assess the patient, please?'

They all did, waiting and watching.

The doctor listened to the patient's chest, checked his pressures and examined the arm, which was still firmly trapped in the machine.

Pete was nearly completely unconscious.

'How long is it going to take to dismantle this machine?' he asked Charlie.

'Two hours, maybe?'

The doctor shook his head. 'The longer he stays trapped in that machine, the worse this is going to get. He's really struggling. His condition is deteriorating. I think we need to do an upper arm amputation and get him out. That arm is pretty mangled. I don't think there's any chance of saving it, and every second he's in there the more chance there is that infection will complicate matters.'

Tom nodded. 'Agreed.'

'Okay—let's do this.'

Charlie and the others backed off, and Tom and the Heli-med doctor set about preparing for amputation. They injected anaesthetic into Pete, so that he wouldn't feel anything, and began to manage his airway.

The doctor and Tom worked fast. Cara watched them. They moved as a perfect team. The doctor in charge, Tom assisting. This wasn't her first amputation, and she could remember being surprised at how fast someone could remove an arm or a leg. In her head, she'd always imagined it would take time. Carefully cutting through bone and muscle and sinew. Tying off blood vessels. Surely that should take hours? But, no. A couple of minutes and it was done.

Soon Pete was freed from the machine and lowered onto a trolley, where Tom and the other paramedics swarmed around him, getting his pressure back up and stabilising him for the trip to hospital via helicopter.

As Tom led Pete off on the trolley, Hodge got back to asking Charlie to open up the machine, so that they could still remove the mangled amputated arm.

Cara wished she'd had more of an opportunity to talk to Tom, but it had been all hands on deck. She would just have to wait to speak to him later that evening.

Tom knocked on Cara's door, trying not to feel as if he was picking her up for a date. Seriously, when had things changed? Because something had and he wasn't sure when. His feelings for her had crept up upon him, lurking like a shadow, always there but not always noticed. But now that he was *aware*, it was as if he couldn't stop noticing them.

He'd taken great care not to dress like a man going

on a date. He wore dark jeans, a black tee, and a flannel shirt over the top. He'd not checked his hair before leaving, despite the almost unstoppable urge to comb it before leaving the house, because he needed this to just be another night out with a mate.

Dress-shopping.

Hmm...

He'd only ever gone dress-shopping before with Victoria, and that had never gone well *at all*. Commenting on the first two outfits had been fine, but after that... He'd always tried his hardest to not seem bored. Once, when one of his friends had passed by, Victoria had let him off the hook and told him he could go. And he had. But when he'd got home she'd called him out on it.

Now, it was a memory that made him cringe. He knew he should have cherished every moment with her. But the truth of the matter was that they'd often let each other down. He wished he'd paid her more attention, but that particular dress-shopping outing had been the day after a huge fight they'd had, and the worse thing was he couldn't even remember what the fight had been about. Maybe work. By then Tom had been working long hours. Picking up extra shifts. Telling himself he was working hard to provide for his family—which he was. He just wasn't always there to enjoy the fruits of his labours. Which Victoria would often complain about.

She'd said she felt like a single mother half the time. And she'd been right. But it had been easier to work than to argue, and he hadn't wanted to argue. They'd had a lovely baby boy together and he'd wanted he and Victoria to work *so much*!

Tom had had dreams of the future in which they were

all together. Going on holidays. Getting close again. Finding the first flush of love that had brought them together in the early days. The feelings would still be there. They just needed rekindling. Somehow they'd both lost their way. Allowed the small things to become big things.

And he didn't ever want to make such a mistake again.

Maybe he wasn't cut out to be anyone's partner if he could screw up something that had once been so perfect? And Cara deserved someone who would put in one hundred percent. All the time. She had got him through his grief at the loss of his wife. Cara had become his rock and he couldn't lose her friendship. He needed her the way he needed air.

But he had to hold back. Not act on the strange feelings and thoughts about her that had often kept him awake at night lately. Wondering what she was doing. Who she might be with. There hadn't been a boyfriend since Leo, and he knew how much of a knock to her confidence Leo had given her. He wanted to be Cara's rock, too.

When she opened the door he smiled and said hello, pushing back the reaction he really wanted to show.

She looked simply and stunningly beautiful. And Cara didn't know she was beautiful, which made her even more so. She was oblivious to how she made him feel. Her hair, usually up in a bun for work, was free and flowing. The orange-red flecks were catching the low evening light. The cool blue of her eyes, sparkling with happiness at seeing him, her friend, warmed his heart and stirred his blood. Deliberately, he stood back, casually turning around to look at the road, as if the traffic or the way the cars were parked were interesting, as he waited for her to grab her keys and phone.

She wore light blue skinny jeans, white trainers and a baggy crimson-coloured tee. Something Victoria would never have been caught wearing to go out. But the colour showed off Cara's pale, creamy skin to perfection, and as she locked her door the loose sleeve slipped down one arm to reveal a shoulder, smooth and toned. Her trapezius muscle, sculpted by many hours spent in the gym, showed the gorgeous slope of her neck.

'Ready?' she asked, turning to him.

'Yep.'

'I'm not. I figure I'm about to look a whole lot of stupid.'

She grimaced, clearly expecting him to laugh, so he gave a small chuckle and led the way to the car, fighting the urge to open the door for her, as a gentleman would. Instead, he walked round to the driver's side and let her get in the car by herself.

As they drove through the evening traffic, a song came on the radio. 'Ooh, I love this one!' she said, and turned up the volume and began singing, bopping away beside him.

She had a good voice. He loved listening to her sing. And the way she was clicking her fingers to the music and swaying beside him made him want to stop the car, throw off his seatbelt and take her in his arms and kiss her.

What the hell am I doing? I can't have these thoughts about Cara. It's not right.

He pushed those thoughts to the back of his skull and tried to concentrate on the traffic, praying for the song to be over. When it was he was able to relax a little more. He found a parking space near to the shopping centre, despite it being busy on a late-night shopping evening, and they got out, paid for their parking and began walking towards the shops.

He knew from experience that there were plenty of clothes shops there, but only one or two that sold the sort of dresses that Cara would be looking for.

'Let's go to Imagine first,' he suggested.

He remembered it from before, and knew it had a large range of dresses. He hoped that would mean she'd find one straight away and then this torture would be over.

'What's that?'

'It's a shop that sells posh dresses. Evening dresses. Ball gowns, wedding outfits—all of that.'

'How do you know about it?'

'It's right next door to the baby shop where we got Gage's pushchair and Moses basket.'

'OK, she said hesitantly.'

'You seem nervous.'

'I am. What if I look ridiculous in these dresses? I've got muscles, I'm broad-shouldered, with tattoos. I won't look right.'

He disagreed. 'You'll look amazing. We'll find you a beautiful dress.'

She bumped into him, nudging his arm with hers. 'Thanks for doing this. I really appreciate it.'

He smiled at her. 'No problem.'

Of course he was worried, too. Worried that he'd see her in each dress and fall for her just a little bit more with every one. He couldn't imagine her not looking good in anything she chose to wear. Cara could wear a potato sack if she wanted to and she'd look amazing. The fact that she didn't understand that blew him away. She was different from most women. She was happy to be without make-up, without having done her hair. She'd never had a manicure or a pedicure, or spent hours in a hairdressing salon, or a tanning booth, and she was *perfect*.

And although he'd kind of been looking forward to spending this time with Cara, now that it was imminent he found himself fearing the evening. He told himself to create distance, not to pay too much attention to how she looked. He'd look at her briefly, tell her she looked good in something, and then they could go home.

And yet... He didn't want to lie to her. He didn't want to dismiss her. But most of all he didn't want to ruin their friendship. Cara would know. Would sense if he was just giving her lip service. And Leo had ruined her self-esteem, so he was damned well going to tell her how gorgeous she looked and try not to give himself away.

Lip service... That just made him think about kissing her.

They headed into Imagine and he stood back as Cara took the lead, checking out the dresses hanging on the racks. There were dresses of all colours. Dazzling to the eye, some of them. He even saw one in bright neon orange, like a highlighter pen.

Cara looked at him. 'I didn't expect there'd be so many. How am I supposed to choose?'

'Pick ones that catch your eye and then try them on.'

'Hmm. I don't know...' She bit her lip, frowning.

'Can I help you?'

A very, tall, thin woman, dressed in a navy skirt suit and a cream silk blouse, approached them. She had glasses on a chain around her neck and wore an alarming amount of perfume.

'I need a dress. For a ball.'

The woman smiled. 'How lovely. Now, let me see...' She ran her eyes over Cara. 'You look to be about a twelve—am I right?'

'I guess...' Cara shrugged.

'You'll want something like...' The woman turned, casting her knowledgeable gaze over her stock. 'This. Or this.' She selected two dresses on hangers and presented them to Cara.

Cara turned to look at Tom, seeking his opinion.

He gave the usual male response and just shrugged.

'Why not try them on?' the woman suggested. 'The dressing room is over there.'

As Cara disappeared into the changing room Tom settled himself down in a chair and waited, pulling out his mobile phone to double-check that he didn't have any messages from the babysitter looking after Gage. The teenager next door often looked after Gage. She used those evenings to study for her exams, saying it was quieter in his house than in hers, where she had to share a bedroom with her younger sister.

There was no message, so he tried to sit back and relax. Eventually the door to the changing room opened and Cara stepped out wearing the first gown. He almost dropped his phone in shock and surprise.

The dress was a dark midnight-blue and on the hanger had just looked like any other swathe of fabric. Nothing special. But on Cara it looked...magical. As if she was wearing the night sky. It was asymmetrical. One-shouldered. Sweeping down across her chest to cradle and hold curves that he hadn't ever quite seen be-

fore. Cara was usually hidden under her firefighter uniform, or in baggy tees and jeans during her off hours.
To see something this tight-fitting on her was…

He swallowed, trying to gather his thoughts, looking her up and down as if he were still thinking about
what to say—and he was. He wanted to say *You look
stunning. Gorgeous*. But he also didn't want her to realise just how affected he was at seeing her like this.

'You look lovely,' he managed, trying to sound normal.

Cara turned this way and that in front of the mirror.
'I don't know… I like the colour.'

The blue showed off her pale, creamy skin to perfection, and the tumble of her fiery hair, which she'd
pulled to one side so she could look at the back of the
dress, revealed to him her neck, her spine, the sweep
of toned muscles beneath her skin.

This was a woman who could carry a grown man
out of a burning building!

She had a waist. And curves that revealed hips that
somehow pulled his gaze.

'I think I'd better try the other one on. What do you
think?'

Tom nodded. 'Sure.'

He cleared his throat and let out a breath when she
disappeared back inside the changing room.

What the hell was happening?

This was *Cara*. Cara! She was just his friend. She
couldn't be anything else to him. He needed to stop
having these thoughts about her. Hadn't she sworn off
guys after Leo? Didn't Reed's daily attempts to wind
her up remind her every day that guys could be idiots

and not worth wasting her time on? Didn't she say that she was happy being single?

And she would never look at him in that way.

So he could never let her know how he was feeling.

It was probably a phase. It would pass! This was silly. He had nothing to worry about, surely? Just a phase...

The next dress was of ivory silk, and when Cara came out she looked like a Grecian goddess.

Tom felt that lump in his throat once again as he saw the draping silk emphasising her breasts, her trim waist, the swell of her hips.

'No, I can't wear this—it's practically indecent!'

Cara crossed her arms over her chest. Clearly it was impossible to wear a bra beneath the dress, and all he could think about were her nipples, which led to him thinking about what he could do to them...

He just nodded and said, 'Yeah, it is a bit...revealing.'

When she'd disappeared back into the changing room he let out a huff of air and got up and paced the shop, trying to make the part of his body below the waist feel a little more...relaxed. He shook out his legs, tried to slow his breathing, and couldn't remember if clothes-shopping with Victoria had ever been like this.

He didn't think so.

When Cara came back out, dressed in her baggy tee once again, he smiled and sighed a sigh of relief.

'Maybe we should try somewhere else?' she said.

'Sure...er...there's another dress shop at the end of this road.'

The besuited woman behind the till smiled as they left, and Tom was glad of the fresh air and the cool evening wind that was beginning to blow. It had got rather hot in Imagine. And now he understood why the shop was called what it was…because his mind had certainly imagined all sorts of scenarios.

The next boutique dress shop was smaller than Imagine, but the assistant was just as helpful. She helped pick out three dresses for Cara. The first was fire-engine-red, which Cara loved, but she really wasn't too keen on the choker neckline as she thought it made her shoulders look too broad. The second was an ombre dress, in seaweed-green, its colour changing to a Mediterranean-blue at the neck, but Cara said she felt like a fairy in it. The third dress was an iridescent black that shimmered and draped her body like an oil slick.

'What do you think?' She turned in front of him, and as she did so revealed a very high split that went almost to the top of her thigh.

He pressed his lips together hard, wondering just what it was that he'd done wrong in this life that he was being punished in such a manner?

Cara grabbed at the fabric to hold it together. 'It's too revealing, huh?' she said, blushing, looking awkward. 'I'll go and change.'

'No. It's…um…lovely.'

Lovely? *Lovely?* Couldn't he think of another adjective? Had he turned into his father? That was what his dad said to things. To a nicely brewed cup of tea. To a nice slice of cake. To a comfy chair.

Cara was beyond *lovely* in these dresses.

'I feel exposed.' She turned to the assistant. 'Have you got anything that doesn't reveal ninety percent of my skin? It's just not me.'

'Let me think…' The assistant turned to survey the shop and then snapped her fingers. 'Do you know? I just might have something in the back. Bear with me for a moment.'

Cara nodded, still clutching the split in the dress to cover her leg.

Tom wished he had a drink to hand. His mouth was so dry! Cara wasn't tall by any means. She was a whole head shorter than him. But that split made it look as if her beautifully toned legs went on for days…

When the assistant came back out, with a dress hidden inside a cover, he found himself hoping and praying that this one would not make him feel as if he wanted to ravish his best friend, as all the others had done.

His right leg was twitching, his foot rapidly tapping the floor in a staccato rhythm as his nerves increased, while he waited for Cara to come out.

When she did he stood up, a smile breaking over his face at the sight of the smile on hers, and he knew she'd found a dress she was happy with.

It was long-sleeved, high-necked and stylishly draped, in a beautiful gold colour. It showed no cleavage. It had no leg-split. But the diamante and sequins that were sewn into the dress in their thousands made her look like a starburst.

'You look…gorgeous,' he said, his breath almost taken from him. She'd looked amazing in everything, but this… This dress made her happy, and that was what counted the most.

She blushed at his praise. 'You think? It's got this at the back, but…'

She turned, and he saw that the dress exposed most of her back, all the way down to the top of her bottom. The gentle swell of her butt cheeks caused the golden shine to blind his eyes. It was just her back, but it seemed to be the most erotic thing he had ever seen and his body stirred in reaction to her.

Tom sat down. Awkwardly. 'It's amazing. What do you think?' He cleared his throat again, trying to regain control of his body. Who knew it could do so many things involuntarily?

'I like it. You don't think the back's too much?' She turned again, giving him another glance of her skin, the curve of her waist…

'No, it's…perfect.'

'It's a good price, too.' Cara admired her reflection in the mirror for a while, before turning to the assistant and saying, 'I'll take it.'

'Fabulous!' the assistant said.

Tom smiled, but inwardly he was telling himself, *Okay, so she's going to wear that dress. Keep your hands high, and when you get to the party you don't have to stay close. You'll have done your part. You'll have warned off anybody wanting to ask her out. You'll just have to get through one dance with her and that will be—what? Two minutes long? Three, tops? Then it'll be a drive home, a quick peck on the cheek to say goodnight and it'll all be over. Easy, right?*

Then they could go back to normal, and eventually the memory of her in that dress would fade, and they could just be mates. That was all he wanted. He didn't want to get involved with anyone again. Not really. It was horrible when you lost someone, and he didn't want to lose Cara if this all went wrong.

No. He could behave himself. He was a gentleman.

And that was what Cara deserved.

CHAPTER FIVE

CARA HAD A day off. And she was determined to use it to get stuff done that she couldn't when she was at work. There was a wonky cupboard door in her kitchen that needed repairing, and a pipe that needed replacing under the sink. She'd bought the parts ages ago but had just never got round to it. So she pulled up some music on her phone and began clearing out all the cleaning essentials she kept under her sink so she could expose the pipe.

As she worked, her mind kept drifting to the previous evening, dress-shopping with Tom.

It had been crazy. Each of those first few dresses had made her feel as if she was naked in front of Tom, and that had done some incredible things to her insides! She'd almost not come out of the changing rooms a couple of times, but she had forced herself, curious as to how he might react. He was her friend, but he was also a red-blooded male, and some of those dresses had been…risqué.

He had looked a little as if he didn't know where to look, and that had embarrassed her to begin with. Clearly he'd believed she looked ridiculous in those exquisitely feminine dresses. Dresses meant for women like Victoria. With long, lean limbs and a flat stomach. Women who were fully in touch with their femininity.

Cara wasn't a girly girl. She didn't get the whole thing about how to be a stereotypical woman, interested in handbags and nails and having her hair done every six weeks. She preferred trimming her own hair in front of her bathroom mirror. Handbags were useless if you had enough pockets. And fake nails? How did anybody do anything with those long claws on? And she bit her nails more than she decorated them.

I was kidding myself if I thought Tom might find me attractive in those dresses.

Cara wasn't a woman who used her womanly wiles. She'd never needed other men to notice her. Tom was the only one who was important. The only one who mattered. And it had mattered what he thought of the dresses—especially when she'd felt so uncomfortable in them.

Except for that last one. The gold one. It had covered all the essentials. The shoulders she thought were too broad, the arms that were probably a little too muscly, the cleavage that was too small anyway and the thighs that were thick with muscle and should only be revealed, if at all, to a physiotherapist or a doctor.

She'd felt confident in the gold dress. As if she could carry it off. Because the evening was going to be difficult enough as it was—what with her father being as annoying as always and it being her mother's birthday and the fact that it would be a fake date with Tom. It all made her feel uncomfortable, and she needed a dress to make her feel okay.

Cara would love it to be a real date, but fake would do. They'd walk in together as a couple. Surprise Green

Watch. But she would explain it to them later, when the party was over. For a few hours she would pretend and be happy.

Maybe they'd walk in arm in arm? That would be nice. Tom would be attentive and at her side all night, with his arm around her protectively, his hand resting on her hip, her body pressed against his. She would be able to get through the evening like that, no problem. Her heart would probably be racing through it all, but it would be worth it.

And then Tom would take her home and escort her to her door and plant a kiss upon her cheek before saying goodnight. And then she would have to fight the urge to ask him in for coffee, knowing that she wouldn't want the night to end. Because when it did they would go back to being normal friends. Which was great. But when the heart wanted more...

I can't make him love me. I can't make him see me as something else.

Plus, there was Gage to think about. That little boy had been through so much, and although she loved him to bits, loved spending time with him and making him laugh, she would never be able to replace his mother and Tom wasn't the kind of man who entered relationships lightly. He'd only ever been in one and that had been with Victoria. He was no gigolo, no fly-by-night, no *wham, bam, thank you, ma'am* kind of guy. Tom only did serious relationships.

Maybe she could talk to him about that? Ask him gently, as his friend, if he'd ever considered dating again? Test the waters?

What would it feel like to see him with someone else? She didn't like that thought.

It would be tragic and hurtful. Make her sad.

The pipe came free and some water splashed down upon her, making her splutter and wipe off the excess. She put the new pipe in place and began to fasten it on, making sure there were no leaks by running the tap above.

It worked perfectly.

If only people could be fixed so easily.

'She's dislocated her elbow,' Tom said to the father cradling his daughter in his lap.

The patient was a young child, only two years of age, and the elbow had been dislocated by her father spinning her around in the garden by the arms. The pulling mechanism of the injury was classic.

'I did it. I feel so guilty. Does she need to go to hospital?'

Tom shook his head. 'No. I can fix it here. It's usually an easy fix, but when I put the elbow back into place she might cry out for a moment. Hey, Lacey? I'm going to fix your arm, okay?'

Lacey snuggled further into her father.

That was okay. Tom was a stranger to her and she was in discomfort—it was to be expected. Tom rolled up the girl's sleeve and held her elbow in his right hand, supporting it so that when he performed the manoeuvre he would be able to feel the elbow pop back into place. He took Lacey's hand in his left hand, as if they were shaking hands, then turned her palm upwards towards the ceiling, straightened the arm, pulling outwards, and felt the elbow snap back into place as he folded her arm at the antecubital fold.

Lacey cried out at the click, but when Tom offered

her a tongue depressor to hold and she used her left
arm for the first time since the dislocation a smile crept
onto her face.

'See? All fixed.'

'It's done?' Lacey's dad asked. 'That's amazing.'

'It's one of my favourite things to do.' Tom smiled.
'Make a patient better quickly. If only all my jobs were
this easy.'

'Well, I can't thank you enough. I really thought I'd
broken her arm.'

'If I could take away your guilt I'd do so, believe me.'
Tom smiled at Lacey. 'Maybe Daddy will find a nice
treat for you because you were so brave?'

'Ice cream!' Lacey said, looking up at her dad.

Tom laughed, just as his personal mobile rang. He
stood up to pull it from his trouser pocket and frowned.
Gage's pre-school was calling him.

'Excuse me. I need to take this.' He turned away
and walked out into the hall for some privacy. 'Hello?'

'Hello, is that Gage's dad?' asked a female voice.

'Yes.'

'I'm sorry to call you. This is Fiona Goddard from
Sunflowers Pre-School.'

'Yes?'

'It seems that Gage isn't feeling very well. He's complaining of a tummy ache and he's not quite himself.
Would you be able to pick him up?'

Tom sighed. 'I'm at work.'

'I understand. But we can't keep him here if he's
not feeling well. Is there any way you could come? Or
a family member who could?'

His mind raced. Who could he call? Who would
Gage feel comfortable with? He knew immediately.

'I'll need to check with a friend. I'll call you back and let you know.'

'Thanks.'

He ended the call and dialled Cara's number. When she answered he heard music playing in the background. 'Hey, it's me. Where are you? Sounds like you're in a disco.'

'You're right. It's 1986 in here.' The music went down a notch. 'I'm fixing a kitchen cupboard—what can I do you for?'

He sighed. 'I realise this is an imposition, but I've just been called by Gage's nursery. He's not feeling well and they want him to be collected, and—'

'I'm on my way. Let them know I'm coming. I'll take him back to yours. Is the spare key still in that fake plant pot?'

This was why she was so great. There weren't many people he could rely on like this. He could have called his parents, but they didn't have their own car now and they lived nearly an hour away—probably more if he took into account how long it would take them to get to Gage's nursery by public transport. Cara knew where it was, and she was close, and he trusted her with his son.

'It is—and thanks. I know this is your day off.'

'I've already done what I set out to do today. All I had planned after this was to sit and watch a movie. I can do that with Gage. What's wrong with him?'

'Tummy ache.'

'Ah… I can deal with that—no problem.'

'Thanks, Cara. I don't know what I'd do without you.'

There was a brief silence. 'You'd do fine.'

'I doubt it.'

He really did. He honestly thought that he'd still be wallowing in grief and guilt right now if it hadn't been for her. She brightened his day…gave him the belief that he could do anything he wanted if he just put his mind to it. She was his cheerleader, his rock, and soon she was going to be his date for a ball. A fake date, but he was looking forward to seeing her in that dress again. Just to reassure himself that she had looked that amazing and it wasn't just his imagination that had made the whole thing up. He was going to feel honoured to walk into Higham Manor with Cara on his arm.

'We'll be fine. What's the safe word?'

The nursery had a safe word system, so if a parent couldn't collect a child any other adult would have to use the parent-created safe word before they'd be allowed to walk off with someone else's child.

He grimaced. 'Don't laugh, okay?'

'I promise.'

'It's banana.'

He heard a muffled laugh. 'Banana?' She was trying to sound serious. 'Interesting…'

'I was eating one when I filled in the form. I never thought I'd actually have to use it.'

'Sounds legit. Okay. See you later.'

She rang off and he stood there for a moment, just staring at his phone, before dialling the nursery to let them know that Cara would be collecting Gage.

When he'd put his phone back in his pocket he went into the living room and smiled at Lacey and her father. Lacey was now sitting on the floor, playing with a toy car, using the arm he'd just fixed.

'See how quickly they forget that they used to hurt?'

'You're a miracle worker,' Lacey's father said.

But Tom didn't think so.

Cara was the miracle worker—not him. She'd got him smiling again, laughing again, when after Victoria's death he'd never thought that would ever be possible.

Cara set Gage down by the front door whilst she surreptitiously located the spare key and opened the front door, ushering the little boy into the living room.

Gage sat on the couch, looking solemn.

She knelt in front of him, smiling warmly. 'Okay. Operation Tummy Ache. What are we talking about here? Does it just hurt? Or are we going to need a bucket?'

Gage smiled. 'It just hurts.'

'Show me where.'

He pointed to the middle of his abdomen.

'Okay. I think I may need to operate. Lie back and be brave. I promise to be quick.'

Gage giggled and lay back. He didn't look comfy, so she grabbed a cushion and put it under his head, and then dragged a holey crocheted throw from off the back of the couch and draped it over his little form.

'TV?'

He nodded.

'What do you fancy watching? Politics? The news? Antique-hunting?'

'Cartoons.'

'I think I can manage that.' She turned and pointed the remote at the screen. It came to life and she brought up the menu to find the channel that showed cartoons all day. 'I prescribe three cartoons. Then I'll read you a story and maybe you can try and sleep, okay?'

'Okay.'

'Do you want a drink?'

'Milk!'

'With a bad tummy? Hmm…how about some juice?'

'Okay.'

She laid the back of her hand against his forehead. He didn't feel hot, which was good. It was probably just a bug, if it was anything at all.

'You watch TV while I make the drinks, and then I'll come back here and sit with you—how about that?'

He nodded.

Cara gave his hair a ruffle, then went to get their drinks. It didn't take long, and she was soon back on the couch with Gage, watching a weird cartoon that she thought was awful but pretended to like. Her gaze kept falling upon the picture of Victoria on the mantelpiece, and all she could think of was how it ought to be Victoria getting the chance to sit with her son. She'd be so proud of him. He was growing into a lovely boy, and Tom was doing remarkable things with him, raising him not to feel out of place because he didn't have a mum, like the other kids did.

What would Victoria do if she was here? Stroke Gage's hair? Keep an eye on him at a distance whilst she got on with some housework? Put Gage in his bedroom?

Tom's wife looked down at Cara on the couch and seemed to say *Well, I'm not there, so do the best for my son. I'm trusting you with him. I'm trusting you with* them.

Cara had become Victoria's friend, however brief that friendship had been. What would she think if she could know that Cara had secret thoughts about her husband? Had *fantasies*? She'd be appalled, that was what.

She wouldn't want Cara to be anywhere near them. She'd feel betrayed.

Guilt swallowed her and she looked down at Gage. What was she doing, having these thoughts about Tom? *I can't! I shouldn't!*

She sipped at her tea, and when they reached the end of the third cartoon she swallowed hard and switched off the television.

'Aww!' Gage protested.

'Storytime, bucko. I can't have you getting square eyes as well as a tummy ache.'

Gage touched his face. 'Are my eyes going square?'

She laughed. 'It's just a saying. Your eyes don't actually change shape.'

'That would look funny.'

'It would. So! Storytime…' Underneath the coffee table was a small pile of children's books. She scooped them out and presented them to him like a magician, saying, 'Pick a card…any card.'

Gage pursed his lips, then pointed at a book.

'Excellent choice, *monsieur*.' She put the others down and then sat back on the couch, draping some of the crocheted throw over her own legs, and settled down and began to read.

As she spoke she held the book to one side, so that Gage could see the pictures. He lay there, listening intently, his eyes growing heavy, until eventually, about three pages from the end, he nodded off and his little cherub face grew soft in repose.

Cara closed the book with a smile and snuggled down on the couch next to him, watching him sleep, thinking how wonderful it would be to have her own little family. What she wouldn't give to have a little boy like Gage. He was perfect and she loved him a lot.

The warmth of the blanket and the softness of the couch soon had their effect on Cara, too, and she fell fast asleep, the book slipping from her grasp and falling to the floor.

Tom's shift finished at midday. He'd been on since seven a.m., just five hours, but when he'd told Control he had a sick little boy at home they'd told him to go home early, which he was really grateful for. Obviously they knew he was a single dad, and they had been brilliant at accommodating him when life got tough. Like today.

He knew he could have stayed, finished his shift in its entirety, but he didn't want to take advantage of Cara's good nature. Despite her protest that picking up Gage from pre-school was just fine by her, he was very much aware that this was a precious day off for Cara and he'd hijacked it. With his family and his problems. That was why he was happy to help Cara out with this ball thing…being her fake boyfriend. Anything to make her life a little bit easier, the way she did so often for him.

Not sure if Gage would be sleeping, he quietly turned his key in the lock and opened the door. The house was pretty silent. Fighting the urge to call out either of their names, he tiptoed down the hall after discarding his work shoes and popped his head through the living room door.

And felt his heart melt with adoration.

Cara and Gage were both fast asleep on the couch, covered in the raggedy blanket that Victoria had made in an attempt to learn something new. It had huge gaps between the stitches. Some of the squares were smaller than the others. The colours clashed. But it had been made with love, and after his wife had died he'd not been able to bear parting with something that had been made by her hand.

For a moment he stood there, gazing down adoringly at both of them. He grabbed his mobile phone, opened up the camera app and took a photo.

The sound of the camera woke Cara. She blinked her eyes open, then sat up in shock, half of her hair squashed to the side of her head by the cushion she'd been sleeping on. Immediately she blushed, then looked down at Gage to check that he was all right.

'Oh, my gosh. I'm so sorry. I must have fallen asleep.'

He smiled at her. 'You did,' he whispered, turning the phone so she could see the picture.

'I must have been more tired than I thought.' She cocked her head to one side and ruffled her hair. 'Do I really look like that when I'm asleep?'

'Apparently.'

'I hope I didn't drool.' She wiped her mouth.

Tom used the zoom function on the photo. 'No drool. How's the patient?'

She smiled. 'Good. Centralised tummy pain, no temperature, no vomiting. He's kept down his juice and…' she checked the time '… I was going to see if he wanted some toast for his lunch.'

'You go. I'll do all that. Enjoy what's left of your day off.'

'Oh, it's no problem. I've enjoyed myself.'

'I can see that.' He grinned. 'I'm going to take this one up to bed. Give me a minute.' Gently, he scooped up his son, who barely woke except to snuggle in closer to his dad's chest as Tom carried him up the stairs.

This was what being a parent was all about, Tom thought. These moments when your kid snuggled into you. When he was dopey with sleep. When he reached for you to provide comfort and love.

'Hello, Daddy.' Gage mumbled.

'Hey, you. How are you feeling?'

His son nuzzled his nose into Tom's top. 'Fine.'

'That must be because you had a good nurse looking after you, hey?'

Gage smiled. 'Can she stay?'

Tom felt an ache in his heart, but he was almost at the top of the stairs and heading towards Gage's bedroom, so he felt it was safe to whisper. 'Not today.'

'You could ask her for a sleepover.'

'Maybe.'

'It doesn't matter that it's not night-time. We had a pretend sleepover at pre-school last week. We told stories and had hot chocolate.'

'Sounds good.'

'She could sleep in my bed with me.'

He smiled, loving the innocence of a three-year-old boy. 'Well, maybe when you're better.'

'And we could look after Cara when she has a tummy ache.'

'We could.'

'You make people feel better all the time, Daddy.'

Tom laid his son in bed and pulled his football duvet cover over him. 'Rest and I'll bring you up something to eat. What do you fancy?'

'Hot dogs.'

'Let's start with something plain, huh? How about some delicious toast?'

Gage nodded from beneath the quilt.

'Okay. Back in a bit.'

Tom trotted downstairs to find Cara folding the cro-cheted blanket and draping it into position on the back of the couch.

'I remember Victoria making this,' she said, strok-ing the blanket.

He nodded. 'Me too.'

'She swore a lot.' Cara looked up at him and smiled.

'She was never very good at making things. Except Gage. He's pretty perfect.'

'Well, you had something to do with that, too.'

'I'm going to make him some toast. Fancy staying for lunch?' he asked, feeling nervous that she'd say no. Feeling nervous that she'd say yes.

'I'd love to.'

The next day, Cara was four hours into her shift when a call came through for a cyclist versus bus. She clam-bered into her uniform with the rest of Green Watch and got into the appliance, and with sirens and lights blazing they made their way through town, towards the co-ordinates they'd been given.

It was a busy high street, and the traffic had come to a standstill because of the accident. Reed, who was driving, had to sound his horn to get people to move, so they could make their way through. Eventually they got as close as they could and Cara clambered from the truck, hearing sirens in the distance as police and am-bulances made their way to the accident.

Hodge led the way towards the bus, which was stopped at a weird angle just past its last stop. It must have been pulling away after picking up its latest passengers and collided with the cyclist. But…where was the cyclist?

Cara got down on her hands and knees and saw a bike and a body beneath the bus. The front wheel of the vehicle was half resting on the cyclist's leg. The cyclist was crying quietly.

'Let's get some stabilisers!' Cara called out, lying down on her stomach and trying to make eye contact with the cyclist, who was just out of reach. Otherwise Cara would have reached for her hand.

As the others placed wheel chocks down, to stabilise the vehicle, Tom arrived alongside her.

'What have we got?'

'Leg entrapment, as far as I can see, but I have no idea if the wheel went over her chest or her pelvis first.'

'She's conscious?'

Cara nodded. 'We'll need to use inflation devices to lift the bus, so that we can pull her out from under there.'

'Okay. I'll get painkillers ready for injection.'

Cara looked back at the cyclist. 'We're going to get you out of there soon, okay? What's your name, love?'

'Penny.'

'Okay, Penny. That's it…just focus on me. There's going to be a lot going on around you, but I don't want you to worry about that. Just keep talking to me. What hurts the most?'

'I—I don't know. My stomach…'

That didn't bode well.

'Can you feel your legs?'

Penny paused, then shook her head, terrified. 'No!'

'Okay. I need you to stay calm. You may just have

spinal shock. We won't know until we get you to the hospital, so stay positive.'

Penny sniffed and nodded. 'Okay…'

'Where were you going today, Penny?'

'The bank and the p-post office.'

'Paying bills or taking money out?'

'Taking out. For a h-holiday.'

'Fantastic! Where are you thinking of going?'

As Cara kept Penny occupied the rest of Green Watch did their thing, finding the correct placement for the inflation devices that would slowly lift the bus from the patient.

'Crete. I have family over there.'

'Parents?'

Penny nodded. 'I haven't seen them since before the pandemic. I've been saving so I can go. Will I be able to go now?'

'Maybe not tomorrow, but let's say yes—you're going to go to Crete.'

'I'm going to go…' Penny looked about her. 'What's your name?'

'Cara.'

'That's pretty. I knew a Cara once…when I was little.'

'Yeah?'

'She went to my school. It was a boarding school. Monrose…'

Cara frowned. She'd gone to Monrose! Wait… Penny… Was this…?

'Penelope Moorcroft?'

Penny blinked. 'Cara Maddox? *Lady* Cara Maddox?'

Cara smiled. 'It's me.'

'But…you're a fireman. I mean, a fire p-person.'

She nodded. 'Yes, I am. I never expected to meet you again like this.'

'You were such a nice girl at school. I remember being f-frightened on my first day, and you took me to the nurse when I got a headache.'

Cara remembered. 'Looks like I'm going to be delivering you to medics again. Maybe we should stop meeting like this?'

'Maybe.' Penny gave a small laugh. Then, 'Why can't I feel my legs, Cara?'

Cara kept her voice calm. 'The doctors won't know until they scan you.'

'Am I going to die? I'm getting cold...'

'She's in shock,' whispered Tom. 'We need to get her out fast.'

'I know.'

'Why are you whispering?' Penny called.

'We're not. Just working out how best to get you out quick.'

'Ideally, I'd like to get some pain meds into her before we lift this bus,' said Tom. 'Let me shimmy under there. You've secured the vehicle—it won't move.'

'Tom—'

'If we lift this bus from her leg it's going to be agony. She could have compartment syndrome and all the toxins will go straight to her heart, putting her into arrest. I need to be under there with her.'

'I can't put you at risk, Tom.'

'I won't be.' He smiled. 'Not with Green Watch's finest looking after me.'

'I'll need to check with Hodge,' Cara told him. 'Penny? I'll be back in just a second.'

But as she got up and turned her back she saw a

movement out of the corner of her eye, and when she turned back she saw the toe ends of Tom's boots as he shimmied underneath the bus, dragging his kitbag with him.

'Tom!'

She couldn't believe he'd done that! It was dangerous. If anyone should have gone underneath, it should have been her. Now Tom could get hurt, and the idea of that happening made her feel sick. Sweat bloomed in her armpits and down her back.

'Hodge! Tom's gone under.' Cara hated hearing the panic in her voice. The fear.

Hodge got down on his hands and knees and spoke to Tom. 'What are you playing at?'

'Keeping my patient alive and pain-free!' Tom's disembodied voice came back.

Cara lay flat on her stomach again, to see what was happening, but Tom was in front of the patient now and she couldn't see what was going on.

'When you get those pain meds on board, you come right back out—you hear me, Tom Roker?'

'Yes, ma'am.'

She cursed silently and looked over at Reed and Garrett and beyond him David Garcia. They all gave a thumbs-up. They were ready to inflate the blocks.

'We're all set out here. Are you done yet, Tom?'

'Nearly... Okay, I'm coming back out.'

Her heart began to slow down as more and more of Tom's body came safely out from underneath the bus. His uniform had oil on it, and he was scuffed and dirty, but he gave her a grin that stopped her from being angry. *He was safe.* That was what mattered.

She turned her attention back to her patient. 'Penny?

We're going to inflate now, and we'll have you out in a jiffy.'

'She won't answer you. I've given her some ketamine, so she's woozy.'

'Okay, let's get this bus off this poor woman,' said Hodge, signalling the lift to begin.

The machines started up, slowly inflating the concertinaed blocks that had been placed at strategic points underneath the bus. It seemed to take ages, but eventually the bus was lifted clear of Penny's legs.

Both Tom, Hodge and Cara helped pull her out, and once she was clear Tom began working on her quickly, alongside the other paramedics who swarmed in from nowhere, along with a doctor who must have arrived in a helicopter, judging by his bright orange jumpsuit.

Cara, Garrett and Reed deflated the blocks and the bus sank back down to the road.

The police had created a barrier around the accident site and were marking the road and taking witness statements. Tom and the others got Penny onto a backboard and whisked her over to an ambulance, so she could be kept warm whilst the doctor oversaw her care.

Cara looked at the giant wheels of the bus and imagined the weight of that vehicle going over a pelvis or a spine. Unless Penny was extremely lucky, her outlook might not be all that great. The likelihood was that there was going to be a lot of surgery and physiotherapy in the months to come.

As the helicopter rose into the air with its patient onboard Cara found Tom, grabbing his arm and making him turn forcibly. 'Don't you *ever* do that to me *ever* again!'

CHAPTER SIX

HE'D NEVER SEEN such anger and fear in her eyes. Cara had been *furious* with him. It was an emotion he wasn't used to from her. In the entire time he'd known her she'd only ever been calm, funny, happy, supportive and caring.

But anger? And fear?

He'd tried to apologise, but he really felt he'd done the right thing. If he hadn't, Penny would have been in a whole world of pain when that bus had been lifted.

Once they'd got her out, they'd discovered she had an unstable pelvic fracture, two broken femurs and a suspected lower spine fracture. That was a lot of injury to one body, and without pain meds it would have been horrific. Penny had been numb from the waist down, but that might have been shock, or her mind protecting her from her horrific injury, but once the adrenaline had worn off she would have felt everything if he hadn't gone under the bus.

It had been safe. The bus had been stabilised. There had been no other traffic flowing around them and he had made a judgement call.

But Cara's response had him flummoxed. Was it

more than the response of just a friend? Or was he trying to read too much into this?

Now, as he drove them both to the shopping centre once again, to help Cara find shoes to go with her golden dress, Cara sat in silence, staring out of the window. It was an awkward silence and one he wasn't sure how to navigate. He didn't want to make things worse, but he really hated not being able to talk to her. And having her angry with him like this made him feel repentant.

'So...are we not going to talk to each other this evening or...?' He let the question hang.

Cara sighed. 'We can talk. So long as you admit you were reckless.'

'I don't think I was.'

She glared at him. 'Silence it is, then.'

'I'm sorry if I scared you by going under that bus. That wasn't my intention.'

'We hadn't had confirmation it was fully stable, Tom! What if the bus had come down on you? You could have been hurt! You could have been injured. Badly. And then what would Gage do, huh? Without his mother *and* his father?'

Tom got what she was saying, but he was also hearing what she *wasn't* saying out loud. Clearly she was worried about how his getting hurt would affect *her*. Wasn't she? And if she was, what did *that* mean? And if it did mean something...if it did mean that Cara had feelings for him that went beyond friendship, then...

No. He was being ridiculous. She was probably worried that if he got hurt she'd have to rescue him too. That she'd have to take on too much with Gage, or something.

He thought for a moment, trying to think of ways to

lighten the mood and take his mind off his quandary. 'Well, I don't have much experience in shoe-shopping with women, but from what I do know it's meant to be a happy experience.'

'Maybe. You could always drop me off. I can go alone.'

'Cara, please. I'm trying to say sorry, here.'

She looked at him. 'You scared me, Tom. Going under that bus like that. It made me feel helpless. That if something were to happen to you I wouldn't be able to protect you.'

So he was right, then. She was just worried about having to rescue two people instead of one. It was nothing to do with her having feelings for him. It was a re-alisation that made him feel glum.

'I was fine.'

'Luckily. Aren't you guys taught not to rush to a pa-tient without checking the scene is safe for you first?'

He nodded. 'It *was* safe. You'd stabilised the bus.'

'But I needed to check with Hodge first. He was in charge of everyone's safety at the scene—not you.'

'I get it. And I'm sorry I scared you.'

He liked it that she cared so much. Just not in the way that he'd hoped for. But he was her friend—maybe her best friend. Either way, it felt good to know that someone cared and worried about him. His parents did, obviously, but it wasn't the same as having Cara care. Knowing that she was thinking about him, worrying about him… What had she said? It had made her feel *helpless*.

He reached over and laid his hand on hers. Her skin was smooth and warm. 'I'm sorry,' he said, and he meant it. It wasn't a half-baked apology just to stop the awkward silence. He really meant it. He didn't want her to worry about him. He knew how it felt to worry over someone you couldn't help. And that helpless feeling…? He was intimately aware of it. 'I promise to never make you feel that way again.'

'And you'll wait for me to say something is safe before you go charging in on your white horse?'

'I will wait.'

She gave him a small smile. 'Good. I hate being angry with you. I'm not used to it.'

'Me neither.'

He drove, still holding her hand, enjoying the way it made him feel, trying not to read too much into it but not keen on letting go, either. If he could hold Cara's hand for evermore, he would. But it seemed they were doomed to be nothing more than friends.

'How's Gage today?' she asked.

'His normal self, thankfully. Back at pre-school.'

'I'm glad.'

'He wanted to know if you were going to come round again soon, to teach him how to do keepy-uppies?'

'Can't you show him?'

'I can't do them.' He squeezed her hand. 'And he wants to learn from the best.'

She laughed. 'Tell him I'll see him at the weekend.'

He had to slow his car as they reached the traffic lights near to the shopping centre, and he had to let go of her hand to operate the gears. His own hand suddenly felt so empty, and he yearned to reach out and take her hand again. But he knew that would seem odd. That was a boyfriend gesture, and he was not Cara's boyfriend.

The moment was over.

They were back to being best friends again.

And even though he feared it would never seem enough, he was willing to take it.

Some of Cara was better than no Cara at all.

The first shoe shop had a display of trainers at the front, and Cara *oohed* and went over to take a look at a black pair that had a flash of neon green near the toe.

'These are awesome,' she said, taking in the neat construction, the multi-coloured laces and the supportive reinforced heel.

But Tom took them from her hands and placed them back down on the stand. 'We're here for something that will match your dress, and I don't think that these will do.'

'Not fair...' she protested, as he led her towards the other side of the shop, where there was a more dazzling array of strappy shoes with heels.

Cara gazed at them, feeling utterly lost. What was she meant to do? She knew nothing about shoes. Was she meant to wear gold shoes with a gold dress? Did they have to match? Or could she wear a neutral colour? A nude? Something contrasting?

'I fail miserably at being a girl.'

Tom laughed. 'You're perfect.'

'Am I? What do I know about shoes? Apart from the fact that they go on your feet and that I'll always choose comfort over style.'

'Last I heard, being a girl didn't mean passing any shoe exams.'

She picked up a pair of pale pink ballet shoes. 'Thankfully. I'd definitely fail. Are these any good?'

Tom shook his head. 'Not with that dress. That dress is...something special. You want a shoe that reflects that.' He picked up a high-heeled strappy shoe in gold. 'What about these?'

Cara turned the shoe over in her hands. 'How are you supposed to walk in these?'

'Gracefully?'

She laughed. 'Have you ever seen me in a heel?'

He shook his head. 'No. I don't think I ever have.'

'Well, there's a reason for that. I look like a toddler who's just found her mummy's shoes. I either look ridiculous or I fall over. These look like they'd break my ankles.'

'Try them on and see.'

'Let's leave them in reserve. What else is there?'

She cast her gaze over the racks. There seemed to be shoes in most colours. There was a lot of black, but she felt pretty sure a black shoe wouldn't look great with the gold dress. She saw a pair that had a small chunky heel. A kitten heel? Was that what it was called? Bubblegum-pink and kind of cute.

'These?'

Tom shrugged. 'Try it on.'

She sat down, pulled off one trainer and a short sock and slid her foot into the shoe. She wondered if she was meant to have painted her toenails. Did Tom think she had ugly feet?

Cara was happy they were talking again. Being angry with him had been incredibly distressing to her. She'd not wanted to fall out with him, but he had scared her so much! If she'd lost him...

Fastening the buckle, she stood up and tried to walk. But it was odd, because she still had a trainer on the other foot. So she sat back down and got rid of that, as well as the other sock, and put on the other pink shoe.

She could barely walk. She wobbled a bit, and had to put her hand out to grab the rack and steady herself.

'Whoa! You okay?' Tom asked, smiling.

'It's like learning to walk again.'

'How do they feel?'

'Awful.'

'I'm not sure that colour would go with the dress.'

'Maybe they have them in gold? I could ask.'

'I think you should try a different heel. You don't look right in those.'

Oh. He didn't think she looked good. And nor did she feel good in them. Not really. They were uncomfortable, and they pinched, and the heel was doing something strenuous to her calf muscles.

Cara sat down to take them off.

'Try on the gold pair,' Tom said. 'What have you got to lose?'

'My ability to walk?'

She grabbed the high-heeled golden pair with reluctance, even though she could see they were beautiful shoes. Elegant...stylish... She just wished they weren't so high!

She tried standing and wobbled.

Tom took hold of her arm briefly, then let go.

Cara stood there, trying to keep her balance, but her centre of gravity seemed way off, all of a sudden, and she was afraid to move.

'They look great.'

'Of course you're going to say that. You're a man.'

'You don't think they look great?'

'I do. It's just... I'm not sure I can move. They're perfect if you plan on carrying me into the ball and then plonking me down by the bar, so I don't have to move all night.'

She blushed at the thought of him carrying her over his shoulder, fireman-style. Caveman-style? As if he'd chosen his woman and now she was his.

'Just try and move,' he said.

'Okay…'

Cara looked about her. No one was watching, so she wasn't about to make a colossal ass of herself. They were all too busy shopping for their own shoes, lost in their own little worlds. It was just her and Tom, and he stood in front of her like a proud parent, waiting for his toddler to take its first steps.

She took an awkward step, but it felt as if she might snap the heel. She was so used to putting her heel down first, then her toe, but that just wasn't going to work. Not for her. Maybe she needed to somehow put the heel and toe down together?

She took another awkward step, and then another, but then her ankle wobbled, and her balance went, and she was suddenly falling forward into Tom's arms.

He caught her, saving her from faceplanting down on the floor. But now she found herself in another strange predicament.

She was in his arms, her head against his chest, hearing his heart pound inside his ribcage. And it was beating fast. Probably from the shock of her falling, that was all. She could feel the muscles in his body…could smell his body spray—something masculine and earthy that performed wonders on her senses. Her cheeks flushed and she looked up into his eyes. Something strange passed through them, and she was so caught in his magnetism she forgot to pull away. Forgot to try and move. Forgot to try and operate her feet.

Because being in his arms like this…so close she could feel every breath…it was a heady place to be.

'Thanks, I…'

His lips were parted and his eyes were large as he stared down at her, but eventually common sense kicked in. He didn't feel anything for her! That was nonsense! He'd just caught her because she'd tripped—that was all!

She coloured and pushed away from him, let go. And somehow, awkwardly, she made her way back to her seat, bending over to slowly undo the buckles, so that her hair would hide her face, her blushing cheeks, the pounding of her own heart.

I wanted to kiss him.

Had he been able to see that? Had she given her feelings away?

She'd wanted it so much. How romantic would that have been? But romance never found Cara. It never had—why would now be any different? Especially with someone who was so off-limits? Her best friend.

Victoria would have been able to handle these heels. She'd have glided down a red carpet. She'd have made her father proud. Tom must think that she was an absolute idiot. Trying to be something that she was not.

'Ankles okay?' he asked, his voice sounding deep and breathy.

'Yeah. They're…they're good, thanks.' She sat up, not sure where to look. She picked up the strappy gold sandals and placed them back on the shelf. 'Maybe we should keep looking?'

He nodded. 'Yeah. I'm parched. Are you parched? Should I fetch us a coffee?'

And he got up and left the shop.

Odd... But maybe he'd seen something in her gaze when he'd caught her, and now he felt awkward because he was going to have to say something about it? Tell her that he'd seen that look in her eyes and it could never happen? They were just friends?

Because it would be so embarrassing if he did. She'd have to protest and lie to him. Say, *Don't be silly! I just fell. Nothing happened...let's move on.*

There was no way she wanted to have *that chat* with him. But clearly he'd felt something, because he'd looked incredibly uncomfortable just now. Probably trying to work out just how he'd tell his friend that he didn't think of her in that way.

Oh, God. This is mortifying.

Tom stood waiting in the queue by the coffee cart, trying to calm his racing heart. Something weird had just happened with Cara. She'd tripped, and he'd caught her...but when he'd held her in his arms she'd looked up into his eyes and...

He swallowed hard. Had he been wrong? He'd thought he'd seen something written across her face—but he had to be imagining things, right? Because this was Cara! She didn't have any romantic feelings for him. And yet he could have sworn that he'd seen something in her eyes. Seen want. Seen desire. Seen...feelings.

But we're just friends.

Those were the parameters of their relationship and that was why they worked together so well. They both knew where they stood, and there was nothing romantic between them—there couldn't be. Maybe he was just being sensitive because they'd had that falling out earlier and emotions had been running high.

He'd reached the front of the queue. 'Two lattes, please.'

Should he say something when he got back to the shoe shop? Should he just pretend that nothing had happened? That seemed cowardly, but he really didn't want to run the risk of making their relationship awkward. He'd hate that. He needed to be able to see her. Needed to have her in his life. If he ruined it he'd never forgive himself.

He headed back to the shop, determined to act as if nothing untoward had ever happened between them.

Cara knew she couldn't risk anything like that happening again, and she kind of wanted the evening to be over—so she could get home and take a bath, or something, pretend that everything was normal. So what if the shoes were too high? All she needed was practice walking in them, and she could do that at home. There was still a week or two before the ball.

So she took the high-heeled shoes to the till to pay for them, and rummaged for her phone when it began to ring.

She had a sudden fear that the caller might be Tom. That he'd gone home, too embarrassed to face her. But when she pulled the phone from her pocket she saw that it was her father.

Great. Just what I need right now.

'Hello?'

'Cara, darling! How are you? Have I caught you at a good time?'

'Sure. I'm just out shoe-shopping.'

'For the ball? Marvellous. I'm so looking forward to it. Seeing you there with all your brothers. The whole family back together again.'

'Is there anything in particular I can help you with?' She didn't mean to sound so sharp with him.

'No, no… I just thought I'd let you know about the latest arrangements. I've been speaking with Hodge, your boss. I know he suggested a deejay or something for the evening, but due to the ball being at the manor I thought a deejay might be a bit tacky, so I've organised an orchestra to come instead.'

She blinked. An *orchestra*? 'Dad…'

'Oh, it was no bother. Nothing fancy—just a local group. But I thought I'd let you know so that you could practise your dancing.'

'Dancing?' She looked down at the heels in her hands. She could barely *walk*.

'You know…waltzes and things. Your mother loved all of that—it will be a fitting tribute. Plus, it will be lovely for people to get on the dance floor and enjoy themselves…not feel like they're only there to open their wallets.'

'Right. Dancing.'

She looked up. She could see Tom coming her way, holding two coffee cups. Dancing. In that dress. With those heels? She'd be clutching onto Tom all night! A few seconds had been awkward enough. How would she ever hide how she felt all night?

Was it too late to get out of going altogether?

* * *

The fire engine raced through the dark streets, lighting up houses in flashes of red and blue. They were heading to an industrial estate behind the one where that guy had caught his arm in the printing press. Ahead of them they could see the night sky lit up by orange flames, with plumes of thick black smoke billowing upwards.

Cara hoped it wasn't the paper factory, because if it was then the fire was going to be intense, with all that flammable material around it, fuelling the flames.

Originally, she hadn't been meant to work this night shift, but she'd offered to work overtime as one of Blue Watch was off sick and Cara didn't feel she wanted to be sitting at home worrying about Tom and the upcoming ball. The whole situation was driving her crazy, and she'd had a headache all day. Every time she thought she'd got on top of her racing thoughts and sorted out how she was meant to be feeling, another thing came along and shook the ground beneath her feet.

When Tom had got back to the shoe shop with the coffees he'd seemed surprised that she was buying the gold shoes that she'd just fallen over in, but he'd said okay when she'd told him that practice would make perfect, and then she'd said she was tired and could they go home?

They'd driven home in silence—a comfortable silence that time—but still her heart had been racing and she hadn't told him about the dancing. He'd barely been able to hold her for a few seconds without looking alarmed. If he heard that her father was meddling again and now wanted them to learn how to dance... Well, she didn't want to see Tom trying to get out of their fake date. It would be embarrassing. Better to just turn up on the night and act surprised, suffer through one dance with him and then go home.

She'd have done her duty to her father and her mother and to the Websters, whose night it actually was going to be. They deserved help to find the best home they could afford. She would do it for them. And if she ended up with a twisted ankle at the end of the night because of it…? Well, fine.

As the appliance pulled up at the fire, another two fire engines that had been called from neighbouring stations arrived, and Hodge leapt out to co-ordinate with the other chief fire officers as Cara and the others began to prepare the hoses.

Hodge came back and gave them their instructions. 'Okay, I want you two over here, taking the east corner of the building. Garrett? They're a man down on Red Watch—can you help them on the west corner?'

Garrett ran over to help the others.

Cara felt the surge of the water as it ran through the pipe and aimed it at the flames, feeling the heat from the fire as it roared high into the sky. The ceiling of the industrial unit already had holes in where the flames had burnt through.

Hodge was yelling. 'Looks like we have a missing night guard! Cara? You're with me. We're going to head round the back and start our search at the guard box.'

Cara passed the hose to Reed and set off at a run with Hodge. They had to give the building a wide berth, mindful of the danger of collapse, and when they got to the guard box it was empty. A half-drunk cup of coffee was cooling on the table inside.

'Damn. Where is he?' Hodge grabbed a timesheet

off the wall. 'Looks like he makes laps of the building at midnight, three and five a.m.'

She checked her watch. A quarter past midnight. 'Think he's inside?' she asked.

They both looked to the building, almost consumed in flames.

'I sincerely hope not,' said Hodge.

By the time they got back to the front of the building, several ambulances and Tom in his rapid response car had arrived.

Her stomach turned at the thought of facing him again, so she went to help with the hoses. The water was having some effect, and they were able to move forward to beat back some of the flames.

As she watched, one of Red Watch came out of the building, carrying someone over his shoulder. The missing night guard? She hoped so. As she moved forward a few more steps she glanced over briefly. Saw Tom ministering to the unconscious patient, placing an oxygen mask over his nose.

I can't concentrate on Tom. I need to focus on what I'm doing.

It felt like a sucker punch to the gut when Tom saw Cara look his way and then turn without acknowledging him at all. He tried to tell himself it was because she was concentrating on her job. Not to read anything into it. But things had been strange between them ever since her fall in the shoe shop.

And that niggled—because he'd spent the entire night tossing and turning in his bed, telling himself that he'd somehow made up the whole thing. But if she *was* avoiding him... Maybe she was embarrassed. Had she seen the look in his eyes when he'd caught her? Maybe she was *appalled*?

There's a fire that needs putting out. She's not going to stop and come over and talk to me.

But a smile might have been nice. A nod of the head. Something was up. He could feel it.

He turned his mind to his patient. He had some mild burns to his hands, and his respirations were extremely low due to smoke inhalation. He had soot in his throat and up his nostrils. God only knew what sort of chemicals he might have breathed in through the smoke. It all depended upon what was burning.

He helped get the man onto a trolley and whisked off into an ambulance, which roared away from him to get him to an Accident and Emergency department.

He hoped the man would live. It seemed they'd got to him in time. But life could be a fragile thing. Tom knew the truth of that better than most.

The fire was extinguished. Only smoke continued to fill the sky. Cara finally had a moment to shuck off her helmet, unzip her coat and allow some of the cool night air to flow in around her body.

She loved her job. She loved to battle against the flames. And although this fire had taken a few hours it was all under control now. The fire investigation team would soon arrive, but Hodge had already come out and said it looked as if some kind of accelerant had deliberately been spilled in the warehouse. He'd found the flashpoint of the fire and the night guard had been found near that.

Whether the guard had started the fire, or someone else had, she didn't know, but the report from the hospital had already told them that the guard was alive but refusing to talk to the police. So...

'Hey.'

She turned. It was Tom. Her heart instantly began to thud again.

'Hey.' She looked away from him awkwardly, back at the blackened building that was now mostly in disarray.

'That was a tough one,' he said.

'It was.'

'I'm exhausted. Looking forward to going home and getting a shower.'

She nodded. A shower sounded great. A shower with Tom would be even better. But that wasn't going to happen anytime soon, so she said nothing about it.

'Gage away?'

'At my parents.' They're going on a cruise tomorrow and taking him with them. They'll be gone for three days.'

'You'll miss him.'

He nodded.

'So will I.'

Another nod.

'Are we okay?' Tom asked.

Her heart leapt into her throat, then began to thump against her ribs. 'Yeah! Of course we are!'

'Good. It's just things have seemed a little funny after...' He tailed off.

'I tripped. That's all. I've just got some other stuff on my mind.'

'Anything I can help with?'

She smiled. Despite it all, he was still willing to help her out. And she couldn't hold it in any longer. 'My father wants me to practise my waltz. He's organised an orchestra for the ball.'

'You know how to dance?'

She laughed. 'Oh, of course! I can cha-cha-cha with the best of them!'

'Really?'

Cara groaned. 'No. I have two left feet. Two left feet that are going to be in vertiginous heels. What do you think?'

Tom seemed to think for a moment. 'That I'm going to need steel-capped shoes.'

'And then some.'

She paused. She wanted to give him an out. Rather than hear him try to worm his way out of his obligation, it would be kinder to just let the man off the hook herself.

'You don't have to do this, you know... I can go alone. You can dance with someone who won't break every bone in your feet, and I will weather the storm with Xander, or Peregrine, or whoever my father tries to set me up with.'

'Are you kidding? I gave you my word. And I don't back out of any promises I make.'

'You sure? I'm not sure our relationship will survive my trying to dance with you.'

She couldn't tell him the real reason. That she wasn't sure *she'd* survive being in his arms all night and not being able to kiss him, or touch him the way that she'd want to, or whisper sweet nothings into his ear.

Tom thought for a moment, then smiled. 'I have an idea.'

'Ditch the night entirely? I can't.' She grimaced.

'No, not that. Daphne—my sister-in-law. She can be our secret weapon.'

'And Daphne will be our secret weapon *how*, exactly?'

'She's a dance instructor. She owns Mango Dance Studio. She could teach you how to waltz.'

A dance instructor? Hmm…

'I know that place. It always looks busy. You think she'll have time to help me?'

'I can but ask.'

'Okay, but be realistic with her, okay? Don't tell her I have promise, or anything. Tell her she's getting a complete newbie, with no sense of rhythm or grace. Tell her I'm like a baby elephant. Or a hippo. Or some other animal that wouldn't be able to dance well but could break her partner's toes.'

He gave her a playful nudge. 'You're not a hippo. Or an elephant. A few hours with Daphne and you'll be as graceful as a swan.'

'You remember me in those heels, though, right?'

'I do.'

'I guess it's too late to find a stunt double?'

He laughed, and she loved the sound of it. Loved how they were talking normally again.

'Much too late. Besides…' He looked directly into her eyes, his voice softening, 'I'm looking forward to dancing with you.'

Her breath caught in her throat. 'You are?'

Did he mean that? And *how* did he mean that? As friends? Or…?

No, it can never be as something more. This man has danced with Victoria. I've seen the wedding video! They were perfect. Graceful.

'Are you kidding me? You'll be the belle of the ball.'

She liked it that he was trying to build up her confidence. He was a good man.

'And you'll stay by my side all night? Because I'm not sure I'll be able to stand upright after dancing in those heels.'

'Always.'

She smiled back at him, then looked away. Because looking into his eyes right now was making all those other thoughts come back. The thoughts she shouldn't be having about Tom. He truly was a gentleman. Her knight in shining armour. But he was also a grieving widower, and she was a very bad person for even entertaining these thoughts about him right now.

'You can dance,' she said. 'I've seen you.'

He shrugged. 'I think I've got some moves.'

Cara nodded. Yes, he had. But even if he hadn't he'd still be a better dancer than her. If the worst came to the worst, she'd throw off her heels and dance with him barefoot, if need be.

Anything to be in his arms a moment longer.

CHAPTER SEVEN

THE MANGO DANCE STUDIO was just off the high street, situated above a Turkish supermarket and a pawn shop.

Cara hadn't been sure what to wear for a practice dance session. The only dance movies she'd seen were set in the past, where leotards and leg warmers were all the rage, but she was pretty sure they weren't in the eighties any more, so she'd decided her usual gym gear would have to do. A sports bra under a baggy long-sleeved tee shirt and some tracksuit bottoms, with trainers.

In a bag, she carried the vertiginous golden heels, in case this Daphne told her that she needed to practise in those, but she really hoped that wasn't the case. Every time she put them on she could feel blisters wanting to make their appearance on her little toes, and her ankles ached in wary anticipation.

And she was also anxious about meeting Daphne. If she was Tom's sister-in-law, that meant she was Victoria's sister, and that meant Daphne would no doubt be curious about this woman Tom was bringing and what their relationship was. She didn't want Daphne to hate her, or to see something that Cara was desperately trying to hide.

As time ticked on she knew she couldn't leave it

any longer, so Cara opened the door that had Mango Dance Studio blazoned across it and headed up a narrow set of stairs.

Once inside, she was amazed. The stairwell was painted in a light grey, and as she took the stairs she saw framed photo after framed photo of dancers in various shows. Ballet, tap…something from the West End, by the looks of it. An entire cast taking a bow in front of a standing ovation, and at the top of the stairs a few dancers standing with celebrities, the photos autographed.

Daphne was serious about her business, clearly. She had ambitions for her dancers, and this exhibition of photos let everyone know that.

At the top of the stairs was a glass door. Cara pulled it open and walked straight into a reception area, where a petite blonde sat behind a desk adorned with orchids.

'Can I help you?'

'I'm here to see Daphne. I have a private session with her.'

'Name?'

'Cara Maddox.'

'Oh, they're waiting for you! Go through the door on the right there and to the end of the corridor.'

Tom must have already arrived. She smiled her thanks to the receptionist and headed down the corridor. Again, there were pictures on the walls. Large poster-sized, this time. Dancers in a production of *Swan Lake*. A line of female dancers all on tippy-toes, arms gracefully arced overhead. Something Christmassy that she didn't know. And another that looked as if it was set in the nineteen-twenties. The costumes were amazing, and all the dancers looked happy and proud.

Could Daphne make Cara look that good?

But as she got closer to the studio door her nerves kicked in big-time, and she froze, her hand on the handle, ready to push the door open but worrying about who and what waited for her on the other side. Tom had a relationship with this woman. She was his sister-in-law. Would Daphne hate her? Think she was replacing her beloved Victoria?

She almost turned back. This whole event was crazy enough as it was! But, unwilling to let her father get any satisfaction from Cara failing them all yet again, she yanked the door open, lifted her chin and went in.

Tom was at the far end of the room, in a pair of dark tracksuit bottoms and a tee shirt, laughing with a tall, svelte, Amazonian woman who was the spitting image of Victoria.

Cara felt a jolt to her system, her mouth went dry, and she suddenly needed a drink very, very badly.

Daphne was the perfect embodiment of Victoria. Every reminder of why Tom had married his wife. She was tall and beautiful and slim. Perky and graceful and stylish. She wore a leotard top that moulded her perfect breasts and showed off her slim waist, attached to which was a diaphanous black skirt that just covered her bottom and hips. And below that were long, slim but strong legs.

'Cara! You made it!'

Tom came over to give her a hug and a quick peck on the cheek, but she was too nervous to enjoy it, her eyes clamped onto Daphne, who was watching the entire thing curiously. She was so keen to give the right impression Tom's kiss hardly registered.

'Wouldn't miss it. Hello, Daphne. I'm Cara!' she

blurted, holding out her hand for Daphne to shake. 'Are you sure you can teach this old dog some new tricks?'

Why was she being so self-deprecating? Was she trying to tell to Daphne that she was nothing special? That Victoria's memory would never be threatened by her?

Perhaps I ought to have completed the image by tripping over my own feet walking in?

'Of course. Cara. Tom's told me so much about you.'

'All good, I hope.' She couldn't stop smiling. She felt like one of those ventriloquist's dummies, her face etched with a permanent rictus grin.

'Tom never speaks badly about anybody.'

Good. That was good. And of course she was right. He didn't. She couldn't recall him badmouthing anyone.

'Great.' She glanced at Tom and could see he was looking at her with amusement.

'So, shall we get started?' Daphne asked.

'Let's do that,' Cara agreed.

'Have you ever danced before?'

Cara set the bag of heels down on the floor by the piano. 'No. Well, I had to do a show once at school, but I'm not sure that counts.'

'Do you ever dance when you're alone?'

'No. I'd rather go to the gym and lift some weights.'

'How much can you bench press?'

'About a hundred kilos.'

'Impressive! You're strong. Tom tells me you're a firefighter, so I guess you have to be?'

'Yes, but I enjoy it. It's not a chore for me, going to the gym.'

'Good. So you're not afraid of hard work?'

Cara shook her head. 'No.'

'Excellent. Because that is what's ahead of you. So!

Let's get started. Tom says you need to know how to waltz, so before we can get into how to do box steps and fleckerls and spin turns we need to perfect the hold. Tom, would you join us?'

Box steps? Fleck-what? Perfect the hold?

That meant being up close and personal with Tom. In front of Daphne! What had she and Victoria been? Twins, or something? Surely she'd remember if Victoria had had a twin? She couldn't remember such a fact, but maybe she'd forgotten?

And right now it very much felt as if Victoria herself was standing there, asking Cara to get into 'hold' with Tom.

'For a standard waltz we need you in a closed frame hold, like this.'

Daphne began positioning them like mannequins. Pushing her and Tom closer together, linking their hands, adjusting elbows, straightening backs, shifting hips, until she felt they were perfect.

Cara couldn't recall ever being this close to Tom.

Daphne stood back, like a sculptor admiring her handiwork. 'Perfect. Now, you'll need to hold this frame throughout.'

Cara glanced at Tom and smiled nervously before looking away. She was up close and personal with Tom. Tom's right hand was under her left shoulder blade. Her left hand rested on top of Tom's shoulder blade. Their bodies were in contact, though they were both slightly off to the right of each other.

'Stop looking at one another. In this dance you both look off to the left,' Daphne said firmly.

Okay. That made it a bit easier. It would have been hard to have her body pressed against his and look at him, too. Thank God her father had told her she'd need to know a waltz, and not a tango or a rumba. She'd seen those on that television show, and there was no way she'd have been able to do either of those with Tom without becoming a gibbering mess.

'You neck looks broken, Cara. Tom doesn't want to look like he's dancing with a zombie. Do it like this.' Daphne tweaked her neck, elongating it. 'This is a dance of grace and softness. Imagine you're exposing your neck so that a man may plant a kiss there.'

Cara flushed, imagining Tom doing just that. Could he feel the heat radiating from her cheeks? She must have squeezed him with her fingers, because Tom squeezed back, as if to say, *You've got this...don't worry.*

'Right, so now I'm going to teach you the left closed change and the right closed change. These are your most basic steps, all right?'

What followed next was the most gruelling thirty-minute session, during which Cara felt less and less that she was learning to dance, but more that she was against an army drill instructor. Daphne was kind and encouraging to Tom, complimenting him on his form and technique, whereas to Cara it seemed she was less acccpting. Everything Cara did was wrong, or out of time, and she kept losing the basic form of their hold.

When she did that Daphne would step forward, pull Cara out of hold and insert herself into Tom's arms and say, 'Like this!'

Cara was beginning to feel like a little girl being told off by a strict headmistress, and inside her rage was beginning to build. She was trying her best! She'd never danced before! Couldn't this Daphne give her a *little* credit?

Cara was sweaty, and tired, and her arms ached from holding them in the correct position. She was tired of counting *one-two-three, one-two-three*, and thinking about how to place her feet, and maintain hold, and look to her left whilst going right, and holding her neck. And Daphne scolding her all the time implied that Tom's last dance partner—Victoria—had been a much better student.

'Can we take a break?'

Cara broke hold and walked away to the piano, where there was some water, and poured herself a drink. She knocked back the entire glass in one go and stood there, hands on hips, breathing hard. She hadn't known what to expect from this session, but she'd expected more enjoyment than this! She was dancing with Tom! Spending time with him up close and personal. And it was being ruined by his harsh task mistress of a sister-in-law!

'You'll never improve if you keep taking breaks,' admonished Daphne, smiling a perfect, un-sweaty smile.

'Yeah? Well, I'll never learn anything the way *you're* teaching me.'

Daphne looked to Tom, as if she couldn't quite believe the impudence. 'I'm sorry?'

'I'm not trying to be a professional dancer! I appreciate your time, Daphne, but you're teaching me like you're trying to get me into a top dance school or a show in the West End! It's just a ball at my father's home. It's meant to be fun!'

'You're not having fun?'

'No! I just want to learn the basics of the waltz, so that I don't fall over my feet in front of my family and friends. No one's going to be scoring me, and no one's going to kick me out of a competition if I accidentally step on Tom's toes! I just want...'

They were both staring at her.

'What?' asked Daphne.

'I want to dance with Tom and I want it to be fun.'

Cara looked to Tom and he gazed back at her with a smile, as if he was proud of her, and in that moment that was all that mattered. When Cara glanced at Daphne, her face said something different.

'I don't need you constantly shoving in my face the fact that Victoria could pick up dance steps easily. I don't need you telling me that I'm not as good as her. I'm not trying to replace Victoria!'

'I'm sorry. I'm not used to teaching for anything but competitions and getting people ready for auditions. Maybe I have been a little...harsh?'

Cara shook her head, wiping the sweat from her forehead with her forearm. 'I need the loo. Excuse me.' And she headed off to find a toilet, feeling humiliated and ashamed.

Had Daphne deliberately been trying to make Cara feel she wasn't good enough? Comparing her to her sister to show her that she could never have Tom, if that was her plan?

She hoped that in her absence Tom would stick up for her and fight her side.

Tom watched Cara go, and when the door closed he turned around and faced Daphne. 'She's right. You were being harsh.'

Daphne had the decency to look shamefaced. 'I'm sorry. It's just...when you said you were bringing this woman I felt like you were leaving my sister behind.'

'I will never forget my wife, Daphne. Never. But life moves on. I've moved on. And Cara is my best friend. She was there for me when no one else could be. She got me through those dark months and she still does it today.'

'You like her?'

'Of course I do! She's my best friend.' He stared at his sister-in-law, hoping that his other thoughts about Cara wouldn't give him away, but he wasn't sure he was that good an actor.

Dancing with Cara had been nerve-racking. A delight. Excitement overdrive. His pulse had been thrumming in the hundreds, without a doubt, and he'd kept sneaking glances at her, even though he'd been meant to look left, away from her. And some of those stumbles had been his fault, not hers.

'I kind of got the feeling she was more than a best friend and that scared me,' said Daphne.

'She's not,' he said, feeling his cheeks flush with the lie.

'Well, if there is ever a chance that you could be something more with this girl, then…you should take it. I want you to be happy, Tom. Victoria would want you and Gage to be happy, too.'

Tom stared at her. He was glad of her kind words, but still all he could feel was doubt. Doubt that he should be moving on already…doubt that he should put his friendship with Cara at risk. What if they did try going out with each other and it all fell apart because he wasn't good enough for her? He'd failed at being with Victoria. Who was to say being with Cara would be any better? He'd been a bad partner.

And why was he even thinking about any of this

when he had no idea how Cara felt anyway? She might laugh in his face at the suggestion that they be more than friends, and he wasn't sure he could stand the rejection. And, maybe it was cowardly of him, but he liked how they were right now. He liked seeing her most days, being able to talk to her and share his life with her. And all those secret feelings...? Well, they felt good, too. He could carry on like this even if it did torture him day after day.

Cara was great. Not only with him, but with his son, too. Gage loved Cara. Adored her. She would fit into his little family easily if she was given the opportunity.

Listen to me! I haven't even asked her out and I'm already imagining us as a family!

But that was a good thing, right? That he could visualise it?

'Thanks. I appreciate it,' he said now.

'She's different,' said Daphne.

'Yes, she is.' He smiled, thinking of how different Cara was. Cara was...unique. And quirky. Not your typical girly girl. But he loved that. Loved her strength. Loved the fact that she had no idea how beautiful she actually was. Her innocence on that matter was engaging.

'And maybe different is what you need?' Daphne suggested. 'I know you and Vic had your problems.'

But what someone needed and what they wanted were two different things. Did he have all these feelings for Cara because he needed her? Was he using her to make himself feel good about the fact that he could help her when he hadn't been able to help his own wife?

Normally when he was having doubts about something he would talk to Cara and get her opinion, but on this he couldn't.

Why do I have such trouble telling the women who are important to me how I really feel?

Cara had splashed her face with water and was now standing in the studio bathroom, staring at her reflection in the mirror and wishing she'd never had that outburst with Daphne. She'd been trying to help, teaching in the only way she knew how. It wasn't her fault that Cara couldn't dance and was having difficulty picking up form and rhythm.

I'll go back in there and apologise.

She patted her face with a paper towel, gave herself one last stern look in the mirror and readied herself for delivering a heartfelt apology. She'd not only embarrassed herself, she'd also put Tom in an awkward position with his sister-in-law. Cara had never meant to cause trouble. That wasn't who she was.

When she reopened the door to the studio music was playing. She recognised the music and could even—miracle upon miracle—count the three-beat, as if her brain had somehow been switched on after Daphne's instruction.

Tom and Daphne were dancing the waltz in the middle of the room and she stood watching them, a smile on her face, wishing she could be as graceful.

When they saw her they broke apart and Tom walked over to her with a smile. 'You okay?'

'I'm fine. And I'm sorry. I didn't mean to raise my voice back there.'

'Don't worry about it. Daphne has something she wants to say.'

'Oh?' She turned to Daphne, who was walking towards her like a dancer, all long-limbed and flowy.

Graceful, like a swan. It was in her bearing and her stature, after years upon years of knowing how to make her body move in an attractive way.

'Cara. I want to apologise one last time.'

'Oh, there's no need for you to—'

'There's every need. I was unnecessarily harsh towards you and that was wrong. I want to help you and Tom learn to dance so that it's fun.' She smiled. 'Take Tom's hand.'

Cara couldn't believe it! Flushing, she stepped into hold with Tom, feeling the strength and kindness of his grip, the press of his firm body against hers, seeing the reassuring look he gave her. Her back protested a little. Her neck ached and her arms felt heavy from all the practice.

But Daphne stepped back and said, 'Listen to the music. Just go with the flow. See what happens.'

So they began to dance.

It was awkward to begin with. Cara stepped on Tom's toes twice. Grimacing, apologising, her cheeks going red every time. But Daphne and Tom both encouraged her to continue, and eventually she began to get the basic box step.

'We're doing it!' she said. 'We're actually bloody doing it!'

Daphne clapped, then strode over to the piano when a trill came from her bag. Cara and Tom stopped dancing.

Daphne looked at her phone. 'Ah, sorry, guys. I've got to go. My husband is not so politely reminding me we have tickets to see a show tonight.'

'Oh!' Cara went to get her own bag, with the heels in it. 'We'll let you lock up, then.'

'No, no! Both of you continue! Naomi doesn't lock up the studio until eight. You've plenty of time to practice.'

'Oh, well… If you're sure?'

'Absolutely! It's been a pleasure to meet you, Cara.'

And Daphne kissed her on both cheeks and rushed from the studio, her diaphanous skirt billowing behind her.

Alone with Tom in the studio, Cara turned to look at him and laughed nervously. 'You want to continue?'

'I don't see why not.'

'All right…'

She nervously stepped forward to take Tom's hand and get into hold. Now they were alone together it all seemed so different from when they'd had a chaperone in Daphne. It felt more intimate, his hand in hers… More personal, her body against his.

Forbidden.

Her heart pounded in her chest—so much so, she was convinced he'd be able to feel it, reverberating through his ribcage, and she didn't dare look at him. It was easier to pretend that he wasn't there, to look off to the left and try to remember her steps.

The music continued to play. They stepped forward, right, together. Left, forward, together. She muffled an apology for stepping on his toes once again, but then they began to get the hang of it. Cara was beginning to remember the flow, now, and feeling more comfortable, more able. And when Tom began to make a turn, going in a different direction, she followed easily, happy to be led.

The music was bright and happy, and it made her think of sunshine, and fields full of wildflowers, dancing in a soft breeze. She and Tom were the wildflowers.

She became comfortable in his hold, laughed when they turned, began to feel the joy of being at one in partnership with him.

If only life could stay like this for ever.

They began to find an easy sway, moving with the music as it built. They were both smiling and laughing at how easy they were finding it in each other's arms.

'We're doing it!' she said.

'We certainly are.'

'Think we should try it with me in the heels?'

She didn't want to break contact with him. She didn't want to stop at all. But dancing in trainers must be easier than it would be in the heels, and although she felt she'd got a good grip on the dance so far, it needed to be rooted in reality.

'Let's give it a go.'

They broke apart, Cara feeling breathless, but full of excitement and drive. She quickly put on the heels, grimacing at the way they made her feet feel. She'd been practising wearing them. Wanted to show Tom she could walk in them now—even if they did make her feel as if she was about to have the worst blisters in the world.

'Wow! Look at you!'

She liked the way he looked her up and down. He was looking at her as if she was a woman, not just his best friend. She saw appreciation in his eyes. Saw... *want*? That made her heart palpitate!

Cara stepped forward and into his arms once again. Her centre of gravity was off, but it didn't take her long to adjust. In Tom's arms, she felt she could do anything. Be anyone. Even a graceful dancer. They swayed and danced, bodies pressed close, enjoying the rhythm of the music, enjoying the feel of being in each other's arms. And as the music came to a crescendo Tom twirled her round and pulled her close, smiling at her, and the intensity of his eyes, so close to her own, caused her heart to pitter-patter.

They stood staring at each other, mere inches apart, but their bodies pressed close. She couldn't help herself. She looked down at his lips. They were parted. He was breathless. And the way he was looking back at her...as if he wanted her... It did strange things to her insides. She reached up, stroked the side of his face, trailed her fingers over his square jaw, and suddenly, somehow, they were kissing.

Her mind was going crazy at what was happening. Disbelief. Surprise. Awe. Terror. Kissing Tom was everything she'd imagined it would be. His lips were soft, his kiss passionate, as if he'd been keeping a secret desire for her hidden and it was now being unleashed, and he was taking every moment of the kiss to enjoy it, in case it ended too soon.

She knew how he felt. She didn't want it to end, either.

Her fingers went into his hair, and he growled deep in his throat, and the sound just turned her on even more. The rest of the world disappeared with the intensity of their kiss. All that existed, all that mattered, was the fact that they were together and that somehow this magical moment was happening. She didn't stop to think of the consequences. She didn't stop to think of what would happen *after* the kiss. All she could think of was his lips on hers, his tongue in her mouth and the way he felt in her arms.

That was enough.

That was all she needed and would ever need in that singular moment.

And then…they both came up for air.

Breathing heavily, Cara stared into Tom's eyes, seeing the want and the need. The real world came crashing back in. The dance studio. Who they were and what they were doing. How they had just changed things between them for evermore.

'What does this mean?' Tom asked, gazing back into her eyes, his hands sitting on her waist.

'I think it means…that maybe we are something more than friends.'

Tom looked down at the ground. 'Is that possible?'

Cara gave a hesitant smile. 'Let's find out.'

It was the day of Gage's birthday party. His grandparents had just brought him back from their three-day cruise to Bruges, and he had returned with a dazzling array of different types of chocolate that he'd bought from the chocolate shops in the Belgian city.

Tom was so glad to have him back. He'd missed him incredibly. Without Gage at home, it had been as if he was living a different life lately. That of a single guy. He'd gone out dancing. Kissed a girl. And now he thought that he might be in a relationship of some kind. His life had gone off in a direction he wasn't sure of.

After he'd kissed Cara, the receptionist had opened the door to the studio and reminded them that she'd be closing up soon. So they'd both very quickly separated and nodded and begun packing up. He'd kept looking at Cara, his heart pounding, his head spinning with possibilities. He'd wanted to say more, to ask her questions, but he'd known it couldn't be a late night—and did he really want to send this blossoming *something* into a downward spiral so soon?

He didn't think they'd ended it awkwardly, but his head was full of questions. What did this mean? Had they stepped over a line that neither of them should have crossed? Could they ever go back to just being friends if this went south somehow?

He didn't want to think it would go bad, but he had no other point of reference. He'd only ever been in a relationship with Victoria and he'd lost her. Their romance had soured soon after the rings had gone on each other's fingers. But that was just life, right? It couldn't be sunshine and roses every day.

Or could it? Maybe it was possible—if you found the right person? His grandparents had never had a cross word between them, and they'd held hands right up until the end of their days. When his nan had left this world his grandfather had pined so much he'd died of a broken heart just weeks later.

That was the kind of love Tom wanted.

But right now he was in his worst nightmare. A soft play centre. He'd tried to steer Gage away from the idea, but when he had asked his son where he wanted the party Gage had said here, so... He was willing to grit his teeth and get through it.

Gage had invited his entire class from pre-school, so there were about twenty-five children. He'd had to sit and make up party bags for them all, and most seemed to have arrived. The play centre was filled with noise and that odd smell of sweat and plastic as children whizzed down slides or swung Tarzan-style into a deep ball pit.

Gage himself had just come down a slide. 'Did you see me, Daddy?'

'I did.'

'I did it head-first!'

He smiled. 'I saw.'

And then he sensed more than saw Cara's arrival. As if his body was attuned, he felt her coming through the swing doors, holding a brightly wrapped parcel that she passed to him.

'Hey.'

'Hey, yourself.'

'Cara!' Gage barrelled into her arms and Cara swung him up and around easily, making him laugh.

'Hey, squirt!'

'You came!'

Cara put him down on the ground. 'You bet I did! I wouldn't miss this, would I?'

'Are you coming in? I want to show you my secret hidey spot!'

She nodded. Glanced at Tom. 'Lead the way.'

Gage ran off into the netted maze, bounding up some soft rubber steps before turning to see that she was following. 'You coming?'

'Yep!' Cara turned and looked shyly at Tom. 'You okay?'

'More than okay.'

He smiled. Things were still good with them. She didn't seem to have had any second thoughts. No one had put any doubts into her head. He was both glad and scared. It meant that they were going to go somewhere with this thing they were building between them.

'I'd better go.'

He nodded. 'Yes, you should.'

He watched her scramble away after his son, loving how Gage took her hand and began to drag her deeper into the maze until he lost sight of them both.

Could he ask for anything more right now?

They were both good. Neither had regrets. And his son *adored* Cara.

So why did he feel as if he was standing on the edge of an abyss?

Cara offered to carry an exhausted Gage up to bed.

'Oh, you don't need to do that,' Tom protested.

'It's my pleasure. I haven't read to him in ages.'

She'd missed the little squirt, knowing he was away for a few days, and that she couldn't see him. But it had been nice too. It had enabled her and Tom to get close. That kiss had been… Well… She kept replaying it in her head. Over and over.

Tom had kissed her back!

She hadn't imagined that part. She hadn't dreamed it. It had been *real*, and he'd seemed to want her as much as she had been wanting him. Which was crazy and wild and…

Part of her had worried that when she turned up for Gage's party Tom might be awkward with her, might have had second thoughts, and would take her to one side and tell her that the kiss could never happen again. Only he hadn't.

She'd played with Gage for a bit, then stood with the parents. And when no one had been watching she'd brushed the side of her hand up against Tom's. It had been exciting, feeling that secret contact, knowing that no one else knew what was going on. It had been their own private thing. And when the children had all sat down to eat their chicken nuggets, or their burger and chips, Tom had squeezed past her in the party room, and the feel of his hand brushing over her hip had been electrifying.

In the car on their way home Gage had babbled away non-stop about what a great party it had been, and how much he had enjoyed his birthday, and Cara had felt glad. He'd not been a sad little boy who missed his mum. He'd been happy and bright and he'd enjoyed himself, and that had been a delight for her, too.

As she laid Gage down in his bed he yawned, and grabbed his teddy bear for a snuggle. Cara sat beside him and began to read him a story. It was often the highlight of her day, reading to Gage at night. She'd not realised how much she enjoyed it until he'd gone away and she hadn't been able to do it. Not realised how often she actually did it.

It didn't take too long for the little boy's eyes to grow heavy, and when his breathing became steady and his eyelids flickered with delightful dreams she crept off his bed, laid the book down on his bedside table and silently left his room, pulling the door almost shut, so that a sliver of light from the hall would show in his room.

When she turned round, Tom was waiting for her, smiling, and he reached up to tuck some of her hair behind her ear.

'He's had a great birthday, thanks to you.'

'It wasn't anything to do with me. You organised everything. I just showed up.'

'Showed up and managed to chase him around that massive jungle gym for almost two hours. Honestly, I don't know where you find the energy.'

'There's always energy if it's something you enjoy.'

She was finding it difficult to concentrate right now. Tom kept touching her. Her hair, her ear, her neck… Now his hand dropped to her waist and pulled her closer, and she almost stopped breathing. How often had she dreamed of this? Wanted this? What was going to happen?

Because if he was going to kiss her again, then maybe they should take this downstairs. Kissing, she could cope with. Kissing Tom had been wonderful the last time, and her lips burned to feel his upon hers again. But if it was going to be something else…

Cara hadn't been with anyone since Leo, and Leo had said some pretty hurtful things about her physical appearance. Things she knew she ought not to let affect her, but they did. Of course they did. How could they not? Tom might like kissing her, and dancing with her, but if he saw her naked would *he* think she looked too masculine, too?

She had short arms, short, stocky legs, almost no boobs to speak of, and muscles aplenty. Her body was solid. Not much wobbled or was soft. Leo had said to her that no straight man would want to be with a woman who looked like a guy. That she wasn't as feminine as she should be. That she wasn't as graceful. And Tom had been with Victoria his entire life, and she had been an elegant, tall Amazon. Blonde and sylph-like. If she'd had pointed ears she might have been an elf. Beautiful. Ethereal. Cara had muscles and tattoos and abs…

What if I'm not woman enough for him?

Tom reached out and pulled Gage's door closed properly.

'What are you doing?'

'I don't want him to hear us.'

'Hear us doing what?'

Tom smiled and pulled her closer, his lips nuzzling her neck, sending delicious shivers down her body.

She closed her eyes in bliss, wanting to give herself up to it, wanting to feel she could be confident in her own body. But she'd always let people down in that way. Her mum had wanted her to be more of a girl, to dress in pink and enjoy the things she did, and she'd gone against that. Playing with her brothers, going hunting, making dens and playing soldiers. Most of her friends were guys and now she was a firefighter, pumping iron in the gym, happy in jeans and trainers or combat boots rather than being the lady her mother had wanted. Leo had said she'd looked like more of a man than he did.

I can't compare to Victoria. I can't!

And so, although it pained her, although it ripped her in two, she pressed her hands against his chest and pushed him away.

'No. Stop. I'm sorry. I can't.'

'What is it?'

'I just… I can't.'

She turned from him and began to run down the stairs, heading for the front door.

CHAPTER EIGHT

TOM LAY IN bed alone, staring at the ceiling, wondering just what the hell had happened? They'd had such a great time at Gage's party. There'd been fun, and laughter, and Cara had been there, looking after his son as if it was her favourite job in the world, happily chasing him around the soft play area, joining in his games, never getting tired.

It had warmed his heart, the way the two of them got on, and it had left him free to socialise with the other parents—chat to them, share stories, and basically talk to other adults for an hour or two. About normal adult things.

He'd noticed the way one of the single mums looked at him. And that was nice, and all, but he'd only had eyes for one woman at the party. And there'd been moments when his arm had brushed Cara's, or their fingers had entwined, just briefly, and they'd shared a secret smile, when he'd felt whatever they had *building*. That build-up—the excitement, the anticipation of waiting to be alone with her—had been intoxicating.

They'd driven home, Cara had carried Gage up the stairs and read him a story, and he'd stood outside his son's bedroom door, listening to Cara doing all the voices for the characters and Gage's little chuckles. Cara made Gage happy. And she made *him* happy, too. He couldn't believe he'd fought this for so long, when clearly there was an attraction between them both. It had been exposed now, through that electrifying kiss, and he wanted more.

When Cara had crept from his son's bedroom, a smile upon her face, he'd just known he had to have her. The idea of spending some quality time in his own bedroom with her, slowly exploring her body and discovering what brought her pleasure, had given him so much excitement he'd thought he wouldn't be able to stand it.

That was why he'd had to touch her. Why he'd had to have contact. And he'd thought that she was enjoying it too. As he'd kissed her neck she had let out a little purr...or had it been a growl of pleasure? He'd exposed her neck even more, so that he could kiss her and taste her and imagine all the wonderfully naughty things he could do to her, and then...

Something had suddenly changed. She'd stiffened. Frozen. Placed her hands upon his chest and pushed him gently away. She'd looked...terrified!

'No. Stop. I'm sorry. I can't.'

Six words that had puzzled him, before she'd stepped past him, hurried down the stairs and disappeared out through the front door!

He'd gone after her. Of course he had.

'Cara!' he'd called.

How was she going to get home?

He'd texted her.

Come back. Please. Let's talk.

But there'd been no answer. No response. So all night he'd lain there, wondering what he'd done wrong. If he'd said something wrong. Or whether she'd simply got cold feet and maybe they were moving too fast.

That had to be it, right? All this time they'd been friends, and then they'd shared one kiss and suddenly he'd been doing things to her that he'd hoped would lead to sex. Perhaps she'd felt that too? Perhaps she'd panicked? Perhaps she feared taking that next step with him—because if they slept together and it wasn't great then there'd be no going back to their friendship.

He couldn't imagine that sex with Cara would be disappointing. His desire for her was almost overwhelming. Sometimes he felt he couldn't breathe. He wanted her so badly.

Or maybe it's that bastard Leo's fault? Those things he said to her. The way he made her feel about herself afterwards. Like she isn't woman enough.

Tom had done his best to build her up, build her confidence and self-esteem, but perhaps she still felt scared? He could only reassure her so much, Cara had to take that final step herself, and believe that she was woman enough for anyone.

Tom hoped that she'd had a good night's sleep and that maybe, just maybe, he'd get the chance to see her today and talk things over. Make her feel a little easier about things. Let her dictate the pace.

Feeling more optimistic, he managed an hour's sleep before his alarm woke him up for work.

Cara kept stirring her tea. Standing in the small kitchen of the fire station, she stared at the hot drink, her mind a thousand miles away.

'Earth to Cara?'

Reed's voice finally cut into her reverie. 'What?'

He laughed. 'You've been stirring that drink for about four minutes now. Something you want to talk about?'

There was. But not to him. Never to a man like him. She trusted Reed, in that he was her colleague and a damned fine firefighter. She would happily place her life in his hands and know that he had her back in such a situation. But as a friend? A *confidante*? No chance.

She put down the spoon and picked up the mug, carrying it over to the table. 'Not really. Not to you, anyway.'

He mimed being stabbed in the chest. 'Oof! That hurts.'

She smiled and sipped at her drink.

'Problems with *Daddy*?'

Cara ignored him.

'Too many Lords chasing after our fair Lady?'

'Shut up, Reed.'

'Or is it lover-boy causing all your problems?'

'I don't have a lover-boy.'

'Because you're too busy fawning over a paramedic.'

'I'm not fawning!'

'No?'

Reed sipped from a big red mug and raised an eyebrow at her, and in that moment she hated him with a passion. Why was he always there? Why was he always pushing her buttons? What did he get from that? Well, if it was a reaction he was chasing, she wasn't going to give him the satisfaction of getting one.

She sipped her own drink. Calmly. 'No.'

'Things are good between you and Tom?'

'Of course.'

'Hah! You paused!'

'I did not!' she protested.

Reed laughed, settling back in his seat. 'Oh, but you did! Something's going on. Come on, you can tell your Uncle Reed.'

'And have my personal life gossiped about throughout the station? Even more than it already is? No, thanks.'

'So there *is* something. You've just confirmed it. Hmm, what could it be?' He seemed to think for a bit. 'You finally told him you fancied him and he turned you down?'

So Reed thought it too? That she was too manly for any man to want her?

Only Tom seemed to fancy her no problem… This was *her* issue. Not Tom's.

Feeling humiliated, she turned away from Reed.

'Was I right?' Reed asked, looking shocked. 'Wow, I can't believe it. I really thought he liked you, too. Would have put money on it. I guess you can't always know a person, can you? Want me to kick his arse for you?'

She turned to look at him, tears in her eyes, grateful, suddenly, for his support. He might rub her up the wrong way most days, and he'd got this totally wrong, but he was there for her. She was part of his team and they were a family.

'Thanks, but, no. It's not like that and I need to handle this on my own.'

'All right. But if you want me to stand in the background—all menacing, like… I could hold an axe and everything. Just say the word.'

Cara didn't get time to laugh. The station bell began

to ring and they both leapt up to respond, running from the kitchen, down the stairs and into their firefighter uniforms. They got into the fire engine just as Hodge arrived with a slip of paper from the printer, outlining the job.

'House fire.'

Cara nodded, strapping herself in, switching from personal mode to work mode. No matter what was happening between her and Tom, she had to forget it for now. Somewhere out there, someone might be about to lose everything.

And she knew how that felt.

Tom had been dispatched to a house fire on a busy council estate. The area, he knew, was compacted. Lots of high-rise council flats, all packed tightly together, with the exception of a few terraces of two-bedroomed houses, built in the Victorian era. If it was one of those, then there would be the possibility of multiple casualties, as a fire in one of them would spread easily to the homes either side.

He was glad to have some work to do. So far, it had been a quiet shift. Not that he liked to use the Q word. There was a superstition amongst health workers that you never said it out loud. Like actors didn't like to say *Macbeth*. It tempted fate and fate wasn't something you wanted to play around with.

As he came roaring into Gardenia Street he realised he was behind Cara's fire engine. He had no idea if she was on today, but he hoped so. It would be nice just to speak to her and reassure her that everything was fine, that nothing had to change yet if she didn't want it to.

They were getting close to their destination, and

thankfully he couldn't see any plumes of smoke billowing into the air. Maybe it was a small fire? Maybe the residents had already contained it?

But when he pulled up at the address and they all got out of their vehicles they saw a bunch of teenagers at the end of the street on their bikes, laughing and cat-calling and whooping it up.

Malicious call? He knew they couldn't just assume that. They still had to check.

He saw Hodge in his white helmet, going over to the house in question and knocking on the door. He hung back, waiting, aware that Cara stood off to one side, beside Reed, who was looking at him strangely. He tried to send a smile to say hello, but Reed just stared back.

Odd…

The door was opened by a woman in a dirty bathrobe, a cigarette held between her fingers. She looked surprised to see Hodge, almost taking a step back when she saw the array of emergency vehicles parked outside her home.

'Yeah?

'Madam, we've received a call that there is a fire in this property,' Hodge said.

'What? No!' She took a step outside, saw the kids at the end of the street. 'Those little bleeders! Wait till I get my hands around their scrawny necks!'

'Am I to understand that everything is fine?'

'Course it is!'

'Can we come in to check?'

'What for? I told ya! It's them kids! They've been winding me up all week. I've had it up to here…' She raised her hand above her head, before backing away and slamming the door shut.

Tom let out a sigh. It was a malicious call, by all accounts. Why did people do this? It was such a waste of resources, and whilst they were driving to a fake emergency it was taking the services away from someone who might desperately need a fire engine or an ambulance. Timewasters could kill someone, and when this sort of things happened it infuriated him.

He glanced over at Cara, caught her eye. He saw her look away briefly, then she took off her helmet and walked towards him. He saw Reed grab her arm and say something in a low voice to her, but she shook her head.

'I'll be fine,' she said.

What was that about? Had she told Reed what had happened? Why would she do that?

As Cara came towards him he felt his heart begin to race. He didn't want to mess this up. 'You all right?'

She nodded, not making eye contact. 'I'm fine.'

'Everything okay between you and Reed?' The firefighter was still glaring at him for some reason.

'He just wants to protect me.'

Understanding came. 'From me?'

'He could see that I was distracted this morning.'

Tom sighed. 'Look… I'm sorry about last night. I pushed. I pushed too fast and you weren't ready. I didn't mean to upset you and I don't want things to be awkward between us. You mean too much to me. Can we go back to the way things were before that?'

Now she looked at him. 'I'd like that.'

'I care a lot for you, Cara. I need you to know that.'

Her cheeks flushed and he liked how it made her look.

'Are we still on to meet at Mango tonight?' she asked uncertainly.

'Dance practice? Sure.'

That made him happy. He'd thought she might cancel. This way they could spend some more time together. It would give them time to talk about what had happened. Or what hadn't happened. If she wanted to. He was wary of pushing her. Wary of scaring her. That Leo must really have done a number on her.

'Okay. Well, good... I guess I'll see you later, then.' She smiled hesitantly and went to walk away.

He watched her clamber back into the fire engine. Watched the fire engine drive away. He called into Control. Reported it as a malicious call and notified them that he was ready and open for anything else.

He'd not been driving for more than two minutes, when a report of a suspected cardiac arrest came through, and he turned on the sirens and raced to his next call.

She almost cancelled. Nerves had got the better of her. Did she really want to see Tom again so soon? Did she really want to see Daphne? But this was their last session. They were meant to be learning turns and fleckerls and transitions, so that their changes of direction looked smooth.

She was beginning to doubt if she could go through with this. Beginning to think she'd made a huge mistake in allowing something to happen between them. Because although she wanted to be with Tom more than anything, she was scared that at the last moment he wouldn't be physically attracted to her—even though he'd told her so many times that she was beautiful, and that what Leo had said had been more about him being a lousy, stupid idiot than it had been about her.

She wanted to believe that. She'd tried to believe that. But…the sting was still there. The doubt.

Cara craved love. Love for who she was. What she was. Love. Acceptance. Pure and simple.

Her father's love was so overbearing it was suffocating, so she ran from it. Her mother's love had been conditional, and so she'd run from it. Leo's love—though you could hardly even call it that—had been critical, and so she'd run from it.

Tom? Tom was meant to be different. He wasn't meant to be like the others. But would Tom always judge her against Victoria? The perfect, slender, soft, feminine Victoria.

Why was finding love so difficult? Why was it this hard?

Could she really afford to risk losing the man she thought of as her best friend, and probably Gage, too? She wanted to punch something because she felt it was so unfair! If she were at the gym she'd tape up her knuckles and go at the punchbag for a few rounds, that was for sure!

She looked up at the windows of the Mango Dance Studio. She could hear music playing. Something hip-hop…the steady drive of a resounding bass note that practically made the windows reverberate.

I can back out of this. I can walk away. I don't have to go to the ball—I'll just make a donation to the Websters.

But something pushed her onwards and she opened the door, walked slowly up the stairs as if she was a guilty person on her way to the gallows, and entered the studio.

Naomi, the same receptionist was on, and she greeted

her kindly and told her to go straight through. That Tom and Daphne were already there.

Oh, God! Tom and Daphne know each other well. Has Tom told Daphne what happened?

Because Daphne would surely hate her, then.

Her steps faltered, but then a small voice in her head said, *No. You've done nothing wrong. Yet.*

So she pushed open the studio door and walked in, smiling, and sent a wave over to Tom, who stood with Daphne by the piano.

Tom's face broke into a smile and he trotted over to her. 'Hey, glad you made it. I was beginning to think you weren't coming.'

'I said I would,' she said, accepting the kiss that he planted on her cheek.

'Good, good… Okay, let's get started. I hope you two have been practising your steps?' Daphne asked, pointing a remote at the sound system, which began to play a classical waltz. 'Let's get you into hold. Show me what you remember.'

Cara hesitantly took Tom's hand and tried to get into position, looking away, over her left shoulder. She didn't want to think of elongating her neck *'as if a man is kissing it'*, as Daphne had said, because when she'd actually done that it had led to her fleeing Tom's home in shame.

'What's this gap?' Daphne protested, pushing Cara's body closer to Tom's. 'I could drive a lorry through there!'

It was hard holding Tom's hand, being pressed against him, when it was both all she'd ever wanted and also the one thing that she couldn't bear right now. With Daphne watching, the whole thing felt excruciating.

Daphne stood in Cara's eyeline and frowned. 'You

had this so perfectly the other day! Have you forgotten everything?'

No. I've just got scared.

'Okay, let's see those box steps. And…*go!*'

Cara tried to remember her steps, tried to use the grace that she'd developed in the last lesson, but it was like starting anew. She felt so awkward and uncomfortable in Tom's arms that she immediately stepped on his toes and broke hold to step back and say sorry.

'Back in hold!' Daphne ordered.

She took his hand again, tried the steps, stepped on his toes again, flushed, felt heat rise all over her. Felt as if she might cry.

'What is going on? You had this the other day? What has changed?' Daphne frowned.

'It's okay. We've got this,' Tom tried to reassure her. 'Cara? Look at me.'

She did so, feeling it was almost unbearable. To look at the man she loved and to know that he might yet reject her, and then she'd lose everything.

'Feel the music. Forget the steps. Let's just try going with the flow,' said Daphne.

She went back into hold and tried, making mistake after mistake, but gritted her teeth and pushed through. This was meant to be enjoyable! This was meant to be fun! Once upon a time the idea of dancing with Tom had been exciting! Being in his arms… Pressed up close… Only now it was like a nightmare and…

Her nose twitched. Could she smell *smoke*?

She broke hold and stepped back, sniffing the air.

'No, no, no! Back into hold,' ordered Daphne. 'You were getting there!'

'I can smell smoke,' she said.

'What?'

She wasn't imagining things. There was definitely a smell of something burning. She was attuned to it. Knew something wasn't right.

At that moment, the receptionist ran into the room. 'There's a fire next door!'

'Call the fire brigade,' Cara ordered, turning to usher Tom and Daphne from the room. 'Exit the building. Let's make sure everybody's out. Do you have a head-count?'

Daphne seemed to hesitate. 'There's a register for each class.'

'I'll need them. Get everyone out.'

Cara rushed from the studio, grabbing the clipboards with a class register on each. She ordered Tom to get Daphne out, whilst she went from studio to studio to make sure everyone else was out. It didn't take long. The three studios had already been alerted and everyone had left the building. Cara went outside and told them all to line up on the opposite side of the street, so they could take a headcount. No one was missing.

She turned to look at the fire. It had broken out in the empty building next door and looked to be on the first floor, flames already billowing at the windows…

Oh, my God…

It wasn't empty. There were people in those windows, banging on the glass. Were they trapped?

'Stay here!' she ordered everyone, then ran across the road and used a chair from outside a café to break the glass of the building's door.

'Cara!' Tom shouted. 'Wait for the fire brigade!'

But she couldn't wait. Those people didn't have time and there still might be a way to get them out.

She knew fire. She knew how to read it. She understood about flashpoints and backdraughts and all the dangers inherent in running into a burning building.

Only this time she wasn't wearing her flame-retardant kit. This time she didn't have breathing apparatus strapped to her back, an oxygen mask upon her face. She could feel the smoke already getting into her lungs and throat and she coughed, looking for a staircase. There was one right at the back of the building. Cement, so it wouldn't burn or collapse. She ran up the stairs, pulling her shirt over her mouth to help filter the air. At the top was a door and it was locked.

Damn!

She looked about her, saw a fire extinguisher on the wall. It was probably out of date, but it would do. She hefted it in her hands and used it to bash open the lock, kicking the door open with her foot.

Flames billowed from each side of her. There were rags and bags on the floor. And what looked like a camping gas tank. Squatters? Had they been using it? It hadn't blown up, but there was a danger of that. She used the fire extinguisher to try and put out some of the flames and fought past them to get to the people at the window.

'Hey! This way!'

'Oh, my God! I thought we were going to die!'

Some of the people rushed past her, leaving behind a woman who was coughing so badly she could barely stand. Cara rushed over to her and hefted her easily over one shoulder, then began heading back the way she had come.

As she made her way down the stone steps she heard

a fire crew arriving and saw the familiar sight of an appliance screeching to a halt outside. Tom was there too.

'I'm a paramedic,' he explained to the unknown fire
crew.

Cara was coughing madly—could feel the smoke
and the soot lining her throat, her eyes burning and
watering madly.

'Cara? Are you okay?' Tom asked.

'I'm fine,' she managed to get out, coughing more
and more, knowing her lungs needed to try and expel
the deadly carcinogens that she'd breathed in during
the rescue.

'You need to be checked out.'

'I'm fine. Just look after her.' She indicated the
woman.

It was odd to stand back and watch the fire crew
work. Despite her almost deadly inability to breathe
properly, she yearned to be part of them—running in,
dousing the flames, bringing the fire under control.
There was something awesome about doing that. Con-
trolling something that was so wild and untameable.
Having to stand out here and do nothing made her feel
useless.

But I wasn't. I still saved a life.

Paramedics arrived to take the woman away, and
another draped a blanket around Cara and steered her
towards their ambulance to get some oxygen. She sat
there, feeling her breathing get steadily easier, until she
no longer needed oxygen therapy.

The fire had been quickly contained and now it was
time for the clean-up. She watched as everyone did their
job.

Tom finally clambered into the ambulance with her

and sat down beside her. He laid his hand on hers and squeezed it before letting go.

'You scared the hell out of me when you ran into that building.'

'I knew what I was doing.'

'Did you? You weren't in your kit. You could have been hurt, or killed.'

'But I wasn't. I'm fine.'

'If you'd have ended up in hospital…hurt…on a ventilator… If I'd had to see you like that…'

She looked at him then. Frowned. 'You didn't. You won't.'

'When I saw you carrying that woman out…' His voice trailed off and he looked into the distance and grimaced.

Oh. It must have been a stark reminder to him that she was just as Leo said. Too masculine for any man to want her. He'd seen her in her firefighter's outfit often, had seen her fight fires—but had he ever been witness to her physical strength? The woman she'd carried out hadn't been little. It had taken all her strength to lift her over her shoulder.

But perhaps it was easier this way? Because now he wouldn't see her naked, and she wouldn't have to be vulnerable and have her heart torn in two by him.

'It's okay. I understand,' she said, trying to make it easy on him. Trying to give him a way out.

Because she wanted to make this easy on him. Then it would be easier on her. They could still be friends. Forget that kiss. Forget the fact that she felt love for him. Admit that all they ever would be was friends. That way she would still be able to see him. That way she could still see Gage. No reason why that darling little boy should miss out, just because the adults had screwed up.

'We both have such risky jobs, but yours is...' Tom shook his head. 'Dangerous! You run into burning buildings, you risk your life, and I... I need stability. Not just for me, but for Gage. He's already lost his mother. I... I'm meant to protect him. Put my son first. And what have I been doing? Chasing after you...'

'Chasing after you...'

As if she was a terrible choice he had made. She nodded, with tears dripping down her cheeks. She could hear in his voice what he was trying to say. He was ending this. Whatever it was that they had begun. And he was right. Gage had to come first.

'That's fine. I understand. It's probably best. You're right.'

She tried to put on a brave smile, though inside her heart was breaking.

CHAPTER NINE

APART FROM AN irritating cough, Cara was suffering no ill effects from going into the fire without her equipment. The cough she could deal with. That was fine. If she had to cough for the rest of her life she'd do it. But the feeling she had in her heart at realising that she and Tom could never be was something much more devastating.

She should have realised from the start! Tom could never love her. He was right. He had to put his son first. And she…? She was not good enough for him.

She'd hoped for so much more, but everyone in her life had been right. People had tried to tell her ever since she was a small girl that she didn't act the way a woman should.

Her mother had tried. For years!

'Wear a dress, Cara! Please. For me.'

'No one will notice you if you dress like a boy all the time.'

'Let's do something pretty with your hair.'

Cara had wriggled free of every attempt to make her more feminine.

Then there'd been Leo. He'd liked the novelty of going out with a female firefighter at first. He'd had a few bragging rights. He'd seemed to enjoy that. But when their relationship had become physical he'd not seemed to want her that much.

She'd not understood it. They'd been young. In their twenties. They ought to have been in the prime of their lives. But Leo had begun distancing himself from her after that first time, and she'd wondered if she'd done something wrong. He'd been her first. She'd adored him. She hadn't wanted anything to go wrong between them. And then he'd told her the truth.

'I'm not physically attracted to you.'

'You're too hard.'

'You've got more muscle than me.'

And now Tom. He didn't want her for who she was. Maybe if she'd chosen any other career than firefighter they might be together now.

She was too strong. Too masculine. Too dangerous.

If was off-putting to some—she got that. Had heard it her entire life.

She'd not thought Tom would be like that.

She stared out of the window of the fire engine as it raced to a fire in a block of flats. Normally, with the sirens going, she could block out what was happening in her personal life. She could enter work mode. But today she was considering her choices in life.

Would it have been different if she'd been more girly? If she'd gone into charity work? Worn skirts and dresses? Not gone to the gym and pumped iron? Not got any tattoos? Maybe if she'd paid more attention to being like other women she'd have true love by now? Maybe if she'd become a 'lady who lunched' she'd be with Tom now, because then she wouldn't pose a threat.

Who am I kidding? If I was a lady who lunched Tom and I would never have met.

Ahead of them, thick smoke billowed into the sky. This was a real fire. Not a malicious call. Residents of the block of flats were gathered in front of the burning building, hands over their mouths in disbelief, some crying, some coughing.

Their appliance pulled up and immediately Cara jumped out to provide assistance. She was tasked with finding out how many people—if any—might still be inside the burning flats.

One of the tenants, a middle-aged guy in his forties, ran his hand through his hair. 'I don't know... Er... I don't see Jason from flat ten—that's on the third floor. And the Kimbles? I don't see them. There's Tansy... she's a single mum...got a small boy...only four. They live next door to Jason.'

'What's his name?'

'Khaya.'

'Okay.'

She thought she heard someone call her name, but she forged inside, breathing apparatus on, and began to search the premises methodically.

It could feel claustrophobic, searching for people in a burning building. Vision was often limited by thick, choking smoke, and being clad in heavy kit and breathing apparatus was hard work. And you often didn't fit in small spaces. Ceilings could come crashing down around you, floors could give way, so you had to go at a careful pace, always checking your exit route, inching forward to rescue those who still might be trapped.

'You run into burning buildings...'

Behind her was Reed, and he headed left down a cor-

ridor as she headed right. Some people had left their
doors open when they'd fled, so she was able to get inside easily, scan the property and then move on to the
next. Others had locked their doors, but she managed
to open them with a couple of swift kicks, slamming
the doors into the walls behind.

She was on the second floor. The missing people
were from the third. But she couldn't miss checking
this floor in case someone had been missed. She would
never forgive herself if someone died because she hadn't
done her job.

Tom had called Cara's name as she'd run into the burning building, his heart sinking into his stomach. This
was a fierce fire. The building looked as if it could collapse at any moment. A fragile prefabricated building,
built in the seventies, it probably hadn't been brought
up to code in an age, what with council cutbacks...

He'd arrived right behind Green Watch. Had run
over to the residents to see if anyone needed medical
help. He'd seen Cara talking to someone and had tried
to catch her eye, needing to talk to her. Things had been
left pretty awkwardly yesterday, after his outburst, and
then he'd had to take Daphne home.

And now she was gone again.

What if something happened to her in that building?

He'd been stupid yesterday. Not thinking about
Cara's feelings, only absorbed in his own confusing
ones. The guilt he'd been feeling about wanting another
woman. The fear he had about ruining his friendship
with Cara. The fear of losing her—of having to sit by
her bedside if she got injured during a shout.

And then last night he'd been chatting with Gage before bedtime?

'I wish Cara were here all the time, Daddy,' he'd said.

'You do?'

Gage had nodded. Yawned. *'I like playing with her. Do you, Daddy?'*

'Yeah. I do.'

'Good. 'Cos sometimes you're sad and I think Cara makes us better.'

And that had made him think about how much Cara loved his son.

Seeing her carry that unconscious woman out of the building had reminded him of how strong she was. Not just physically, but mentally. Her determination to put others before herself was one of her greatest traits.

If only it was that simple. She runs into burning buildings.

They could collapse. This block of flats could collapse, with her inside, and he would lose everything all over again!

He couldn't do that.

And he certainly wouldn't put Gage through it.

But his heart thudded against his ribcage as he waited for Cara to emerge from the building all the same. His head might be wary of the risks in getting too close to Cara Maddox, but his heart had only ever known how to love her.

Cara paired up with Reed as they took the stairway to the third floor. The stairs were concrete, the only part of the building not on fire, yet still the air billowed with smoke that curled and danced to its own tune.

As they reached the fire door to the third floor they could see flames roaring when they looked through the small window.

'We stay together!' Reed shouted.

She nodded, yanking the door open and hugging the wall that would take them through the flames down to the two flats on the left-hand side.

The heat was fierce. Sweat was pouring down her back, but she barely noticed. They made it to the first door, saw smoke issuing out from behind it, indicating a possible active fire beyond. The door was locked. Reed gave it a hefty kick and they were in.

There was a long corridor, with rooms going off it left and right, thick with black smoke and flashes of orange and red. Cara heard something shatter, off to her left, and entered the first room. Empty. She checked beneath the bed, inside the wardrobes—anywhere someone might think was a good place to hide.

Nothing.

They moved on. Found a bathroom with the door locked. Another kick and it came open easily, and inside was a man, cowering in the bathtub fully clothed, water running over him.

'You Jason?' Cara yelled through her mask.

He nodded.

'Come with me,' Reed said, grabbing his arm and pulling him out. Before he left, he turned back to Cara. 'Be safe!'

'I will!'

With one missing person found, Cara knew they were not going to find the Kimble family in this flat. They were next door, the tenant had said, but she still had to sweep this flat. She entered the room at the end

of the hall. A living room, with a small kitchenette off
to one side. The ceiling had fallen through here and fire
raged above. There were collapsed struts and beams
lying haphazardly on the floor, smoking wildly. But
there were no other people here.

Cara backed out of the flat and went on to the last
one on this floor. The door was closed, but it felt hot.
There had to be a fire raging behind it.

She kicked it open and stood back, waiting for the
surge of flame, watching as it licked up to the roof beyond. Could she hear something? Screams? Someone
crying for help?

She kept low and made her way in, her arm above her
head to protect it from any falling debris. It was hard to
see in here. The smoke was thick. She got out her torch
and switched it on. A television still played in the living room—she could see the flicker of images—and
by the window stood a woman, holding a small child in
her arms. A child who looked unconscious.

Cara carefully made her way forward, jumping to
one side as the ceiling above her collapsed, raining
burning plaster and wood down on her. She fell, slamming into the wall, but soon was kicking off the burning joist and getting back to her feet, finally making it
to the Kimbles.

'Tansy? Khaya?'

The woman turned, her face filled with fear. 'I can't
wake him!'

'It's the smoke.'

Cara took the boy and laid him down, where the
smoke was thinnest. She pulled off a flame-retardant
glove and touched her fingers to the boy's neck. There
was a pulse, thankfully.

Behind them, the ceiling crashed down completely, blocking their exit with a roaring flame. There was no way they could go back the way Cara had come in. They would have to find another way.

The window was slightly ajar, but didn't fully open. Cara looked around, saw a wooden chair, and told Tansy to stand back. She picked up the chair and swung it at the glass, shattering it into a million pieces, then she cleared away the last remaining shards around the frame and peered out to see if the ladders were being sent up.

They were!

Cara flashed her torch and waved to her crew below, indicating that she had two people to rescue.

Hodge was coming up the ladder, with Garrett behind. One for each of them.

Cara dipped back inside and took off her breathing mask. She secured it to Khaya's face, then double-checked the window frame once again, to make sure that no one would suffer a nasty cut as they were carried out through the window.

'Nearly out,' she reassured Tansy.

'I'm afraid of heights!' she yelled back, coughing.

'You'll be okay. Don't worry.'

Cara covered Tansy's body with her own as the flames continued to get near. Then Hodge was at the window and Cara passed out Khaya. Garrett was there too, and they gently coached the petrified Tansy out onto the ladder. As something exploded behind her Cara ducked, feeling something explode as it flew past her.

What the hell was that?

But then she was up at the window and climbing onto the rescue ladder herself.

It slowly began to lower. And the air became cleaner and easier to breathe. Cara let out a heavy sigh. They'd done it. They'd got everyone out, as far as they knew. If there was anyone else still missing it would be up to the others to find them. She knew Hodge wouldn't let her go in again—not until she'd been checked medically.

She saw Tom at the bottom of the ladder, waiting for his patients to be brought down. His face was etched in a deep frown. She wished she could run into his arms and just hold him, tell him she was safe and hear him say, *Thank God. I was so worried about you!*

But she knew that was never going to happen. If she wanted someone like Tom then she would have to change who she was, and she wasn't sure she could do that. It would all be pretend. She'd be playing dress-up—something she'd hated ever since she was a child.

No. She would have to look elsewhere for love.

Or maybe she was destined to be alone for ever.

As they reached the ground, Tom set to working on Khaya immediately.

'Is he going to be okay?' she asked, knowing how hard this must be for him. Working on a child the same age as Gage.

Tom looked up at her, his face strained. 'I'm doing my best.'

He was right. He had a job to do. Save the boy, not answer her inane questions! Angry with herself, she walked away, back to the appliance, where her feelings about everything that had happened lately threatened to overwhelm her.

Tears in her eyes, she lashed out, kicking the tyre of the fire engine over and over again.

* * *

It was the day of the charity ball for the Websters. Her mother's birthday. Cara's night. She was supposed to be going with Tom on her arm, looking like a lady.

What a joke that was going to be!

They'd both know that she wasn't, and everyone else would too. All her family would be there, no doubt laughing about her behind her back. And all her fire crew family. Reed would no doubt have something to say. And Tom? He would probably feel the most awkward of all.

If he showed up.

She'd not heard from him since he'd called things off between them. This was the longest they'd ever gone without speaking. She'd tried texting, but had got no response. She'd even left a message on his voicemail. Surely he wasn't going to stand her up for this? However wrong things had gone between them romantically, he was still supposed to be her best friend.

She'd hoped for so much more from Tom. That he would *see* her. That he would see the woman she was beneath the firefighter's suit. Yes. She was totally different from Victoria. They could never be compared. Clearly. But they'd had something…hadn't they? Apparently not.

Maybe she was just terrible at reading men. She'd made a bad choice yet again.

Will I ever learn?

Still, Tom deserved to be with someone who didn't put her life at risk every day. She couldn't expect him to live like that. Wondering if she'd make it home every day. She'd witnessed the trauma he'd gone through after his wife's death, so she understood his reticence as his heart began to get involved.

Cara sighed. It was time to put on the dress. Do her hair. Make-up. Wear those dreaded heels! Instead, she checked her phone again. Surely Tom should have called her by now? Or maybe his silence was telling her all that she needed to know? That he wasn't going to show. That she would have to walk into her childhood home without a date on her arm?

She sat down in front of her mirror and started combing her hair, trying to decide which was the best way to wear it.

If she could get out of this night right now she would. But she'd made a promise and she wouldn't go back on it. And if she turned up alone and anyone had anything to say about it, then she'd just lift her chin, square her shoulders, and walk away.

She decided to wear her hair up. She'd been to the shops and bought some fancy pins. But every time she tried to make her hair stay put, it kept falling down.

How do other girls do this?

In the end she resorted to an instructional video she found online.

Ah. That's how.

She'd been doing it all wrong…she needed to put it up in sections, not all at once.

It looks pretty.

Next, she got out the make-up palette that she'd bought at the same time as the pins, wincing at the extortionate cost, and sought another online tutorial for something called 'a smoky eye'.

The first attempt made her look like a panda, and

then she'd begun to cry, so she had to wipe it all off with wet wipes. But the second time was much better.

I'm a quick learner.

She put in some stud earrings she already had, and then slipped out of her robe and put on the dress. It clung to her in all the right places and she sat down to put on the heels. When she looked in the mirror to check out her reflection, she gasped. She'd never seen the entire look put together at the same time! It was astonishing! It was…dizzying! Suddenly she understood why girls did this. They could change who they were. Show different sides of themselves. Looking as if she ought to be walking down a red carpet made her feel…*special*.

Suddenly she wished her mother was there to see it. She would have been proud. She would have cried, without a doubt, and Cara knew that because she felt like crying again, too.

'What do you think, Mum?' she said to the empty room.

Of course there was no answer.

What would Tom do, seeing her look like this? Would he have second thoughts?

No. It takes more than a pretty dress and some heels to change a man's mind.

She checked the time. The car would be here at any moment to collect her. Tom ought to be here, only he wasn't, and the rejection she felt was absolute.

She sniffed, realising that she had to put this disaster with Tom behind her. It hadn't worked. They'd both been stupid to think that they could take their friendship and make it into something more. She could only be a stereotypical woman for this one night, and Tom would want someone who could be beautiful and feminine for ever.

There was a knock at her door.

Cara answered it. Her father's chauffeur, Jamison, was waiting.

'Lady Cara.' He gave a brief nod of his head. 'You look stunning.'

'Thank you, Jamison.'

She closed the door and walked down the path, feeling terribly alone, unaware of the ringing phone in her hallway.

The car carried her up the long driveway and she let out a small sigh at seeing her childhood home once again. She had lots of great happy memories of here. Playing in the stables. Going horse riding. Making dens with her brothers and playing hide and seek in all the attic spaces. Cara could hear her mum's voice now, calling to them all to come down for tea. She missed it. Missed her. Wished she'd had the opportunity to show her how she looked today.

I may have totally ballsed up my love-life, Ma, but look at me in a dress!

She had no doubt her mother would have squealed in delight at seeing her. She would have wanted to take many pictures. Pictures that would have been framed and set in pride of place for everyone to see.

Lady Cara Maddox. How she was supposed to be.

But she'd never fitted into anyone else's mould. Cara had always done her own thing and walked tall, and she would walk tall now, no matter what anyone said. Even if it meant walking in her own lane…even if it meant that she walked alone.

Suddenly the car door was being opened and her father was there. 'Cara! Look at you! Oh, my gosh, you're so beautiful.'

Her father took her by both hands and kissed both cheeks, before stepping back to take another look.

'Stunning. Simply stunning.' He smiled at her, proud, then looked behind her and frowned. 'No gentleman paramedic?'

She shook her head, determined not to cry. 'He couldn't make it.'

She had no idea if it was the right thing to say. Maybe it would have been better to say he was running late? But then when he didn't show at all, she'd get those knowing, pitying looks.

Poor Cara. Lost another guy, huh?

This way, if he did show up—which she doubted very much now—it would actually be a pleasant surprise.

'That's a pity. Everything all right between you two?' her father pressed.

'It's fine.'

'All right. But I can't have my daughter having no one to dance with tonight. You'll dance with me, and then I think Xander or maybe Tarquin will want to whisk you around the dance floor looking like that.'

'I'm quite happy not being on the dance floor, Dad. These heels aren't best suited to fancy footwork.'

'Nonsense! Your mother danced in heels, and you've been practising, by all accounts!'

He disappeared into the crowd before she could find out who had told him she'd been practising the waltz.

Cara gazed out over the ballroom. It looked magnificent, as always. Tall marble columns stood all around the edge of the room. Long, red velvet curtains hung in between. Beautiful paintings and portraits of Maddox ancestors adorned the walls. The dance floor was filled with couples—men in tuxedos, women in all colours. It was like watching a garden of flowers, dancing in the breeze. To one side was an orchestra, currently playing a gentle number, and in between them all uniformed butlers and waitresses mingled, offering flutes of champagne and trays of hors-d'oeuvres.

She was surrounded by people, but she'd never felt so lonely.

'Can we get there any faster?' asked Tom from the back seat of the cab, trying his best to tie his bow tie, but failing terribly.

'Traffic, my friend. Nothing I can do,' said the cab driver, chewing his gum.

They were in a long stream of cars waiting to go up the long drive to Higham Manor and, unable to wait a moment longer, he flung some notes at the cabbie, darted from the car and began to run—with a large box under his arm.

He'd been a fool. An absolute fool! Thinking that if he removed Cara from his life he wouldn't have to worry about her. Since telling her he couldn't be with her, he'd not been able to get her out of his mind. And then there'd been that conversation with Gage...

'We...er...won't be seeing much of Cara from now on,' he'd told him.

Gage had looked shocked. Then sad. *'Why?'*
'Because...'

He'd struggled to think of a way to explain it to his

son that he would understand. But that had been hard when he still wasn't sure he understood his own feelings.

'*Because she's busy.*'

'*Has she got a new job?*'

'*No.*'

'*Then why can't she see us? She's always seen us. Always played with me and read me bedtime stories.*'

'*I know. It's just that things happen when you're a grown-up and life gets complicated.*'

'*If she came to live here then it wouldn't matter if she was busy.*'

He'd stared at his son. '*What?*'

Gage had stared up at his father with wide eyes. '*I want to be able to see Cara!*'

'*She has a dangerous job, son. She might...*' His words had got caught in his throat.

'*Might die? Like Mummy did?*'

He'd nodded, barely able to speak at such a thought.

Gage had been quiet for a while, then he'd sat up in bed and said, '*Daddy? If she can be brave, then we can too.*'

He'd stared at his son, surprised at the wisdom that came from a four-year-old boy. He'd been avoiding Cara's calls, sitting on the stairs as his phone rang with her name on the caller ID. He'd hated himself for ignoring them, knowing he needed to keep his commitment to their fake date at the ball but not knowing how he was going to bear the pretence now that things were over between them.

But now Gage had made him think that maybe it could be different.

Cara was a firefighter. She'd always wanted to be a firefighter. That was who she was and he loved her for it. And, yes, she was brave. Perhaps braver than them all. She'd defied everyone who had tried to change her and stuck to her guns. She had been there for him and his son in so many ways and he knew she had strong feelings for him. She had been devastated when he'd said they had to end.

Staying away from Cara for the rest of his life? That wasn't saving his heart—that was killing it! Why stay away when he could be with her? Any time he got to spend with her would be a gift. And if she got injured or, God forbid, something awful happened to her...? That would be terrible, obviously, and he didn't want to think of it happening at all. But if it did then he and Gage would have been blessed by having known her at all. Being part of the love that she gave so willingly.

So, yes. He'd been a fool and he needed to tell her.

She must be thinking he had backed out of their fake date. Well, he wasn't that kind of guy. He'd said he would be there and he was looking forward to dancing with her. Besides, they needed to talk about things.

When he reached the doors to the manor, he stopped, and asked a uniformed butler who was wearing a perfect bow tie if he could help him with his.

'Absolutely, sir.' The butler smiled patiently as he tied the tie, and then he reached into an inside jacket pocket. 'Might I suggest, sir...a comb?'

Tom glanced down at the man's hand and laughed. 'Yeah, thanks.' That was probably a good idea. 'Where's the ballroom?'

'Straight ahead, sir. Just follow the music.'

He nodded and walked towards the ballroom. When he got there someone presented him with a flute of champagne and he took it, downing it in one, before placing his empty glass back onto the tray.

He was looking for the most beautiful woman in the world, who would be wearing a gold dress.

His gaze scanned the walls, where groups of people stood in groups, chatting, but he couldn't see her there. Then he looked on the dance floor, and his eyes caught a glimpse of glittering gold and flaming red hair. She was dancing with her father.

Feeling his heart pound out of his chest, he stepped forward into the dancing throng. 'Excuse me… Sorry, could I just…? Excuse me…thank you.'

And then he was there, right next to her, and she looked stunning, if a little uncomfortable.

'Might I interrupt?'

Cara's head swivelled in his direction at the sound of his voice and she might even have gasped a little.

Her father smiled a greeting and nodded, stepping back. 'Of course. Be my guest.'

He stood in front of her, smiling. 'I'm sorry I missed your calls.'

'Where have you been?'

'Practising being an idiot. You look beautiful.'

She blushed.

'I've brought you a gift. I almost brought you a corsage, but then I saw this, so…' He proffered the large box that was tucked under his arm.

It was wrapped in gold, with a gold ribbon, which she tore open, smiling when she saw inside, nestled in white tissue paper, a sparkly pair of golden trainers.

'I thought these would let me dance with you for longer.'

She bent down to take off her hated heels and slip her feet into the trainers.

Tom took the heels, put them in the now empty box and passed it to a bewildered waitress. 'Could you get rid of these, please?'

The waitress took them and Cara stood up, gazing at him with apprehension. 'I thought you weren't coming.'

'I would never have missed this. I'm sorry I had you worried.'

He stared at her and stepped closer, holding out his hands for her to step into the hold they knew.

She did so.

And as she slipped hand into his he felt that somehow this was all going to be all right.

'I need to tell you how I feel about you,' he said.

She looked apprehensive. 'It's okay. I know. I'm not like Victoria. I never will be. But I am a firefighter and that will never change.'

'I'm not looking for another Victoria and I don't ever want you to change.' Tom waited for her to look at him. 'I've been an utter fool,' he said. 'A coward.'

'And I've been too caught up in myself,' she told him. 'I forgot you needed to think about Gage, too. My job makes me a risky prospect. I get caught up in what I do. I run towards danger. I go into burning buildings and I give up my oxygen and I use my body to protect others. Gage doesn't need someone like that. Neither do you.

'Are you kidding me? That selflessness? That bravery? Both of those things are wonderful! I would never change you. Not in a million years! You're perfect exactly as you are. And when I saw you carrying that woman from the burning building I realised just how much you terrified me.'

She frowned. Puzzled. 'What are you saying?'

'I'm saying that I realised I could have lost you, and

that thought was too terrible to contemplate…because I'm in love with you.'

A small smile broke across her face. 'You're in love with me?'

'I am and I always will be. And I'd like to think that you will forgive me for running and being afraid, because I'm not any more, and I'd like to make this a real date between us. Not a fake one. What do you think to that?'

'I don't know what to say…'

She flushed, her cheeks pinker than he'd ever seen them before, and he just wanted to kiss her in front of everyone. Make it real. Let everyone in this room know that he loved this woman. Because she was all woman. No matter if anyone else had made her feel that she was somehow lacking. She was the best woman. The only woman for him.

'Say you'll be my girlfriend for real?' He smiled, pulling her back into hold and pressing himself up against her, imagining more.

Cara laughed, and looked around her before looking back at him. 'I've loved you since the moment I met you, Tom. Do you know how hard that's been for me?'

He nodded. 'You still haven't answered my question.'

'What was that?'

'Will you be my girlfriend?'

She nodded, beaming. 'I will.'

'Good. Now kiss me. Kiss me before I spontaneously combust.'

Cara laughed, bringing her lips to his, and kissed him as he'd never been kissed before.

EPILOGUE

The double doors to her old childhood bedroom opened, and she turned just as her father gasped in surprise.

'Cara…you look beautiful,' he said in awe.

She flushed and turned to check her reflection in the long mirror. She was bedecked in white. A beautiful fishtail wedding gown with a sweetheart neckline, covered in lace and crystals. A diamond tiara and a long, floaty veil.

'Thanks.'

'If your mother were here…' His voice choked in his throat.

Cara reached out a hand to take his, squeezing his fingers in solidarity. She knew what he wanted to say.

If your mother were here, she'd be crying with happiness.

And he was right. She would be. Seeing her daughter like this. About to be married. Looking like the perfect bride. The fact that her mother would not be with her at her wedding hurt a lot. But Cara knew that wherever she was she would be looking down at her and smiling, full of pride and joy.

'I wish she was here.'

Her father nodded. 'Me, too. You know, I'm very

much aware that I've been a bit...*overpowering* at times. What do you call it? Sticking my nose in where it's not wanted?' He smiled.

Cara smiled back. 'A bit. But it doesn't matter today, Dad. Today is for happy memories.'

'You're right. But I wanted to have this moment before I pass your hand over to Tom to try and explain.'

He paused for a moment. Checked his own reflection in the mirror and rearranged his cravat. Plumping it to perfection.

'When your mother died, I was distraught. We all were, I know. But in you I saw your mother. You're so alike in so many ways. The way you smile. The way you tilt your head when you're listening to someone talk the way you're doing now.' He smiled again. 'The way you laugh. And when you moved out I couldn't bear to be separated from you. I still needed that contact with her through you. I kept trying to mould you to be like her and I should have known better. You're your own woman, just as you should be, and I wanted to tell you today that I've realised what I was doing and it was wrong. So... I apologise.'

'Oh, Dad!' She stepped forward to wrap her arms around him and held him tight.

They stood in an embrace for a while, until the wedding planner, Harriet, came in with her clipboard, clapping her hands.

'Time's tight, people. Ready to go?'

Cara let go of her father and stepped back, just as he reached into his jacket pocket.

'Your something borrowed.' He passed her a velvet box.

She frowned in question, then opened it. Inside, lying

on a green velvet cushion, was her mother's diamond necklace. 'Dad...'

'She'd want you to wear it. She wore it on her wedding day. But you know you don't have to, if you think I'm being—'

'Dad, it's perfect. I'd be honoured.' She turned so he could fasten it at the back of her neck.

Cara looked at it in the mirror. Her mother would always be with her, but this was extra-special and made her feel close to her once again.

'Ready to go?'

Her father held out his arm and she slid hers into it. 'I'm ready.'

Harriet left the room and signalled to someone at the bottom of the stairs. Music suddenly bloomed through the high hall and up the stairway of Higham Manor. The 'Wedding March'.

Cara took a brief moment to adjust her veil, so it lay perfectly, and then began the slow walk from her bedroom, all the way down the sweeping, staircase which was adorned with fresh flower garlands.

Beneath them in the grand hall were all their guests. Friends. Family. Work family. Everyone she knew. People whose lives she'd saved and stayed in touch with. Everyone. She saw all their happy faces, all their smiles, and saw how beautiful everyone looked. But there was one person she wanted to see the most.

Tom.

He stood in front of a flowered arch, dressed in a suit like her father's, his lovely face looking up to her as she descended the stairs. Beside him, in a miniature top hat and tails, stood Gage, holding a red cushion with their wedding rings on it.

Her heart pounded with joy as all her dreams began to come true.

People whispered their good wishes and love as she passed them. She met happy gaze after happy gaze. She got a cheeky wink from Reed. A bow of the head from Hodge.

And then she was standing next to Tom and her father was letting go of her and stepping back.

Tom reached for her hand, smiling. 'You look stunning.'

'Thanks,' she answered shyly.

'Are you wearing them?' he whispered.

Cara lifted up her skirt slightly, to reveal the bridal trainers that he'd bought for her. White. Studded with crystals that caught the light.

Tom laughed. 'You look perfect.'

She smiled, covering them up again. 'So do you.'

* * * * *

STRANDED WITH
THE PARAMEDIC

SUE MacKAY

MILLS & BOON

For all our friends who helped each other throughout the storm that decimated our area.

It has been quite a ride.

CHAPTER ONE

'HEY, BROOKE. I don't know when, or if, I'll get to join you. But it won't be today. The ferries are cancelled, and there're no flights into Blenheim either. Add to that, Wellington Airport's on an extreme weather alert.'

'No surprises there.' Brooke shivered as the gale slammed into the house, almost as if it knew it was being talked about. 'This weather is unbelievable,' she told her sister. 'I'm amazed we're even having this conversation. I had no power or cell phone coverage for most of the night. It came back on ten minutes before you rang.'

'The weather app looks as though it's going to get a whole lot worse yet. You stay safe, you hear?'

Saskia was wearing her big sis hat, the one that said, *I'm always here for you, Brooke.*

As she was for Saskia. 'Not a lot I can do about anything. The rain's torrential, and the house shakes with every blow. The wind's like nothing I've known, and that's saying something.' Having spent her childhood in Wellington, the world's supposedly windiest city, she was used to gales, but this one was something else. 'Seriously, sometimes I think the house is going to take to the sky.'

'Jeez, Brooke, I don't like the thought of you dealing with that on your own. Wish I was with you.'

'No, you don't. You'd be changing your knickers every five minutes.' Brooke managed to laugh even as the large bay window overlooking the storm-tossed sea sounded as though it was about to implode. So much for taking a relaxing break from her hectic job over in Nelson where she worked as an advanced paramedic.

Saskia laughed. 'True. I am such a scaredy-cat when it comes to storms.'

Brooke was meant to be having a week with her sister, lazing around catching up on what they'd both been up to over the past few months. Brooke sighed. As much as she was comfortable with her own company, she'd been looking forward to spending time with Saskia. They never shut up when they got together, always had plenty to say. Her sister was one of the few people in her life who hadn't tried to make her do things their way. She and their dad. Saskia never came up with nasty surprises like their mother used to do such as 'You're changing schools today'. It might have been because she was being bullied, but some warning would have made the change less stressful and given her time to get used to the idea.

Like the morning when she awoke to be told she wasn't playing with her friends. Instead, she had an appointment with the dentist to have six teeth removed because they were growing wrong. No one had mentioned there was a problem when she'd first gone to the dentist with her mother. The *surprises* didn't stop there. Not all so drastic, but each one undermining her confidence and taking away her right to face her own problems. Their mother used to say it was her way of protecting her girls from unnecessary worry. Eventually, as she grew older, Brooke understood where her mother was coming from, but her mother couldn't accept that was not how she liked to face these things. She preferred to be prepared.

Her ex had been no better. In fact he had been worse, surprising her with shocks such as 'I've found somewhere better to rent and we're moving on Friday. You'll have to take time off work to pack up the house.' There had been another instance when he'd flipped her life overnight, and by then she'd had enough so she had packed her bags for the last time and left him. She should have done it sooner but in her book loving someone meant accepting them for who they were, even if it meant giving up some of her own dreams. Up to a point, and she'd reached that point then. It seemed she was always having to stand up for herself. Even her first boyfriend used to hide what he was up to from her, not telling her he intended going offshore as soon as he qualified as a doctor until one day she overheard him talking about it to another medical student. No wonder she found trusting people difficult.

Saskia cut through her memories. 'Who else is in the bay that you could spend the night with?'

'I'm fine, really.' Who was she trying to convince? It was a little creepy sitting here, listening to the weather beating down on the house so fiercely, hearing the boards groan and the roof creak. But there was nothing she could do about it. She'd cope without knocking on doors for a bit of company. She had a pile of books to read, and the fire was cosy.

Plus, she was still having much-needed time out from work. This break was essential for her sanity. The weather wasn't wrecking that, although the beach walks looked as though they were off the menu at the moment as well as the talking she and Saskia would have done. Recently, along with a shortage of qualified paramedics, there'd been an abundance of patients with severe injuries that had tested her skills to the limit. A couple hadn't been saved, which got her down at times. It didn't always pay to be too caring. Would she have been happier to still be working in a laboratory sitting behind a microscope and not having to front up to people while dealing with their health issues? No way.

Strange how she'd always liked the idea of working in the medical world, and because she'd loved science at school and always got top grades she'd thought being a lab technician would be the ideal career. The problem was that she loved being involved with people and the lab just wasn't right for her. Test tubes and microscopes were kind of dull, even though the work was fascinating. After working as a volunteer ambulance officer in her spare time Brooke had quickly known where she wanted to be, and had become a full-time crew member on the ambulances, advancing up to an advanced paramedic in little time. It seemed she'd found her niche— hands-on helping people was a perfect fit.

'You still there, Brooke?'

'Yeah.' Miles away. 'The only lights I saw before we lost power during the night was next door in Mike and Paula's place, and a car there I don't recognise. It was bucketing down when I got up an hour ago, so I haven't gone to check to see if Lloyd's here. I'll go shortly. I presume he's tucked up inside.' Old Man Duggan had lived in the bay since well before their parents bought the small, basic beach house next door to him thirty-odd years ago and it was a family thing to always knock on his door whenever they came here for a break.

'It's not like he'd have his lights on,' Saskia said. The old man went to bed when the sun went down, summer and winter.

'It was spooky not being able to see what was going on in the dark,' Brooke admitted. There were no such things as streetlights out in the Sounds so the only light at night was from the stars and moon, which were notable by their absence due to the dense cloud coverage.

'Stay in contact,' her sister said. 'We know what major slips have done to that road before. They're saying this is a one in one hundred years storm.'

The only road giving access to the area cut along the edge of the hills rising above the sea and didn't always remain in place when bad weather struck, bringing landslides spilling across the road.

'Don't panic if you don't hear from me. It's more than likely there'll be other power outages before this is over.'

Right then the lights flickered.

Brooke held her breath.

Flick, flick.

The light settled, became constant again.

'Talk about tempting fate.' Outages had happened all too often in the past for her to think today would be any different. Besides, if this storm was battering the rest of Marlborough, the power company would be crazy busy.

'What happened?'

'Power nearly went off. Right, the gas bottle's going to need changing soon so I'd better go get the spare from the shed. I'm not looking forward to getting blown about and saturated to the skin.' It looked a bit spooky out there too. While it was daytime, outside was dark as dusk. 'Talk later, if we can.'

Placing her phone alongside the lantern she'd put out along with matches last night, ready in case of problems, Brooke got the shed key, slipped into gumboots and a rain jacket and headed out into the maelstrom. *Should've done this when I first arrived yesterday*, she thought as a gust shoved her sideways. So much for being prepared for the worst-case scenario, something they'd been taught as kids by their father. Unlike their mum, he always prepared them for the worst, which was something their parents never agreed about, thereby causing a bit of friction at times, their mother thinking they should just get out there and enjoy themselves without worrying about anything. Dad believed staying at the beach might be all about having fun but remembering that things could go wrong when the weather decided to flick from good to bad was equally important. Saskia was Brooke's opposite; she always avoided problems until they could no longer be ignored. But she still supported Brooke in her decision to face up to those same problems.

When she'd arrived last night the wind had seemed to be abating, so she hadn't worried about getting the gas bottle. Instead, wanting to keep warm throughout the night, she'd replenished the firewood inside the house from the stack by the garage, then called it quits, needing food more than anything else, having missed lunch. Within hours of that decision, the storm had picked up to become more ferocious than she'd believed possible.

All around the property and in the neighbours' places, trees groaned and creaked as though their branches were about to fly off. Small branches and twigs were scattered across lawns, snagged in fences and hanging from washing lines. Water poured down from the hills, and a small torrent cut through the lawn where she was headed. It reached her ankles when she tried to stride across what was usually firm ground. The soil sucked her feet downwards. It was unbelievable. She shivered, tucked her arms around her waist and, head down, pushed on.

The ground felt as though it was moving, but that had to be her imagination. How could it move? It was the water, wind and rain making this feel foreign, nothing like the place she'd known all her life and spent wonderful summer holidays lying on the grass in the sun, wearing a bikini and working on getting a tan.

Splat. Brooke landed on her backside in mud. Great. Shoving upright, she took more tentative steps towards the shed in the back corner of the property. Her feet went from under her. This time she landed on her side, her thigh taking the brunt of the impact. How come it was such a hard landing when water and mud were supposedly soft? On all fours, she pushed up and back onto her feet. Did she really need the gas bottle so badly? If the storm went on for much longer then yes, she did. What had she been thinking, not doing this last night when it would have been easier? And safer. She shivered. This was no picnic.

Slowly, one step at a time, she finally made it to the shed.

'Hey there. Are you all right?' A male voice reached her during a brief lull in the wind.

It wasn't a voice she recognised. The owner of the car at Mike's? 'I'm fine. Getting a gas bottle. Do you need something?' she yelled back.

'Just checking up on people,' came the shouted reply.

That was nice of him, whoever he was. He certainly wasn't a regular, she knew them all, so he must be staying next door. Moving away from the shed to go around to the side door, her feet once more shot out from under her. This time she managed to keep her balance. 'I am so over this,' she groaned. She'd be turning black and blue all over.

'Wait there. I'm coming to help.'

'I'm fine,' she muttered, saving her energy for crossing to the door. Then she swore. The key was no longer in her grasp. Which fall had she lost it in? Looking over the ground she'd skidded over, she couldn't see the yellow plastic tag holding the key. 'Where is it?'

She tried the door in case someone had forgotten to lock it. Yeah, well, that was wishful thinking. Rule number one: whenever leaving the beach house make sure everything's locked. So, back the way she'd come, head down, this time scanning the mud and lawn. It was going to be a longer fifty metres than it had been on the way over.

Deep rumbling made her pause and look around. What was that? The ground seemed to shake. An earthquake? In the middle of all this? No way. That would be nature having much too big a laugh. But mud *was* rushing at her, pouring around her feet, up to her ankles, while her chest was thudding hard. Storms were bearable, but earthquakes were her nightmare. The lack of control and fear of what damage could be caused always turned her into a blithering idiot during one of those. But there hadn't been an earthquake. It was the storm dealing more blows she had no control over.

Crack, bang, smash.

The kowhai tree next to the shed bent towards her,

a large branch snapping off as though it were a twig, hitting the ground hard, sending water and mud in all directions, a lot of it over Brooke as she tried frantically to get out of the way of the rest of the tree. Too late. The trunk landed beside her, branches entangling her legs and dragging her down into the muddy water, taking her down the sloping lawn towards the usually quiet creek that was now more like a river. She swore as her body tensed. This was ridiculous. She'd been taken down by a tree and if the noise was anything to go by there was more trouble coming. She needed to get away from here. *Yeah, right.* Like her feet were helping. Or her legs with their shaky muscles.

Get a grip.

'Hey.' That voice again. 'I'm here.' Then he swore. Must be catching.

At least she wasn't alone, which made her feel infinitesimally happier. If she was in trouble, far nicer to be there with someone else. Even a stranger was preferable to being alone. She might have toughened up when it came to men but nature could still undermine her resolve to cope with anything that was thrown her way. There was just no fighting nature, no winning against storms or quakes or seas that could devour a person in an instant.

Weird how she was moving, out of control, being pushed further down the lawn by the sheer volume of water and mud and getting closer to that torrent that was normally a small creek. It only ended up in one place— the sea—where thunderous waves were pounding the shore. Something wound around her arm, pulled against the flow. Something strong and determined to keep her from disappearing further down the way. Something soft yet firm. Human.

'I've got you.' A man. 'Try digging your feet in to get a purchase on the ground.'

Easy said when everything was so slippery. Was she going to get out of this at all? Safely?

'You can do it.'

The deep male voice beside her ear gave her confidence, something she hadn't realised she'd lost in the last few scary seconds. Brooke shoved one foot hard against the slithering ground, gained some purchase. Then she shoved even harder with the other and felt a brief shot of relief as that too dug in deep. Pushing upward, she came upright against the man saving her from sliding further down what had only minutes ago been an overgrown lawn. When she tried to pull a foot free to take a step, her foot came out of her boot. 'Great.' She reached down to tug the gumboot out of the mire. No easy feat, but eventually it was swinging from her hand.

'Let's go carefully. We'll do this together. Put your arm around my waist and hold on tight. I've got you.' The guy's voice was deep and edgy, but he seemed to know what he was doing.

Which made her relax further. She wasn't in this mess on her own, not that it was dangerous now, mostly annoying. Then she looked around her and shuddered. It could become bad very quickly, the way the water was streaming down the hillside. She'd seen the results of heavy rain in this area before and wasn't silly enough to believe a massive landslide couldn't happen here.

'Right.'

Let's do this.

She placed her arm around him and began the laborious job of getting out of the mud, one squelching step at a time.

Whoever he was, Brooke wasn't worried that she was about to be abducted so he could have his wicked way with her once they were free of the mud. For starters, she'd belt him around the head if he even so much as looked as if he might try. Right now, she was more interested in getting onto safer ground. She'd find out who he was later.

'We need to go the other way.' Her house was in front of them. There was a new river running between her family's house and Old Man Duggan's. 'I want to go check on my neighbour, make sure he's all right.'

'Let's wait until this torrent is done with wreaking havoc all over the show. I'd hate to be caught in a further rush of water, or mud and trees,' her rescuer said as he turned them back towards her place.

He mightn't be from around here but apparently he was more aware of what was going on than her, because she hadn't noticed other trees now bouncing down the slope.

'Good call.'

'I thought so.' He sounded almost light-hearted. Almost. Some tension was underlying his words, and definitely in the arm gripping her close to his body. Then he slipped, and she was going down with him as his arm held onto her.

Digging her feet in hard, she tried not to topple. 'I've got you,' she repeated his earlier words.

He barked a sharp laugh as he struggled not to fall flat on his face. 'Yeah, right. Think I weigh a load more than you.' His feet did a couple of quick slides but he remained upright. 'Thanks. This is getting ridiculous.'

'Come on. A few more steps and we'll be out of the worst.' The unscathed part of the lawn was close, unless there was something she wasn't seeing in the whirling leaves and pieces of bark being thrown around by the wind.

'You're right.' Her companion pulled her along, hellbent on getting free of the mud. Sensible man.

Suddenly they were standing on terra firma, not being sucked into the mess that used to be a tidy grass yard. 'Thanks for coming to help me out of that,' she said. 'To think when I arrived here yesterday I thought I'd mow the lawns when the rain let up today.'

'Chance would be a fine thing. It's going to take a digger to clear away all the debris.'

'As far as I know, there isn't one anywhere near here. A guy has one in a bay further along the road, but he'll probably be busy clearing storm damage there once the rain and wind stop.' Brooke began crossing to the house. 'Let's get out of this.'

On the porch she shrugged out of her coat and hung it on a peg by the door. Relieved to be safe, she turned to the man who'd helped her and tensed. He was dropdead gorgeous. Even when covered in mud splatters and with his sopping-wet hair flattened on his skull, he was—stunning. Lifting her arm, she was about to wipe a splodge of gunk from his cheek, but realised just in time how stupid that would have been. He was a stranger. She did not touch strangers—except in her work, trying to help someone. So what was it about this man that had her wanting to run her hand over his face? It must be a reaction to the last few minutes, worrying about getting back to the house in one piece.

Taking a step back, she tried for normal, which was

hard to do when her heart was suddenly beating as if a wayward drummer had taken over. 'I'm Brooke Williams. Are you staying in the cottage next door?'

He nodded. 'My name's Danny. I came a couple of days ago with Paula and Mike. They went back to Blenheim yesterday morning, and I'm staying to enjoy the quiet for another couple of days. Except—' He gave a wistful glance over the yard. 'Nothing quiet about this.' There was a definite Aussie twang going on in his voice.

'You're not the only one hoping for some relaxation. We were going to have some quiet time. My sister was meant to come over from Wellington, but that's not happening any time soon.'

Too much info, Brooke. You don't know this man.

But he had come to help her and didn't look evil.

'I wouldn't want to be crossing the Cook Strait in a plane or ferry. It'd be diabolical at the moment.'

'Everything's cancelled. You said you were checking up on people. Who else is staying in the bay?'

'As far as I could ascertain, only the man in that house beyond yours. I was coming this way when I saw you heading across to your shed. Thought you must've needed something important to be out in the weather so figured I might be able to give you a hand.'

'That was kind. I had intended getting the spare gas bottle but must've dropped the shed key when I slipped.' The remaining boot wasn't coming off easily. It was moulded around her foot. Using the top of the step as leverage, she pulled hard and finally it shot off, sucking at her foot as it went.

'Is there a spare key? I could get the tank for you.'

'Thanks, there is, but I'll make do in the meantime.' She'd go light on using the stove top. 'You'd only get

into the same trouble I did.' She mightn't be so good at
hauling him out of the mud as he'd been with her. Now
she had time to really look him over there was a lot
standing before her. At least two metres tall, she reckoned. Her head barely reached his shoulder. Hard to see
his outline with the heavy wet weather gear he wore,
but he didn't appear to be carrying excess weight. More
fit and muscular, if what she'd felt when he had his arm
around her holding her tight was anything to go by. 'I
still want to check up on Lloyd though.'

'Let's see what happens over the next hour. The
weather might clear a bit and the water running off
the hill might slow some, then we can tackle getting
to the house and possibly your shed.' His mouth was
sexy when he smiled. There was a cheeky twinkle in
his eyes now they were out of the rain and safe from
the sliding mud. 'So you're on your own?'

Forget sexy or beating heart or good-looking. 'I think
I'll go inside now. Thank you once again.' She put her
hand on the doorknob, ready to go in and lock him out.
She didn't feel vulnerable, but she also wasn't stupid
enough to take any risks. He was a stranger, and if that
smile was anything to go by, a right charmer when he
put his mind to it. There were other people in bays along
the road if she had concerns, but it wouldn't be easy
getting around at the moment. Attracting someone's
attention if she needed to would be near impossible,
especially with the likelihood of phones not working.

'Hey, I'm sorry if that sounded bad. I was merely
thinking that you might prefer to join me rather than see
this out alone.' He stepped off the porch onto the path.
'I only had your safety and comfort in mind.' Danny
sounded genuine. What was more, he looked it.

Brooke felt awful for doubting him. Kicking her boot aside, she said, 'It's me who should be apologising.' She needed to accept not all people came with hidden agendas. 'I'm used to hanging out here on my own. My parents own this place, and my sister and I also like to spend time here together for catch-ups whenever our busy lives give us a break,' she said in a bid to be friendly. 'We've been coming here since we were toddlers.'

Talking too much now, Brooke. He doesn't need your life history.

'What I'm saying is I'm fine on my own.'

CHAPTER TWO

DANNY BREATHED DEEP, exhaled slowly. For one worrying moment there, when Brooke went all stiff and tight
on him, he'd thought she'd recognised him. But she
hadn't, had only been responding to his offer of company, and he'd overreacted. Nothing new in that. He
did it so often, it was a habit. One meant to save him
a lot of aggro or harassment, but which didn't always
come out right. Come to think of it, she'd looked cross,
not about to hug him and try to become his instant best
friend. That made him happy.

'I'll head back to the cottage then.' Where he could
breathe easier. Not get sidetracked by an interesting
woman who might, for once, not want anything to do
with him other than what he had to offer today. Company and help if required.

One of the best things about this working trip to New
Zealand was that not as many people recognised him
as in Australia and he could occasionally move around
uninhibited by overzealous fans wanting to offer com-
miserations about his failed, once stellar and rising career as a professional golfer. It was great being able to
go where he liked without ducking out of the way of
eager individuals wanting to talk to him, especially fe-

males who wanted to be joined at the hip with the offer of the hottest sex he'd ever get, supposing he'd fall in love and not let them out of his sight. Unlike at home in Oz, in this country he could breathe a little freer and be himself—a medical intern—and enjoy everything that came his way without looking for hidden agendas. Except he was always on his guard, because the times he relaxed were when he got caught out. He had been busted in Blenheim, but for some reason the fuss had died down fast. A small town with lots going on and no time for outsiders maybe? Who knew, but he'd been happy.

Brooke seemed to be wanting to make up for her blunder because she started talking again before he'd made it off the deck. 'Hopefully there'll be access out of the bay soon after this weather bomb has finished. The road gangs are usually quick to clear the road enough for the many people relying on it for getting to work or going to doctors, getting groceries, you name it, to be able to get out.'

'Good to hear. I'll need to leave on Monday.' How long was this gorgeous woman staying? She'd said her sister was meant to join her so surely they'd planned on a few days here? Now that the sister mightn't be able to get through for those few days, Brooke's plans might change, whatever they were. Crazy, but he'd like to spend a little time with her, get to know her some.

Which was so out of the blue it made his stomach squeeze. He had no idea why he felt that way. His usual practice was to avoid getting close to anyone other than mates and family. She'd rattled him with that sudden sharp look when he'd asked if she was alone. As if she was on alert, but he sensed she was also quite capable of looking out for herself. The hint of wariness shifting through her expression suggested she had seen another side to men she did not like.

'I'll leave you to it. But I'm serious about going with you to check on the neighbour.'

Her smile was brief. 'I'll be fine.' With that, she stepped inside and shut the door without another look his way.

Danny shook his head, grinning stupidly. This was getting better by the minute. He was so not used to people doing that. Brooke didn't know who he was and, even better, didn't appear to want to know. It had been a very long time since he'd been ignored, and he loved it. Plodding through the sodden long grass to the house he was staying in, a trickle of amazement—even excitement—heated his groin.

Settle, man. This can't last.

His secret was so well known, eventually someone would let her know who he was, even here in New Zealand. But wouldn't it be great to let loose for a change? Have some fun with a gorgeous woman for once? There'd been a couple of looks from her suggesting she was sizing him up. Was she contemplating the same thing? Fun out here where they were alone with no one to spoil it for him would be amazing. And who knew what might come of a few minutes of relaxed conversation with a lovely-looking woman? In a couple of days he'd be out of here, on his way to Nelson and work, while who knew where Brooke would be? There wouldn't be any follow-up to a brief tryst even if she was single and happy.

He was so damned cautious these days it made for loneliness and longing for what there was to take if only he could lighten up. Not easy when most women he'd dated and thought he could get to know well and possibly fall for were more interested in his fame and money than in Danny himself. Brooke wasn't rushing to get to know him. Which was exactly why his blood was heating.

Talk about getting ahead of himself. Which only went to show how long it had been since he was seriously involved with a woman. The ones who dropped in and out of his life these days weren't welcome to hang around. They always wanted something he wasn't prepared to give. They believed they'd be the one to change his mind about getting into a permanent relationship. Nearly every woman he'd dated in the past six years had thought that and had wanted him to accept they were right for him, that they'd be the one to turn his life around.

The one exception had been refreshing. At first Brenda had been unaware of his background and accepted him as he appeared to be. He'd met her when he did a spell at an outback medical centre, and they'd had a fantastic few weeks together—then the time had come for him to return to med school in Melbourne and she had followed to spend some time in his territory, so to speak. Within hours she'd learned the truth and greed filled her eyes. She had started demanding more of him, a house in the most expensive area of Melbourne, trips overseas, clothes to die for. It wasn't happening. He had a medical degree to finish, followed by specialising in radiology. Then there was the way Brenda had changed so fast, her love no longer about the man she'd met in the outback and all about what he could bring her. He was out, done with her. Another layer of hurt added to his problems. It had been hard enough dealing with losing his career at a time when it was going stellar without adding the way he was treated by women.

So far he hadn't found that woman who'd take him on for who he was these days, the man who'd put his golf clubs away and hunkered down to study medicine. He'd love to find a woman who was more interested in all the characteristics that made him who he'd become. Not only in the man who'd earned a small fortune playing professional golf before the incident that killed his career, but a guy with dreams to be a doctor, a husband, a father.

Leaping into a pool to save the son of a world-renowned businessman from drowning had made him even more well known around the globe. He'd smashed his shoulder and all the ribs on one side of his body when he'd hit a concrete bollard he hadn't seen in the pool. The shoulder had never been the same. It was the end of golf. The end of a lot of things. But the boy had survived, and for that he was grateful. Maybe if that had finished the media following him everywhere he went things might have turned out differently, but he was still loved so much for his fame rather than who he wanted to be. Not being seen for everything he was wasn't good. It made him feel he wasn't loved for the right reasons.

Danny made his way up to the deck of the tidy little beach house—Kiwis called them bachs, he reminded himself—and kicked off his boots. His gaze cruised over to the next-door property. Being stuck here might prove interesting. *If* that meant catching up with Brooke Williams again. It wasn't as though he had much to do now that the other two had gone back to town. Spending time with Brooke and having a chat about anything that came to mind was the best option to fill in his days he could come up with. That could be fun, and he'd be careful, wouldn't push himself into her space, but he was here if she needed help with anything.

Crack.

A loud sound broke through the bay.

Crack, crack.

'What the—?' Danny froze to the spot.

Whoosh. Bang, Thud.

Rushing water tore down the hillside beyond Brooke's house. Right at the spot where he'd helped her. Mud followed. Then rocks, a boulder and trees were heading towards the neighbouring house. This was getting out of hand.

Bang. Slam. Crash.

'That's too close for comfort,' he muttered. 'Forget close.' The house had taken a slam dunk. Boots back on, Danny began running towards the flooding between that house and Brooke's.

Brooke appeared on her back step, shoving her arms into her wet weather jacket as she charged down the step and onto the lawn, her focus entirely on her neighbour's house.

'Be careful,' he shouted. 'Everything's moving fast.'

'I need to get Lloyd out. If he's there.' She didn't waste time looking his way or slowing to let him catch up. She was on a mission.

So was he. Keeping her safe was paramount. 'Brooke, slow down. Carefully does it.'

She was slogging through the mud that had previously trapped her, but this time it wasn't holding her back. The determination in the set of her jaw said it all. She was going to the other house come hell or high water. Both of which they were already dealing with.

He caught up with her and grabbed her arm. 'Take it slowly. Falling and injuring yourself won't help your neighbour.'

Crack.

More rocks pelted down in front of them, banging into the building. 'This is way serious.'

Brooke stopped abruptly, looked all around and back to him, worry blinking out of those hazel eyes. 'You're right. What was I thinking?' She tugged her arm free of his hand. 'Not one of my brightest moments.'

'You're concerned for your neighbour.' Something he'd appreciate if he was in a dire situation, especially coming from this woman. Water was pouring through the shed door, which had been slammed back on its hinges. Mud and debris were also heading inside. The wooden structure groaned as a boulder slammed into the wall and widened the doorway.

Danny grabbed Brooke's arm again as she started ploughing through the mud. 'We're doing this together. We need to keep an eye on what's coming down that hill. Getting knocked off our feet by more mud or even a boulder won't end well.' That was putting it mildly. One of those rocks could kill anyone in its path.

She jerked her arm free and stared at him. 'You think I'm stupid?'

Well, she had been charging across without taking any notice of what was happening before he'd intervened.

It must've dawned on her what she'd said because she suddenly laughed, and it was a surprisingly light, sweet sound that touched him tenderly. 'Yep, I'm stupid. Come on, let's get to Lloyd's before anything goes horribly wrong. I think I owe you a coffee when we've got a free moment.'

'Sounds good to me.' He'd prefer something stronger, but he wasn't saying.

She stomped through the mud as though that'd stop her getting stuck.

A deep rumbling sound ripped through the noisy air, tightening Danny's spine as he spun around to see what was happening now. 'Crikey.' He'd been wrong to slow her down. 'Run, Brooke.' He tried to get his feet moving but they were glued to the ground in mud, sucked down hard. 'Run!' he shouted. Brooke mustn't get caught in the landslide heading straight for them.

'Here.' She was tugging at his left ankle. 'Pull hard.'

Slurp. His foot came free. 'Get away from me, Brooke.'

She had his other ankle in her hands. 'Pull.'

Quicker to do so than argue. He hauled at his leg, pulling and pulling, then *bang*. His foot was out and he was sprawled on his back on the ground.

Brooke had her hands held out to him. 'Grab hold.' Her eyes were wild with fear as she looked up the yard. 'Most of it's going beyond us. But hurry.'

Shoving up, he reached for her hands and abruptly stood up, swaying with the intensity he'd risen. 'Go. Leave me. I'm fine.'

'Look out. Run.'

Danny didn't stop to look at what might be rushing at him, instead he did exactly as Brooke said. He ran. Slipping and sliding, gripping her hand, trying to keep them both upright. The woman beside him was all over the place. Every step she took became a skid in a different direction.

Then she went down.

And he was on his knees beside her, falling so his shoulder took the brunt. Bad move.

A tree rolled over them. The branches scratched at the skin on his face and hands. Then the trunk slammed into his ankle, bounced away.

'Jeez,' Brooke gasped. She was in the midst of smaller branches and stone-laden mud, scrambling to stand up. 'Danny? Danny, are you all right?'

His name sounded wonderful on her tongue. 'I'm good.'

How had she moved from the branches to right beside him so quickly when her legs were entwined with a wild passionfruit vine? 'Get away from here before something else comes down the hill,' he growled. 'Go on. Move.'

'I'm not going anywhere without you,' she snapped and reached for him with a grimace.

'Are you injured?'

'Just a few bruises. Nothing to worry about. What about you? Any damage?'

She was assessing him as though she knew what she was doing. Medically trained?

'I'm fine.' Above the wind he could hear groaning as outside boards popped off the framework of the house under the strain of the heavy layer of debris that had built up against the back wall.

'Crazy,' Brooke said as she approached. 'I've never seen anything as bad as this before.'

'Can't say I have either.'

'Lloyd's eighty-one, and while he's spry for his age, he's not going to come leaping out a window. I have concerns. Who knows what it's like inside? This will break his heart.'

'I'm coming in with you. I'm a doctor.'

'I'm an AP.'

An advanced paramedic. Then if Lloyd was injured he was going to be in good hands. Brooke was probably a better option than him. She'd be used to major trauma on site without all the medical equipment that came with an emergency department, whereas he was a trainee doctor who usually only dealt with trauma after the patient had been brought into hospital.

'Right, let's do this.' She shuddered, then braced herself.

Crack.

A loud sound broke through the bay.

Crack, crack.

'What the—?' Danny froze to the spot.

Whoosh. Bang, Thud. Rushing water tore down the hillside right where they'd walked moments ago. More mud followed. Then rocks, a boulder and trees.

'Dangerous.'

Bang. Slam. Crash.

'Yes.' Brooke's curt reply made Danny smile. 'Definitely dangerous.' But she didn't move, as though afraid of what might happen if she went inside. Or of what she might find.

Danny gave her a gentle nudge. 'I'll go first.'

She shook her head. 'No. I can do this.'

'Then I'll be right behind you.'

'Thank you.' She shuddered, then braced herself. 'I'm going in through the kitchen window. It's already broken.'

Danny nodded. Whichever one that was, the sooner they did this the better for all of them, especially the man inside. 'I'll give you a leg up once I've knocked out the remaining glass.'

'No need.' She was there, reaching inside, avoiding the sharp pointed pieces of glass still attached. 'I've got the latch.' With that, she pulled the window frame open. 'Amazing it's still straight. Thought it'd be out of whack after what's happened.'

'Is there another door that might open? That would be easier than trying to climb in through there.' Danny nodded at the window.

She stared at him. 'I'm a dope. Of course there is. Just around the corner, at the front, which might not be in good shape either.'

She was nothing like a dope, but he wasn't wasting time telling her, only to be rebuked. 'Worth checking out.' He was already on his way, followed by Brooke. 'Doesn't look too bad,' he said the moment he set eyes on the door. 'But we need to be careful after what's gone in through the back of the house.' He tried to open it. It didn't budge.

'Let me help.' Brooke came alongside him.

For an instant he breathed fruit. Light and sweet, and appetising. Her perfume? He couldn't think where else that intoxicating scent came from. Together they pushed into the panels with their shoulders. Nothing happened. 'We're wasting our time and energy. Back to plan A.'

Brooke stepped further along the front of the house.

'Hey, come back. That's not safe.'

'It's all right. I'm just grabbing this.' She lifted a wooden crate from the wonky deck. 'I can stand on it to get inside through the window.'

'I'll go in first. Then I can help you on the other side.'

'That's not necessary. Anyway, I know Lloyd. You don't.'

And apparently her pride was on the line, if the way her shoulders lifted a little and her eyes turned steely meant anything. 'Call out to him and see if you get a response.' He was still going in first. They had no idea what it was like inside, and he didn't want Brooke getting caught in there.

But she was ahead of him, stepping onto the crate she'd placed below the window and leaning in. 'Lloyd, it's Brooke. Can you hear me?'

'I'm in the kitchen.' The reply came loud and clear, though a little wobbly.

Shock? Or pain from an injury? Danny wondered. Likely a combination of the two.

'Are you all right? Can you make it through to the lounge, where I've got a window open?' Brooke called out.

'I'm stuck. There's a lot of mud in here and I'm on the floor. Think I've done in my leg and I banged my head when the microwave flew off the shelf.'

'We're coming in. The guy staying in Mike's place is with me. He's a doctor.'

Danny drew a deep breath. 'You're way more qualified than me. I'm still an intern.'

Her eyes widened. 'You started late in life?'

'At twenty-four.' That was all he was telling her. For now at least. Which was more than he told any woman he met who hadn't recognised him. Because then they wanted to know where he'd been before he started his medical studies and why hadn't he gone from school to university and a hundred other questions he wasn't keen on answering.

She blinked, smiled and started to clamber through the window space. 'Sometimes older students are more prepared for what lies ahead. From what I've seen, anyway.'

Her smile loosened some of his determination to remain aloof about his past, though not enough to spill the beans on the career he had begun his working life in. Or the accident that had killed that dream. Or the fame and fortune he'd earned in a very short time. Anyway, they didn't have time for deep and meaningful conversation at the moment.

'Know what you mean,' he blurted. Because he truly did. He studied and worked mostly with med students six years younger than him, and there was a lifetime in those years that had matured him well beyond them. He no longer looked at life as being there to do with as he chose. Now he trod carefully through the mixture of good and bad, the expectations that were doused by any number of obstacles and understood how easy it was to decimate a person's hopes and ambitions.

'Ouch.' Brooke had dropped into the room and slipped on the sodden carpet. Looking around, she grimaced, her eyes widening as the house seemed to shudder. Her shoulders tightened as she squeezed her arms close to her sides. 'I don't like this.'

Creaks and groans made Danny tense and at the same time drove him to hurry and rescue the old man lying in the kitchen. Who knew how long this house was going to stay upright? He climbed in to join Brooke, but she wasn't waiting around for him.

'Lloyd?' she called. 'Where are you? I can't see you.'

'There.' Danny pointed to a foot poking through a

broken cupboard as he joined her, trying to ignore the sounds suggesting there was more trouble to come.

'Sort of in the pantry,' came a terse reply from beyond the smashed bench. 'Be careful. I don't know how long that bench's going to stay upright. It's wobbling back and forth like nothing's anchoring it to the floor.'

'No surprise there,' Brooke muttered as she squeezed around the offending counter and bent down. 'Am I glad to see you.'

Danny concentrated on checking out the situation and the safety hazards. The kitchen was pretty much wiped out, cupboards askew or torn from the wall and tossed aside, and there was a load of mud covering every surface. He tensed, not liking being in there at all. It was dark and broken and not exactly still. From where he stood, Danny thought the dining area hadn't been damaged beyond water and mud on the floor. Stepping through the doorway, he saw the hall walls were warped yet the first room he peeked into, a bedroom, was all right.

'The damage seems random,' he told Brooke. 'I think the main damage has come from where that boulder struck in the centre, but we need to work fast at getting your friend out of here.' And them.

Her face was grim. 'I know. But it's not going to be simple. Lloyd, your left ankle appears broken.' She glanced at Danny. 'He's taken a huge knock on the head and is bleeding profoundly. I think there might be other injuries too.'

'Yet he's coherent.'

'That'll change once shock sets in.'

'He's shivering hard. His clothes are sodden.' Danny crouched down beside her and surveyed the man before them. 'This isn't going to be fun, I'm sorry, but getting you out of here takes precedence over everything else.'

'Leave me here with Jean. Get out yourselves.' The man's voice was wobbly.

'Who's Jean?' Another person to save?

'His late wife.' Brooke sounded sad. 'He's not as coherent as I thought.'

'That crack over the head might've done some serious damage.' The man's age wouldn't be helping. Danny carefully felt the offending ankle. 'Definitely fractured. We'll strap it once we're out of here.'

'Going out via that window isn't feasible,' Brooke said as she wiped blood from Lloyd's face.

'I'll see what's holding the front door in place.' Danny stood up.

'Please be careful,' Brooke said quietly, giving him a quick glance. 'I don't want you tripping up too.'

'Same back at you,' he said as she moved around Lloyd to where his arm was caught under a pile of broken plates and bowls that must've poured off the pantry shelves. A loud noise that sounded like timber twisting reached them and her head shot around. 'Where's that?'

'Get Lloyd as ready as you can.' Danny found the front door. 'No wonder we couldn't open it.' There was mud and stones in a pile about half a metre deep against it. 'I'll work at shifting these. Fast.'

'There should be a coal shovel by the firebox.' She stepped around the decimated pantry and bent down. 'Here. Something's on our side.'

He reached for it. 'I'll do this. Stick with Lloyd.'

Digging deep, Danny worked hard and fast from the other side to move the pile blocking the door. Apart from the fact they needed out of here as soon as possible, Lloyd would be getting colder with every minute they took to free him. There wasn't a lot to him so there was every chance of hypothermia setting in, adding to his woes.

'How are we going to move Lloyd? I don't have a stretcher on hand.' Brooke gave him a tentative smile, as though worried he might think she was being flippant. She began scraping away mud with her hands.

'I'll piggyback him.' When her shapely eyebrows rose and her mouth twitched, he grinned. 'I know. But seriously, it's the only way I can think of. If we took this door off its hinges and loaded him on that it would be too heavy to carry across to your house.'

'It would also take a lot longer to get out of here.'

'You're onto it.' They were in this together, thinking along the same lines all the way.

'I doubt Lloyd weighs too much. He's always been lean, but now he's downright skinny.'

He hoped she was right. His right clavicle didn't take kindly to a lot of pressure since being broken in two places when his dive to save the kid had turned into a direct hit for him. It had never been the same since, and while swinging a golf club was still possible, he'd never returned to his peak game.

'Age does that to a person.'

Brooke stood up. 'I'll try moving the door.'

They'd cleared most of the debris. Danny reached for the handle and pulled firmly. The door ground hard across the floor but it did open. 'Not bad. Let's get our man out of here.'

Brooke looked around as more creaks came from the walls and ceiling. Shaking herself, she headed back to the kitchen. 'Lloyd, we're getting you out of here. Danny's going to carry you on his back.'

'Haven't done that since I was a kid.' The old man tried for a smile, but pain and worry dimmed it fast. He was staring around his broken home. 'I'm sorry, Jean. I'll be back as soon as I can.'

Danny swallowed hard. The poor old guy was tearing apart inside. 'Come on, the sooner we're out of here the better.'

Brooke nodded, understanding reflecting back at him. 'I hope so.'

Between them they got Lloyd standing on his good foot and then, with help from Brooke, Danny lifted him onto his back.

'I'm right beside you both,' Brooke said. 'In case you slip, Danny.' Her worry over what they were about to do was pouring off her.

'Going to catch us, are you?' He smiled at her.

'You're not going to fall.'

'You're right. I'm not.' He was going to be very careful so that he got Lloyd to safety, which meant Brooke would be safely out of here too. One firm step at a time, he reached the door and went out onto the deck. Down the two steps, across the lawn, through the mud and water, which had slowed considerably since he and Brooke had first approached the house. He slipped, felt Brooke's firm hand on his arm as he righted himself and moved forward. They were a team. Both knew instinctively what had to be done and got on with it. But he wouldn't relax until they were inside her house and Lloyd was lying down.

'The wind's abated somewhat,' Brooke said. 'Might be calm enough to get the rescue helicopter in.'

He hadn't thought that far ahead. 'I guess that's the only option. The sea's too rough for a boat to come in.' Waves were breaking on the beach, pounding the sand as though with a massive mallet. 'Do you know for sure the road is blocked?'

'No, and I could go along on the four-wheel bike to check it, but I can't imagine it's clear. Not after all that rain and wind. This won't be the only slip between here and Linkwater. Even if it was, the Queen Charlotte Drive will have slips for certain.'

No access to Blenheim and the hospital that way then. 'First we need phone coverage.'

'It was working earlier, and now that the wind's dropping hopefully it still is. Otherwise I'll have to use the marine radio on Mike's boat and get them to organise a rescue.'

She had it all under control. He was liking Brooke more and more by the minute.

CHAPTER THREE

'POWER'S ON,' BROOKE told the men as Danny stepped through her back door in his sopping socks, still with Lloyd on his back. He'd insisted on getting his shoes off, which had been a mission. She'd pulled at them while he'd balanced precariously on one foot then the other. 'Bedroom this way.'

'Can we have a towel?' Danny asked as he followed her.

'No problem. I'll grab some of Dad's clothes too. Lloyd needs to get out of his wet gear.' She pulled back the bedcovers and helped lower Lloyd onto the bed, where Danny began removing the shirt from the shivering man. 'Be right back.'

'Where's Jean?' Lloyd groaned through blue lips. 'Is she safe?'

'Yes, Lloyd, she's safe.' Brooke sniffed. She wasn't going to cry. Not now, not in front of Lloyd. Or Danny. Jean had died four years ago and Lloyd had never got over losing her. But then who would when they'd shared a love like her neighbours had? Something she hadn't experienced. She'd loved Brad, but they hadn't been as connected as Lloyd and Jean. Not many couples were.

'Brooke?' Danny nudged her gently.

'Sorry.' Looking away from Lloyd, she focused on what was necessary. 'I'll get some scissors. Otherwise those trousers aren't coming off without causing added pain.'

'What's she's saying is I'm not to tug your pants over that ankle that's giving you grief,' Danny said to Lloyd, even when it wasn't likely the old man heard, which told her Danny was a compassionate man. He gave her a wink. 'Okay?'

'I'll be fine.' That wink caused a softening in her stomach. He appeared cheeky *and* confident, yet there was something intriguing about him she couldn't ignore. Every now and then caution seemed to slip across his face and he'd tense a little. What that was about was anyone's guess, and she wasn't about to try and figure it out. She had other, more important, things to do. Like supplying towels and dry clothes and getting Lloyd warm. Followed by calling 111.

'Here.' She placed towels and scissors on the bedside table. 'I'll see if I can get through to the emergency services. While I'm at it, I'll get the first aid kit. By then you'll have Lloyd ready to be checked over.'

A frown appeared on Danny's brow. 'What's in the bag?'

She was an AP, remember.

'Most things we might need. Except no serious pain-killers, only analgesics.'

He put his hand in his pocket and removed a set of car keys. 'Front seat of my vehicle. There's a bag with something stronger in it.'

Like any doctor she'd met, he obviously went every-where prepared for a medical event. Like herself, though she didn't carry the serious drugs as that was not allowed.

'Back shortly.'

'Brooke,' Danny called after her. 'Go carefully. It's still dangerous out there.'

'I won't be anything else. I'll check the phone's got coverage too.' If Lloyd's ankle was busted then he should be taken to hospital, but whether that was possible was another thing.

It was a lot easier going across to Mike's house than it had been in the other direction, with no slips or racing water to contend with, and she quickly found Danny's small bag and got her much larger kit from her car before heading back inside.

In the bedroom, Danny was checking Lloyd's foot. 'Have you got something we can make a splint with? The ankle's fractured and I think so are some of the metatarsals.'

'Here. Use this.' Brooke pulled out a thick plastic sheet that could be wrapped around the ankle. 'Lloyd, I'm going to look at that wound on your head. I'll try not to hurt but let me know if it gets too much.'

'Where's Jean?'

'Do you know if he has any health problems we should be aware of? Does he take medication for anything?' Danny asked.

'I haven't a clue. He's never talked about prescriptions or the likes.' She pushed her sleeve up to reveal her watch and reached for Lloyd's wrist to find his pulse and began counting silently. If only she'd thought to find out, but she hadn't expected to be in this situation. The pulse was a little rapid, but that was more likely due to mental anguish and nothing to be concerned about. Despair was mingled with pain on his face.

Pulling her phone from her pocket, she sighed with relief. 'Three bars. That's not bad, even on a fine day.' One of the few downsides to staying out in the Sounds was poor internet coverage in many areas. Too many hills to interfere with it. 'We're going to get you out of here as soon as possible,' Brooke said to Lloyd, mentally crossing her fingers.

'I don't want to leave Jean.' His voice broke and tears dripped down the sides of his wrinkled face.

She gently wiped them away. 'She'd want you to get help.'

'Emergency service. Do you require Fire, Police or Ambulance?'

If only it were that straightforward.

'I have an eighty-one-year-old man who needs to be hospitalised. He has a head wound, fractured ankle and possible internal injuries, but we're in the Marlborough Sounds, where road access is probably unavailable due to the storm going on. I think sea access is also unfeasible, and I'm not sure about the rescue helicopter with the wind factor.'

'Are you medically trained?'

'I'm an advanced paramedic, not currently on duty.' She glanced at Danny. 'There's also a doctor here.'

'That's fine, just making sure you understand the man's condition. Is there somewhere close a chopper can land?'

That was the problem.

'No. They've used our front lawn before, but that's not a goer today. They'll have to lower the medic and a stretcher.'

The woman said, 'I'm putting you on hold while I talk to the helicopter rescue service. Don't hang up.'

'I won't.' Digging in a drawer, she found a pen and paper and began writing down Lloyd's scant details to go with him, including Brad's phone number which was in her father's notebook. He didn't keep it because he liked the man who'd screwed with his daughter's heart, but because he cared about his friend and neighbour. Could she leave it up to the hospital to phone Brad? She could, but she wouldn't be able to look herself in the eye. This was about Old Man Duggan, not his grandson.

'What's happening?' Danny asked.

'The operator's onto the chopper service. They'll know what's going on here and if the weather's safe enough to fly in.'

'They'll come from Nelson, won't they?'

'Most likely, unless they're too busy, then it's possible the service will send one across from Wellington if the wind's quietened over the strait.'

'That's a big if.' Danny smiled. He really did a lot of that. Was he used to getting his own way by doing so? Or was he just a genuinely nice guy? Instantly she relaxed a little. How did he do that to her with simple smiles? But they weren't simple. They came with understanding and thoughtfulness. Almost as if he knew she liked having him on her side at the moment. But then why wouldn't he? She hadn't tried to push him out of the picture. So far he didn't seem overly assertive, nor wanting to please her all the time like some of the men she'd recently dated. But she knew they didn't tend to show their true colours immediately.

Her ex-fiancé, Brad, certainly hadn't. He'd been accomplished at fooling her into believing everything he did was for them and with her best interests at heart. He wouldn't explain why he'd signed them up for a second house before the contract for the sale of the first one had gone through. When the sale had fallen through they'd survived the threat of bankruptcy by the skin of their teeth and a load of luck. But their relationship hadn't. That was when she'd left him. Brad was never going to change. He acted impulsively, causing a lot of harm along the way.

Like her first long-term boyfriend, who'd been reticent about sharing his ambitions with her. No wonder she didn't trust people to be honest with her and why she now refused to let any man take control of her. Except, by avoiding those sorts of men, she'd found herself dating men who enjoyed her strengths and wanted her to be in charge so they could go along for the ride, being compliant with her dreams. That didn't make her happy either. Relationships were meant to be equal on all counts. Even the one with her mother, though nowadays they'd reached an understanding and got along a lot better.

She was happy being single. There was no one to disrupt her plans or decisions. Then it hit her. Brad. She did have to call him. Lloyd's family needed to be told what had happened. She'd wait until he'd been evacuated before she dealt with that devil.

Danny was talking, calming their patient. And her? 'I've never experienced wind like we've had these past twenty-four hours. I'm from Melbourne,' he added.

Then his mouth tightened, and his eyes became wary. He hadn't meant to tell her that. Why ever not? Millions of Aussies lived in that city.

Did he think she might recognise him from somewhere? Maybe in a previous life, she thought as the operator returned.

'Are you there?'

'Yes.'

'It's your lucky day. There's a chopper leaving Blenheim to return to Nelson so they're diverting to come to you. Can you give me details re the location?'

'I can do better than that. I have the GPS coordinates.' Something her father kept on his desk for this exact reason. Yes, he tended to be a pessimist, but sometimes it was just as well.

'Excellent. Fire away.'

Brooke read out the numbers and heaved a sigh of relief. Help was coming, and sooner than expected. She gave Danny the thumbs-up. 'Fifteen minutes tops, I reckon.' A smile spread throughout her, lifting some of the chill that had settled when she'd gone inside Lloyd's house. Things were looking up. And the man crouching at Lloyd's side was looking better by the minute, mud-splattered and all. If she didn't get wound up about him possibly being secretive. But they'd barely met so there hadn't been time to talk much about themselves. She'd move outside in preparation for the chopper—now.

Danny lifted his end of the stretcher Lloyd was strapped onto and they headed outside with the rescue doctor, keeping one eye on their patient and the other on the slippery ground. Brooke was calm at the other end of the stretcher. The ideal paramedic to have by your side in an emergency. How did she download afterwards? Go for a run? Talk to a friend? A partner? Pour a stiff drink?

Lloyd had started slipping in and out of consciousness minutes after they knew the helicopter was coming for him. Danny's heart squeezed for the old boy, who'd been upset about leaving his wife. What was it like to have a love like that? If only he could find it and learn the answer.

Briefly he studied the set shoulders and slim feminine frame in front of him. Not beautiful in the traditional way, but Brooke had an inner beauty that shone through even when she'd been trying not to freak out inside Lloyd's house with the boards creaking and groaning, sounding as if they were about to spring free and let the outside in further. His skin had lifted in bumps and the hairs on the back of his neck stood up. A similar reaction to Brooke's, if he'd read her correctly. She'd shivered and rubbed her arms a couple of times while peering around the space they were in. But she'd carried on checking over Lloyd as though she hadn't a care in the world other than making sure her neighbour was going to be all right. She was one cool woman—with a whole lot of apprehension going on in that trim body.

The medic was talking into his radio, presumably telling the paramedic still on board the chopper to lower the winch because Danny could see it beginning to drop from the side opening.

The downdraught from the rotors pelted them and flicked up water. No one bothered to talk. They wouldn't be heard above the racket the helicopter made. It didn't matter. The medic had everything under control and it was obvious Brooke had been in this situation before as she knew what was required, which was for them to continue holding the stretcher while the winch was attached. Within minutes Lloyd was on board and the medic was spinning in the air as he was lifted up to join his crew.

'See you around, Tristan.' Brooke had her hands around her mouth as she yelled at the swinging medic, who waved back.

Danny turned for the house, grabbing Brooke's hand on the way, leaning in to shout above the noise, 'Let's get out of this.'

She didn't even blink, just went along beside him, almost running, her shaky hand in his. So she wasn't as calm as he'd believed.

'It's been quite a morning, hasn't it?' he said when they charged up her steps.

Her boots went flying, followed by her jacket and then she was pushing the door open. 'Come in.'

Not the most enticing invitation he'd had, but probably more genuine than any he could recall in a while. He could get used to this anonymity. Except—His heart lurched. It wasn't good to be dishonest and not saying who he was might be construed as that. Anyway, eventually the truth would out and moments like this would disappear once more.

'Yes or no?' Brooke stood there, hand on hip, a look of *What are you waiting for?* on her gut-stirring face.

His shoes hit the wooden deck with a clunk and his jacket joined hers on the wicker chair. 'That's a yes,' and he grinned. 'If you don't mind a bit more mud around the place.'

'Couldn't care less,' she said over her shapely shoulder as he followed her to the kitchen, where she went to stand in front of the firebox, rubbing her arms hard.

'Cold?' A chill was creeping into his body now that they were out of the wind and downdraught. He removed his damp jersey and moved beside her, stretching his hands out to the heat like she was.

'A bit.'

Another thing he liked about her was she didn't yabber on for the sake of it. Strange how that had him wanting to hear more from her.

'Is that why your hands are shaking?'

She stared at her hands, fingers splayed, then turned them over, flexed her fingers. 'That and the tension finally easing off. Now Lloyd's safe and we're out of the way of any harm, it's all catching up.'

'It was scary in that house, with all the noise making me think the roof or walls were going to collapse in on us at any moment.'

Her eyes met his. 'Think I'd have preferred being at work dealing with a worst-case scenario than in there.'

He couldn't help himself. He took her hands in his and rubbed the backs with his thumbs. Her skin was freezing. 'You were great. I couldn't tell that you were so worried.'

Her hands tightened around his. 'Same back at you.' The tip of her tongue appeared between her lips. 'Thanks for helping me and Old Man Duggan.'

'No problem.' As if he wouldn't have. Even if she'd been falling over in her haste to get him to notice her he'd have done his darnedest to get her neighbour to safety. It was a bonus she hadn't acted in that way.

'It was heartbreaking, listening to him talk about Jean. Asking if she was safe.'

'It made me sad, and also thinking how much in love they must've been.'

'They were.' She nibbled her lip with a faraway look in her eyes. Then she straightened, once more appearing focused. 'Do you want a tea? Or coffee? Or something stronger?' She still hadn't pulled her hands away.

'I'll go for stronger if you don't mind. It might warm me up a bit more than tea.'

Her eyes were large and now filled with relief, not a hint of the wariness that had been there when he'd first left her on her back porch. The shaking in her hands was easing, and she'd moved ever so slightly closer. It would be effortless to wrap his arms around her and hold her close, sink his chin into that damp, dark blonde hair and absorb some of her strength and warmth. She'd kick him where it hurt if he did. Wouldn't she? He wasn't about to find out. It wasn't the way to get to know her better. He stepped back, pulling his hands free.

Disappointment met his gaze. Then she shook her head. 'What's your preferred drink?'

'Scotch, if you've got it.'

'Dad's favourite. And mine.' Then she grinned, as though a load had fallen away.

Danny felt as if everything was right in his world. Which had to be a first for a long time. 'Something else we seem to have in common.'

Her left eyebrow rose. 'Along with what?'

'We worked on Lloyd as though we've always worked together. We helped each other through the mud and water, got in and out of the wrecked house without any explanations required.'

'True, we did,' Brooke agreed.

'I take it you've been on other cases where the flying rescue service attended. You knew that medic.'

'Often. I work for the Nelson ambulance service.'

A gentle nudge in his gut. 'Another thing we share. I'm starting work at the Nelson ED this coming week.'

Brooke laughed as she crossed to a cupboard and poured two generous drinks. When she handed him a glass she tapped hers against it. 'Here we are, warming up in front of the fire, having a drink and admitting we got a little scared in there. I'm glad I met you today, Danny.'

He looked right into her, felt heat spear through him. Never had he known anything quite as right as this. It was as though he'd found something he hadn't been aware of searching for. 'Back at you, Brooke.'

She seemed to be considering something as she sipped her drink. Then she stretched up and placed a light, whisky-flavoured kiss on his mouth. All the while her eyes never left his.

The heat flared, spread like wildfire throughout his system. The last of the tension was unleashed inside, pressing into his gut, his groin and, dare he admit it, his heart. Surely not. His hand trembled, sloshing his drink to the rim of the glass. Putting it down, he reached for her. 'Brooke, can I kiss you? Properly?'

Her glass joined his before her breasts pressed into his chest and her arms reached around his neck. Her lips met his. 'Yes,' she whispered between them. 'Yes, please.'

She was to die for. All heat and tenderness and strength and giving and demanding. He devoured her with his kiss. And gave as good as he took. It wasn't enough. He should stop, but there were no brakes available. His body leaned further into her, bending to fit against her torso, to feel more of those exquisite breasts, her stomach, her hips and thighs up against him. It still wasn't enough. She made him feel safe. Safe from the danger of the storm. From the women who tried to tell him how to run his life and grab what they could for themselves along the way. He was safe from the world for a short while.

Don't ask him how it happened. Not even torture could make him answer the question, but next they were lying on the mat in front of the firebox, naked as the day they were born, and warm for the first time in hours. Hot, not warm. Heated beyond reason, need pouring through him as he reached to hold her tight, and to touch every inch of her skin, to feel her softness, her moistness.

Brooke wasn't lying still. She had an agenda of her own. Her hands were all over him, touching, rubbing, teasing, setting him further alight. Driving him insane with need. To the point he had to grab her hands to slow her down. She came first.

Nope. They came together. Both ready in such a hurry, impossible to ignore.

The conflagration was over almost before they'd started, and it was the best he'd known. Brooke was beyond any encounter he'd ever experienced.

Reluctantly he slid off her, but immediately took her in his arms as he lay on his side, breathing long, deep lungfuls of warm air as his heart rate slowly returned to normal. Under his hand he felt Brooke's heart rate slowing too. It was so cosy—and surprisingly intimate—lying on the mat with the fire's glow touching them. Especially since they hadn't met until a few hours ago. But *what* those hours *had* delivered. Could be this was the way to go—leap in and see where he landed? It had been quite the morning. Quite the introduction.

Long may this last. But it couldn't. He knew all too well how it would play out. Not necessarily today, or even tomorrow, but one day she would learn who he was. That was if they saw each other once they returned to their real lives in Nelson. What were the chances? He'd like to follow up and spend more time with her, which was bizarre in itself. He actually wanted to spend more time with Brooke, have more than a passing moment with her in front of her fire. Usually it was the other way round, and he'd be walking away.

Brooke ran her finger down his cheek. 'You're exactly what I needed.'

His gut tightened, and his heart lightened some. 'Know what you mean.' Except he thought he might need more of her, not less. Whatever had caused them to fall into each other's arms, share their bodies, it had been so good he felt relaxed in a way he'd forgotten was possible. That should be a warning, right there. This wonderful woman was doing things to him that he hadn't felt since he was an innocent nineteen-year-old heading up the chart towards number one for the under-twenties in international golf.

His girlfriend, Iris, had believed she was on that chart with him, and grabbed every opportunity to make a name for herself as his partner. That had been hard to deal with when she was back in Australia while he was playing around the world. He couldn't quieten her down, no matter how often he told her he wasn't interested in putting his whole life on the platform, only his golfing skills. Worse, she would often get a part in the interviews on TV whenever he was featured, either at his side or as an added feature. He'd loved her, but possibly not as much as he'd believed because his love had dried up the more demanding she became. She'd given up studying for a degree in accountancy because he was going to make a fortune and she'd be able to help him spend it. He suspected he hadn't listened hard enough to her earlier on in their relationship.

Then he had got it wrong again with Brenda. Hard lessons, but hopefully they'd pay off one day. Despite a major career change, and less fame, he was now so cautious of women and their intentions he could almost sign up to work in a monastery. Almost. He still enjoyed women, as long as they kept their mouths shut when it came to his past and wealth. So far they'd all had one feature in common: they thought he needed them more than he did.

Yet here he was, getting wound up over Brooke, whom he'd met only a few hours ago. A few hours that had included danger, saving someone, and the most exciting sex he'd had in forever. They were going at breakneck speed with getting to know each other. He should get up and head over to the other house, stay away from this distraction before she became more endearing. Before she got any deeper into his soul, because there would only be one ending, and he really did not want to face it with Brooke. Not that he could explain that to himself.

She fascinated him with her determination to get on with whatever had to be done, without stopping to make sure he was following. She'd been rattled in the house and again outside when the hill slid down towards them, but she'd dug in and continued doing what she'd set out to accomplish. And then she'd fallen into his arms and made out like he was the only man on the planet.

Long may it last, and he grinned.

Except he shouldn't be so idiotic. He sighed. High expectations always tipped over the edge into darkness.

CHAPTER FOUR

LYING IN FRONT of the fire where she'd just had fast, mind-blowing sex with a near stranger, Brooke stretched her legs as far as they'd go—not as far as she'd like—and raised her arms over her head. Incredible. To think she'd been wary of the guy when he'd first appeared. But Danny wasn't a stranger, not any more. If she could be so intimate with him, then he was in her blood now. Possibly only for a few hours, or even a couple of days, which was probably as far as this would go. They knew nothing about each other. Although that wasn't strictly true.

They were both medics, and were good at what they did, if helping Lloyd had shown her anything.

They had helped one another out of the mud and water whenever either of them got stuck or fell.

They both enjoyed a whisky. Of which neither of them had had more than a sip. She smiled to herself.

Their bodies had recognised each other in a flash of heat and desire—as if they'd been waiting for one another. She looked at the man who'd woken her up so thoroughly.

What they'd had added up to far more than the last man she'd dated and had a dull round of sex with. Her smile grew wide. Yeah, she'd just had an amazing experience. Now she'd better go remove the mud from her face and hair, then put on some clothes because the air was getting cooler as she lay naked on the floor. First the fire needed more wood.

Sitting up, she found Danny's gaze on her. 'I'm going to take a shower. Then I might heat up some soup.' Suddenly she felt awkward and wanted to cover up, but all that was on hand were her wet, muddy clothes she'd dumped in a pile as they'd got intense. It wasn't as though he made her feel inadequate or unattractive. It was… It was because she suddenly felt overwhelmed by the way they'd connected so fast and had seemed to be able to read each other without trying. If they were like that physically, how would it go on other levels? She would like to find a man to share her life with, one who'd accept her for herself, but it wasn't something that would come easily. She'd tried, and been disappointed, become cautious. Possibly too cautious. The disappointment was worse than not trying, so she'd given up and got on with doing the things she loved, like work, and more work, preferring that to being disenchanted again and again.

Danny's finger ran down her arm. 'You're getting goosebumps.'

'So are you.' The hairs on his arms were standing up too. Getting cold, or overheating with need?

Then he smiled, and her world tipped on its axis when he said, 'Go get warm and clean. I'll head over to where I'm staying and do the same. Am I invited to share the soup? I can bring bread rolls.'

Definitely a charmer. But that was okay as long as he didn't overdo it.

'See you shortly.' She pushed to her feet, fully aware of him watching as she straightened, making her feel wanted. He probably wanted more sex. She did, no hesitation. There wasn't going to be much going on for the rest of the day, apart from checking out the situation up on the road, so why not think they might get together again?

'You've got some bruises from those crash landings you took.' Danny touched her thigh and butt.

'I'm not surprised.'

Walking out of the room, her backside seemed to have a mind of its own, sort of wiggling in a sexy way. Her over-kissed lips presumed a smile. Sexy, or looking silly? Who cared? She wasn't a beauty queen, nor did she care. She'd leapt in and had sex with him, and that was huge. That was not something she'd normally do. Which went to show she trusted him to be good to her, physically at least. There might be time later on to learn more about him. She wasn't getting in a quandary about that at the moment.

By the time Brooke pushed the tap off in the shower her skin was wrinkled and red, but did she feel good. She'd applied a treatment to her hair after washing out a ton of mud. After rubbing moisturiser on her face, then doing the same for her arms and legs, she dried her hair into its neat bob, applied a light coating of make-up and went to get dressed, laughing at herself all the time. Make-up? Out here where the only person she'd probably see was Danny, and it was a little late to be trying to look her best. He'd seen her slip-sliding in the mud and water, crawling through a window into Lloyd's house. And naked by the fire.

Lloyd. How was he doing? Were they already operating on his ankle? What about the other injuries? Oh, no. Lloyd. Brad. She hadn't called Brad to let him know about his grandfather.

Picking up her phone, she tapped the number she'd found earlier in her father's notebook.

'Hello?'

Deep breath. 'Hi, Brad. It's Brooke.'

'Ahh, she deigns to ring me. It must be my lucky day.' Sarcasm was another one of his talents.

'Your grandfather has been taken to hospital.'

'Which is why I'm sitting in Christchurch Airport waiting for a flight.'

So the hospital had contacted him. 'That's good. He'll be pleased to see you.' Hopefully. It wasn't her place to be the judge of that family's problems, but Lloyd did need someone by his side at the moment and since Brad's parents now lived in Rarotonga he was the only person available.

'Why are you calling me now, and not earlier? I'd have thought I deserved that much of your time. I'm presuming you're at the bay.'

'I am. You don't understand. It's a disaster area around here. Just going over to Lloyd's house took forever as there's so much debris in the way. The landslide that came down behind his house is huge.' Another deep breath, because that was what she'd done a lot of in the last years of their relationship. 'Brad, I hate to tell you, but Lloyd's house has been badly damaged when the hillside came down. The house's not safe any more. I doubt it can be repaired. Probably have to be pulled down.'

'A complete rebuild is long overdue. I don't get why Granddad was so stubborn about hanging on to the place when it's so out-of-date and too small for the family and friends to visit. At least something good's come out of his accident. I can get a place that I like to spend time at.'

You selfish git. Lloyd hasn't wanted to change a thing because his memories of Jean are in every corner, on every shelf, in every room, and you don't give a toss.

It also wasn't her place to say what was on her mind, but she'd have loved to.

'Brad, tell Lloyd I'll be in to see him as soon as I leave the bay. We don't know what state the road's in yet, but I'll go when I can get out.'

'Did you help him out of the house?'

'Yes. Me and a doctor staying at Mike's.'

'How was he? The hospital said something about a broken ankle and a head wound. They're going to do some X-rays to see if there was an internal injury of some sort.' Brad finally sounded worried and sad.

'He didn't want to leave, was worried about Jean.'

'She's not there, so what's his problem?'

Lost love. To think she'd once believed they might have shared lifelong love.

'He took a hard knock to his head when the microwave came off the shelf.' Lloyd hadn't been his usual gutsy self, not by a long shot.

'That would've hurt. Got to go. My flight's been called.'

She tried one last time to make Brad understand his grandfather's plight. 'He was very distressed. Shock will be a big part of that, but I saw how worried he was about not being able to stay with his memories of Jean.'

'He'll get over that when he starts feeling better. See you.' The phone went dead.

'Not if I see you first, you jerk.' She dropped her phone on the bench in disgust. How had she ever loved him?

'Someone rattle your cage?' Danny stood in the doorway, looking good enough to eat dressed in black jeans hugging his hips and a grey jersey that did nothing to obliterate her memory of the chest underneath. A bag of buns swung from his fingers.

'Lloyd's grandson.'

'You're not mates, then?'

'He's my ex.'

'That explains a lot. Still want my company? You can throw things at me if you need to get him out of your system. I'm pretty good at dodging flying objects.' His smile was kind and understanding.

Damn it, but she laughed. And as she did, Brad's selfishness disappeared from her mind. Done and dusted.

'I wouldn't waste my time or energy.' Brad wasn't worth it. 'Come in and close the door before all the warm air disappears outside.'

'The wind's dropped further. It's almost hard to believe how strong it's been.' He left his shoes on the porch and a jacket on a peg by the door, as though he felt right at home already.

This was getting a little interesting. Where would they go with this? How far?

'The rain's letting up at last. I'll take the four-wheel bike out later to see what the damage is along the road. For as far as I can get, that is.'

'Mind if I hitch a ride? Might as well see what I'm in for when I come to leave.' He placed the buns on the bench, then crossed to lift the lid on the pot warming on the firebox, leaned closer to sniff. 'Pea and ham. Great. You make it?'

'Found it in the freezer. Mum will've left it there a few weeks ago, knowing Saskia and I were coming to stay.' Their mother did spoil them when it came to home comforts.

'To think I nearly didn't come to the Sounds this weekend. I'd have missed out on all the fun.' Danny picked up the two glasses of whisky they'd been side-tracked from earlier.

She glanced at the microwave clock. Much earlier. It was now gone two. Time did fly when you were having fun rescuing a neighbour and getting to know a stranger intimately.

Handing her one of the glasses, Danny said, 'To us and one heck of a morning.' His mouth was wearing that delicious smile.

'It had its highs and lows, for sure.' She sipped the liquor and sat down on one of the two recliner chairs on either side of the fire. 'Know which I prefer.' Though the high wouldn't have happened if she hadn't been wound tight over getting Old Man Duggan to safety while hoping the house wouldn't collapse completely, trapping them all inside.

'Me too.' Danny lowered his sexy butt onto the opposite chair. 'Even if you can get out in the next couple of days, are you going to stay on for the week as you'd originally planned?'

'Haven't had time to think about it. There is a fair amount of cleaning up to do outside, which I can't leave for Mum and Dad next time they come down. Think I'll get some of Lloyd's clothes out of his place to drop into hospital for him too.'

'We'll do that one together. Though we probably shouldn't go inside again. That house is a menace.'

'True. But I keep hearing Lloyd calling for Jean and I want to give him something that's familiar to cling to. Maybe a photo of their wedding.'

'He's still got those? That says a lot about their relationship.'

'They were so close it was awesome to see.' So lovely, and she'd truly believed she'd have that with Brad. Silly woman. But there you go. Not everything turned out as expected in this world. She'd get it right next time—if she met the right man. Her eyes slid to the one sitting opposite, and a warmth bubbled through her. He mightn't be the one, but she could enjoy the time they did have together.

'Have you always been a paramedic?' he asked.

'I qualified as a medical laboratory tech, did that for six years. During that period I volunteered as an ambulance officer and found I loved it so much I swapped careers. I like helping people hands on, not from sitting behind a microscope.' She'd always been a caring kind of girl, looking out for pets, birds that flew into windows, or other kids at school when they hurt themselves at playtime. She should have known from the beginning that working in a lab wasn't her. 'I enjoy the intensity of the situations we go to. They keep me on my toes, and at my absolute best.' People died on her watch in the ambulance service, and it got to her, but somehow she coped because a lot more people made it home again, not only because of her but because of the way she helped their recovery. 'What did you do before setting out to become a doctor?'

He winced. 'I tried a few things, got into sport for

a while, then decided it was time to settle down and get on with what I really wanted to do.' Danny stared at the mat where they'd had sex earlier. 'My father encouraged me, said that he didn't believe in going from school to university and diving straight into a full-on career. He thought I needed to get some life skills and experiences under my belt first.'

'And did you?' He wasn't very forthcoming about himself. Should she be getting worried? Though why not sit back and enjoy his company? She wasn't committing to anything with him.

'Yes.' He sipped his whisky. 'And now I'm getting some more.'

He was looking everywhere but at her, shifting that butt on the chair as if a change of subject was required. She could do that for now, though it felt familiar— Danny not talking about himself as if he had something to hide. Strange when they had barely started getting to know each other. Should she be wary? Or give it a rest and go with the subject change? See where it led? She didn't know, which was odd in itself. She usually ran a mile from people who kept things from her.

'Where will you be living in Nelson?'

The relief was huge. His eyes lightened, his mouth softened and he looked directly at her again. 'I've rented a fully furnished apartment around the waterfront. I'll be there for about six months. I've been working in Blenheim since January.'

The same health board covered both regions. 'Nelson will be a lot busier than Blenheim, though I guess if you did your initial training in Melbourne it'll still seem quiet.'

'Friday and Saturday nights are the same in any hospital. Bedlam with drunks and motor vehicle accidents, to name a few of the problems we face.'

'And the drug-enhanced people demanding to be seen by doctors when they aren't urgent. I hate dealing with those and dread weekend night shifts.'

'You'd have to be insane not to.' Danny was settling deeper into the chair, his fingers not so tight around his glass.

She followed suit and relaxed. To heck with her concerns—for now at least. She'd go with the flow and enjoy Danny's company on this storm-battered day when there was little else to do.

'My grandmother was a nurse, and she can't believe some of the stories I've told her about over-toasted patients and having to have security guards in the department.' The whisky was smooth on her tongue. The atmosphere was calming and quiet. Just right. Outside the tempest was dying, leaving behind the shambles it had created, going on to deliver more havoc elsewhere, hopefully out to sea.

Danny's laugh was deep and heart-warming. 'What I saw today when you were with Lloyd, I cannot picture you in a lab coat studying a blood film down a microscope.' He grinned. 'Nor does it compare with another picture I have of you.'

Heck. She blushed, bright red by the feel of the temperature charging up her neck to her cheeks. 'You are a right charmer, aren't you?' she said a little too sharply.

'You don't trust that?'

Breathe deep. 'Not always. Well and truly bitten, now totally averse.' Crikey, she was being honest, and saying things as they were when she didn't normally talk about private matters at all. Clearing the air before she got too interested in him?

'The grandson, for one?'

She should have kept her mouth shut. But then again, Brad was her history and she wasn't ashamed of her role in their relationship. 'Afraid so.' She got up to stir the soup. Dipped her finger in and didn't get burned. 'Not quite ready.' Crossing to the kitchen nook, she put the oven on to heat the buns, got out soup bowls and plates, cutlery and salt and pepper.

'Whereabouts in Nelson do you live?'

'I'm central and can walk into town for my coffee. I bought a little cottage on the bank of the Maitai River. It's a nineteen-twenties house, cold as a snow field in winter and warmer than this oven in summer, but I love it. The maintenance is ongoing.' She placed the cutlery and serviettes on the table.

'Want me to do anything?'

'I've got it, thanks.' Suddenly she felt awkward again. Who was this man? Like really, who was he? She'd had sex with him, was sharing a drink and soup, and didn't have the foggiest. For all she knew he could be lying about being a trainee doctor and using his charm to get whatever he wanted. There again, he knew Paula and Mike, a surgeon at Blenheim Hospital, and they wouldn't have left him in their bach if they didn't think he was trustworthy.

The soup spoons hit the table with a clang. She turned to look at Danny without blinkers on. He still looked good. Kind and caring. And charming, which wasn't a fault if used appropriately. He'd been gentle with her, then strong and sexy, and then gentle again.

'Brooke?' Danny stood in front of her, not in her

space, giving her room. 'It's hitting home what we've done, isn't it?'

Was that it? Leaping to have sex with a stranger was new for her, yet at the time she'd known what she was doing and had still wanted it. After what they'd been through outside she'd needed that affirmation she was okay. But was she now looking for reasons to doubt herself? Or Danny?

'It's okay. I'll head back to the house and let you have some time to yourself.' No charm, no heart-melting smile, just a genuine look of understanding.

She watched him walk out of the door, her hands pressed to the tabletop. She shouldn't have had sex with him. Tell that to someone who believed her when she had felt so good afterwards. They'd both been coming down off an adrenaline high and it had felt right. Not that there'd been a lot of considering about what they'd been about to do. She'd just known she had to have him, and he'd appeared to have felt the same about her, which was a turn-on too, if she'd needed another one. He was so sexy. He'd been a generous lover. It hadn't been all about what he wanted. Was she being selfish, letting him walk out of the door because she was in a quandary about herself, and him?

Pulling out a chair, she sank onto it and put her elbows on the table to drop her chin into her hands. What a screwed-up woman she'd turned out to be. She'd just had the most amazing sex with a lovely man, make that a sexy, good-looking man, and now she was doubting herself.

Get over yourself, Brooke. Don't you want to find a man who'll treat you well and accept who you are?

The only way that will happen is if you let go of the past and have some fun.

Was it that simple? Anyway, hadn't Danny come out to help her when he could've stayed in the house pretending nothing was going on? Didn't he just show how much he understood her by saying their moment on the mat was hitting home?

So what if he was charming? It could be a good thing, and it never hurt to be complimented once in a while. Didn't mean it came with a price tag. She had become a little twisted when it came to men. Time to change that.

Getting a grocery bag from a drawer, Brooke started packing it with everything she needed for lunch.

That went well, Danny thought as he stared into the fridge, trying to decide what he'd have for lunch now that soup was off the menu. Not a lot of choice in front of him. He'd come prepared with basics, but what had seemed good when he was in the supermarket now made him shake his head in disappointment. He could still smell pea and ham soup.

Closing the fridge, he plugged in the kettle for coffee and pulled out a stool to park his backside. No new messages on his phone since the one from his mate who owned this place asking how he'd fared overnight and if the property was still intact.

The house hadn't taken a hit. The yard had its share of debris, including small branches and lots of leaves, but otherwise it looked much as it had yesterday.

But he wasn't quite the same man who'd woken up this morning after a night of intermittent sleep while the house was being slammed with wind and rain. No, that guy had had a wake-up call in the form of one dark blonde woman with a slim, short frame, and a lot of determination. Determination and uncertainties. Strength and fears. He hadn't met her in anything close to normal circumstances, but she didn't seem overly fazed about getting to know more about him in a hurry, and when he'd backed off talking about himself she'd been quick to pick up on that and let him be. That alone earned her more points than just about anything a woman could do for him. The fantastic sex had been a bonus. If only she hadn't got cold feet. When they'd had sex they'd been coming down off a high of nerves and adrenaline, and it was only natural to reach out to each other.

More than reached out, as far as he was concerned. He'd mentioned the fact he'd been interested in sport before he took to studying medicine. He *never* said that to anyone who didn't already know. He was always on his guard. Not around Brooke, it seemed. Saying things like that always brought on more questions, or shocked surprise when the realisation dawned. 'You're *the* Daniel Collins, as in famous golfer.'

As in the egotist who went off the rails when his career disappeared overnight. Young and unable to cope with suddenly being incapable of hitting a golf ball with the accuracy that had won him many tournaments, he'd found fault with Iris and dropped her. Then he'd taken to dating every woman who glanced his way. He had used women to feed his ego, something he was now appalled about. Until his father had stepped in and made him look at himself with a frank and hard conversation about how he was letting everyone down, especially himself. Dad had followed up with a reminder of how he'd once dreamed of being a doctor and how that option was still there if he settled down and pulled his head in. That conversation had flipped his life around, possibly because deep down he'd wanted to be normal again.

Brooke hadn't a clue, and he liked that so much. Not that she knew him by any other name than Danny. If he did get to spend more time with her he'd have to fill her in about his past, but surely he was allowed to have some fun without turning it all on its head straight away? They had only met that morning, and once he left here they probably wouldn't see each other again except at work.

Yeah, right, who was he fooling? He wanted to see a lot more of her. Was it possible that once she knew about him, Brooke still wouldn't care two hoots about the money he'd earned and how he was still put on a pedestal all these years later? She appeared to hold herself tall without needing to lean on someone else's accolades to get through life. She didn't shy away from problems or blink coquettishly at him. Then again, he'd seen it all before. Yeah, he sighed, he was jaded.

But he sensed there might be more to Brooke that he'd enjoy being a part of, sharing good times and the bad stuff that life might toss at them. There was a depth to her he hadn't encountered in a long while. Obviously she'd also taken some knocks. The grandson was not on her Christmas list by the fed-up look in her eyes as she'd hung up from talking to him. Nothing like her feelings for the grandfather. There'd been nothing but care and concern as Brooke saw to that man's needs.

She could care for his too—as much as she liked. Except he didn't really have any other than wanting a life partner somewhere along the way to old age. A woman to share everything with, and possibly have a family together. Here he went—getting ahead of himself. She'd been happy for him to walk away from lunch, hadn't tried to call him back. She'd got the jitters. It was plain in her face and how her hands kept flexing against her thighs. Funny, because it so rarely happened, but he'd known when he wasn't wanted. Another point to mark up in her favour. She wasn't all about doing whatever it took to make him happy.

Which made him very happy indeed.

Knock-knock.

Hope soared. It had to be Brooke. Who else would be out and about in this weather? There was only one way to find out. Before she disappeared on him because obviously he wasn't interested in opening the door to her.

'Brooke.' His heart did a little skip. 'Here, let me take that.' He reached for the pot she was holding in one hand. From the fingers of the other swung a laden bag. 'How did you manage to knock on the door?'

Her pert nose screwed up as she laughed. 'Used my heel.'

'Come in.'

'There's too much soup for me.' An olive branch by any other name.

'I'm glad. I wasn't getting enthused over what's in the fridge.' He closed the door behind her and followed her into the kitchen with a bounce in his step. Sometimes things had a way of working out. He was going to hang on to that idea for as long as possible. He might even thank the weather gods for sending the storm, if not for the people who'd been injured or lost property or would be stranded for days to come.

'Didn't you bring food with you?' Brooke was looking at him in surprise. 'You're not exactly within walking distance of a supermarket out here, even on a good day.'

'There's plenty here, just nothing I fancied after the idea of hot soup grabbed me.'

'That's better. For a moment I thought you were saying you didn't prepare for your stay, though I can't imagine Paula not making certain you were left with everything you'd need.'

So Brooke thought he might be a bit useless when it came to looking after himself, did she?

'I am very self-reliant. I've had to be.' Whenever he couldn't face being accosted by ardent fans at the supermarket or a takeaway outlet, usually after another tedious news slot on television or in the internet media.

Unpacking the bag she'd brought with her, she handed him the half-full glass of whisky he'd put aside when he left her house. 'Here, can't have you saying I neglected you.'

Obviously not a wasteful woman then. Because she had to be careful? Or didn't believe in acting like a spoilt child? Whichever, he liked that about her. Removing the plastic wrap she'd sealed the glass with, he laughed. 'I've never taken so long to finish one drink. Did you bring yours?'

Reaching into the bag, she lifted out another half-full glass. 'I don't usually overindulge, but today is like no other I've encountered. Not for a long time, anyhow. Cheers.' Her lips were soft on the rim of her glass.

'Cheers.' He joined her in savouring the whisky. 'I'll put that pot on to heat a bit more.' He wasn't in any hurry to eat. She might leave the moment her bowl was empty, and he didn't want that. It had been a long time since he'd enjoyed a woman's company so much, so why cut it short if he didn't have to?

Brooke sat at the table, crossed her legs and focused on him. Not in a *What's in this for me?* way, but with an open and honest look, as though she genuinely wanted to get to know what made him tick. 'You said you've had to be self-reliant. In what way?'

There wasn't much Brooke seemed to miss. He'd be wise to remember that. 'Just a few hiccups along the way. Life throwing its curve balls at me, as it does everyone,' he added in an attempt to divert her away from him in particular.

'Know what you mean.'

He'd got away with it. The sudden tension backed off. 'Like today for Lloyd.'

'I hope he survives this. Not the injuries he sustained, but the loss of his home and those wonderful memories of Jean.' She sipped her drink. 'My largest curve ball was Brad, the grandson. But he's firmly in the past now.'

Hadn't the man wound her up tight during that phone call earlier?

'You see him occasionally down here?'

'Not if I can help it. I do my best to avoid him just to save hearing all the reasons why I'm such a cow. I take it you're single or we wouldn't have got close earlier. Or am I being naïve?' Her eyes had become very focused on him.

Where did that come from? Had Brad cheated on her? 'I'm definitely single, and no, I would not have touched you, let alone made love, if I'd been in a relationship.'

'Thank you.' She sipped her drink. 'You didn't come to New Zealand to get away from someone, did you?'

And he thought he'd distracted her. A whole load of someones was the answer he wasn't sharing.

'No.'

Then she blushed, and sputtered, 'I'm sorry. Take no notice of me. I'm being nosey. It's just that I don't usually let any man near so quickly and I'm trying to figure out why I did with you.' Her elbow banged on the top of the table. 'Now I'm talking too much.'

Had he got to her in a similar way to how she'd got to him? It would be kind of fun if he had. If he wasn't looking for something that wasn't there just because this didn't usually happen to him.

'Perhaps I'd better dish up the soup after all.'

'You think a mouthful of pea and ham will shut me up?' Her mouth curved into a soft grin.

A grin that went straight to his gut and sent tendrils of longing spiralling through him.

'I can always hope so.' He remained on his chair and sipped his whisky. 'How often have you been caught out here by a storm?'

'Only once before and it wasn't as severe as this one. The roading gangs had the slips cleared within twenty-four hours. I have a feeling we're going to be stuck for longer than that. You might have to call in the water taxi when it comes time to leave if it's really bad around here. That'll get you to Havelock, but what you do about getting to Nelson I don't know. There's probably a bus going through from Blenheim.'

'I'll worry about that when I know what we're dealing with.' He'd need his car in Nelson, if at all possible. 'This is a new experience for me.'

'How long have you been working in New Zealand?'

'Six months. My initial term with the local health

board is for a year, but I'm thinking of asking for an extension. This is a great region, with the Sounds and the vineyards. I like the smaller towns too.'

'Careful. You'll be settling down permanently before you know it.'

Not likely. The whole idea of stopping in one place permanently was ideal, if not on his agenda. People would invariably find out who he was and then he'd lose the comfort of being anonymous. Glancing at Brooke, he had to admit it mightn't be so bad with a woman at his side he could trust to accept him for who he was and not only for what had made him famous.

'I'm not ready for that.' Yet here he was, only hours after meeting Brooke and having the strangest thoughts about what might lie ahead. For the first time he wasn't ducking for cover, instead felt they were level pegging so far.

'Did you grow up in Melbourne?'

'Victoria.' He instantly regretted his terse answer. Another ingrained habit.

'Plenty of vineyards there too.' That eagle look was on him again. She knew he was avoiding giving her a specific answer. But to say Ballarat might start some bells ringing inside that lovely head that he wasn't ready to deal with.

'Some superb reds are made there.'

'So you'll return to Australia to further your studies?'

'Probably. Once I finish my medical degree I intend qualifying as a radiologist.'

Her eyes widened. 'Radiology? I thought that was for medics who didn't want to have too much interaction with patients.'

'Yes, and you have doubts about that?' X-rays couldn't ask him questions about golf or saving Toby Frank. They'd show him what was wrong with a patient, and he'd pass that on to the doctor dealing with the patient.

A frown had formed on Brooke's brow. 'Here I was thinking how personable you are. But then I have been known to get my people reading skills wrong.'

'Haven't we all?' Danny tried for a laugh to lighten the heaviness settling in his gut. It didn't come off. Brooke was right. He did have the gift of the gab— because he liked people, was interested in what made them tick, and had a way of drawing them out. Of course that was when they weren't trying to dig into his background. Draining his glass, he rose to get their lunch. He'd dodged enough bullets for now.

CHAPTER FIVE

'YOUR MUM MAKES a great soup,' Danny said as he scraped up the last smear from the bowl with a piece of bun. 'Delicious.'

'I agree.' Brooke leaned back in her chair, feeling the most relaxed since she'd gone to bed last night to the sound of the wind ripping through trees and hitting the house.

'Tea, coffee, whisky or wine?'

'Tea, thanks. I'll wait until after we've done a recce of the road for something stronger. Though it might be a short ride if there's a slip beyond the bay on the way back to the main road.' The only good thing about the slip that had come down while they were outside was that it hadn't blocked the road in that direction. No doubt there'd be a lot of people living further out who wouldn't agree with her.

'What are the chances there haven't been any other landslides?'

'Zilch. Big storms nearly always cause slips around here, and this one was exceptionally rough.'

'All part of living in such a beautiful place, I suppose. Sitting here, looking out over the bay towards the Sound beyond, it's hard to imagine scenery more stunning.'

'It's a great location.' A perfect bolthole too. She and Saskia came here whenever they needed a break from work or other problems. It was here, walking on the beach for hours, that she'd chosen moving on from Brad to regain control over her life. For her, moving on with life had meant stopping still, having one job to get totally involved in without waiting for the axe to fall, and settling into her small cottage and making changes to it that were for her and not the next person to live there. To be able to plant daffodil bulbs and be there to see them flower in the next spring. To choose colours that she liked for her curtains, not what would appeal to a prospective buyer when she'd finished re-decorating the house.

'Did your family spend all your summers here when you were growing up?' Danny brought her back to now.

'We did. Dad would go back to work after two weeks, but he always returned for the weekends. It was much the same with most of the bachs in the area. I've still got friends from those days. Of course everyone's now scattered across the country, even around the world, so we don't catch up often, but when we do it's usually one heck of a party.'

Strange how Danny wanted to know about her time here but when she'd asked where he came from his reply had been Victoria, one of Aussie's states. He hadn't mentioned where he lived in that vast area. It *was* as if he didn't want to talk about himself, which bugged her. She wanted to know more about him, even under-stood she might be rushing him if she dived in with questions, but it still irked. If they were spending time together, what was wrong with talking about himself a little? He reminded her how often people close to her had kept things from her.

She would never forget that day her mother had picked her up from school and said, 'You love those stories about girls in boarding schools, don't you?'

If only she'd known what was coming, she'd have answered differently, said, *No, Mum, I hate them.* Instead she'd said, 'Yes,' and had got home to find her bag packed and two airline tickets to Auckland on her dressing table. One for her mother, and one for her. At least Mum had gone with her to the school, explaining it was an opportunity for Brooke to get away from those bullies.

But what if Danny was hiding something important from her? Or was she looking for trouble because of her past? Not everyone kept important things from her, but she was braced to look for it.

Dishes clattered into the sink. Brooke jerked around to see Danny rinsing their bowls. 'Sorry, I was miles away.' She needed to take a break from worrying about who he was and what was behind his abrupt answers to some of her questions—for now anyway.

'Teach me for asking about your family summers.' He wore a gentle smile but there was contrition in his eyes, as though he regretted it even when he couldn't know what he might have triggered. Could be that he understood being hurt by someone you loved.

She wasn't asking who. That was getting too personal too soon, she supposed. Not that she'd held back over Brad, but that was her way of dealing with her past.

'Shall I get the bike?' Why was she asking? She was supposed to be doing as she saw fit, not getting permission. Those days were over. 'What I mean is, are you ready to go for a look-see?'

'You bet.' His eyes lit up in anticipation.

'It might be the shortest trip you've had anywhere,' she warned despite the happiness spilling through her, brought on by this man, who seemed to tweak her strings in good *and* worrying ways.

'You're a dab hand at driving a four-wheel bike? I'm not risking life or limb?' He was grinning at her as if she was the best thing to happen along today.

'Never driven one before.' Her dad had taught her to ride a smaller, less powerful bike when she was nine. Far too young, her mother had said, which had made her more determined to do it and she had become very proficient very quickly, impressing her father and winning a few extra hugs.

'Then I'm in for an adventure,' Danny said with a laugh, obviously not believing her.

'If I were you, I'd delve through the gumboots at the back door for some that might fit. We'll probably end up tracking through more mud at some point.' She'd take a shovel in case they lost footwear, but with their height gumboots were easier to retrieve.

'I'll join you shortly. Unless you need a hand getting the bike out?'

'No, I'm good. There doesn't appear to be anything preventing access there.' She still had to get that gas bottle before the day was out. Danny could give her a hand. More getting stuck and muddy and needing a hot shower. More getting close and—

Stop it. Go get the bike.

For all she knew, Danny mightn't want a repeat of earlier. She shouldn't either. She should be getting to know him better before thinking of stripping naked again. Her skin tingled at the thought of his fingers teasing her and his lips kissing trails all over her breasts. Mentally flapping her hand in front of her overheating face, she headed for the cool air outside. There was a time and place for everything, and this wasn't it for having repeat sex with Danny. Which was a huge shame. She grinned and hummed a tune as she collected her coat and gumboots, and the keys for the shed and bike. Danny would have to sit behind her, his thighs on either side of hers, hopefully his arms around her waist—though that wasn't necessary it would feel good.

The bike bumped over the lawn as Brooke drove towards the road, avoiding branches and other debris. 'The road's full of ruts,' she said over her shoulder to Danny—who *was* tucked in close to her back, and yes, he did have one arm around her waist. Oh, so cosy. She grinned like the proverbial cat with the cream.

'There's been a lot of water running across to the beach,' he said right beside her ear, his breath teasing her skin.

'Still is compared to normal. Hold on.' Revving the motor, Brooke negotiated a deep gouge and a small rise taking them onto the road. Turning left, she started along the road.

Nearly a kilometre on, just around a tight corner, they came to an abrupt halt. The hillside had come across the road and down into the sea fifty metres below. Massive trees were contained in the clay and rock, and over the road and down the bank to the tempestuous water.

'There's our answer,' Danny said as he swung a leg over the back of the bike and stood up in ankle-deep mud. 'We're not going any further today.'

Switching off the bike, Brooke surveyed the sight before her. He was right. Nothing or no one was getting over that slip in a hurry. 'It's going to take heavy equipment to shift that,' she agreed. 'I'm going to try and see what's on the other side.' She started for the slip and a large pine tree stuck on the side.

'Brooke, that's not a good idea. What if there's more hillside to come down? Or a boulder or two?'

She stared up the hill. 'I don't think that'll happen. It's clear above this. You can see the rock face now.'

'Yeah, and I don't want to be pulling your broken body off there if you're wrong. Don't do it.' Seemed he could be bossy when he chose.

But he might have a point. She didn't do standing back and waiting for help to arrive very easily though. Her motto was to get in and do it herself, and all she wanted to know was how bad this blockage was.

'I'll only be walking across.'

Danny's hand took hers in a gentle grip. 'Yes, and I'll only be holding my breath and wondering what would happen if you slipped and went over the edge into the sea.'

His look was serious and made her draw a breath.

'Fair enough. Anyway, even if I got across there's no knowing where the next slip is. I can't hear diggers at work so I'm picking they're working near the start of the road.'

'Is there anyone you can ring to find out what's happening?' He was still holding her hand.

She kept still, enjoying the warm, firm grip and the hot tingles on her skin. 'There's a local company that does work with diggers and bulldozers that is usually called in to help whenever something like this happens.

But I don't know the family personally so I'm not going to harass them when they're probably getting lots of calls while trying to get on with whatever needs doing.'

'Fair enough.' Danny didn't appear at all worried that he might be stuck here for a few days.

'When did you say you start at Nelson ED?'

'Monday afternoon.' A flicker of concern crossed his face. 'I'll give them a call tomorrow to let them know my situation, and I'll also find out about water taxis and buses then. It looks too rough for any boat to come into your bay today, but hopefully it'll have calmed down some by later tomorrow or Monday morning.'

'What about Mike? He might be able to sort out transport to Nelson for you.'

'I'll add him to the list of calls.'

She leaned her head to one side. 'You're obviously comfortable with how things are today.' It wasn't bothering her as she had all week for the road to be cleared enough to get out, and neither did she mind being here alone.

'Couldn't be better,' he said with a grin. 'I'm happy to be out of—' He stopped, drew a breath. 'Happy having some time without patients and emergencies to distract me.'

Once again he'd cut himself off from saying what he'd first intended. Interesting. There was more to this man than she was getting. But for now she wasn't pushing, which was so unlike her these days. It seemed she wanted to enjoy his company more than to be wary of him.

'Now that Lloyd's safely tucked up in a hospital bed, you mean?' She couldn't stop grinning right back at him. What was it about Danny that had her reacting in ways she thought she'd forgotten? She should be acting more cautiously, not ready to dive right in and make the most of him.

He started walking towards the edge of the road where it dropped away to the beach that was being pounded by an angry sea, his hand still wrapped around hers. 'There seems to be a lot of logs and trees heading this way.'

'They'll be from the Pelorus River. Most of the tree trunks on our beach come from there after even a small storm or high tides. Some locals cut them up for firewood.'

'Doesn't the salt cause rust in their fireboxes?'

'That's why my dad isn't a fan of driftwood for our fire. He's had to replace ours twice after the chimney split due to heavy rust.'

'Look at that sea. It's relentless.'

'The power of nature is amazing and frightening at times.' She admired the natural forces she saw here. The wind, tide and rain made changes large and small all the time. 'Let's hope we get a clear sky tonight and you can see the sky like you've never seen it before. Unless you live out in the back of beyond back home, that is.' She paused, got no answer, so continued, thinking he was definitely keeping quiet about his private life. Why? It was starting to grate. Was she being impatient? On a disgruntled sigh, she let it go. 'There are so many stars above us it's incredible. I love nothing more than to lie on the beach and just stare upwards.'

'I haven't had the opportunity to see that. But the chance of a clear sky tonight is nigh on impossible, surely?'

'You'll be surprised how quickly the clouds will clear

away, unless there's more bad weather to come, and when I checked earlier it seems we're done for now.' No one needed any more rain, not for weeks at least. There was water everywhere. Water. Of course. It was the first thing she should have thought of. 'I need to check the house tank and the supply pipe from up the hill.'

'Aren't you on a community system?'

He had to be a city man to ask that. 'No one out here is. We all collect our water from uphill streams or underground sources. Ours comes from underground, but the pipe is above ground and could've been damaged by falling trees.' It was always her father's first priority to check the water flow to their tanks after a storm or earthquake. She'd been distracted more than she'd realised. Her elbows hugged her sides as her body smiled. Who'd have thought that amidst the carnage and noise and mayhem of the past twenty-odd hours she'd have been distracted by a sexy man? Also a kind, understanding, gentle man. That said a lot about him. Or her life. Her feet were light on the ground as she headed to the bike. 'Let's head back.'

Danny climbed back on the bike, his arm again around her waist.

'No quick fix for this,' she said.

'I hadn't quite grasped the extent of the damage.' His sigh tickled her neck. 'I might be a day or two late getting back to my real life.'

'If the sea drops further I can launch Dad's boat and take you to Havelock rather than getting the taxi.'

'How will you get the boat out of the water on your own when you return?'

'There's a winch on the tractor.' But the water would

have to be calm or she'd be struggling to align the boat with the rollers on the trailer.

'I'll call the taxi if necessary.' He spoke in a don't-argue-with-me way.

Brooke grinned. 'Yes, boss.' Pressing the starter, she headed back to the house.

'Glad you understand,' he said close to her ear, his breath sending tendrils of heat over her neck.

'Um…would you mind checking the water system with me?' *Or shall we head inside and get warm together again?* 'If I find a break in one of the joins my hands aren't strong enough to put it back together. Especially when water is rushing through it.'

'Of course I'm coming with you.'

She softened some more towards Danny, let go some of the angst about how he dodged answering her questions in depth. He was so easy to get along with and didn't make a big deal about helping her. *Early days, Brooke, early days.* Besides, who said this encounter with Danny was going anywhere? A great bit of sex, some time together checking out the results of the storm, sharing soup and a drink, didn't add up to something deep and meaningful, or even the beginning of such. More likely, come tomorrow or Monday and they'd be saying, 'Bye, see you around.'

In the meantime, he was going to give her a hand.

'Thanks. First, I'll see if the water is coming through. We might not have to do anything else.'

Not so much as a trickle dripped from the outside tap. The pipe leading down from the water source sounded hollow when Brooke tapped it further along.

'Dad keeps a small backpack ready with wrenches and screwdrivers and replacement fittings. I'll go grab it.'

'Gumboots all right for this?' Danny asked.

'Maybe not. We're going over rocks and through a waterway that's higher than normal. Gummies won't have enough grip.'

Footwear changed, the pack on Danny's back, they set off, following the pipe up the hill. When it went under the road, Brooke led him across the other side where it was again visible. Every fifty metres or so, she tapped the pipe to see if it was still empty. As the climb got steeper, their feet slipped and slid on the wet ground, making the going slower.

'There.' Danny pointed to the other side of the racing stream. 'Is that what you're looking for?'

'Where?' Brooke followed the direction he was pointing at. One end of a black pipe was bobbing on the edge of the water. 'Got it. That's what we're after. Now to find the other end and see if we've still got the connection.' Thankful her father was always prepared and that there were five connectors in the pack, she began to step through the water, watching for unsteady rocks to avoid.

'There's the other end,' Danny called behind her. 'It's caught in a tree.'

Reaching the first piece, which was coming from further up the hill, Brooke lifted it and grunted with relief. 'This appears to be the only fault. Water's flowing fast. But it means reconnecting the joiner will be difficult.' She was glad Danny was with her.

'There's only half a connector on this end.' He dragged the pipe free and walked it up to her.

'There's a spare in the pack.' She reached for it,

touching his shoulder with her fingers as she caught the strap. Not that he'd have felt it with the heavy wet weather jacket he wore.

Danny turned and locked his eyes on her. 'You think?'

So he might have sensed her hand on his shoulder. Yes, she'd like some more time with him, but that didn't come in a pack. Time to be serious and stop wondering what could happen if she let her guard down some more. Not that it was anywhere near as high as usual.

'I know.'

'Damn.' His grin was infectious.

It went a way to lowering that guard further, and she grinned back. How great it would be to have a man to spend time with outside of work, to share meals and a bed, to talk about anything and everything with, and even argue sometimes. So far, she was enjoying Danny. But first impressions weren't always totally true. Brad had been a charmer and full of fun when they'd been getting together. No change from the boy she'd known on the family summer trips here when she was growing up. There'd been no inkling how he'd turn out. Same as her first boyfriend, all fun and excitement until he got what he wanted.

'Here.' She handed Danny the connector. 'Have you ever used one of these before?'

'Can't say I have.' He took it and pulled the two sections apart. Definitely not a country boy or he wouldn't have done that so abruptly.

'Careful. Don't lose the O-rings.'

'Sorry. Tell me what to do.'

Within minutes they had the pipe fixed and the lower section weighing heavily in Brooke's hand. 'I'll wait a few minutes to make sure the supply doesn't run out because of another break further up.' Hopefully there wasn't. She was ready to head home to the warmth. It was getting colder here under the trees showering them with water with every gust of wind. The afternoon was closing in and soon night would fall, lowering the temperature further.

'You know what you're doing, don't you?' Danny looked at her with something like admiration.

'Comes with growing up here. Dad made Saskia and me learn about this and many other things that kept the house running because we never knew when it could go wrong and being so far from town isn't always ideal.' She'd put extra effort into making sure she was *au fait* with the essentials in an attempt not to be sent away to boarding school every year, but her mother always won out on that one. 'Right, let's go home and get warm and dry.'

It wasn't so easy going down, with water and mud making traction harder than it had been on the way up, but finally they walked out of the bush at the edge of the road.

'That wasn't what I expected to be doing during my stay in the Sounds.' Danny laughed as he crossed the road and stepped off into mud. He sank up to his ankle, then his calf, and higher. 'Great.' He wrenched his leg hard and groaned as a loud popping sound reached Brooke.

'What's happened?' she asked.

His mouth was tight, his hands clenched on his thighs.

'Danny?' She reached him, keeping clear of where his leg was buried.

'I've wrenched my knee. It's a bit painful,' he gasped.

So he wouldn't be pulling his leg free, not easily anyway. 'Keep still and I'll try to scoop the mud away.'

'Get a trowel or spade.' His voice was strained.

'No, I'm doing it as fast as possible.' He was in pain and the sooner she freed him the better.

'You'll wreck your fingers doing it by hand.'

'Too bad.' Mud flew as she scraped around his trouser-covered leg.

Above her, Danny was alternately holding his breath and groaning.

'I'm getting there.'

Scoop, splat. Scoop, splat.

A fingernail tore. 'Is the pain only in your knee?'

'Yes.'

'One to ten? Which is it?'

'Five.'

Bad but bearable. If he was being honest. 'Right, there's your shoe. I'm going to try and free it without putting any pressure on your leg.'

'I'll try lifting it.'

'No, Danny. That'll only add to the pain level. We'll do it my way.' She already had most of the shoe exposed and began digging underneath with her fingers. Another nail broke. Time for a manicure when she got out of the bay. 'Right, here we go. No, wait. I'll remove more mud from in front of your foot so you don't have to bend your knee.'

He huffed out a breath. 'Glad you're thinking clearly. I don't think I can bend it at the moment. Wonder if I've dislocated the kneecap again.'

'You've done this before?' Using a flat rock, she

scraped a narrow trough from the foot to the top of the ground.

'Unfortunately, yes, a few years back. But it's usually a quick fix, and I'll soon be fully mobile.'

'Though in some pain.' She'd seen patients with dislocated knees and kneecaps. The kneecap was a better option, easier to get moving after it was put back in place, but painful discomfort came with that.

'I have painkillers.'

'I know, remember?'

'Of course. Lloyd.'

'What are they for?'

'In case something like this happens.'

That was all she was going to find out. He certainly didn't talk about himself. Did that mean the pills were his, not in case someone else needed them? If she got into questions he might head back to the other house without her. Once he could walk, that was.

'After we've got your foot free I'll get the bike to take you down to the house.'

He shook his head. 'I'll take a look at it before you do that. It might be as easy as straightening my leg to fix it and then I'll be able to hobble across the lawn.'

'I've seen that done a couple of times.' She'd also seen the pain that happened as the cap moved back into place. 'I agree the sooner we do that the better off you'll be.' She sat back on her haunches, ignoring the cold where her trousers were now wet through. 'Let's get you unstuck. I'll lift your leg. You try to remain loose and relaxed.'

He touched her shoulder, gave her a gentle squeeze. 'I'm ready. Get on with it.'

Placing her hands palm up under his lower leg, she

counted, 'One, two, three.' Pushing firmly without jerking, she raised his leg, bringing his foot free.

'That was nice,' Danny grunted. 'Right, can I put an arm around you for balance while I straighten my leg?'

'Don't you want to take a look to make sure it is dislocated first?'

'I'd have to drop my jeans and that wouldn't be easy standing on one leg.'

'Fair enough.' He seemed to know what he was doing. Brooke moved beside him, wound an arm around his waist.

His fingers were tense as they wrapped over her shoulder. 'Here we go.' Without any hesitation Danny straightened his leg. The knee gave a loud popping sound. Danny groaned louder, his fingers digging into her shoulder.

The knee popping suggested he'd fixed the problem, but she'd still check his knee once they were inside. 'You need to elevate your leg and put ice around it.'

'True,' he muttered through a stalled breath.

'Let's go to my place. It's closer. There's ice and chicken casserole in the freezer, and I'll make you a drink to warm you up.'

'I'm all for that. Could you get my toilet bag for me? I put the painkillers back in it.'

'No problem.'

He took a step, paused. 'Actually, no, I'll get it.'

'You're going to walk an extra hundred metres when I can get your bag?' What was he so reticent about her seeing? 'Worried I might go through your bag?' Tempting as it was, she wouldn't.

'Of course not,' he said hurriedly.

Too quick? Her stomach clenched. She wanted to

believe he wasn't hiding anything, but history taught her differently.

'Would you prefer to go to the other house?' she asked sharply.

'I'm being an idiot. Sorry.' He looked repentant, as if he finally understood he'd upset her.

'It really doesn't matter which house we go to. I'm not leaving you on your own.'

Danny grimaced. He'd walked into that one. Too eager to hide his identity, he'd suddenly worried Brooke might open his toilet bag to get the pill bottle and read his name on the label—Daniel Collins. She might recognise it. Or she mightn't, but she could look him up on the internet.

Or it was possible she'd do neither, and carry on treating him as she'd been doing so far. Why was it so hard to accept Brooke might be unfazed by who he might be and liked who she'd met? He wasn't used to it. That was why. There were times when he met a woman and the reaction was similar to Brooke's, until they learned more about him. Right now the last thing he wanted was Brooke changing towards him. This could only last until they were away from here, maybe for a while longer, but it would come to an end and, more than anything, he'd like to have made some inroads with her, so she knew he was more than that public image.

'Hello, Danny? You listening?'

To trust or not to trust? The million-dollar question. Breathe in, hold, breathe out. He looked at Brooke, drank in the genuine concern for him in her eyes and sighed. Sometimes he just had to take a chance.

'I'd love to doss down at your place, and yes, if you'd get my bag that'd be great.'

'That wasn't so hard, was it?' she said with a smile.

His heart lightened. *If only you knew.* But for once he was glad he was risking everything. Brooke could prove to be worth it.

'Want to hobble down to your house with me?'

Those golden-green eyes lightened and her smile grew as she took a firmer hold around his waist. 'Best invitation I've had all day.'

'Doesn't say much for your day then,' he said through the pain radiating out from his knee. It would soon improve enough to be able to move more freely. Last time he'd been about to tee off for a friendly match between club mates when someone shouted a warning about a snake coming onto the ground. He'd spun around without moving his right leg and pop went the kneecap. It hadn't taken long to recover fully, and this would be the same. The pain was annoying more than anything.

'Anything else I can grab while I'm at it? Those clothes look a sight.'

His wet jeans clung to him, making him shiver. On the plus side, that might help with any swelling. 'My overnight bag's in the bedroom with everything I need, except my phone, which should be on the table.'

He hobbled up the step to Brooke's back door where, to his embarrassment, she insisted he sit while she knelt to remove his shoes. He held his breath and pretended this was a routine medical situation. Which in most people's eyes it was. Should be in his, but that was Brooke down there, and while she was only doing what she probably did many times in her work, he didn't like being the recipient for some inexplicable reason. She was getting to him in the strangest ways, getting under his skin little by little.

Standing up, Brooke said, 'There's a towel in the bathroom cupboard and plenty of hot water if you want a shower while I get your gear. If you think you can manage by yourself, that is.'

'Can't be too hard.'

That could not be disappointment widening her eyes. Did she want to get into the shower with him? Hold him steady? When he had a wall to lean against? Did she want to wash his back? His gut tightened, quickly followed by his groin. *Steady, Danny boy. Don't rush things.* This was a rush? He wasn't going nearly as fast as earlier. That'd been whizz-bang, great sex all over in no time at all. Though the memories were vivid, and likely to remain so for a long time.

Stepping off the porch, Brooke said over her shoulder, 'Back in a minute. Make yourself at home.'

'Brooke...' Danny called softly.

She spun around to stare at him. 'Yes?'

'Thanks for helping me. You're a legend.' He faltered to a stop. So much for going slowly. Next thing he knew, she'd be using that to get to him even further.

'As if I wouldn't look out for you. Or anyone in the same situation.'

'It's what you do. I know that, but still...' He shrugged.

That's not disappointment beating in my chest because you accepted my comment as though it was nothing out of the ordinary.

If only she knew. He didn't want her to know. Not yet, when he was happy enjoying her company without looking over his shoulder. Hard to believe they'd only met that morning. Everything could, most likely would, come to an abrupt end when she learned who he was. But that was not happening. Not today. Or tomorrow. Having some uninhibited fun with this wonderful woman was holding him back from opening up.

He *was* getting stirred up in a hurry. There was a lot of ground to cover before he could even let words like that enter his mind. Lots of ground.

'Go get out of those wet clothes, will you?' Brooke sounded impatient.

Fair enough. His feet felt as though they were stuck to the deck. Even his bad knee felt heavier than it should. 'On my way.'

When I can move.

'You want a hand?'

'No, thanks.' Taking a tentative step, he reached the door, grateful his legs were obeying his messed-up mind. Removing his jacket, he slung it on a hook by the door and hobbled inside, where the warmth hit him, making his wet clothes cumbersome. His skin tingled as bumps rose. Where was the bathroom? Down the hall he found what he was looking for. Shucking his shirt, he tried to remove his jeans, but being wet they clung to his skin. Getting his injured knee out was going to be fun.

'Let me do that.' Brooke stood in the doorway.

'Thought you'd gone to get my gear.' His gaze dropped. His bag swung from her hand. 'Have I been that long getting absolutely nowhere?' All he'd done was enter the house and get half undressed. When had he become such a geriatric? She'd be thinking he was useless.

'It's not like I don't know my way around Mike's house.' Her laugh lifted his suddenly despondent spirits. 'Sit on the edge of the bath so I can roll your jeans off without hurting too much.'

'Anyone ever tell you you're bossy?'

'My sister does all the time. She's the oldest and thinks she still holds the boss card. It's been my life mission to show her she's wrong.'

Whip.

His leg was free with hardly a stab of pain.

'There. I'll leave you to get showered.' Standing up, Brooke glanced at him, and her smile wavered. 'Unless you need me.'

Don't look below my waist. I need you, all right. Nothing to do with getting warm and clean, and all to do with letting go and enjoying you and giving you something back for making me feel this way.

'Are you any good at washing backs?'

'I could be.' It wasn't a whisper, but neither did Brooke yell. 'Do you think that would be wise, given your—' Her gaze dropped, and her mouth opened, turned into a big smile. 'We have to be careful.'

'We'll manage.' While their minds were still working, but for how long was anyone's guess. His being that it would be many minutes.

Then Brooke went all serious on him. 'Are you sure? I'd hate to bump that knee.'

'Do I look uncertain?' he asked with a cheeky grin.

'I guess not.' Her fingers were already working at the buttons of her shirt. Then she stopped.

Another doubt coming up?

She crossed to turn the shower on. Then she got towels off a shelf. Finally she went back to stripping out of her clothes.

The room warmed up fast. Nothing to do with the

steam beginning to rise from the shower. All to do with the sight unfolding before him. If he hadn't been hard before, he certainly was now. So much he barely felt his knee as he moved to the shower and stepped under the water, closing his eyes to take a moment to settle the pounding under his ribs.

Soft circling movements on his back. Brooke had slipped behind him as he let the water pummel his face. Her hands were firm yet gentle as she caressed him. So much for quieting his heart. She was winding him so tight he might burst apart. Turning carefully, Danny reached for Brooke and leaned in to kiss her. Ignoring the painful reminders to go easy coming from his knee, he leaned back enough to touch her breasts, leaned close and kissed them, drawing her nipple into his mouth to run his tongue over the tip.

Above him, Brooke gasped, and her hands dug into his backside to pull him closer. His arousal pressed hard against her stomach. He had to have her. If she was ready. He'd make her ready. When his finger found her need, she cried out. Then encased him in her hand, rubbing him hard, taking his breath away, turning him tighter than ever.

'Brooke,' he gasped against her breast. 'Slow down. I can't take much more. I want to make you come first.'

Using the shower wall as leverage, she lifted up and hooked her legs around his waist. 'Now, Danny. Right now,' she groaned by his ear. 'Please.'

Happy to oblige, he pushed up into her. Once, then again, and again, until she cried out and tightened around him. His heart belted against his ribs. His mind was blank apart from the heat and relief rushing through his body. His hands held Brooke's backside, feeling her quivering as she came and came. Then he lost all control and joined her in wonder.

CHAPTER SIX

BROOKE DRIED HER HAIR, staring at the smile on her lips. No way could she stop her mouth beaming. Her whole body was limp, happy, sated. Danny was one heck of a lover. He'd brought her to a peak in an instant and delivered on his promise fast and wonderfully.

They'd had sex that morning. Now they'd made love. It didn't mean they were in love, but what they'd shared was more than a rip-your-clothes-off-and-get-it-together act. There'd been a tenderness amidst the heat and speed of that moment that she couldn't describe other than she'd felt beyond wanted and free, beyond having fun to something deeper. Yeah, and she had ripped her clothes off.

Of course she was overreacting and jumping in too fast. A day ago she hadn't known Danny. Still didn't really. Like Danny who? Did it matter? Only if there was an ominous reason for him not saying. She could ask, but for once she didn't want to spoil what was going on between them. She wanted to enjoy the rest of the weekend and see where it led. That seemed perfect, and what could be better than perfect?

'Knock, knock. Did you mention ice in the freezer?'

Danny stood lopsidedly, taking the pressure off his injured leg.

'I'll get it, and the casserole.'

'How many meals did your mother leave for you?'

'Plenty. She loves cooking. There's cake and some desserts too.' These days her mother tried to make up for the past hurt by doing lots of loving things for her. Brooke had finally explained to her how much her mother's approach to certain situations took away Brooke's control. Her mum had apologised profusely, and said she finally understood her daughter's stance. Brooke had forgiven her in an instant. Grudges were a waste of energy and, no matter what, she was her mother.

'I don't need those.' Danny rubbed his stomach. 'As tempting as they sound.'

'You like to keep fit?'

He nodded. 'I run a lot, though that's going to take a rest for a little while. I also work out at the gym. It's what I've always done. I see too many unhealthy people through work to want to give keeping fit a miss.'

'Know what you mean. Though I'm not a fitness addict, I do run and cycle.'

'It shows. You look good.'

She blushed, something that was happening too often today. 'Thanks.'

'You're not used to compliments.'

'Can't say I am.' There wasn't anyone to give them out. No one important, any rate. 'It's been a while,' she said in a strong voice. It might be true but she wasn't looking for sympathy. She probably shouldn't have said it, but it was just another effect Danny was having on her—she was talking too much. 'I'll get the ice while you find somewhere to make yourself comfortable.'

She all but danced out to the laundry where the freezer stood. This whole scenario was so bizarre it was funny. Interesting and exhilarating. Then she looked out of the window and her smile faded. Old Man Duggan's house was destroyed enough to suggest he probably wouldn't be moving back. It would take at least a year to clear away the wreckage and get planning permission for a new house, to draw up plans and have it built. He would likely end up in a retirement home, a place he'd often said he never wanted to go. Her heart broke for him. She loved the old man. He was like a second granddad to her, hence calling him Old Man Duggan.

'Here you go,' she said, handing the ice to Danny, who'd claimed the couch to sit on with his legs up.

His knee was red and swollen, yet he wasn't having too much trouble moving it. 'It's not bad,' he affirmed. 'I'll strap it later.'

Winding the ice bag around Danny's knee, Brooke tried not to think too much about his firm muscles and how wonderful it'd felt wrapping her legs around his waist in the shower. It seemed she'd flipped a switch and her life was now exciting and fast filling with all sorts of possibilities. She hadn't realised just how much she was missing having a man in her life. She taped the bag in place.

'Hello? Where have you gone?' Danny tapped her shoulder. 'You have a habit of going off somewhere I can't follow.'

Brooke crossed to sit on a lounge chair. 'I don't mean to.' It wasn't something she usually did, but the more time she spent with Danny the more she was comparing her previous relationships and seeing him for the great guy she hoped he really was. She shook her head. 'I'm doing it again, aren't I?'

He laughed, apparently unfazed by her lack of attention. 'No problem. It's not something I'm used to, that's all.'

'Used to women swooning at your knees, are you?' she said with a chuckle.

His laughter died away, and for a moment he said nothing. Until—'I like genuine women, and you certainly seem to be that. I can't believe we've only just met. I feel as though I've known you far longer.'

Talk about upfront—for once. 'The circumstances have been demanding and exceptional.'

The laughter returned. 'That explains it. Your normal first date is at a café for a coffee and muffin.'

Brooke relaxed. She didn't like it when he went all serious. 'More like a pub and a wine.'

'I'll take note of that.'

He was going to ask her out? On her thighs, her fingers were doing a little dance. Bring it on.

Danny fed more wood into the firebox, biting down on the sharp stab of pain from his knee. Time for more painkillers. Brooke was snoozing in her chair, the day having finally caught up with her.

They'd eaten dinner sitting here in the warm glow from the fire, and he'd cleaned up the kitchen afterwards despite Brooke saying he should take it easy. She didn't know him well enough to realise he wasn't one for sitting around even when injured, and today's injury was minor.

A little snore reached him and he wanted to run his hand over her silky hair, to feel her warmth on his skin, to be close. Danny returned to the couch. He should wake her and insist she go to bed, but it was great sitting here watching her. She was lovely. He was so sure of that he could almost feel the truth slipping off his tongue between them as he explained who he was and why he tried to downplay the past so hard. One day wasn't enough to be certain she would remain so accepting of who he presented himself to be.

It wasn't as though he was being dishonest. He *was* a medical intern who revelled in the work he did, because he liked to help people and because he enjoyed the medical puzzles that presented themselves with every patient. Yes, he'd been an avid sportsman and fitness freak. He'd also always been fascinated with medicine after listening to his grandfather tell him stories from his private practice. He'd revelled in his ability to outplay other golfing champions. He also enjoyed putting people back together both physically and mentally after they'd copped one of life's arrows.

In that way he was luckier than some. His golf career had crashed and burned, and for a while it had been hard to get back on his feet and face the future. His family had rallied around him, giving him time and encouragement to get it right. His body had recovered quicker than his mind, but he'd made it because he did believe in himself, did understand he could do well in whatever field he chose to work in.

Medicine was interesting, exciting, and hard on the heart at times. Patients didn't always make it out of the front door of the hospital. That sucked. But it was unavoidable. He did his absolute best to be there for them and their families. He had no regrets about his career choice, and sometimes even admitted to himself that it might have been for the best he'd had to stop playing golf. He'd been getting too big for his boots. Hard not to when the television crews were always tracking him, when women were all but begging to be his next bed partner. It was his family who'd kept him mostly on track. He owed them for that.

If only he could find a woman who'd be the perfect match, who'd support him without looking for what she wanted from his past, his future, his bank account. Sure, sharing a home and family was his dream, but could he please have that without all the nonsense?

His gaze never left Brooke for a moment. Her breasts rose and fell gently under her cream angora jersey. Her hair fell across one side of her face, highlighting her fine bone structure. She was lovely, heart-warming. There'd been concern in her eyes as she'd tried to rescue her neighbour, and when she'd dug his foot out of the mud so he didn't have to yank it free, causing added pain. Not that he wouldn't have done so if he'd been on his own.

Yes, he liked Brooke Williams a lot already. Already, as in he hoped to spend more time with her. She hadn't backed away when he'd said he'd remember she liked going to the pub for a wine. Nor had she leapt in and demanded an instant invitation. This was a special time for him, and he was afraid to ruin it by bringing in the past. Then again, he might wreck any chance with her if he didn't fill her in soon.

'You're staring,' Brooke murmured as she straightened her legs out from under that firm, sensual backside he'd held in the shower. 'How long have I been asleep?'

'About thirty minutes.'

She glanced at the wall clock. 'Might as well hit the

sack and get some real sleep. Do you want a bed or are you happy staying on the couch?'

'I'd prefer a bed, so I'll head over to Mike's.'

'There are beds made up here.' She paused, looked at him with a hint of a smile. 'Or you could share mine and we'd be warm together.'

Danny was already getting warmer and he hadn't moved. The idea of curling up with Brooke was perfect, making him smile like a kid in the lolly shop. 'Yes, please.'

She blinked and stared at him some more. 'You're sure?'

What had brought on that sudden doubt?

'If you're changing your mind I won't get upset.'

'Not at all. This is quite unexpected, that's all. I don't usually get so close to a man I've only just met.'

Somehow that didn't surprise him, despite how fast they'd torn each other's clothes off that morning. She seemed too contained to be anything but cautious with a stranger. Yet she hadn't been like that with him, which made him soften more towards her and want to protect her. Could be that she didn't think of him as a stranger.

'You can still say no to sharing your bed.'

Her hair flicked around her head as she shook it. 'I'm looking forward to it. Come on, let's move. Unless it's too early for you. It's barely past nine.'

'Feels more like midnight. It's been a day and a half for real.' He stood up slowly, favouring his knee. Brooke's fingers had been so gentle as she'd wound the crepe bandage round his leg he'd almost enjoyed the process.

Stripping down to his underpants, Danny slid between the sheets and studied the photos on the wall.

One was of an older couple and Brooke with another woman. The sister she'd mentioned? And her parents? In another a much younger Brooke was laughing at the camera as she held up a large fish, which he didn't recognise, with both hands. Brooke's face was split with a grin and laughter lit up her eyes. He'd long forgotten what it was like to feel so relaxed; he was always wary and distrustful of people's motives. Strange he didn't feel that way with Brooke. He almost had to remind himself to be careful.

She entered the bedroom, dressed in winter pyjamas that wouldn't have won a glamour award and made her look soft and cuddly. 'That's a snapper.' She tapped the photo he'd been looking at. 'A big one. Eighteen kilos.'

'You wound it in?' That would take some effort if it fought.

'Every metre of the way. I wasn't letting Dad take over, though he was itching to. Mostly afraid I'd lose it. Best fish I've ever eaten.' Her face reflected the same laughing smile she'd worn in the photo.

'I've never done much fishing. I might have to give it a go while I'm here.'

Slipping in beside him, she rolled onto her side and looked at him with interest. And puzzlement.

He could see she was tossing up questions, wondering which to ask. Instead of cutting her off, he held his breath and waited, hoping it wasn't going to be something he'd have to dodge.

'How long do you think you'll be in the country?'

So far he was safe. 'I'm here until the end of the year, when I'll return to the hospital in Melbourne where I did my junior training.'

'Is that where you want to specialise?'

'It seems appropriate to carry on there. I'm not sure where I'll go once I'm qualified. It'll depend on where I get a job.'

'You might come back to New Zealand.'

'I might.' At the moment he didn't want to leave at all. Didn't want to go to Nelson yet either. Being with Brooke was tantamount to being in paradise.

'I'm guessing since you haven't done much fishing you haven't lived on the coast?' She was clever. That was a tactful way of asking where he grew up.

'I grew up in Ballarat, well north of Melbourne.' Under the sheet, Danny's hands clenched. He was being honest. Too damned honest. What was he thinking? Getting to know Brooke better didn't have to mean talking about himself. Not yet. Not while he could relax and have some fun without waiting for the truth to hit.

'It's okay. I won't tell anyone,' she teased with a mix of fun and concern in her voice. 'Your secret's safe with me.'

Loosening his fingers, he reached for her and pulled her into a body-length hug, an arm over her waist, thighs pressing against hers, shins feeling her toes, chest to breasts.

It wasn't a secret as such, more a way of having some freedom for a little while. He definitely would talk to her about his past one day—if they saw more of each other once he left here. But not today. Nor tomorrow. The thought of seeing recognition dawn in those beautiful eyes made him tired and sad. There was a chance she wouldn't have a clue who Daniel Collins was, but past experience told him that it wouldn't take long for her to look him up. He'd tell her everything, but reality was clearer when seen in the media. Damn, he was bitter. How about giving Brooke a chance? It was early days, and there was a possibility what they'd started could come to more.

'Your turn to spacewalk?' Her voice was muffled by his neck, where she'd placed a light kiss.

'I'm right here with you.' He reached across to switch off the light and snuggled down with Brooke, ignoring the painful twinges in his knee. Nothing was going to get in the way of this moment. Or the next ones. His mouth sought hers, covered her lips, and he began kissing her, slowly, tenderly. A kiss like no other. Brooke did that to him. She'd changed him already. Was this love at first sight? No, he wasn't in love. But he might be falling into it.

His kiss deepened, and Brooke responded with an intensity of her own.

And he fell a little bit more.

It might have been too cloudy to view the stars above as Brooke had suggested, but right now there were stars aplenty in his head. And his heart.

'In my mind I keep hearing Lloyd calling for Jean.' Brooke placed a plate of toast on the table. 'I'm going to look for some photos for him this morning.'

'Don't you think it'll be too dangerous to go inside that house?'

'I'm hoping nothing much has changed overnight. If there's more damage I'll rethink the idea, but at the moment I'm going in.' She'd be careful—and fast. She knew where there'd likely be some framed pictures. 'It'll be a snatch and grab.'

Danny said, 'I'm not missing out on the raid.' He

wasn't smiling or laughing; he was serious. He was that kind of guy.

He hadn't baulked about helping her yesterday and, apart from querying the safety factor, he hadn't now. In her mind that made him a keeper. First tick to becoming one anyway. 'Thanks,' she said. 'But only if you're not going to mess with that knee.'

'The knee's good.'

'So that wasn't a groan of pain when you got out of bed?'

'You would prefer me to be a wimp?' he asked with a little smile tipping those erotic lips upward.

'Nothing wimpy about you so far.' Danny had been hard as rock when they'd made love during the night. A generous lover, he gave more than he took, making certain she was ready and willing. Except he'd have had to be deaf, blind and dumb not to know when she was ready, all but begging for release.

'Are you going to start clearing your backyard today?'

Blowing on her coffee, she watched as he slathered butter on his toast, remembering those fingers on her body. She blew harder on the coffee. 'Maybe.'

His head came up and he locked his gaze on her. 'Maybe?'

Her cheeks heated. 'We'll see.'

We might have better things to do.

When Brooke went outside she heard a digger working on the road. 'Sounds like the road might be open later today,' she called to Danny.

'I'm quite happy being stuck here for another day.'

'You're due at the ED tomorrow afternoon.'

'I've got a good excuse not to be. I don't usually try

to get out of turning up for work. It's only that I'm so relaxed I don't want to leave.'

She knew what he meant. For her, it wouldn't be quite the same when he did head away. 'Do you think you'll be able to drive with your bung knee?'

'It's improving all the time, and tomorrow's a while away. I'll see how it is then.'

'I can drive you to Nelson if need be.' A three-hour round trip wouldn't be a problem, especially spending half of it with Danny.

'Thanks for the offer, but hopefully I'll be fine because I'll need my car. It's also got all my worldly goods in the back. As in clothes, books and laptop.'

Which would be easy enough to transfer to her car, but Danny seemed determined to drive himself. She doubted he'd do it if his knee wasn't up to it, though he might not be insured if he had an accident. His fault or not.

'Insurance?'

He looked away. 'I can cover it.'

She'd mentioned insurance, nothing about his wealth or lack of. Her eyes cruised over his wet weather jacket and trendy trekking trousers, down to a pair of fashionable walking shoes. No lack of funds there. A glance next door at the latest model four-wheel drive vehicle parked outside Mike's house backed her thoughts. It made her second-hand wagon look worn-out when it was barely five years old. It was solid, reliable and went like a cut cat when she was out on the open road. What more did she need?

'I'll get the gas bottle while I'm out here.' She'd never got around to it yesterday, what with everything else going on.

'Let me do that.' Danny was already striding unevenly for the shed.

The tank was heavy, and weight was the last thing he needed to put on his knee. About to say so, she stopped. He wouldn't like her insisting she carry the tank. He seemed to be a man who helped women and wouldn't step back for any reason. She wasn't ready to upset him by demanding he back off when they were getting along so well. Besides, it was great having a man taking care of her. She could get to like it. She wouldn't mention her aching bruises. He might get too protective.

'Here's the key.'

Danny was back within minutes, the tank swinging from his hand as if it was light as a football. 'I'll put it on the porch, shall I?'

'That's fine.' At least she wouldn't have to go out to the shed in the dark now if it ran out during the evening.

Brooke headed for the house next door, or what was left of it. Without the rain and wind buffeting her, she could see how bad the damage was. The boulder that hit the back wall was wedged firmly between the doors to the kitchen and laundry. The wall where she'd been going to climb through the window now leaned at a precarious angle.

'Looks worse today.'

'It does.'

She jumped. She hadn't heard Danny coming closer.

He laid his hand over her shoulder to draw her near. 'Sorry. I should've been puddle jumping and then you'd have heard me approaching.'

For a brief moment she snuggled closer, enjoying his strength. It felt solid, reliable, with a sense of safety and comfort. 'Let's check the front door, see if there's any change.'

'If it's too dangerous, please don't go in.' Danny's arm was still around her shoulders, keeping her with him as they made their way through the debris. 'I understand it's important to you to find some photos, but your safety has to come first.'

Her heart melted a little bit. Whether he was being friendly and caring or he really was concerned for her, it didn't matter. It sounded great and it was something she'd needed to hear from a special person for a while. Danny mightn't be her man, or so special she couldn't live without him, but he was getting further and further under her skin every minute. Waving him off tomorrow would be a wrench. If only she could go ask the digger driver to stop what he was doing and go move another slip further out. But the day would still arrive when Danny left.

'Lloyd wouldn't forgive me if I got hurt trying to help him.'

'No, he wouldn't.' Danny hugged her before going around to the front of the house. As though they were both used to being together and getting on with whatever called.

Joining him, hands on hips, she stared at the gap they'd come through yesterday. 'This doesn't appear to have moved at all.'

Stepping onto the wobbly deck, Danny peered inside. 'Looks pretty much the same at it was.' He moved inside.

Brooke followed. 'You don't need to be in here. I know what I'm looking for.'

She worked her way over the muddy floor. The bookcase had toppled over so books lay on the floor, ruined. As were the first three photos she found. Her heart sinking, she kept searching. 'Yes—' she sighed as she lifted a frame from the couch '—Jean and Lloyd on the beach.'

'Here's another one.' Danny passed her a silver frame.

'Their last wedding anniversary, on a cruise down Australia's east coast.' The building creaked, sending shivers down Brooke's spine. 'Two's good. Let's get out of here.'

'What about clothes for Lloyd?'

Along the hallway, one wall was on a slant and a panel ceiling had fallen to the floor. 'His bedroom's past that buckled patch of wall. Think I'll give it a miss.'

'Wise decision.' Danny turned for the front door. 'Let's get out of here.' So he wasn't comfortable either.

'Next stop the bike shed. We'll see how that digger driver's getting on.' It was always good to know what the options were. One never knew what might happen, especially after the storm they'd been through. The hills were unstable, and the roads would have been undermined by all the water still pouring down. As much as she'd like Danny stuck here a few more days, getting caught in another slip wasn't an option they needed to deal with.

Slip, slide, all the way to the shed, and Brooke was out of breath as she struggled to stay on her feet. 'Who needs to go for a run when I can walk around the yard all day?'

Danny grimaced as he lifted his injured leg free of a puddle of mud. 'Should've worn those boots you offered.'

'I do know what I'm talking about sometimes.'

'I'll remember that,' he muttered as he raised the shed door for her.

Brooke drove the bike forward and waited for Danny to climb on behind and wrap an arm around her. They had a routine going. Were they falling into sync too fast? Possibly, but it was fun.

Rounding the corner, Brooke brought the bike to a halt well away from the slip, where a digger was moving bucket-loads of clay and rotten rock onto one of two trucks lined up.

A driver spotted them and sauntered over. 'Morning. Bit of a mess, eh?'

'Worst storm I've been in out here. My family has a bach in the next bay,' Brooke explained. 'What's it like before here?'

'Three massive slips, which we've managed to clear enough so essential traffic can get through. There's also metre-deep mud covering about half a kilometre of road that's being cleared as we speak. A narrow track was made for us to get through, but you wouldn't want to be taking a car along there yet.'

Danny asked, 'How long before the road's passable? I'm hoping to get out first thing tomorrow.'

'You'll be right, mate. The guys reckon they'll have it cleared by tonight.'

Brooke swallowed her disappointment. Danny had to leave. But for once she wanted to be difficult and keep him here. *Toughen up, woman.* Danny had a life. So did she. If he was as keen as she was, they'd make it work. Only not for the next few days.

They got back on the bike and returned to the house.

'Is there a trailer we can use to cart away those branches?' Danny asked as he gazed around the yard.

'Or should we stack them somewhere for firewood?' He started wandering towards a broken tree, totally disregarding his knee.

'You're okay with the pain level?' It was as though he'd learned to cope with pain before.

'It's not bad.' He lifted a heavy clay pot that had rolled down from the shed and winced as he straightened.

'How come you already had painkillers in your bag?' she asked.

Lowering the pot back on the stand it had fallen off, he looked around then over to her. 'I injured my shoulder years ago and sometimes I get a few niggles, especially when I've been sitting too long.'

'How did you do that?'

'Slammed into some concrete. Now, what do you think? Stack the bigger pieces by the woodshed, or put them on the trailer?'

'Firewood's always useful.' She got it. Shut up and don't ask any more. Well, tough. 'Did you fall off a bike or something?'

'No, I dived into a swimming pool badly.' He didn't even glance her way. 'Now, are we doing this?'

'Yes,' she snapped. Why he didn't like talking about something that didn't sound like a major catastrophe was beyond her. More than annoying. More like infuriating. Was she expecting too much too soon? Could be. A deep breath didn't help her relax any, so she grabbed a shovel to dig mud away from the trees.

He banged a heavy branch against the shed. How he managed to drag it through the mud without putting pressure on his knee was beyond her. But he was a man, and from her experience they did like to prove they weren't wimps. From what she'd seen so far, Danny got on with whatever had to be done, and didn't try to find an excuse not to do so. Her kind of man—if he didn't keep major secrets from her in the future.

Spinning around, Brooke stomped over to another fallen branch, trying to ignore the sudden thumping going on in her chest. *Her kind of man.* What planet was she on? She didn't have a type. Sure she did. Strong and gentle, serious and fun, kind and sexy. Definitely sexy and generous in that department. *Tick, tick, tick, tick, tick, tick and tick.* So—her kind of man.

How could she think so when she was worried about his caution? Because her pulse had raced pretty much all the time since she'd met him and went crazy when they kissed and made love. Because she felt safe around him. Because…because of a hundred reasons. *Scary.* Last time she'd fallen in love it had all turned to trouble, so much so that she had come to enjoy living on her own, being in charge of her choices about everything. That was something she'd find hard to give up.

Getting ahead of yourself, Brooke.

She sure was. It was exciting and frightening. And possibly a total mistake. How could she trust Danny when she had this sense deep inside of being kept in the dark? He was probably having fun and wasn't thinking past when he drove out of here tomorrow morning. He certainly wasn't talking non-stop about his past or even his future, which most guys she'd dated recently seemed to do. They came with an agenda that included saying what they wanted for the future and why couldn't she see they were right for her. Was she getting too used to doing things her way now? Was she looking for trouble because she couldn't let go the past hurts?

She did want to find a man to love and make a life with. But, whoever it was, he would have to accept she wasn't a pushover. Glancing at Danny, air stalled in her lungs. So far he was looking better and better by the hour. She hadn't had such amazing sex in forever, or enjoyed sitting around talking or not, sharing a meal and a whisky so much. She was relaxed with him, wasn't looking for trouble. He was something else.

'Coffee and muffins on the front deck. Who'd have believed it after yesterday?' Danny stretched his legs out as he looked over the lawn, running down to the beach where driftwood had piled up haphazardly. This place was magical, despite showing how rough it could be. There had been beauty in the storm too, though it'd been worrying once the hills started sliding down.

'A normal day in paradise,' Brooke said. 'In summer we get severe storms as well as stunning hot, cloudless and windless weeks on end.'

'I hope to be here for some of those.' Sitting on this particular deck with this particular woman.

'Thought you said you'd be back in Melbourne by then.'

She didn't miss a trick. 'I might be able to drag out my start date over there for a little longer.' If he put in for a change now. To be fair, which he usually tried to be, hospitals were always crying out for staff over the summer break, and him wanting to have an extra couple of weeks off before turning up might be a problem. If he and Brooke were still getting along as well as they'd started out, he'd look into it. 'Do you spend Christmas and New Year here?'

'I come back and forth, depending on my roster. Next

summer I'm due to have two weeks off since I've stood in for everyone else the last two years.'

Why didn't that surprise him? From what he'd seen so far, she was kind and generous.

'Your whole family comes here?'

'It depends on what Saskia has on, and who she's with, but Mum and Dad are always here. No exception. They spend more time together these days, now Dad's no longer working. Does your family do joint holidays?'

'Not often now. My parents like to go over to Wales to stay with Mum's sister. Mum's Welsh and met Dad when he was over there on a golfing trip.' Oh, oh. Mentioning golf not clever. Move on. Fast. 'My brother's married and lives in Vancouver.'

'So golf is a family pastime?'

Serve him right for mentioning how he'd first done in his knee. Golf and Daniel Collins were synonymous. All Brooke had to do was look up either and she'd learn all about him. No, not all. There was the part of him that thrived on becoming a doctor, and another that wanted nothing more than to fall in love with a woman who accepted him for all his faults and wealth without making demands on him to change. That was not recorded on any website or in any interview.

'Dad and I play the occasional game.'

'Who's the best?' Brooke was grinning. She really had no idea. Thank goodness.

'Me, of course.'

'You'd say that anyway, wouldn't you?'

'Yep.' Because it was true, and because when she did find out she couldn't say he'd lied. 'You ever given golf a go?'

Laughter filled the quiet. 'Once. I was hopeless. I

have more chance of winning millions in a lottery than coordinating a club with a ball, let alone getting the ball in the air.'

'Not many people can on their first attempt.' He'd been lucky. He really had. 'If you had those millions, what would you do with them?' He was on a roll, wanting to learn how she might react to his situation.

'Get a newer car and change my carpet.' She grinned. 'Naturally I'd share with my family. Otherwise—' she shrugged '—I really have no idea. Of course I'd spend more, have some fun, but it seems almost more of a problem than anything else. Having that much money would be a responsibility. I'd want to give some to charities, but choosing which ones wouldn't be as easy as a stab in the dark.' She sounded completely genuine.

Danny didn't know whether to be impressed or sceptical. He'd heard it all before, yet knew how, when people did have access to so much money, they changed. He had. No denying it. He'd become arrogant and cocky, until the accident that had changed everything. It had taken a while, but eventually he'd learned how lucky he'd been and to make the most of what he'd got.

'A lot of people who win big lose it all within a very short time.'

'So I've heard. What would you do?'

'Employ my brother, who's an accountant-cum-business CEO, to invest it and oversee any donations I made.' That was exactly what he *had* done. Cooper was the financial brains in his family.

'I might buy a ticket when I get out of here. Maybe the luck of not getting hit by that landslide will continue.'

'Go for it. Who knows? You might get lucky and I can

introduce you to my brother.' *Yikes*. His tongue really did run away with him around Brooke. He was talking so much about himself it was ridiculous. Because he felt close to her. Very close. Too close? So what if he did? He liked her. A lot. *And* he wanted to follow through. He really did. A knot formed in his gut. The standard warning sign for him. *Don't trust her so readily. Wait, be patient, learn more about her.*

But he'd been waiting for Brooke for years. Now he'd found her, he didn't want to let her go. He was already halfway to falling for this beautiful woman and he hadn't checked her out enough. *Let go of the past and move on with the future.* His new motto? Or a damned stupid idea? The knot wasn't getting any tighter, if anything it was loosening. A sign he was on the right track? He hoped so. More than that, he was prepared to find out. Slowly, carefully, but definitely, he wanted to get closer to Brooke.

Brooke tapped his foot with hers. 'You've gone quiet again. You got something to hide?' There was concern behind her smile. Had someone hurt her by hiding the truth?

If that was so, he didn't want to be the one who repeated it. But, even feeling ready to make some attempt to let go of what had held him in place for so long, he couldn't quite bring himself to act on his feelings for her. They were too new, too raw, and might turn out to be a complete mistake.

'Sorry, it's a bad habit.' That was true. 'I've done it for a while now.'

'Why?'

He'd set himself up for that. 'I'm not good at sharing

myself.' Also true. She was going to ask why again. He could feel it. 'You're very open with people, aren't you?'

'Up to a point. But I have been hurt more than once by people hiding important things from me and the idea of it happening again gives me chills.'

'You're honest.' He wasn't. He was being dishonest in what he wasn't saying. He could hurt her badly.

So, tell her the truth.

If only he could guarantee she wouldn't turn out like the others. What if she didn't? He just wanted these two days with her, happy and relaxed, before putting his heart on the line. There was a real possibility of losing her trust if her reaction was what he wanted, but he wasn't quite ready. It was too soon.

Standing up abruptly, he held out his hand for her mug. 'Want another coffee?' He didn't, but he'd have one if it meant the end of this particular conversation.

Brooke shook her head. 'Sit down. I won't eat you. Or demand answers to questions that obviously bother you.' She watched as he slowly placed his butt back on the outdoor chair. 'We hadn't met until a little more than thirty hours ago and we seem to have got on faster than I've experienced with other men. Let's leave it at that for now.'

For now meant hope for the future, didn't it? He reached for her hand and wound his fingers between hers. He wanted to tell her she was special. The words were there, on the tip of his tongue, pushing to get out. Breathe in, one two three. He couldn't do it. Not yet.

'Despite the storm, I'm glad I came to the bay for the weekend.'

'So am I.'

His fingers tightened briefly. Brooke was wonderful.

Patience, man. You're going like a bat out of hell over this, and the result is likely to be you'll scare the pants off her and you'll never see her again.

He had to take his time so no nasty surprises arose. So he could tell her everything that'd made him who he was. Mostly so he could enjoy the whole journey, not stop halfway along. Except he knew better. The past always caught up.

Huffing out his disappointment, he asked, 'I'm serious about another coffee. I could do warming up.'

'I know another way to fix that.' Now it was Brooke's fingers tightening their grip around his. Her eyes had widened and were filled with an invitation.

He kissed her knuckles. 'Sounds more than good to me.' Standing, he pulled her up against him and held her close as he kissed her. Deep and filled with longing. A kiss meant to tell her how he was feeling about her. A kiss to replace the words he couldn't put out there.

A shiver tripped up Brooke's spine. Danny kissed like the devil. He brought her awake in an instant, tightening all of her body so it was crying for release. His kisses were temptation on lips. They didn't take away her confusion about letting go her fear of being duped again. If those nearest and dearest could hurt her by not being open and honest then what was to say Danny couldn't? He'd dodged questions non-stop over the hours they'd been together.

His mouth left hers. 'Brooke? Are you all right?'

Yikes. She'd been doing a Danny, losing focus. What was more, she'd done it when his kisses were sensational. Was she rushing this? Probably. And enjoying it.

Stretching up on tiptoe, she whispered, 'I'm fine.

Very distracted at the moment. By you,' she added in case he backed off, feeling unwanted.

'You're sure?' He was aware of her feelings. She'd never been good at hiding them.

'Very. Kiss me again,' she begged. She'd given in to these new feelings too easily, so she was going to make the most of them.

His reply was to place his mouth over hers and return to making her toes tingle, her skin lift and her heart dance. As simple as that. As complicated as that. She'd go with simple for now, drop all the questions threatening to return and upset the moment. Pushing her tongue into his mouth, she tasted him, absorbed his heat, breathed in the outdoorsy male air about him and gave her mind over to desire and pleasure.

As they lay entwined under her bedcovers, regaining their breath, Brooke heard a knock on the back door. 'Who can that be?' she said as she scrambled upright and grabbed her jeans. 'As far as I know, we're the only ones in the bay.'

Danny got out of bed too and began dressing. 'I'll come with you. Could be someone needs medical help and have heard you're here.'

When Brooke opened the door the truck driver from earlier stood on the porch with his hand raised, about to knock again. 'Howdy. Is the man who mentioned trying to get out here?'

'He is. Danny, someone to see you.' She smiled to herself. Didn't they sound like a regular couple?

'I'm Connor, by the way.'

'What's up?' Danny stepped out onto the porch.

'You were saying you had to get out tomorrow for work.'

'That's right.'

'Seems I was wrong about the road being open by then. It's likely to be two or three days before people will be allowed out, except for emergencies.'

Danny grimaced. 'Not much I can do about that. I'll try the water taxi.'

'Hang on,' Connor said. 'We have a truck going out to Blenheim to collect some gear required for the digger. The driver is happy to escort you as far as Picton. Without an escort you aren't allowed to go. It's too dangerous. They're not letting anyone else out. You also can't go the other way. That will be closed for a week at least.'

'When's the truck leaving?' Brooke could feel her heart beginning to speed up. Was her time with Danny up already?

'As soon as Danny's ready. We need the gear urgently.'

Danny looked from Connor to Brooke and shrugged. 'I'll go and throw my bag in the car.' He looked sad.

As sad as she suddenly felt. She would miss him, even if she could expect to see him in the ED next week. It wouldn't be the same with doctors, nurses and patients all around them. They'd basically been alone and she'd loved it. It seemed the storm had brought them together, and in a roundabout way was now pulling them apart.

'That's a yes then,' Connor said with a grin. 'I'll go tell Geo to wait for you. He'll explain what you've got to do.'

'Basically stick to his tail,' Danny said with a weak smile as he rubbed his shoulder against hers.

He didn't want to go. She'd swear it. Lifting her shoulder up and back down, she acknowledged his touch.

Connor stepped off the porch, then paused. 'I'm hearing you two saved Lloyd.'

'We got him out of the house and gave him medical attention until the chopper arrived,' Brooke said, nodding. 'Have you heard how he's doing?'

'He's had surgery and been put back together. That's all I know. But the whole community is grateful you were here, or who knows when he'd have been found, or if he'd have survived his injuries.'

'You couldn't have stopped Brooke getting in to him. She was a woman on a mission.' Danny looked at her, admiration obvious in his eyes.

'You weren't so bad yourself,' she said quietly. Connor probably thought this was gag material.

'Right, see you shortly.' Connor strode away.

She said to Danny, 'I suspect they're helping you because we helped Lloyd. He's adored around the area.'

'It's good of them.' Danny took her shoulders and turned her so she was looking up at him. 'This has been very special, Brooke. I can't believe what's happening between us. Thank you for being...you.'

She sniffed. A flick of her hand over her eyes. 'It has.' She swallowed hard. 'I'll see you at work.' Not the same, but better than nothing.

'I hope so.'

That was it? He wasn't suggesting they get together in any other capacity? Her heart sank. She had no right to get upset. It had been a short acquaintance. He'd said the loveliest things, but she must've read too much into them.

You could ask him to meet up at the pub or go for a meal next weekend. And be turned down? *Nothing to lose except your pride, and that was used to taking a knock in the past.*

'Danny...'

'I'd better go. I got the feeling these guys are in a hurry to get to town.' He started to lean forwards, as if about to kiss her. Then he stopped, stepped back, rubbed a hand over his face. 'Take care.'

She grabbed him, placed her mouth on his and kissed him. Not softly. Not lightly. But hard and full of the passion that had simmered from the first time he'd helped her up out of the mud. A kiss that was a message—*I'm available if you want more time with me*. Pulling back, she told him, 'Be careful out there.' She spun around to head inside. Watching him walk away wasn't an option. It was too hard when she longed to hug him, kiss him again, tell him he was more than a two-day fling.

Thankfully her brain was running this, or her heart might have shouted out something like *I care about you and want to be with you*, and that would have been a deal-breaker for sure.

'Brooke, wait.'

Her breath stuck in her chest, like a stab of pain. What had he forgotten? Turning slowly, she stepped back onto the porch.

Danny had his phone in his hand. 'I don't have your number.'

The breath whooshed out as relief took hold. He wanted to keep in touch. It was a start.

He stood in front of her, an expectant look on his gorgeous face. 'Brooke?'

She rattled it off. 'Send me a text so I get yours.'

'Will do.' Leaning in, he brushed those gorgeous lips over hers. 'We're not done, Brooke.'

Returning his kiss with one of her own, she smiled beneath his lips. They weren't finished. Stepping back, because he did have to go, she asked, 'By the way, Danny who?'

He took a deep breath, held it a moment, then said quietly, 'Danny Collins.'

'Thanks.' No problem with that. Or was there? He had hesitated. No doubt she was looking for trouble. 'Let me know how you're settling in to Nelson, will you?'

I really want to hear from you.

Reaching for her hand, Danny looked right into her eyes. 'Brooke, if you're back by then, would you like to go out for a meal on Friday night?'

'I should be and I'd love to.' No thinking required. It was exactly what she'd love to do with Danny. A real date with a man who had her heart pounding and her brain wondering if she'd found the one.

'I'll call and let you know what time I'll pick you up when I'm clearer on what's happening with the job.' He kissed her again, a kiss that went right through her and touched her heart. 'See you later.'

And he was gone.

CHAPTER SEVEN

'DANNY, YOU TAKE THAT,' Gayle, the head of the ED, called over the blaring sound of the emergency bell ringing from the ambulance bay.

'Onto it.' Striding purposefully through the emergency department, Danny was quickly joined by Sarah, a nurse, pushing the resus trolley. 'Wonder what's going on,' he said.

'Cardiac arrest or seizure?' Sarah said.

'Bleed out,' Brooke told them even before they'd reached the ambulance to find a man lying on a stretcher on the floor of the parking bay. 'Cardiac arrest.' She was doing compressions while her offsider prepared the defibrillator.

At the sight of Brooke, Danny's eyes widened. She was meant to still be on leave. Kneeling beside the patient, he surveyed what injuries were apparent. 'Fill me in.'

'Stand back,' the other paramedic called.

The man jerked as the electric current hit him. The line remained flat.

Brooke continued with the compressions, totally focused. 'Brett Gibbons, thirty-seven, trauma from being struck by a truck as he tried to cross a road. Multiple fractures, internal injuries, head trauma.'

Anyone would be happy to have Brooke at their side when their life was in jeopardy, Danny thought. Including him.

'Where are we at with the bleeding?' There were swabs on most exposed parts of Brett's body, soaked through and still oozing.

'It's slowing, suggesting there's not much to come.' Brooke was breathing hard. Compressions were tough work.

The defib beeped. 'Stand back.'

Another jolt, another flat line.

And again. The fourth electric current was coming up and Danny held his breath.

Ping. The line moved up, down. Up, down. Not high, but it meant life. The heart had started. They'd been running out of time. Much longer and the man would be pronounced DOA.

'All hands to the stretcher,' Danny demanded.

Brooke already held one corner. Damn but she was smooth—and fast. And, in that green and black uniform, every bit as sexy as he'd dreamt all week.

'On the count,' Danny said. 'One, two, three.'

He, Sarah, Brooke and another nurse carefully lifted the stretcher onto the trolley and started back into the ED, the other paramedic following with the ambulance ECG still attached to their patient at her side.

'Emergency bed,' he said, though everyone would know that. This man needed the highest standard of care the department had. He wasn't out of trouble by a long shot. His heart rate was erratic and slow. He needed blood fast. Another cardiac arrest was very likely. That was only the beginning. There'd be sutures, X-rays, surgeons putting him back together, to think of a few.

Danny instructed the staff. 'Courtney, call for blood, three litres to start with. Hugo, let Radiology know we need them here with the portable unit. Sarah, start checking those bleeds.' He turned to Brooke. 'Tell me everything you've found.'

'Fractures in left femur and lower leg, right femur, and the left arm appears to have fractures.' Brooke turned a tight face towards him. 'There's swelling in the upper abdomen, and ribs are possibly broken. There's also a soft area at the front of his skull.'

The sorrow in her eyes for this man made Danny want to reach out with a very big hug. Instead he started on a thorough examination of Brett, speaking into the microphone attached to his tunic.

The ECG monitor was swapped over to the hospital one, leaving Brooke and the other paramedic free to leave, but she remained, standing to the side, watching everything he did.

A shrill sound filled the room. 'Flat line,' Sarah called.

Here we go again.

Danny began compressions while the defibrillator charged.

'Stand back.' Sarah pressed the button to send the shock into Brett's heart.

'Yes. Good result.' Danny wiped his brow with the back of his gloved hand. 'Get me the cardiology unit on the phone, Hugo.' This man needed a cardiologist right now. 'Where's that blood?'

'The lab's sending down interim red blood cell units and will take a sample for a cross match for later. They should be here within a few minutes,' Courtney informed him.

'Thanks.' Danny only hoped there was a later. At the moment this man was in a very dire situation, but he'd got this far, with help from Brooke no less.

'What do you want me doing?' Another doctor had arrived.

Where to start? 'Start suturing the severest lacerations so the blood loss doesn't continue after transfusion.'

'Here's Radiology,' Sarah reported.

They all got busy and when Danny finally straightened up his back ached, but they were getting somewhere. Brett was heading to Theatre for surgery on his liver and spleen, and a neurosurgeon would do what he could for the severe head wound causing a lack of consciousness. The fractures would have to wait until the more urgent problems were dealt with.

Brooke was long gone, back to her work of helping someone else. He smiled to himself as a picture of her in her uniform came to mind. Lovely even when fighting for someone else's life. He looked around.

An orderly stood ready to wheel their patient wherever the surgeons now examining Brett demanded.

Danny touched the man's hand even though he wouldn't feel it. 'Good luck, Brett.' Then he turned away. This was the difficult side of what he did. Not knowing if the patient would survive or not, or whether he'd be returning to his normal life in the future, took its toll. But he wouldn't change his job for anything else. Not even to return to being a top-ranking golfer. Being a doctor was about helping others, not looking after his own ego. There was a bit of that in the mix, Danny admitted as he threw his gloves in the bin. He was proud to be able to help people in pain, to make them well again, or at least comfortable. But there weren't any glaring lights and flashing cameras because it was more about the patient. He'd come a long way.

The next time Danny saw Brooke, she was wheeling in a little boy with his left arm in a sling. 'Danny, meet Thomas. He had a fight with the jungle gym at school.'

Danny crouched down so he was eye to eye with the little man. 'Looks like the jungle gym won, buddy. What have you done to yourself?'

'My arm's broken.' The kid sounded proud, not upset.

'You reckon? I'll have to have a look and make sure you're right.'

'I am.'

'We got a doctor in the making?' Danny straightened and asked the woman standing by the wheelchair, looking distressed and amused all in one.

'It's one of three occupations he has in mind this week.' Thomas's mother shrugged. 'Better than last week's, which was to be a bank robber.'

Danny chuckled. 'Okay, Thomas, let's get you onto a bed first so I can have a look at your arm and check out the rest of you.'

'Nothing else hurts,' Thomas informed him, looking very serious. But that changed as he was helped onto the bed. He cried out, 'Stop it. I don't like that.' Tears spilled down his face.

'Does something else hurt besides your arm?' Danny noted Thomas wasn't putting any weight on his left side.

'He complained of pain around his hip when we first loaded him into the ambulance,' Brooke told him. 'Another boy who was there said Thomas landed on his hip and arm. There's swelling and bruising in that area. Otherwise nothing to report.' She handed the paperwork to Hugo, who'd just joined them.

Stepping away from the cubicle, Danny asked Brooke, 'You okay now? You looked shaken earlier.'

'I'm good. I get a little rattled once I've handed over a serious case. It's as if the tension lets go and I turn to jelly. Any news on how Brett's doing?'

'He's still in Theatre and will be there for quite a while.'

'I figured.' She sighed. 'Right, I'd better get going. We're having quite a busy day.'

'I thought you weren't back at work until Monday.'

'I was asked if I minded coming in, so I came back last night. Another AP's wife went into early labour. I could hardly say no.'

Of course she wouldn't. 'Still up for dinner?'

Brooke's face lit up. 'Try and stop me.'

'It's a date.' He headed back to Thomas, his feet skipping, his heart beating a happy rhythm.

Taking the washing out of the dryer, Brooke began folding it as she waited for Danny to turn up. He'd texted to say he was running late due to an emergency just as he was due to leave the department. She grinned. The joys of dating a doctor. When the text pinged on her phone and she'd seen his name, her stomach had dived. He was going to cancel, had changed his mind now he was back in town amongst more interesting people. Of course he hadn't. Danny wouldn't do that, would he? Her stomach had returned to normal. As normal as having a cage-load of butterflies flapping around in there could be. She couldn't understand this nervousness.

He'd looked surprised, then pleased to see her in the ED so what was there to be edgy over? She'd missed him like crazy since he'd left the bay on Sunday—which was crazy in itself after such a short time together.

Was it because she really liked him and wanted to get closer? Probably. It couldn't be because she was falling for him.

It could be.

But there were all these doubts whenever he didn't tell her things about himself. Was she overreacting? It'd been a while since she'd felt this way about a man, long enough for her to start wondering if she'd always be on her own and that it wasn't such a bad state to be in because at least no one else was taking control of her day-to-day actions—and reactions. But she couldn't help thinking something was about to implode. That whatever Danny was keeping to himself might hurt her, or them.

Did she look all right in her black trousers and white frilly blouse? Crossing to the full-length mirror, she assessed her clothes. They fitted perfectly, accentuating all the right places. Black and white was ordinary. It was her go-to style because it didn't draw a lot of attention. Didn't she want to attract Danny's attention? Sure she did. Then she should have put on the ruby-coloured leather trousers and cream jersey. Her silver earrings swung when she turned her head this way and that. Her hair shone where it fell over her shoulders. The leather boots gave her some much-needed height for standing close to Danny.

The doorbell rang. It was too late to make changes. If he wasn't impressed then too bad. She was in control of herself, right? Yes, right...

Pulling the door wide, her heart lurched at the stunning sight on her front step. Danny was wearing a tan leather jacket, an open-necked white shirt and black trousers. Simple, and perfect. She could remember the body underneath, could feel his warmth against her skin.

'Hey,' she managed around the lump blocking her throat. How had she managed to get this man to even look at her, let alone want to take her out for a meal?

'Brooke, you look wonderful.' He stood watching her.

Managing not to say *You think?*, she smiled and felt goofy, as if his compliment was beyond amazing. 'Thanks.' When he said nothing else, she burbled on. 'Do you want to come in? Or should we get going?' It was nearly eight and her stomach had been crying out for food. Earlier her appetite had disappeared when Danny sent her hormones into a spin in the emergency department. Baggy scrubs weren't sexy, but picturing the fit body inside them was.

He nodded. 'Let's go eat.'

The fluttering slowed. This wasn't the Danny she'd spent time with last weekend. That Danny had held her hand at every opportunity, had smiled a lot. Was he regretting his dinner invitation? She thought about her unusually tidy bedroom, the bedcovers straightened and the pillows all fluffy. Her clothes might be ordinary but underneath she wore the sexiest G-string and bra she'd been able to buy when she'd got back to town late yesterday. She could have been wasting her time.

'Where are we going?'

'Do you know the Dock?'

Everyone talked about it. 'I haven't been there, but

I've driven past numerous times.' It was small and supposedly quiet, sitting over the water on the edge of Nelson Harbour. 'This is going to be a treat.' She slipped into her vinyl jacket and zipped up the front.

'I hope so. It was recommended by one of the specialists at the hospital. She said it's a great place to go when you don't want to be surrounded by lots of people. Plus, the food is apparently simple but excellent.'

'You're spoiling me.'

'I'm glad to.' He opened the door to his car for her.

She slid in, pinching herself. When was the last time a man had taken such care of her getting into a car? Never, was the blunt answer. It might be an old-fashioned thing to do, but it gave her a sense of worth, as if she deserved to be treated well. He might also be being polite rather than relaxed and happy with her.

Danny got in but, instead of starting the engine, he turned to look at her. 'How have you been?'

'Great. I did quite a lot of cleaning-up outside, though the lawns still look a mess. It'll be a while before everything dries out and then there'll be dust for weeks, but the trees are all gone.' She'd put a fair bit of effort into hauling some of the branches away and her muscles had known about it for a couple of days.

'I kept wanting to walk out of the ED and come down to give you a hand. It would have been more fun than dealing with broken legs and heart attacks.' At last, a smile that went straight to *her* heart.

Where she shouldn't be letting it in. Not until she understood what had been behind his cooler approach when she'd opened her door. 'As a trainee doctor you're not meant to say things like that,' she retorted. 'How's your knee? You don't seem to be limping.' They hadn't talked all week. She'd tried phoning, but the connection in the Sounds was still intermittent, and unclear when it was working. Had Danny tried calling her?

'It's fine unless I make an impulsive turn or step too hard. Right, let's do this. We can talk over food and wine.'

And get the evening underway. She got it. 'Is the Nelson department busier than Blenheim's?'

'Lots more patients, but there are more staff to cover the cases most of the time. Though it was already heating up into the usual Friday night chaos when I left. One ED is the same as any other.' His voice had lifted and was filled with happiness.

'You like the work, don't you?'

He nodded.

'So why not specialise in emergency medicine? It's far more exciting than sitting at a computer reading X-rays, surely? You deal with people, not pictures.'

His smile slipped, and his hands tightened on the steering wheel for a moment. Concentrating on his driving a little too much, he didn't answer for a few minutes.

Here we go again.

Like those other times when she'd tried to delve a little deeper into what drove him. Maybe she should tell him to pull over so she could get out and walk home.

Then he said, 'You're right, but I like the idea of studying those images and making decisions based on what's in front of me.'

No mention of patients. Was that a problem? Was there a reason involving a patient in the past behind why he wanted to be a radiologist? It didn't add up.

'You were good with the two people I delivered to ED earlier.'

'We all were. But there's something about radiology that fascinates me too.'

'I think I'd go raving mad not talking to people about what I was looking at. It's one of the reasons I left the lab.'

Danny's smile slowly returned.

Brooke worked on breathing easier. They were on their first date. She'd enjoy it, no matter what. Danny might relax a bit and talk about himself some more.

'I have hours on my own with no one to talk to, so to go to work and carry on the same would send me insane in a very short time.'

'Why don't you get a flatmate?'

'I didn't say I don't like being on my own. I just don't want to be that way twenty-four seven.' Leaning back in the seat, she watched the traffic going past in the opposite direction. 'I'd never lived by myself until I separated, and I enjoy it. Most of the time. There are days when I find myself talking to the birds, but usually it's great.'

'No arguments with yourself?'

'They're the best kind. I always win. And lose.'

'Here we go.' Danny parked opposite the restaurant and got out to open her door.

She could get used to this. It wasn't the most important characteristic in his make-up, but being a gentleman was always a bonus. 'Thank you.'

Taking her elbow, Danny walked them across the road and inside, where they were greeted by a young man dressed in black trousers and white shirt, who took their jackets before leading them to the furthest corner, where the windows looked out over the harbour.

'Look at that,' Brooke said with her heart in her

throat. A ship was being nudged through the Cut by a tug with another one at the front with a wire strop running from the bow of the ship.

'Pretty awesome, isn't it?' Danny held her chair out, taking the job away from their waiter.

'Is the ship the reason for the slight shaking of the building?' Brooke asked the young man.

'Yes. Some people say it feels a bit like an earthquake.'

Exactly what she was thinking. Relief was instant.

'You've been in a few earthquakes?' Danny asked as he sat down opposite, his back to the rest of the restaurant.

'You're in New Zealand now, Danny. They're a regular occurrence, though not often very big. Growing up in Wellington, I've had more than my share of them. It's a shaky city, as well as the windiest.'

'Melbourne had one not too long ago which did some damage in the city centre. It was a complete shock to the locals. I was working on the children's ward and hadn't a clue what was going on. When someone yelled out "Earthquake!" I didn't believe them at first. They're rare there. But when people began diving for doorframes I got the idea it was for real.'

She was watching the ship as it was turned towards the main wharf further along. 'Incredible how something so huge can be manoeuvred like a floating toy.'

'Until it needs to stop.' Danny picked up the wine list. 'What wine do you prefer?'

'Chardonnay.'

Taking the menu the waiter was offering her, she began reading through the courses on offer. It was a short menu but looked awesome. 'How am I going to choose? Each dish sounds delicious.' Eventually she decided on the blue moki and salsa verde.

'I'm having the steamed mussels. We can share. Here's to us.' Danny tapped his glass of wine against hers. 'I am so happy to see you again.'

Here's to us.

That sounded as if he meant to continue their relationship a little longer at least. He was relaxing more and more.

She tapped back. 'To us.'

'Tell me more about what you do when you're not in the ambulance.'

'Apart from the upkeep on my house and going for runs, I like to spend time with my friends. Fairly ordinary, but I'm happy.' She wasn't about to mention she had begun writing a crime story. It was a work in progress with a long way to go.

'That's the main thing, isn't it?' He was watching her with something like envy.

'You're not happy doing what you do?' Would he answer, or once again dodge the question?

'I love my work.' So the problem was in his private life.

'What do you do for rest and relaxation?'

'Not a lot of time for those while I'm studying.' His gaze shifted to the night view outside.

Dodging was how it was going to be. Why? This was beginning to annoy her. If he had secrets then fine, but weren't they supposed to be getting to know each other?

'Fair enough,' she said a little too abruptly. 'Danny, I like you a lot, but you do seem to keep things close to your chest.' Not a bad chest either, but right now she wanted him to open up a little.

He came back to looking at her. 'You're right. I do.' He paused, seemed to be studying her and making up his mind about something.

She waited, the tip of her left boot tapping the carpet softly.

'It's a defence mechanism I've developed over the years. One day I'll explain why, but not tonight?'

She could see he was holding his breath. This must be important to him. Unfortunately for her, she understood how important it was to be allowed to have freedom to do and say whatever when it suited.

'All right.' Would she come to regret giving in to him so quickly? She *had* given in to him. Like she always had with her exes. Gave in. But Danny had asked for her patience. That was different. Or was she making excuses for herself? For him?

Looking away, she saw the lights of a small boat heading in through the Cut.

'I've let you down,' Danny said quietly.

She might have let herself down. Turning back to him, she saw the man she'd spent last weekend with, the kindness, the strength, his readiness to accept her as she was, and she sighed. She was taking a chance on Danny. She might be being gullible accepting his reticence to be open with her so far, but she'd give him the space he'd asked for, and wait until he was ready to talk—as long as he didn't take too long.

'No, you haven't. I'm fine with what you've said.'

His eyes widened in a startled expression, and now he reached for her hand. 'Thank you.'

Her heart expanded at the genuineness in those two words and his touch. With her free hand, she raised her glass. 'Let's enjoy our night out.'

'Let's.' The tension in Danny suddenly fell away and he gave her the devastating smile she'd been longing for all week. 'Here's to more of these.'

Yes, please. No matter what his problem, she wanted to spend more time with Danny Collins.

'Are you ready to order?' The waiter was back.

The food was delicious, and the company just as delicious. She put everything behind her and enjoyed Danny. 'Do you want to come back to my place?' she asked as they walked hand in hand out to his car.

'Yes, please.' He kissed her. 'This is a great evening, Brooke.' And he kissed her again.

'I'm going to the market this morning,' Brooke told Danny as they stretched out in her bed after more sex. 'Want to come?'

And be surrounded by hundreds of people, any one of whom might recognise him? 'I don't do markets. I'll head back to the apartment and get some chores out of the way. Maybe catch up later? Go for a walk somewhere?'

'You don't know what you're missing out on. The Nelson market is one of the best. Everyone goes.'

Exactly. 'You're not going to change my mind.' He wrapped an arm around her waist and hugged in an effort to shift her off the subject.

Under his arm he felt her breathe deep and huff it out. 'So it would seem.' She sounded peeved.

'You don't understand.'

'You're darned right I don't.' She pulled away, rolled out of bed.

He was still getting his head around the fact that Brooke hadn't learnt who Daniel Collins was. He'd been ultra-wary last night, unable to relax for a while. She obviously hadn't rushed to look him up on the internet. Not everyone did that, but he was so used to it happening to him he was struggling to accept Brooke hadn't. If she had and accepted him for himself, she'd still have said something or shown some reaction.

She knew his name, but nothing had really changed. He wanted to be with Brooke. He was close to loving her, if not already in love. It had happened fast. Possibly because for two days he wasn't looking over his shoulder for someone to shout out, 'Hey, Daniel Collins, what are you up to these days?'

Brooke was coming to mean so much to him, so that meant the time was fast approaching when he'd have to explain. But it was getting harder to face, not easier, because he had more to lose. He'd have to risk her changing to one of those women who'd let him down in the past. Granted Brooke was worth the risk. He knew that. So why not get it over with? The sooner he found out how she'd react the sooner he could really let go the ties around his heart and be happy. Or the sooner he could tighten the knots and move on—again. He so wanted to know because he wanted to believe she would be different, because he longed for that future he'd dreamed of for years, and he wanted it with Brooke. It was early days as far as their relationship was concerned, but deep down he knew she meant so much more to him than he could've believed possible.

So do it. Tell her. Get it over with. Find out where he was headed. Suddenly it didn't seem too hard. He relaxed some and felt good. This would work out.

'Brooke…'

'I'm making the coffee and having a shower. I like

to get to the market early, while the stalls are still full.'
She headed out of the door, taking his chance to be
open with her.

'Hang on. What's the hurry?'

Give me a minute. More like half an hour.

Glancing over her bare shoulder, she shrugged at
him. 'Whatever you were about to say will have to wait.
The best fruit and vegetable stalls sell out fast.'

He swore under his breath as he watched her walk
away. Women didn't walk off from him. They swooned
and made all sorts of ridiculous promises. This was
new, and he liked it, but his head thumped with despair. What if he never got it right with Brooke? He'd
finally decided to do the right thing and the opportunity walked out of the door. He could've called her back,
but it didn't feel right. Brooke was on a mission, and
not happy with him. To stop her to talk about himself
might not start off well.

Not using that as an excuse, by any chance?

He didn't think so.

'I'll make the coffee while you're in the shower,' he
called after her, shivering as he tossed the covers aside.
This was one cold house. Being a nineteen-twenties
building, there probably wasn't any insulation in the
walls or roof. What would it cost to fix? Was it even
possible? The inner walls would have to be pulled apart
at some place to be able to spray the insulation behind
them. A costly job which might be beyond her. Plus the
rooms he'd seen appeared to have had a lot of decorating
done, which no doubt Brooke wouldn't want ruined. He
might be able to talk to her about it later, if they were
still getting along. They had to be. There was no other
way forward.

Showered and dressed in last night's clothes, Danny stood at the bench gulping coffee and toast. Brooke's foot was tapping the floor and she kept glancing at the oven clock.

'It's meant to rain later. We might have to postpone the walk. Do you do movies? As in go to a theatre?' She was watching him carefully. Waiting for him to say he didn't do movies either?

'A bit old-fashioned, isn't it?' Even if the place was full they'd be in the dark, so no one would notice him. 'But, yeah, why not? What's on?'

Brooke passed over her phone and he read the list of films showing locally. 'Not a lot of choice unless you like dancing piglets.'

For the first time that morning she laughed.

And the tension in his gut backed off some. He wasn't out of trouble by a long shot, but he had a bit more time on hand. Brooke really did have him wound around her little finger.

'I'll settle for the crime wave if that suits you.' He'd seen the pile of books beside her bed, all thrillers. Something else they had in common. The list grew every day. The time to be upfront with her was rushing at him.

Do it. Get it out of the way for ever so you can relax completely.

'Perfect.' She gathered up some shopping bags. 'Not rushing you but I'm heading out in a few minutes.'

'Yes, you are,' he told her, relieved there wasn't time to talk now. She was in a hurry, and he was backing away from opening up to her. This had to stop. 'Brooke?'

'Yes?' Her foot was tapping the door mat impatiently. This was clearly not a good time to hold her up. So,

'Which time slot do you want to go to the movie?' He'd probably come up with that excuse to save his heart. Too late now. He'd have to wait it out for another appropriate moment.

'How about five? Then we could grab a meal at the pub afterwards.' She was heading for the door, not realising he wanted her to stay so he could talk to her.

'Or we could get takeaways and go back to the apartment.'

She blinked in surprise, looking a bit like a dingo caught in headlights. Except no dingoes in NZ. 'We could?'

'Why not?' Because he had been closed off so far. He understood her surprise and felt ashamed. 'I'd like to show you where I'm living while I'm here.' He'd go to the supermarket this morning to get some steak and other bits and pieces to cook for dinner and show her he was more than a doctor of no long-term abode. He'd let her in a bit more by sharing what he had here. 'The views are stunning.'

It would be pitch dark beyond the harbour, but the Western Ranges would become visible when the sun rose in the morning. To see the mountains beyond Tasman Bay was magic, unlike anything he'd opened his curtains to in Australia. It didn't matter how chilly the mornings had been in the past week, he'd taken his first coffee of the day on the deck, absorbing the sight.

At last Brooke relaxed fully. 'Meet you at the theatre? I'll walk. You know where it is?'

'I have a phone. Sure you don't want me to pick you up?' Every minute spent with Brooke was another enjoyed—until she learned the truth.

'It's only five minutes from here.'

There was no arguing with that tone. It dawned on him Brooke wanted time to herself. She had said she was happy with her own company, and here he was wanting every minute with her he could get. Was it because she wasn't as keen on him as he was her? Or had she become ultra-cautious after her failed relationship? He couldn't see that, considering how quickly they'd first got together sexually, and how he'd stayed in her place for the rest of his short time in the bay. So she was used to being alone and having him here in her space was fine until she was ready for a break.

'Not a problem.' She wouldn't know what he was really referring to. 'I'll see you there.'

'That wasn't the most enthralling script,' Brooke said, slipping her arm through Danny's as they walked to his car. 'I worked out who the antagonist was about halfway through.' All the notes on writing crime came with one firm instruction—be sure not to give away too many clues too early.

'I wasn't far behind you. It was disappointing considering the fantastic cast.'

He was right. They were all big names in the film industry. 'Still better than the dancing piglets.' A cold, wet gust of wind hit them, and she snuggled closer to Danny. He felt so good, like the man of her dreams. She could get used to always having him at her side. If he wasn't only a dream. Her elbow nudged into his side. No, he was real. Sexy real. Fun real. Interesting real. Make that not entirely real yet, because there were things he hesitated to talk about.

But had she told him all her problems? she wondered. Her problems weren't so bad she couldn't talk about them. She wasn't mentioning them to Danny yet because it was too early in their relationship, which might be his answer to her concerns. Too early to be delving into the deep stuff. So when did they? His hesitancy made her cautious, and worried she'd be sorry for giving him space. It would be too late if they waited until they'd fallen in love, and it hurt more if the other person wasn't happy about what they learned.

Only one way to find out. If she wanted to, and she could say for certain she did. She was falling for this gorgeous man, fast and deep. Even when she sensed there was a lot to learn about him, like that morning when he didn't want to go to the market with her. It was only a market, not a major event. But, despite her caution, he was getting to her in ways she hadn't known before. He was different to other men she'd been serious about in that he put her first, or at least was at her side. He'd been quick to help with Lloyd, while not acting as though he'd done all the work, had credited her with saving Lloyd with her insistence on going into that house. Not once had he put her down or questioned her take on something. She couldn't stop feeling Danny would never do that. This wasn't a charade to be dropped once she'd been sucked in. He read her well, hopefully not so well that she couldn't keep some things to herself for a while.

'Where have you gone again?' Danny asked as they climbed into his car. 'Not going over what happened in the movie, I hope.'

'Wondering what you're cooking for my dinner.' See? He did get her. He'd caught her out mind-wandering and hadn't demanded to know what she was thinking about or what had he done to upset her. He wasn't putting himself first. That was special in her book.

'Wait and see,' he said with a laugh. 'But don't get too excited. I'm not a gourmet chef.'

'Steak then. Or fish.'

Another deep belly laugh filled the car. 'I knew you'd get it. I can promise you it's not kangaroo. There don't seem to be any in this country. Plenty of wild wallabies though, I'm told.'

'They're taking over some of the bush country. You might be able to find some in the ranges. Might keep you from getting homesick.'

'*If* I was ever homesick it wouldn't be because I hadn't seen a kangaroo in a while.'

He was still laughing happily, tempting Brooke to ask what might cause that emotion, but she didn't want to bring on that stillness some of her questions invoked. Old Brooke to the fore? Protecting herself from being lied to or conned into doing something she didn't want? She didn't believe so. That Brooke was gone. This Brooke wanted to enjoy being with Danny and still be true to herself. She didn't need to dig into who he was. She could wait to be drip fed bits and pieces as they spent more time together.

'Have you eaten kangaroo steak? I hear it's to die for.'

'*Delizioso.*' He smacked his lips together. 'This is making the steak seem ordinary.'

'No way. I love steak but hardly ever cook it.' They were passing a supermarket. 'Can you stop? I'll get a bottle of Pinot Noir.'

'All sorted.'

'Damn, but I could get to like you.' Too late. She already did, and like had already turned into something closer to love.

'So my plan's working.'

The rest of his plan appeared straightforward. They shared dinner, coffee and bed. And in the morning they made slow, idyllic love and ate breakfast wrapped in blankets sitting on the tiny deck overlooking the harbour and out to Tasman Bay. The day flew by. Brooke enjoyed doing nothing, lazing around talking, being quiet, laughing, making love again, eating. Perfect, really.

After a light snack on Sunday night, she finally pulled on her boots and headed for the door, Danny behind her. Turning around, she wound her arms around him and held on tight. 'Thank you for a great weekend.'

He kissed her forehead. 'Back at you.'

'I'm on nights this week.' At work, that was, not getting close and sexy in her bed.

'I've got a mix of afternoons and mornings. We'll probably cross paths in ED some time.'

He could've sounded a little disappointed that they wouldn't have time together.

'I'll wish for an accident where no one gets hurt but needs to be taken to ED anyway.'

'You'd never do that.'

No, but it had been worth saying just to see that ridiculously sexy smile. If only she didn't feel so happy with him, didn't feel a growing apprehension that there was a bomb waiting to explode.

CHAPTER EIGHT

'Hey, sis, how's things?'

'Apart from missing out on our week together, I'm good,' Saskia replied. 'Though the bank account took a hit last week. I mean, what's a girl supposed to do when her holiday plans are changed?'

Laughing, Brooke retorted, 'Hit the shops and buy an outrageous number of clothes.' She got it. 'New suits to wear to court, matching high end shoes and handbags.' Saskia was a lawyer and liked to look the part. 'I should've come over to join you instead of staying on at the bach.' It would've been hard to walk away from the mess that had become the yard, though. She hadn't wanted her parents to have to go there to do the job.

'I did say that.'

'I know.' They'd talked a few times over the week. Brooke hadn't mentioned Danny other than to say he'd helped her with Lloyd and some cleaning up. 'Like I need more clothes.' Her wardrobe was chock full of lovely clothes from previous shopping expeditions with Saskia, and she wore a uniform to work.

'You sound tired. What's up?'

She could never hide anything from her sister. 'Had a busy weekend, that's all.' She had spent a lot of time worrying about what was going on with Danny and herself. Even more time having fun, and not a lot of sleep last night as they'd got together in his oh, so comfy bed.

'You weren't working, so what kept you busy?'

This was really why she'd rung. She wanted to talk to Saskia about Danny, but still she hesitated.

'Come on. Spill. Is it something to do with that doctor staying at Paula and Mike's?'

'How do you do that?'

'I know you. So it was. Danny, wasn't it?'

'Yeah.' She sighed. 'I… We got close, very close.'

'He must be special then.'

Brooke agreed. *He is.* 'We'd been rescuing Lloyd from his falling down house, and me falling and being swept towards the beach, and, I don't know, just having a few frights. Afterwards we kind of came together and let rip.'

'Have you seen him since he left the bay?'

'We spent the weekend together. He's working in Nelson ED.'

'What aren't you telling me, Brooke?'

She sighed. She shouldn't have rung Saskia, but her sister was her best friend. 'I really, really like him, as in I might be falling for him.'

'You're afraid he'll hurt you.'

Got it in one. 'I get the sense that he's holding back on me. Am I being too cautious? It is early days, and I'm probably expecting too much.'

'You could try looking him up on the internet,' Saskia said, then laughed. 'You won't though. You want him to talk to you straight up.'

'I do. If we're going to have a relationship then it should be open and honest.'

'Then you're going to have to be patient. Not one of your strongest traits these days,' Saskia said. 'It is only a few days since you met though, and in that time you were stranded together in the midst of chaos, then returned separately to Nelson and your jobs. Give him a chance, Brooke. Someone might've hurt him in the past too, making him as wary as you.'

'Thanks, Sash. I had considered that, but needed to hear it from someone else. It's just that he is gorgeous and I can feel myself falling under his spell.'

'Then get out there and make the most of him, leave the worries alone for a bit. You are stronger these days, you can fight for yourself.'

Brooke put her phone down with a sense of relief. Nothing had changed, or been solved, but she was ready to continue with Danny as things were for a while longer. Hopefully he felt the same. And if he didn't, then so be it.

Really?

No, but she was trying to be positive about the future.

Danny watched the young woman on the bed. She was calming down as the anaphylaxis stopped, the panic slowly fading from her face. The epinephrine he'd administered within minutes of her being brought into the department had prevented serious constriction to her breathing.

Relief poured through him. With anaphylactic shocks there was always that moment when he didn't know which way the outcome would go. The paramedic's urgency and one fast check of Jamie and he'd been drawing up the drug to save her. Turning to the man standing in the corner of the cubicle looking frightened by what had happened, Danny said, 'You did the right thing calling the ambulance as soon as you did and bringing that bottle of pills was even better. It gave us a heads-up to what was causing Jamie's distress.'

'You think the penicillin did this?'

'Yes.'

'She only had one tablet. It wasn't like she'd taken too many.' The guy didn't relax.

'Sometimes the drug will build up in a person's system until the body can't take it any more and then they'll have a reaction. Unfortunately, a small percentage of people have an instant shock and that's often severe.'

'What happens now?'

'I'm keeping Jamie here so she can be monitored for a while, and we can make sure she's going to be all right. Then she'll go to a general ward and be administered a new antibiotic for the infection in her surgical wound.' Jamie had had her appendix removed the previous week.

'I can't thank you enough, Doc. I'm going to be paranoid about any pills she takes from now on.'

'You can relax. Her doctors will be aware of what's happened and they'll make sure she's safe. Pull up a chair and sit with her. I'll be back later.'

Danny checked the case list, found no one needing him and went to grab a much-needed coffee at the cafeteria. An hour to go before knock-off time, which meant nothing, as none of the staff left just because the clock had ticked over to shift-finish hour.

'How's it going?' The cardiologist he'd called in earlier for a patient with heart oedema was sitting at a table near where he was waiting for his coffee.

'I've had better days.'

'Haven't we all? What do you do for relaxation?'

'As little as possible. Go for runs mostly.' Spend time with Brooke now she was back in town.

'You don't play golf?'

Alarm bells rang, but when Danny looked directly at the guy he wasn't staring at him as if it was a loaded question.

'Not at all. I'm useless at it.'

'I'm sorry to hear that.'

Jackson knew. Danny could swear he did.

'Can't be helped.'

'If you ever want to hit a ball around on a Sunday morning give me a bell. I'm not great, but I like getting out and stretching the body a bit.' Jackson drained his coffee and stood up. 'No pressure. Just thought you might want to meet some of the crew away from here.'

'Thanks.' If he was going to be comfortable living here then this was what he should do. The day would come when he'd have to get over himself.

'Greg from Radiology plays too. You've met him? He's a good bloke.' That was a recommendation? Probably as good as they got from this man.

Danny couldn't help himself. He said, 'I don't have any clubs. Not with me anyway. I presume the club hires them out.' What was he doing even considering this?

'They do.' Jackson handed him a card. 'My numbers if you decide to join us.'

'Again, thanks.'

'No problem. By the way, you did a good job with Mrs Hogarth. She's got a good chance of a full recovery, thanks to your fast action.'

Danny shook his head at him. 'Not me. It's the paramedic, who saved her first time round when she was at

her worst.' Not Brooke this time, but another compe-
tent medic. Would he see Brooke before he left for the
day? He hoped so.

Jackson smiled. 'You should definitely make an effort to join us for a game. See you around.'

The guy headed away, leaving Danny feeling as
though he'd just made a friend without even trying.
Nelson was turning out to be good for him.

'Morning.' Danny was leaning against the wall at the
central ambulance station when Brooke walked outside
the next morning at the end of her shift.

'Howdy. What are you doing here at this hour?'

'Waiting to take you to breakfast before you hit the
sack. And I don't mean I'm joining you in said sack.
You've worked a twelve-hour night shift. I'm sure you're
exhausted.' There was a twinkle in his eye that said he
might be available if she wasn't shattered.

'What other plans have you got for the morning?'
she asked, stalling on her answer just to tease him. She
was tired, but not so much that a good romp in bed was
off the list.

'Study.'

'What about getting out and about?'

'On a Tuesday morning when everyone I know is
working? Not that I've had time to get to know people
very well, other than you.' His eyes widened a little,
then returned to normal. Had he just lied?

That unease was back. That romp not quite so enticing. Not make love with Danny? Impossible to turn
down. This was getting silly.

'Since you said you play golf occasionally, why not
have a game at the club and meet people there?'

'I might just do that,' he said indifferently. 'One of the surgeons suggested it the other day.'

Danny had answered her, no hesitation at all. That threw her. She was used to him avoiding questions. She could relax a bit for now.

'Where shall we go for breakfast?' No more questions about golf or friends or he might clam up again.

'I was hoping you'd know somewhere good. I feel like a full works brekkie.'

'Let's go.'

'Thought you were never going to say yes.' He led her to his car.

Maybe I shouldn't have.

'I've been asked to cover for someone on Sunday.'

'The reality of being a paramedic, eh?' Danny said. 'No matter, I've got plenty to be doing. I've been ignoring study over the past few days. A certain lady keeps distracting me.'

'Don't go blaming me if you fail your exams,' she warned. 'I take no responsibility at all.'

'Now there's a surprise. You're not geared to spend your time trying to please me, are you?' he said with his best sexy grin.

Little did he realise how close he was to knowing who she used to be. 'Never,' she replied a little too sharply.

His grin dipped. 'Did I hit a nerve?'

There was nothing to lose by explaining and it might encourage Danny to be more open with her. 'I'm not a pleaser.' Not any more. 'Not to the point where I give up everything I want anyway.'

'Go on.'

She had his full attention now, almost as though he

wasn't used to people talking about themselves in more than a casual way. 'One day my ex picked me up from work and said we were moving to a new flat at the end of the week. I hadn't even known he was looking to change homes.'

'Hardly fair or thoughtful.'

'Another time he nearly bankrupted us by buying a property before we'd sold the house we already owned. We couldn't afford that.'

'You weren't consulted about that move either?'

'No.'

'No wonder he's your ex.'

'I didn't walk away easily. We were a couple. Don't couples support each other? There was the rub. He was never going to change. I was the one who was supposed to get over it, move on, be happy. Great when I didn't know when I got home every night what shock might be awaiting me. I was the one who'd have to sort out the financial losses and work extra hours to pay the bills. I left him.'

'How'd he take that?'

Danny got it in one 'He hated it. Me. I was supposed to love him and understand he was trying to do great things for us.' *Yeah, right.* 'If only I'd seen him for what he was a lot earlier.'

'But you did eventually, and that's what counts.' An arm went around her shoulders and he drew her in close. 'You're tougher than you realise.'

'Most of the time. I know I won't let anyone control me like that again.'

'No one should want to. Nor do they have the right.' Danny kissed her forehead.

'It's made me very wary of people keeping secrets.

I always wonder what their agenda is. Am I being duped again?'

The arm around her shoulders tensed. Danny drew a long, slow breath. Then he said quietly, 'Stay strong. You'll be okay.'

'What are you not saying, Danny?'

'That I think you're amazing. Everything I've seen about you, from that storm to bringing patients into ED to spending time with me, you're strong, considerate and kind. Your ex was a fool.'

Brooke relaxed. He'd tensed because she'd been hurt, no other reason. She'd been letting her suspicious mind take over the logical side. Or had she excused him because she didn't want to go there?

'Do you want to come home with me for an hour or so?' They could talk over another coffee, clear the air a bit.

'Now let me think.' Danny looked around with a smile crossing his mouth. Then he turned and grabbed her to him and began kissing her like there was no tomorrow.

Brooke wanted to pull back and have it out with him, but his kiss was burning her up, turning all sensible thought to chaos. She gave in and went with him. There wouldn't be a lot of talking involved right now.

So Brooke had walked away from her ex because he was unstable when it came to being settled. It sounded to Danny that financially they'd been doing all right until Brad got carried away and nearly bankrupted them.

After returning to his apartment to let Brooke get some much-needed sleep, Danny sat on his deck, looking out over Tasman Bay, the view not quite as beguiling today. Hearing Brooke's story, however brief, gave him more insight into who she was and why she was wary of him when he didn't always answer her questions about himself. She'd had a few hard knocks along the way, but she seemed to have done fine by herself. She had that house right in town and was doing it up. She was a top-notch paramedic and was happy with her life.

What did she want for her future? A partner to have a home and family with was probably part of her dreams. Did she want a grander lifestyle? To be financially secure? Not be the only one paying the mortgage on that house? Houses in Nelson didn't come cheap. He'd looked them up the other day for interest's sake. Or in case he got close with Brooke and decided to make this town his home. But now the old doubts were tumbling back into his head. Would she see his wealth as something to grab hold of, so she didn't have to fear losing everything? Brad hadn't kept her up-to-date with his plans. *He* hadn't told her his past. Was she going to see *him* in the same light as her ex?

It did explain some things. But he was none the wiser about how she'd react to his past. He very much doubted Brooke would turn out to be like the other women in his life and see him as a ticket out of her life—which she said she was happy with—to something bigger and more secure.

He had no issues with making her feel secure, he even wanted that. He especially needed to make her feel loved for herself. The feelings he had for Brooke were special, and overwhelming, and loving. He loved her. But was he ready to lay his heart on the line and wait to see what she did with it?

The clock was ticking, and he would be outed if he delayed any longer. Brooke hearing his story from him was better than someone else telling her. It was a matter of trust, which he'd deliberately been overlooking in a bid to protect himself. It was going to backfire if he didn't pull his finger out and get on with it.

His phone interrupted his gloomy thoughts.

'Hey, Danny, it's Jackson. I know I said to give me a call if you wanted a game, but Troy and I were booked to play this afternoon and he can't make it. I see you're working the night shift. Want to take his place?'

He didn't hesitate. Brooke was getting much-needed sleep before her next shift, and he needed a distraction.

'Count me in. What time and where?'

As he listened to the details, Danny couldn't believe he'd accepted Jackson's offer so readily. It would be a badly needed distraction and might go some way to quieting the turmoil in his head. He did love Brooke, and the deeper in he got, the more concerned he was about to have his heart slammed.

But there was a conversation he needed to have with her. The sooner the better. Not today though. He had a game of golf to play.

'Marie Coupland, forty-one, fell down flight of stairs in her home, suspected fractured right arm, shoulder damage, lacerations to head and legs.' Brooke handed the paperwork to the ED nurse indicating which cubicle to take the patient.

'Any obvious head injuries?' Danny came up behind her.

'There don't appear to be. Conscious level's good,' Brooke answered, trying not to smile too wide as everyone lifted the woman onto the bed from the stretcher. This was the first time she'd seen Danny since Tuesday morning in bed. Their rosters hadn't matched and besides he was supposed to be studying. It wasn't for her to keep him away from that. But now it was Friday, she was coming towards the end of her shift, and she had tomorrow free. So did Danny, if she'd read the roster correctly.

'Marie, I'm Danny, the doctor who'll be attending you. Did you at any time lose consciousness? Maybe before the ambulance crew reached you?'

'I don't think so. I had to crawl a few metres to get my phone to call 111. I felt a lot of pain but I was aware of what I was doing all the time.'

'We had to untangle her legs when we got there,' Corina, the ambulance officer on with Brooke, told Danny. Her eyes lit up with excitement as she locked them on him.

Brooke was not amused. They were here for a patient, not to flirt with the staff. Was that a twinge of jealousy? Glancing at Danny, she relaxed. He was focused entirely on Marie, carefully touching her scalp, searching for any tender spots. She hadn't found any, but it was his job to make certain. Then she noticed his mouth had flattened. Because he had found an injury? Or because Corina had annoyed him?

The pager on her belt beeped. Time to go. Another callout needed an urgent response. Reaching for the stretcher, Brooke started for the ambulance bay. 'Come on, Corina. We've got a Code Three down at the port.'

'Coming. See you later, Doctor.'

Danny didn't respond.

Brooke smiled to herself. She might tease him about

this when they next got together. Hopefully that night when he finished at eleven, except he rarely walked off the job immediately. There was nearly always a patient he was midway through helping, or an influx of urgent patients just as shift change was occurring.

'What've we got?' Corina asked as she strapped herself in and began driving out of the bay.

'A crane driver loading logs has fallen off his machine and is unconscious.' Brooke put the siren and lights on to alert the traffic. 'Our patient's going to have more than a head injury. Those cranes are so tall it's creepy.'

'That's what I'm thinking too.' Corina's disposition was calm as she weaved through cars moving out of the way. Same as when she dealt with severely injured patients. She'd make a good paramedic by the time she'd finished her training. It was how she'd behaved around Danny that annoyed Brooke and, to be fair, she wasn't sure if that was her being antsy because he was her man.

Swallowing her annoyance, she said, 'It's been a night for falls.' First Marie, and now this case.

Mark Dixon wasn't going to be driving a crane for a long time to come. 'Severe head injuries, fractured upper arm and shoulder, query spinal damage as there was no reaction to pressure on his feet. He was lying at an odd angle when we got there.' Brooke filled Danny and another doctor in when they brought him back to the ED. 'Fortunately no one tried to move him. His heart rate dipped, then stopped on the way in and I had to get Corina to pull over so we could resuscitate him.'

Mark was transferred from the spinal board to a bed in Resus. Brooke read through the notes she'd written up so far, added more while watching Danny and the female doctor begin assessing what lay before them. Where did they begin with a case like this? Damage to the spine needed urgent attention, but the head injuries were worse, and if there was internal bleeding, as she suspected, that would need fast intervention. Who'd be a doctor?

'Here you go.' She handed the paperwork to a nurse.

Danny took the pages from the nurse, gave it a quick glance. 'That's one heck of a fall.'

'Yes. Right onto concrete.' She gave him a small private smile. 'We'll leave you to it.'

'See you, Dr Danny,' Corina called over her shoulder as she took the stretcher away.

Again, Danny's mouth flattened, and he turned back to his patient without a word. Corina was undoubtedly annoying him.

'You do know who he is, don't you?' Corina asked the moment Brooke got into the ambulance, this time as the driver.

'Who?' But she knew who Corina was referring to. Dr Danny.

'Danny…aka Daniel Collins. I'd swear that's him. He's got the looks and the body, and his smile is to die for.'

'So?' Now she thought about it, his surname wasn't on his badge. Most doctors at the hospital had their full name on their badge, but Danny wore one that wasn't hospital issue, reading Dr Danny. Why not Daniel Collins if that was who he really was? Was he hiding something? Like who he was?

'So Daniel Collins is famous.'

'For what?' The steering wheel was tight in her palms,

and her foot hit the brake too hard as she slowed before driving out onto the main road. Had she been burying her head when it came to Danny not talking about himself? But everyone had the right to remain silent unless it affected someone else, and she couldn't see how anything about Danny being famous could affect her so there wasn't an issue.

Except he didn't tell me. Not even a hint.

She had given him some leeway, hoping she'd hear more soon. Had she been too trusting? Or too far in love to look beyond the surface? Not again. Anything but that. No, this wasn't her doing. Danny had held back, not her. He hadn't trusted her with the truth. He'd been happy to listen to her past problems and keep his own to himself. He'd betrayed her trust. Betrayed her love. It was beyond hurtful. He knew how she'd been hurt and yet he hadn't said a word. Not one. Well, Daniel Collins, you're done for.

Corina was looking at her phone. 'Daniel Collins, Australian, thirty-two, three times junior world golf champion, winner of US junior competitions, Australian, Asian, New Zealand, British competitions. Want me to go on?'

'Not really.' Not at all. She didn't want Corina reading out anything to do with Danny. Sorry, Daniel Collins. She'd look him up herself when she got home, and the door was locked and she'd had a shower. Why had he stopped playing? The next step would surely have been into the open league.

'Base to Nelson Ambulance One.'

Thank goodness for radios and work. Brooke held her breath while Corina took the call. If this wasn't a case to attend, she'd go back to base and hide out in the bathroom until home time.

'Nelson Ambulance One receiving.'

'Possible breech birth, woman alone, says she's bleeding.' The woman at base gave an address.

Corina acknowledged the call and began writing down the few details they were receiving.

Brooke turned on the lights. 'Here we go again. It's been a busy shift.'

Thank God it was nearly over. She kept talking to shut Corina down about Danny. Her head was whirling. Danny wasn't Danny. He was Daniel Collins, apparently a famous golf player. Big deal. It wasn't something she couldn't handle—other than that he'd never mentioned it. What else hadn't he mentioned?

Daniel Collins…born and raised in a comfortable lifestyle in Ballarat, Victoria. He had a brother who was a CEO of some technology company in Canada, and his father owned an investment company that was rated very highly.

Daniel Collins had done exceptionally well in his golfing career, winning all those competitions Corina had read out and plenty more. He'd earned millions after he turned nineteen and became a professional player.

Daniel Collins's career had plummeted at age twenty-one when he dived into a pool to rescue a drowning four-year-old boy at a millionaire's home in Los Angeles. He'd damaged his shoulder and ribs and could no longer swing a golf club as well as he had in the past. But he'd become an overnight hero for saving the film producer's son. He had wanted to make a movie featuring Daniel. Daniel had talked him out of it.

There were many photos of Daniel Collins with glamorous women hanging off his immaculate suit-covered arm. Brooke swallowed the urge to throw up.

Daniel Collins was now studying to become a doctor in Melbourne.

That was slightly out-of-date.

Brooke pushed her laptop away and picked up the mug of tea she'd made after her shower.

Daniel Collins.

The name went round and round in her head.

Not Danny, but Daniel.

He had hidden who he was from her. Fair enough? Or plain, damned insulting? Was he hiding the truth from her in case she thought she could make the most of his wealth? Or want the limelight? Though when she thought about it he seemed to want to avoid that at all costs. This explained the restaurant table by the window where he sat with his back to the other diners and preferring to eat at home than go to the pub, and wearing that name badge at work.

Another gulp of tea. He had hidden who he was from *her*. Okay, she got that he mightn't want to spout off about his past, but not to tell her his name or where he'd grown up or the places he'd visited? No, she wasn't letting him off so easily. She'd been sucked in before, and now Danny had done the same. She'd thought he was a regular, good guy working hard to become a doctor. He *was* all of those, but there was so much more. What happened when the media confronted him? Did he play up to them, or go all quiet? Did he love or hate the limelight?

More tea went down her throat. Whatever. She didn't care. He'd been playing her along. And she was done with men who did that. Even her mother had had to learn not to keep things of importance from her. What Danny—he was still Danny to her despite what she'd learned—had done wasn't as bad by a long shot, but it was wrong as far as she was concerned. More than that, they were barely two weeks into their relationship. What would happen further down the track?

It was time to have a talk. He deserved the chance to explain.

Problem being he was at work and wouldn't finish for another five hours. By then she'd be wound up like a clock, her springs ready to burst wide, opening up to let everything through without touching the wires that usually kept her together.

She texted him.

Please come here when you finish work.

Then she sat back, finished a second mug of tea, and waited. And waited.

He didn't answer. By eleven she was pacing the floor. Would he drop by? Would he go to his apartment for a sleep after a busy night? Well, he wasn't getting one. She snatched up her keys and headed out of the door.

Danny heard the buzzer. Someone wanted to see him. As far as he was aware, only Brooke knew where he lived. Had to be her. Had to be. But he'd replied to her text saying he'd catch up later when he'd had some shut-eye. He needed time to himself.

He'd been outed earlier by that ambulance officer. Corina had been waiting for him when he took his dinner break at the staff cafeteria. He'd known immediately by the way she'd smiled at him. It was all so familiar, so gut-wrenching. He didn't want this now, not when he and Brooke were getting on so well, when he'd begun to think he could have a normal life.

He loved Brooke. He'd held off telling her who he used to be for too long, and now he'd pay the price. It was all very well feeling relaxed and happy in a way he hadn't for so long—maybe since he'd first begun to make a name for himself in golf—but he'd known this day would arrive.

The buzzer sounded again, almost angry with him.

'Yes?'

'Can I come up?'

Brooke's voice was angry. Corina had probably filled her in on all the details.

'Of course.' His heart dropped. What was she going to say? Do?

He opened the door and waited. His heart was now pounding, and his legs didn't feel strong enough to hold him up for much longer. Everything rested on the next few minutes.

The elevator door slid open and there she was, looking fierce. 'Daniel.'

Bang. Daniel. She knew.

'Brooke.' He stepped back, his hand holding the door to the apartment wide. 'Come in.'

She strode past him, back straight, head high, and went through to the lounge, where she stopped by the glass doors looking over the bay. Her gaze was directed outside, but he knew her mind was right in the room, focused on him and how he'd let her down.

'I'm sorry,' Danny said with everything he had in him. He was so sorry it hurt.

Brooke spun around. 'Not good enough, Daniel.'

That made him mad. He wasn't Daniel to Brooke. He was Danny. Had always been Danny, the man who was at ease with her.

'Don't, Brooke. I've messed up, but don't make it worse.'

'Really? Finding out from someone else who you are doesn't make this worse? For me, it does. What's more, you know why I feel like that.'

'Let me explain.'

'You've had two weeks to explain, or at least give me an inkling. You could've told me when I talked about Brad and how he'd hidden important stuff from me.'

'I wanted to.'

'Then why didn't you?' she snarled. 'It's taken me finding out from another source for you to offer that.'

She wasn't making it easy, but who could blame her?

'I was wrong. But I was so happy with you and I didn't want it to stop.'

'You didn't—'

He held his hand up in a stop position.

'Brooke, believe me when I say I knew I was dicing with trouble, but I've never felt as relaxed with anyone as I have with you these past weeks. It's not what I'm used to, and I couldn't give it up.'

'You already made up your mind how I'd react? Good one, Danny. Thanks for the vote of confidence.'

Breathe in, slowly breathe out. This wasn't Brooke's fault. He shouldn't be angry with her. But there was so much to lose. If he hadn't already lost her. *Breathe in, slowly breathe out.*

'Please sit down. This could take a while.'

For a moment Brooke didn't move.

Breathe in, slowly breathe out.

She crossed to the couch and sat upright, her hands clasped in her lap. Not a Brooke pose he'd seen before. It suggested she was more than angry with him, she was hurt. He had to fight himself not to haul her into his arms and promise everything would be all right. That wasn't the way to go with Brooke. She'd never let him get away with that. She deserved his story before anything else.

Sitting on the arm of a lounge chair, he swallowed hard. 'I take it you've read about my career in golf?'

'It's all there at the tap of an icon, every last detail. You were quite something. Still are, from what I gathered.'

'Yes. It doesn't go away, even though I no longer have anything to do with the upper echelon golfing world. I'm being unrealistic to even wish it would, I know.' Had always known. 'I was young when I first caught attention from players, coaches, and the media. I tried not to let it go to my head, but I lost that battle. I enjoyed being in the limelight. Reporters wanted to know everything about me, and I mean everything, right down to the brand of socks I wore for a golf match. Some people love that. It drove me crazy at times but it was the price I had to pay for being famous.' Along with the women who liked to cling to his arm.

Brooke stared at him. 'I can believe that.'

So she wasn't going to knock him down over everything. Dared he relax? Her gaze remained steady and didn't show any of her usual friendliness.

So stay on guard, protect your heart, though it's probably too late for that.

'Then I was invited to a pool party at a friend's in

LA and everything changed.' She'd have read what had happened so no need to recount the details that had heightened his fame. 'My golfing career was over, and I struggled for a while. I wasn't hopping on planes to fly all over the world. I didn't have to get out of bed to go to the range to practice a stroke. I didn't have a purpose in life. It was strange, and yet reporters were still following me, asking what I was going to do next. Would I become a coach? Would I do this…do that? Blah-blah-blah.'

'Plus putting it out there that you were a hero for saving that little boy.'

He sighed. 'Yeah. As if anyone wouldn't have done what I did. I happened to see Toby go under for the second time when no one else did. He wasn't moving his limbs and I reacted.'

'You injured yourself and still pulled him out, probably adding to your injuries.' Was that admiration in her voice?

If it was, he didn't want it. She didn't owe him a thing.

'True.'

The doctors told him he'd also tweaked his spine lifting the boy off the bottom of the pool.

'So why couldn't you tell me this? It's part of who you are.'

'There's an ugly side to all this.' *Breathe in. Slowly breathe out.* 'I was in a relationship when I had to give up golf. Iris loved being in front of the cameras and wasn't pleased she hadn't been there when I saved Toby. Like it was my fault for not taking her with me, but she wasn't in the US at the time. Whenever I was interviewed about that day she made sure she was there.

Then she started going on about how I should start touring countries and get paid to talk about my career and encouraging others to do the same.'

Brooke remained quiet. He wasn't sure what that meant.

'Money was right up there with the glamour for Iris. The crunch came when I decided to apply for med school back in Melbourne. She was furious, said it wouldn't bring in the same money, and that I'd be stuck looking after people and unable to socialise with important people. I began to see I mightn't have loved her as much as I'd thought. I certainly didn't want to continue with the relationship the way it was, and she didn't want to go with my plans. We split up. To this day I think she probably sticks pins in a voodoo doll before she goes to bed every night.'

'No wonder you wince in your sleep sometimes.' Brooke's posture had softened a little.

Hope flared, until Danny knocked it back in place. He had hurt this wonderful woman by not sharing who he was. All he could hope for was that she'd understand what had driven him.

'That could be due to many reasons,' he replied.

'Why medicine?' He had once mentioned this briefly.

'Before golf became my career, I thought I'd study medicine. I was good at science subjects at school and fascinated with biology, and especially after the conversations my grandpa and I had when I was younger. When I finally got over what had happened it was a given really that I'd go to med school. I had to do a fair bit of study to get in, it having been a few years since I'd looked at a science book.'

'You're obviously happy with your decision. You're

good at what you do.' Brooke stood up and paced to the glass doors and stood staring out.

He waited, heart thumping.

Finally, she turned around and came back, but she didn't sit down.

Not a good look, from his perspective.

'Danny, I understand your reticence over telling me all this. You're afraid to be used again. Fair enough. But the fact that you didn't trust me enough to tell me some of this is a game changer. I won't be treated like that again, by anyone. Not even you.' She spun away, looking outside again, before turning back slowly. 'I thought we were getting on especially well.' Sadness lined her words and his heart sank further.

He had failed her. But he wasn't giving up that quickly.

'We are. I care a lot for you, Brooke.' Actually, he loved her.

'Yet you continued to hold out on me. Surely when I told you how Brad used to hide deals from me until he had to come clean so I could figure a way to pay the loans you must've seen how your reticence would hurt me? How he lied to me. It hurt—a lot. So much I walked away from our relationship, and that was not something I did lightly. I'd vowed to be there through thick and thin, good times and the bad. But when I'm being used, lied to and treated as though I don't deserve the truth, then I'm out.'

'Brooke.' His heart had gone into overdrive. She couldn't leave him. They needed to talk some more. 'I made a mistake because I was afraid. I would never lie to you about anything else. I promise.'

'I'm sure you mean that, but I'm struggling to accept it. You did lie to me. It's just as bad when you do it by omission. I have learnt to protect myself, yet I still talked to you about my past in the hope you'd reciprocate. I knew you were holding something back and I tried to be patient. Where did that get me? Nowhere. It was early days, but starting a new relationship means getting to know the other person. I came to you tonight, not the other way round.' Her back was straight again, her hands tight, and a solitary tear trailed down her cheek.

Brooke was going, getting out of his life, taking his heart with her. How to prevent this? He'd said everything he could think of. Except lay his heart in her hands. Looking at her, he choked on the words *I love you*. She wasn't ready to hear them, might never be. Deep inside he could feel her need to walk away, her longing to be strong and look out for herself. If only she could understand he'd do that for her, for ever.

'I'm here for you.'

'Goodnight, Danny. I'll see you around.'

At least she had called him Danny.

CHAPTER NINE

BROOKE SAT IN the car, unable to drive with tears filling her eyes and streaming down her face. Danny hadn't been honest with her. She might have read it all, but hearing Danny put it into words—his words—made it more real, more true. It also underlined his dishonesty by omission. He'd been hiding who he really was. Sure, with good reason, but he must've known he couldn't get away with it.

Wrong, Brooke.

He hadn't hidden his kindness or generosity. Nor how he had listened to her and supported her. He was a good guy. He was also made to be a doctor. He had a firm but compassionate approach to his patients that went over very well most of the time. No one could please everyone all the time, but he came close. None of that meant he could get away with how he'd treated her. None of it.

What about the fact he'd been a famous golfer and a hero for saving the young boy? That only made him more interesting. Did it though? Why not tell her? He must've known it would come out sooner or later. It always did, he'd said. Why risk her finding out from another source and feeling let down—as she was feeling right now? She'd have heard him out and carried on as normal, not felt so devastated. She'd have loved him more, not less.

I was falling in love with you, Danny. Truly, I was already there. You're in my heart, and my head. I get so much from being with you, I didn't want to lose that.

But now she had. Their relationship was over, gone before it had really got up to speed. She couldn't countenance Danny not owning up to his past sooner. She got why he hadn't during the first weekend they'd spent together. At the time neither of them knew how it would pan out. It might have been a weekend fling so his reticence was natural. But they'd carried on when she'd returned to Nelson. He'd had opportunities to talk to her.

She knew how this went, having learnt the hard way to be super-cautious when anyone hid something from her.

Damn you, Daniel Collins. We had something good going.

A car with a radio station's logo screeched into the parking space in front of her and two people leapt out. The woman held a microphone and camera, the man had a pen and pad in his hand. They charged up to the apartment entrance and read the residents' names. They were out of luck if they were looking for Danny. Was that their purpose? The truth had come to light yesterday, so it was likely. Obviously the reporters were trying every apartment, pushing buttons and leaning in to speak.

So this was what Danny had to put up with. It would drive her crazy. From what he'd said, he felt the same. He no longer wanted to be the focus of bored reporters and TV viewers. Would he come down to talk to them? She doubted it.

Brooke picked up her phone, pressed a number.

'Brooke? Are you all right?'

'Danny, don't open your door. There are two reporters trying to find you by pressing every button on the board.'

'Great. And thanks. This is part of what I've been trying to keep from you.'

Only one part. How she'd have handled it was anyone's guess, but she would have stuck by him, and not looked like she was there for what she could get.

'Goodnight, Danny.' Stabbing the ignition button, Brooke swiped a hand over her eyes, flicked on the windscreen wipers and leaned forward to see through the moisture stinging her eyes as she made her way home. Her safe place.

The house felt cold and lonely when she stepped inside and locked the door behind her. Danny had left his mark already. The couch in front of the fire where he liked to sprawl while she prepared something to eat after a difficult day at work. The cups and plates stacked in different places in the cupboard to where she'd always kept them. In her bedroom, she stared at her big bed, too big now that Danny wasn't here to share it with her and wouldn't be again. She used to love her bed. It was warm and cosy, not too hard when she went to sleep, her favourite place to read a book. The place she'd had the best sex she could remember.

She needed to forget that.

Opening a drawer in her dresser, she dug deep for a pair of fluffy pyjamas. Ugly but cosy, she didn't wear them in front of Danny, but today she needed the comfort they brought. Along with a mug of hot tea in bed, while she tried to read the thriller she'd started two days ago, because sleep wasn't going to happen any time soon, despite being exhausted after a busy shift on the ambulance and all the grief eating at her heart.

When Brooke gave up on the book after rereading the same page four times, she turned off the light and snuggled down on her side facing where Danny had lain the other morning after they'd been to breakfast. Picking up his pillow, she breathed in the smell of him. Hugging the pillow tight to her breasts, she took more deep breaths.

How could you do this to us?

Tossing the pillow aside, she flipped onto her back and stared at the darkened ceiling. Should she forgive him and take another chance? He did appear genuinely upset he'd hurt her.

So had her mother, and her exes. Then they did it again. She had to protect her heart. No one else could. Or would.

Oh, Danny. Why, why, why?

Tears flowed again. Her eyes were going to look awful when she turned up for work. Puffy and probably still red. Not that she cared. She'd say she had a touch of flu and hopefully be sent home, away from ED and any chance of bumping into Danny if he was called in to cover for someone.

Seriously? Pull your big girl pants on and go to sleep.

Just like that? Sure thing. She did have soft, comfy pants on, though they didn't make her feel like a tough warrior. She was exhausted, but the tears weren't abating. Yet. Give it a few minutes, and hopefully the salt water would run out.

* * *

The ringing of her phone woke her. The caller ID shocked her. So did the time. Six-thirty.

Grabbing the phone as she leapt out of bed, she answered, 'Pete, I'm sorry. I've overslept.' She never, ever did that. 'I'll be there ASAP.'

'Glad to hear. Thought you might be sick. See you shortly.'

Click.

'Guess you don't want to waste time chatting.'

Brooke dropped the phone on the bed and headed for the bathroom, trying to ignore the pounding going on in her head. Hard to believe she had slept at all, let alone through the whole afternoon. Even harder to believe she had managed to fall asleep with all the hurt and thoughts about Danny and what they'd lost going on in her head.

'Here, get that into you.'

Pam, her crew mate for the night, handed her a covered paper mug of hot coffee the moment she raced into the station. Thank goodness it wasn't Corina.

'We've got a call. I'll drive while you down the caffeine fix.'

'You're a champ. I need this more than anything else.' She sipped the coffee and winced as it burned her lip. 'That's fresh.'

'Just made it. Come on. I've checked over the ambulance, restocked and we're good to go.'

'I'm really sorry I'm late.' Was she going to spend all night apologising to people for one thing or another?

'Brooke, cut it out. You've done the same for me. It happens, okay?'

Not to me, it doesn't.

She'd start setting the alarm as backup to her errant brain from now on. 'What've we got?'

'Little old lady—eighty-three—found lying on the floor of her bedroom. She's lucid but complaining of hip pain and a sore arm.'

'Ouch. Let's hope the hip's not fractured.'

'Don't like the odds.'

'Me either.' Brooke sipped her coffee, not burning herself this time. 'Just what the doctor ordered. Thanks, again.'

'Talking of doctors—did you realise who Dr Danny really is?' Pam asked.

Here we go.

'I heard.'

'Seems Corina has been making a fool of herself around him. But that's Corina for you. Danny's probably used to it.'

'Most likely.' Definitely. Deep in her heart she felt a twinge of sympathy for him. There would never be any getting away from what he used to do, and how famous he'd become because of it. But he took the good side, so he had to accept the other side too. Thankfully Danny had the weekend off so there was no chance of running into him. But that wasn't going to last. He did work in ED, which was also the destination of the patients they picked up.

'Joseph White, twenty-two, head knock in a rugby tackle. Lost consciousness for about five minutes,' Brooke said, looking stunned as she filled Danny in about the man she and Pam had brought into the department towards the end of her shift.

Of course he wasn't supposed to be working this

weekend but, like ambulance crews, there were often staff shortages in the ED.

'Any other injuries?' he asked, trying not to stand there drinking in the sight of Brooke. It hadn't been twenty-four hours since she'd walked out of his apartment, yet it felt as if he hadn't seen her for weeks. Looking wicked in her fitted uniform, he could only think about the woman underneath the thick fabric, and not touch her or look as though he wanted to race her away and make up to her for his foolishness.

'Not that we could ascertain. We put the neck brace on in case there's been some spinal damage when Joseph was taken down by two players.' Tension tightened her slight body. She was not comfortable with him.

'That was wise. Rugby tackles are hard on the players' bodies.' He had really blown it with Brooke. Instead of getting excited about who he was, she was staying away, not trying to gain anything more than he'd already offered, and even that wasn't wanted any longer.

He looked around, found Sarah had joined them. 'Sarah, did you hear Brooke?'

'Yes, I did.' She took the notes from Brooke. 'Has anyone been notified Joseph's with us?'

'The coach was calling his partner when we left,' Brooke informed them. 'Let's transfer him and we'll get out of your way.'

Away from me, Danny thought, as they moved Joseph to the bed on the count of three. Talking to Brooke yesterday hadn't gone anywhere near as well as he'd hoped for. It had been so different to any reaction he'd had from people, especially women, that he'd been stunned. Though not surprised. Brooke had always been honest with him and had never shown any interest in him other than who he was now. His lifestyle was very wealthy, but when he'd mentioned it she'd hardly blinked. There'd certainly not been any sign of avarice lighting up her face or putting hope in her gaze.

'Anything else you need to know?' the woman who'd given him a sleepless night asked politely.

Quickly dumping the worry, he looked from Joseph to the notes Sarah held out and scanned them. 'Looks like everything I need is here.'

'Right, we're off.' Brooke was already pushing the stretcher trolley towards the ambulance bay, her shoulders tighter than usual, back straighter than straight.

His heart plummeted. Well, it would have if it hadn't already been as low as it could go.

I love you, Brooke. I know I've blown it, but can we talk?

'Do you want Joseph to have a CT scan?' Sarah brought him back to what he should be focused on.

'I'll arrange it once I've given him a complete examination. Joseph, can you hear me?'

'Yeah, man. My head hurts like stink. Those guys gave me the roughest tackle ever.'

His speech was clear and his mind was lucid, as Brooke had said.

'All part of the game, eh?'

'Yeah. Prefer it when I do the tackles, not the other way round.'

'You lost consciousness for a few minutes, so we're going to send you to Radiology for a scan. Are you hurting anywhere else?' The neck was Danny's concern, but he wasn't about to say so and give Joseph the idea. If he was in pain, he'd say so. Then again, rugby players didn't like to admit to pain very often.

'All good,' Joseph replied. 'Don't like that thing you've got around my neck. It's awkward.'

'We'll remove it soon.'

'Cheers, man.'

'You've got off lightly,' Danny told Joseph an hour later. 'But no playing rugby for at least ten days. Go back to your GP then for a clearance. Okay?'

'No.' Joseph grinned. 'I hear you. I'll behave 'cos I've got a trial with a team in Auckland next month. Missing that would be the pits.'

'I like your attitude. Good luck with the try-out.' He remembered those occasions when he'd be hyped up to do better than his best, and terrified he'd play golf like a five-year-old. Winning or getting accepted by a new coach or being included in a greater team was always the goal. 'I'll watch out to see how you do.' He'd probably just added to the man's tension.

'Thanks, Doc.'

Danny filed his report and glanced at his watch. Five forty-five. Brooke would be finishing for the day in a quarter of an hour. Chances of seeing her again today were unlikely. Unless he rang and asked if he could visit after his shift ended. But that would be late, and she had looked beat when he'd seen her earlier. Despite holding herself tall and proud, her feet had dragged when she'd been focused on the patient and not on avoiding him.

Best leave her alone, give her space so she could think about everything. Who knew? He might get a second chance.

Dreams were free.

'Want another game of golf at the weekend?' Jackson had appeared out of nowhere. 'Troy's keen to knock your socks off.'

Danny managed to laugh. This man was befriending him and hadn't once mentioned the past. 'Bring it on. What time are we booked to play?'

Another week, another payslip.

Whoop-de-doo. Exciting. Not.

Brooke threw her keys on the table and opened the fridge to get the bottle of wine she'd been into for the last couple of days. Every day had dragged since Danny's revelations. The days or nights she'd been on shift had been lacking the thrill that usually came with helping people in scary situations.

The fact was, she missed Danny. In every way imaginable. Talking on the phone late at night when they were in their own beds, sharing a meal here or in the back of a restaurant or pub, making love. It wasn't even the same seeing him in the emergency department any more. Danny was as friendly as ever, which made her uncomfortable as she tried to keep her distance, protect her heart.

It seemed all the staff now knew who they were working with, and there'd been quite a buzz for a couple of days, but it had died down pretty quickly. Corina had kept pressing Danny for attention, and no doubt a date, but she hadn't succeeded in getting even a smile. Now she was busy telling anyone who'd listen what an arrogant man he was. Brooke didn't bother telling her how wrong she was.

Flicking the igniter against a fire starter, she watched as the flames caught on the wood she'd set that morning. Winter was beginning to slip away into spring but the nights were still chilly. Especially so now that Danny wasn't around to cuddle up to or share the air with.

What if she was being unreasonable by not accepting his explanation and apology for being afraid to spoil what they had going? Had she been unfair? Possibly. But instinct was hard to ignore, and these days her instinct with relationships was to protect herself. Which could mean she'd never have another serious one, might never marry a man she loved beyond reason or have those children she'd dearly love one day. Over the years since she'd become single again she'd accepted that she mightn't have either of those, and had carried on with the things she could control. Work, home, friends. Now it wasn't enough. Because of Danny.

If she'd understood him correctly, he was missing out on the same needs too. And he seemed to want to try to have that with her, or to find out if they were compatible on all fronts at least. Had she let him down by not giving him a chance? All because he'd pushed her caution button.

Ding-dong.

'Who's that?' She didn't usually get unexpected visitors on a weeknight. Putting down her glass, she headed for the door and swung it open. Her head spun and her heart flipped. 'Danny.'

'Brooke, mind if I come in?'

Not at all. 'I suppose.' She held the door wide, shut it firmly after him. It was tempting to lock it so he couldn't walk out again. Hang on. She'd walked away from him because he'd lied to her and broken her heart along the way. 'Can I get you something to drink?' Why bother? He wasn't staying long, she'd make certain of that. He didn't belong with her any more.

'Whisky'd be great.' He seemed surprised she'd offered, as though he'd expected to be tossed out within seconds of hearing why he was here.

Why was he here? Her hand shook as she poured the whisky into the glass.

'Easy,' he said and took the bottle from her.

There was no getting away with how she felt about him being here. Nervous was one word for it. The one she hoped Danny came up with and didn't realise she was also angry at him for turning up unannounced.

His smile was bleak. Was he struggling too?

'Let's sit by the fire.' Hopefully they'd both feel a little more at ease. 'If it's still going. I'd just started it when you rang the bell.' Sure enough, the flames had died to a glow. Using the metal bar, she prodded the pieces of wood and started some small flames. 'I'll leave the firebox door open until it starts blazing.'

'Here.' Danny handed over the wine she'd left on the bench in her hurry to move away from the tension.

Sinking into her seat, she tucked her legs underneath her butt and sipped the wine. 'How was your day?' She hadn't seen him in the ED.

'Day off. I walked up to the Centre of New Zealand and along the hills to Atawhai, did a lot of thinking.' He sipped his whisky and put the glass aside. 'I miss you, Brooke.'

Her heart banged against her ribs. Wine sloshed over the rim of her glass before she put it down too. 'I—'

I can't give in without learning more.

But how she wanted to.

'Maybe you do, Danny, but I can't forget what you did that easily.'

He winced. 'Hear me out before you say anything else.' Settling onto the couch where she had those wonderful memories of him stretched full length, sometimes nodding off for a few minutes, he twisted his glass back and forth in his fingers.

Unfair advantage, she thought as she waited for him to get to the real reason he'd come here.

'I know I should've told you who I am right from the get-go but, like I said, I enjoyed spending that weekend with you and being able to pretend none of it mattered, that you didn't need to know for that short time. Then, when we carried on seeing each other, I sort of got swept away with the normalcy of it all, not having to watch you for trouble, pretending to be like any other guy you might have dated. I felt so free, even when I knew it couldn't last and that one day someone was going to recognise me and it would all blow up in my face.' He paused, regarded her as though looking for understanding.

'The perfect reason for explaining everything to me, I'd have thought.'

'True.' He sipped his drink. 'I was playing with fire.'

'I understand to a point. But you'd found a woman who had issues about having info withheld from her, and you still didn't think to come clean.'

'It made me feel guilty more than anything else. I know how dealing with what other people have thrown at you in the past has made you jittery about revealing yourself. Yet you did tell me, and I still hung on for a few more days because I was so relaxed and happy with you.'

What else would he do that about? Brooke wondered as she tried to sip her wine without spilling any.

'What else should I have known that could've affected our relationship?'

'Like I told you, my partner, Iris, loved the money and, even more, the adulation. When the lights went out, so to speak, she wasn't as keen on being with me. I was still sought out by the media, but I wasn't heading for bigger and better things in the golfing world. I chose to step away, not linger on the periphery as a mentor or coach. No more cameras in my face, or so I thought. I know I'm repeating what I told you last week, but what I didn't say was how much it hurt. I had loved Iris for who she was, accepted everything about her. She was kind, loved kids and would go out of her way to help other people. But she changed, as I did.'

Brooke sat and waited for him to go on. She didn't want to interrupt and send him off on a tangent.

'My next relationship was short-lived for much the same reasons. That woman was more interested in living in the best house, having a top-of-the-range car, buying clothes for every time she went out the front door. She wasn't into me for me after she found out more about me. She made me cautious, which I should have learned by then. But I'd been thinking, hoping, Iris was a one-off and the next woman would see past the glamour to the real me. I've dated sporadically ever since, until I met you.' He reached for his glass, took a mouthful of whisky and set it aside again. 'You answered my dreams. You saw me for me, and I didn't want that to stop.'

'It didn't have to. I didn't know you for who you really are.'

'I know, but I didn't want to risk it.' He sighed. 'Nothing ventured, nothing gained. Only it was wonderful being so at ease with you, and I've had some hard knocks so I kind of believed there'd be another one coming. When you told me how Brad had kept important issues from you I nearly blurted it all out then, but caution won out and I shut up.'

'Come on, Danny, get real. Like you said, it was always going to come out.' Brooke studied the man in front of her. The man she'd started falling in love with one stormy weekend down in the Sounds. He was everything she'd dreamed the man in her life would be, and more. But how well did she know him? She could no longer just dive in and take a chance. She couldn't forget the lessons she'd learnt in case she got to have the life she longed for. The reality was she could very easily end up heartbroken again. 'Is there anything else you should be telling me, Danny?'

'Not about the past, no.' He took a deep breath. 'I was going to suggest we date some more, see how it works out. People are starting to find out about me and you might not like the consequences.'

'But?'

Taking another deep breath, he looked straight at her. 'Brooke, I love you.'

'Brooke, I love you.'

The words spun through her head, filled her with hope and happiness and relief. Brought tears to her eyes. Danny loved her. She loved Danny.

He hadn't finished. 'Are you willing to take a chance on me? On the crazy things that occur because of my past? They can be annoying at best, infuriating at worst, but I'll do whatever it takes to save you from the worst.'

Wine splashed over her thighs. 'Danny, how do I know I can trust you?'

'I swear I'll never hide anything from you again. I promise.'

Easy to say.

'How can you know that? Nothing's ever that straightforward.'

The eyes that met hers were laden with sadness, and love. 'I mean it. I'll do anything in my power to be open with you about everything. There's nothing else I can say.'

She had to accept that. There was nothing more to be done at the moment about that. But her heart was shaky, and her head spinning. He said he loved her. She believed him. Did she trust him to love her for ever? To always have her back?

'What do you want for your future, Danny?'

'You. And a family, if you're willing. A home that we create together. I don't care where I live as long as it's with you.'

'You could live here in Nelson?' She wouldn't mind moving but she was testing him.

'I certainly could. It's a great place.' He gave her a hesitant smile.

Brooke nearly choked over her wine. She couldn't go on asking him questions when her heart was filling with the love she had for Danny. He was everything she'd been looking for. Everything and more. Despite what he'd done, she knew he wouldn't do it again.

She stood up on shaky legs and moved towards him. 'Danny. I love you too.' She couldn't go on. She was so overwhelmed. She'd been hurt because he hadn't talked to her about what mattered and made her think he was like other people who'd hurt her. But he loved her, and had finally told her what was important when he'd been afraid of the consequences too. This wasn't all about only her.

'You'd take a chance on me?'

'There's no taking a chance. I'm in. For everything that gets thrown at us. For all the love and fun and pain. It will be an adventure.'

Danny was standing in front of her, reaching for her hands. 'I still struggle to believe how lucky I was to meet you that day. You are awesome, Brooke. I can't explain how much I love you.' Then he was kissing her, not letting her tell him again how much he meant to her.

She leaned into his body, absorbed his strength and gentleness, drank in his kiss, felt his love in his touch, in the air around them. She kissed him back with everything she had. No doubts. No what-ifs. Just her love. They'd already wasted too much time.

Then Danny pulled back, his hands on her hips as he looked at her very seriously. Her heart thumped. What was wrong? She held her breath.

'Brooke Williams, will you do me the honour of becoming my wife?'

A smile expanded across her face. Marry Danny? 'Yes, yes, yes.'

'You're not giving in too quickly?' he asked with a cautious grin.

'Of course I am.' Brooke paused, fought the need to fling herself into his arms and get back to kissing him senseless. 'I was hurt by you not talking to me until someone else told me who you were. But—' She tapped his mouth with her finger. 'I've also been too wrapped up in my own concerns over getting hurt that I didn't really accept that you had similar concerns about being accepted for yourself.'

No caution in that grin now. It was wide and genuine and full of love. For her.

'I'll tell you something else. I've already started making enquiries about positions in emergency departments in the district.'

'You're going to specialise in emergency medicine? Not radiology?'

'You were right. I love the work I do. Why would I want to hide behind a computer screen all day? I've also had a couple of games of golf with two guys from the hospital. One of them approached me suggesting I might like to join them, obviously knowing who I was but not making any big deal out of it.'

'So you've started to get out amongst it?' Her heart was thumping. This was good for Danny, and maybe the benefits would rub off on her too, making him more relaxed whenever he went out. 'You do need to stop and settle in one place, make some lifelong friends.'

'Yes, Brooke.' He laughed. It was a sound that warmed her from top to toe. He was happy. So was she. More than happy. 'We have a lot to look forward to.' He took her hand. 'Starting right now.' His kiss was soft.

And then it wasn't. It was demanding and enticing and had to be followed up on. Brooke didn't stop kissing him back as she tugged her fiancé down to her bedroom.

* * * * *

COMING SOON!

We really hope you enjoyed reading this book.
If you're looking for more romance, be sure to
head to the shops when new books are
available on

Thursday 27th
October

To see which titles are coming soon, please visit

millsandboon.co.uk/nextmonth

MILLS & BOON®

Coming next month

CHRISTMAS WITH THE SINGLE DAD DOC
Annie O'Neil

Harry was still on the ground, and although he'd definitely grazed his knee, he somehow seemed entirely unfazed by it. Normally there would be howling by now. But the woman crouching down, face hidden by a sheet of glossy black hair, was somehow engaged in a greeting ritual with his son.

'How do you do, Harry?' She shook his hand in a warm, but formal style. 'It's such a pleasure to meet someone who loves Christmas as much as I do.'

If she was expecting Lucas to join in the I Love Christmas Every Day of the Year Club she was obviously recruiting for, she had another think coming. It was only November. He had enough trouble mustering up excitement for the day of December the twenty-fifth.

Clearly unperturbed by his lack of response, she smiled at Harry and pointed at his grazed knee. 'Now... Important decision to make. Do you think you'd like a plaster with Santa on it? Or elves?'

'Elves!' Harry clapped his hands in delight.

The woman laughed and said she would run into the house and get some, as well as a cloth to clear away the small grass stains Lucas could see were colouring his son's little-boy knees.

Her voice had a mischievous twist to it, and underneath

the bright, child-friendly exchange was a gentle kindness that softened his heart.

'I'm ever so sorry. Harry is just mad for—' Lucas began, but when she looked up and met his gaze anything else he'd planned on saying faded into nothing.

Though he knew beyond a shadow of a doubt that they'd never met, his body felt as if it had been jolted into a reality he'd always been waiting to step into. Every cell in his body was supercharged with a deep, visceral connection as their eyes caught and held. Hers were a warm brown…edging on a jewel-like amber. Her skin was beautiful, with an almost pearlescent hue. Glowing… Cheeks pink. Lips a deep red, as if they'd just received a rush of emotion.

Perhaps it was the unexpected excitement of a three-year-old boy careering into her front garden. Perhaps it was the fresh autumnal weather. Or maybe…just maybe…she was feeling the same thing he was. A strange but electric feeling, surging through him in a way he'd never experienced before.

She blinked once. Then twice. Then, as if the moment had been entirely a fiction of his own creating, realigned her focus so that it was only on Harry.

Continue reading
CHRISTMAS WITH THE SINGLE DAD DOC
Annie O'Neil

Available next month
www.millsandboon.co.uk

MILLS & BOON

THE HEART OF ROMANCE

A ROMANCE FOR EVERY READER

MODERN

Prepare to be swept off your feet by sophisticated, sexy and seductive heroes, in some of the world's most glamourous and roman locations, where power and passion collide.

HISTORICAL

Escape with historical heroes from time gone by. Whether your passion for wicked Regency Rakes, muscled Vikings or rugged Highlanders, av the romance of the past.

MEDICAL

Set your pulse racing with dedicated, delectable doctors in the high-pr sure world of medicine, where emotions run high and passion, comfor love are the best medicine.

True Love

Celebrate true love with tender stories of heartfelt romance, from the rush of falling in love to the joy a new baby can bring, and a focus on emotional heart of a relationship.

Desire

Indulge in secrets and scandal, intense drama and plenty of sizzling h action with powerful and passionate heroes who have it all: wealth, sta good looks…everything but the right woman.

HEROES

Experience all the excitement of a gripping thriller, with an intense ro mance at its heart. Resourceful, true-to-life women and strong, fearles face danger and desire - a killer combination!

To see which titles are coming soon, please visit

millsandboon.co.uk/nextmonth